What are re

". . . a whirlwind of suspense, tragedy, justice, inspiration, and more. The characters, for the most part, are so well-developed that you can almost cast the parts yourself for the "movie!" "

"Made me think about choices I make and how they affect others. We never really think about the long term effect of one simple choice"

"Warm, down-to-earth, and honest! A very satisfying feel-good story."

"The author's character development in this book was such that I felt I knew and cared about each person. . . . I didn't want it to end and hope he writes a sequel."

" I felt that I knew each character personally and laughed when they laughed and cried when they cried."

"I am amazed at how well the author was able to capture my heart and allow me to be able to be drawn in to the lies, revenge, deception, greed, love, friendship, and most importantly the love of Christ in this book. It was beautifully written."

"I was not able to put this book down. . . . It was one of those books that endeared you to each character, even the bad ones, hoping that something good would happen to them in the end."

"I laughed, cried, and rejoiced throughout this book. What a witness to those who feel that their lives have gone too bad for forgiveness . . . a great lesson that we can never go too far from God who gave the ultimate sacrifice for our sins. Loved the book and cannot wait to read more from this author!"

Troubled Fields

a novel

by Dennis Manor

Published by Dover Road Publishing

Copyright 2011 Dennis Manor

all rights reserved

This book is dedicated to my wife, Sharon, and my daughters, Amy and Carrie for your patient support and encouragement during the how-long-I'm-not-going-to-say process of bringing this story to life.

Thank you to Angie, Bettie, Melissa, Sharon (the other one), Laura, Mandy, and Victor, as well as many others who have encouraged me to keep writing. I hope ya'll weren't just foolin' around.

I'm also thankful for "my raising" which planted the characters and places of "Troubled Fields" in my mind.

Dennis

1.

"You want me to scratch off and throw some rocks on 'em?"

"No, sir. We'd best not do that. They'd be liable to haul me back in there and take you, too. I'd say we just git while the gittin's good!"

As the barricade dropped into place behind the truck, Ray reflected that it was a good day to get out of prison. Immediately he laughed to himself to be thinking such a thing. Any day should be a good day to be leaving Parchman Penitentiary as a free man, but, he recalled with unexplained clarity, it had been raining, storming actually, on the day he had arrived. Almost sixteen years of all kinds of Mississippi weather had passed since he had last been on the better side of that gate. Still, over two hours driving time lay before him and his father. He was glad the miles would be spent on dry pavement . . . especially so since his father had not changed his old driving habits. 'Any place worth goin' to is worth gittin' at as soon as you can,' Pat Bennett had always replied to his wife's admonitions to slow down.

"What're you grinnin' about, son?" Pat asked, then sheepishly said, "Well, I guess it don't take no rocket scientist to figure that out, does it?"

"Oh, I've been kind of scared thinking of all that's bound to have changed since I was locked up. I'm not sure I'm ready for it."

"There's nothing out here you can't handle, son. We're all behind you, and you know we'll help you anyway we can."

Ray patted his father's shoulder. "Don't worry about it, Pop. Just keep us out of the ditch and out of trouble 'til we get home."

"Well, you know that any place worth goin' to is worth gittin' at as soon as you can!" Pat chuckled.

Ray laughed, "Never more so than today, Pop. Just don't get us arrested. These local cops get kind of nervous up here sometimes. We wouldn't want to give 'em the impression that you're helpin' me escape, would we?"

"Not today, son. I'll admit I've thought about it plenty, though. I just never could talk your mother into bakin' a file into a cake for you!" They enjoyed laughing together for the first time in many years.

Ray had always taken advantage of an opportunity to laugh. It was good to laugh, and to smile, and Ray did both well. He had not laughed much during his first few years in prison. He was angry and bitter over the circumstances that had placed him there. He resented the power one man could wield over another. He had not begun his stay at the Mississippi State Penitentiary as a model prisoner, certainly not a model human being. It was as if the gate that shut him away from the world he had grown up in had shut him away from the young man he was. After a few fights, some won, some lost, all he had to show for his attitude were some scars and hard, cold eyes. Then one Christmas his grandmother, Gran, he called her, sent him a present that changed, or more accurately, gave back, his life.

She had been able to visit him only a few times, but when she had come along with Pat and Mary before Thanksgiving she saw the hardness creeping into Ray's eyes where it was likely to take up permanent residence. She realized that it was not just a face he put on for survival in Parchman, but was the face of the man he was becoming. So, when Ray opened the package he received from her just a few weeks later, a card taped to the top of the flat box said simply, "Some things are better forgotten. Some should always be remembered. You'll have a merrier Christmas, even there, when you've sorted the two." Inside the box was a small photo album. There were pictures chronicling Ray's life from infancy through high school graduation. Ray alone, Ray with family members, Ray at Christmas, Ray on his grandfather's tractor, Ray riding his horse, Ray . . . living. The photos, at first a curiosity, took Ray back to those places and times in his life. He remembered the easy going boy and the life he had looked forward to. Looking from his graduation photo to his mirror, Ray suddenly saw in himself the thing that had so frightened his grandmother. And he decided, then and there, that he liked the young boy in the pictures more than the hardened man in the mirror. He couldn't quite reconcile it with himself, though, considering what had put him there in the first place.

The change was gradual. He realized that no matter where he was there were still choices that were his alone to make. In a place where so many choices were stripped from him and made for him, he could and must chose what kind of person he would be, how he would live his life - even within the confines of prison walls. He lowered the walls he had built within those walls of the prison. He looked for humor, and found it in strange places, but he learned to laugh again. He made an effort to get to know and understand other prisoners. His former reputation stuck with him to an extent like some kind of legend. To the newer convicts he was described as a nice guy that you don't want to mess with. One person did. His last fight, actually, over a rather trivial matter, had earned him some more time on the worst of work details, but it had ironically introduced him to the only person he would truly call friend on the inside. So here he was, on the outside at last. He had made the best of his "home" for fifteen years and now he was to make a new home. There would be trials and troubles, and he could treat them as just that, or he could view them as experiences to grow by . . . and smile at. After all, just the thought of having "free" troubles as opposed to prison troubles would bring a smile to any incarcerated face in the country.

Much of the remainder of the trip passed in silence. Pat couldn't help smiling. He'd never been able to give Mary the kind of gifts he thought she deserved, but nothing he could dream up could ever top the present he was bringing home on this crisp October day.

Ray was awash with emotion. Excitement, fear, joy, melancholy. He had no idea of what to expect of his life from this moment on. For the past fifteen years, he had known pretty much what would happen moment to moment, day to day, week to week, year to year. Now, so much of his life had passed by outside that gate. He had spent many hours making plans for the day that he would be set free for the life he had always wanted. Sorting dream from reality, he had decided that he would start small. Maybe stay small.

His grandfather's place was waiting for him. There was a small amount of acreage; too little now to operate as a farm. There was equipment Joseph Winstead had used in his own successful custom farming business. But the tractors and the cotton pickers and combines were old and unused for years. Could they be pressed into service now? If not, there was no living to be made on that old place. Even if everything worked, who would do business with an ex-con? And not just any ex-con, but the one who put Carl Sullivan in a wheel chair. His old high school friends would certainly have moved on. Even though most of them were probably still living in Winstead County, they most assuredly had moved on in other ways. Few, if any, would consider him as a friend by now anyway.

All that time in prison, his day dreams of being on the outside, always centered on the life he had known. But that was the life of a boy, a teenager who hunted and fished and drove too fast on gravel roads, and partied and worked for whoever needed him at the time, and swam in ponds, and had no responsibility.

He was a man now. He had little idea of what normal thirty three year old men did. It had to differ greatly from what they did in prison. And it had to differ somewhat from what they did on television. And . . . he was not normal. He was a convict. Parole had merely gotten him out of prison; it had not cleared his name.

He still had to live with what happened, even if he couldn't remember it, and didn't know for sure one way or the other whether he had done the deed. His family had always been convinced that Ray was innocent. But, in fifteen years, he could come up with no answer other than the same one those twelve people on his jury had. He must have done it. There was no other way it could have happened. Ray had a feeling that the stigma of prison would be like the stench of a skunk . . . He would be a long time getting shed of it.

As Highway 49 brought them near Delta Hills, Ray's stomach churned. He remembered how the town had received its name, for, sure enough, right here the flat fertile Delta farmland gave way to the tall hills and bluffs overlooking the Yazoo River. Delta Hills stretched, if stretched is what you could call it, from the flat lands just east of the river until her streets and houses and buildings rose up into the great bluffs that cradled the bulk of the county seat. It was a sight Ray had long ago forgotten and had never appreciated as much as he did now.

Other more intense memories engulfed him as they drove on further into his old stomping grounds.

Going up Broadway past Main toward Monroe, Ray glanced to the right to look at the Delta Palace Theater. There was nothing there but an empty lot between two old three story brick buildings. Delta Hills skyscrapers. He wondered why anyone would tear it down if they had nothing else to build in its place. Most any movie Elvis had happened to make, Ray and his family had seen at the Delta Palace. From 'Wild in the Country' to 'Change of Habit'.

He remembered wondering as a child why the black kids got to have all the fun of sitting up in the balcony. He had thought that he might like to go up there when he was older and see what it was like, but by the time he grew old enough and Elvis all but quit making movies it seemed that Jackson was the place to go to see a good movie. By now people were sitting pretty much where they wanted to and Ray understood more about the balcony anyway.

His father pointed out many of the changes in the town, and told the stories that accompanied those changes. The old Tastee Freeze was gone, but now there were a McDonald's, a Dairy Queen, and a Pizza Hut! Howard Brothers was long gone, and a new Super K Mart was soon to open on the plot of land that once held the Five Points Motel. Ray had missed the "regular" K Mart altogether. A newer, nicer motel and a few small office buildings and medical offices occupied the place Ray had last visited as the Delta Drive-In. The closest thing to a dirty movie he would see, he had seen there.

All through town, he had noticed kids driving nice new expensive cars. The fifty-sevens, and sixty-sixes and sixty- nines he had known would be scorned by these kids. He shuttered to think of what his standing would be in his old sixty-four Biscayne. Obviously, the days of "a car, any car" were gone with the drive-in they once inhabited. He blinked as he felt tears running into his eyes. So much change. It was well that the years could not be given back to him so that he could return as an eighteen year old. He doubted that he would know how to live as a teenager in 1987.

Highway 49 had been four laned south of Delta Hills. The kudzu, that all consuming vine that Ray had marveled at as a child and could scarcely remember now, seemed not to look quite the same. He remembered being angry at the kudzu when he was a boy. What a marvelous gigantic playground it covered in the hills and hollows along the highway! His young dreams of somehow making it over here to play were soured by the fact that the kudzu, more than the miles from home, kept him from reaching this cowboy's paradise.

Now the great green vine held a different fascination. Even at this time of year it was still lush and bright. The kudzu vine was very much alive. Alive and growing. And as it grew it covered any and all things in its path. His grandfather had once warned Ray not to take a nap too near the kudzu. He might wake to find he had been swallowed up by it. So it was with the land and the grass and the trees that one day found themselves covered, smothered and dying. The bright green blanket, teeming with life, hid beneath it the dry crumbling brown remnants of death.

Ray remembered seeing a man standing beside his parked car on what they once called Mile Hill. He held a camera to his eye, pointed at the vast green hillside before him. "Why would that man want to be taking a picture of all that kudzu," Ray had asked. Noting the out of state tag, Mary had replied, "Because Yankees think it's pretty!" Young Ray shrugged and went back to his daydreams. There wasn't much he would put past a Yankee.

He was glad the trip from Delta Hills took only fifteen minutes. Moving through all that change with too little time to process his thoughts and reconcile his emotions was almost over whelming. It would be well to be still for a while. The tears he had successfully fought in town wouldn't stop as the Dodge truck turned onto the short gravel driveway that led home. A strange black and white mutt ran alongside the truck barking happily. "I forgot that Rebel died," he said softly. Pat, half thinking himself that he was bringing home an eighteen year old boy, said, "Yep, son. This is Sport. We got him from the Strong's not long after Pappy died. As a matter of fact, I recalled how Pappy would always pick a puppy from Queen's litter and name it Sport. I didn't want a dog named Pappy, or Joe, so I named him Sport for him anyway!"

Before the wheels of the pickup stopped rolling, the front screen door burst open and out ran Mary. Ray bolted from the moving truck, and met his mother in the middle of the yard. They both stood there hugging and sobbing, unable to speak for several minutes. "You look . . . well, son," Mary finally managed to say.

Lying to her children was something Mary Bennett had never been able to do. She always managed to tell something near the truth when necessary to spare feelings or bolster confidence or do whatever else was best for them. The truth was that today Raymond Lee was as pretty a sight as he had been on the day he was born. Of course, to anyone other than his mother, he was no Ivory Snow baby. But, he had been a handsome young man by most accounts by the time he was a teenager. He was still handsome, but a few scars on the outside, and some obvious inner scars that showed through left her saddened. Her youngest boy was supposed to have the face of a man with a good life, a happy life. Now, at thirty three, he had the face of a man with no life. That would change almost immediately, though, and Mary wanted so much to radiate hope, not to spare feelings or bolster confidence, but because hope was there.

At just over six feet tall and one hundred sixty pounds or so, Ray had enjoyed good health throughout his life. He had grown accustomed to letting his dark brown hair grow a little too long between haircuts and even now it was a bit shaggy, contrasting with his clean shaven face. Too many hours indoors had left his complexion light, pallid looking. Even though he was obviously thrilled to be home at last, there was no spark in his eye, no snap to his step. The spoils of the war between time and spirit weighed heavy upon him.

"Well, Mama," Ray replied, "you're beautiful as always." Mary started crying and hugging again. "You look especially good out here in the daylight instead of in that dark old visiting room up . . . up yonder.

"It's so good to have you home. You must be hungry. Your grandmother is inside. And you need to get in out of this cold!" Mary almost scolded.

Ray smiled, "It's good to be home, Mama." So far, about the only things that had not changed beyond his recognition were his home and his mama and his daddy. Of course he had seen the both of them quite a bit through the years. But still, they were not much different than they were the day before Carl Sullivan lost the use of his legs.

"Raymond Lee," Gran said softly as he entered the cozy living room. She reached up to cup his face in her trembling hands and gave him a gentle kiss on the cheek. "I was beginning to wonder if I would live to see you again. And I'm glad I did, because you are still as handsome as my Uncle James. I only wish your grandfather could be here now." The slight eighty one year old could scarcely hold back her own tears by now.

Gran always had a way of making each of her grandchildren feel special, like each was the most important, even as they all sat at her feet at the same time. Totally equal, yet most special. Sibling rivalry makes this an impossible task for parents who want so much to instill these feelings deep within their children. But, for one such as Gran it seemed to come effortlessly, and truthfully.

"I know, Gran. I wish he could, too." Ray bent to hug his grandmother. "I thought an awful lot about him, and he was a big help to me, even after he died. But, I'm glad you're here, and to tell the truth, there have been times when I wondered if I would live to see you again." He laughed, but the pain of better forgotten memories showed in his eyes.

"I know it must have been terrible for you. But, let's don't talk about all that right now."

Ray wondered if his grandmother thought he would be better off not remembering the past fifteen years, or if she and the rest of the family would be better off not hearing about them. In any case, he was not anxious to discuss his life in prison under any circumstances.

"Well, I finally get to see this room ya'll built on. It's real nice." Ray looked around at the expansive den that had been stuck onto the south side of his home. Vaulted ceiling, fire place, two full size couches and chairs of all descriptions. What family gatherings he must have missed!

"It's kind of funny, ain't it, son?" Pat said. "We raised all you children in this little old house, and then when everybody is grown and gone, we start addin' rooms!

Seems like folks would start out with a big house and then go to takin' off rooms they don't need no more. Instead we live for years all bunched up and trippin' over each other and then start stickin' on rooms we don't need."

"Pat, have you been running on like this all the way home?" Mary scolded. "And, besides, I don't hear you complaining about all this extra room when you have a house full of grandchildren! I only wish Ray had been here to enjoy it with the rest of us all these years. He would have if Carl Sullivan had been a half way decent human . . ."

"Now, Mary," Pat interrupted, "Let's not bring all that up!"

Mary sighed deeply, "I'm sorry, Ray. Here it is your homecoming and I'm acting ugly."

"No, you're not! You're just acting like my mama," Ray said. "And I mean that in a good way!" he hastily added.

"Dinner is ready, and we'd best get in there and eat it before we have to cook supper," Gran reminded. "I reckon this boy is past ready to sit down to some good home cooking!"

The house smelled of roast beef and carrots. Black eyed peas and hot fresh cornbread would certainly be waiting. A hint of the musky odor of mustard greens hung in the air. And though there was no fragrance to announce its presence, there was undoubtedly a banana pudding in the refrigerator.

Ray enjoyed this noon meal as much as he had any Thanksgiving or Christmas dinner he had ever had in his whole life. All of his old favorite foods were laid out. And he ate and caught up on many of the family and local goings on.

After dessert he excused himself to walk around outside. His mother tried to insist that he put on one of his old coats that didn't fit, but he finally convinced her that he would be fine in the denim jacket he brought with him from Parchman. A heavier coat was packed with the rest of his belongings, but he didn't feel like dragging it out at the time.

There really wasn't much to look at. The Bennett spread took up all of an acre. There was a new, at least new to him, storage building in back of the house. The interior was kept in the usual Bennett style, disorganized. A few of his and his brother's and sisters' old belongings were there. Piled on shelves, stashed in trunks and boxes, or strewn on the floor. The old shed, beside, but out from the house, still held the lawn mower and garden tools. There in the back, a familiar shape sat covered by a tattered old tarpaulin. Ray smiled and licked his lips. Pulling back the tarpaulin, he found his motorcycle, a Honda 550 four cylinder, looking to be in pretty good condition.

He straddled the bike and worked the throttle, clutch and brake. It was already old when he bought it. After fifteen years, it was too much to hope that it would start, but, if he could remember how, he would soon do what he needed to get her going again.

"I told your folks that I would get you to drive me home," Gran said startling him. "I need to get my nap before we do this all again tonight."

"Sure, Gran," he said hurrying to meet her. "Let's get in the car. It's too chilly for you out here."

As he turned to drive down the gravel road that led to his grandparent's home, Gran said, "Go over to the old barn. I've got something to show you."

As Ray complied more memories flooded over him. How many times had he driven the dirt road to his grandfather's barn, the center of operations for his small farm before he had gone into the custom farming business. The weathered old structure was not much to look at. It had not been painted, as few barns were. Boards had broken away in places, doors and gates hung on worn out and broken hinges. Implements that were lined up outside the barn were covered in vines and rust, some worse than others. Weeds surrounded the barn and filled the yard around it. And yet, it was still obvious to Ray that this barn stood on the most beautiful part of the whole place. Overgrown and unkept as it was, it was still beautiful. One of his adolescent dreams had been to someday build his own home on this piece of land.

"Have you thought about what you are going to do?" Gran asked.

Ray knew what she meant. Generally speaking, "What are you going to do?" doesn't apply to a specific situation or problem. It means, "How are you going to make your living?"

"I haven't thought about much else since I got my parole," Ray replied. "I know the place is in rough shape. The good thing is that I have all winter to try to get the business going before I might be needed. The bad thing is I don't know what I'll do to make a living until then. I know the bag plant is closed. A lot has changed in town. Something will turn up. About all else I know about is farming from what Pappy taught me and what I learned in Parchman. Maybe I can drum up enough work on the farms around here until I can figure something out. What do you think, Gran?"

"I think I'm glad to hear that you are still interested in farming," his grandmother smiled.

"Ma'am?" Ray questioned.

"It's yours, man," she still called him "man". "The farm, such as it is, and the business, tractors, pickers, combines and all! Here's the deed and titles to everything except my house," she said handing him a folder filled with ominous looking paper. "You'll work it out and you will do fine. It may take some time for people to come to trust you. But they will."

"Gran, I . . . I ain't thought about much else but makin' something out of this place again," Ray stammered. "But, I feel bad takin' it all for nothin'. There's the others," Ray said thinking of his family. "Why don't you just let me work it for you? That way you can keep everything and do what you want to with it later. Maybe I can turn it back into something for you. But, I can't just take it like this."

"Of course you can turn it into something," she retorted. "And I am doing just what I want to with it now! Your grandfather wanted you to have this place. You're the only one who ever showed any interest in it! Besides, your brother and your sisters have all gone off to their own lives that don't include anything here. And, I'll tell you now, young man," she almost scolded, "this is it for you. When I'm dead and gone my last will and testament will say nothing about Raymond Lee Bennett except that he can keep the looks he inherited from his Great Uncle James. You are getting yours right now. Understand?" His grandmother cast a stern eye his way.

"Yes, ma'am. I understand," he said reverently. "I just don't know how to thank you, Gran."

"Raymond. You've had fifteen years of your life taken away from you. You probably would have been working this place for your grandfather years ago and would have wound up with it anyway. Besides, it is not such a great prize right now. You see the shape it's in. The rest of the acreage is pretty run down, too. Bad fences, dry water holes in the pasture land, broken up feed and water troughs. The truck runs, both of these tractors run. I had Lester come over and take care of them day before yesterday. He moved them over from the big shed. You have three horses somewhere on the place that are probably half wild by now. As of now, it's yours. You run it like you see fit. It will be hard. There are plenty of people around here who would love to see you fail. Just give it your best and take as good care of it as your grandfather did. That will be plenty of thanks for me. Now, I'm going in the house to get my nap. Here are the keys to the truck. I'll drive myself across the road."

Ray walked his grandmother to her car, and saying nothing, hugged her tenderly. He watched as she drove her old Buick across the road and up the driveway to her own home, and waved one more time as she disappeared through the front door.

The afternoon passed into evening unnoticed. What had begun as a nostalgic tour around the old barn ended up as a work day. Ray could hardly stand to see the place so grown up with weeds, so he greased the old bush hog, sharpened the blades with a rusty file he located in the barn, hitched it to the little Massey Ferguson tractor, and clipped the barnyard. Then, with a sling blade, he trimmed close to the fence and the building itself. He could come back tomorrow with his father's line trimmer and do it right. He found some old hinges, tightened some others, and rehung the doors and gates that were visible from the front of the barn. Rusty nails found in a coffee can worked fine to shore up lose boards and replace broken ones. By the time he heard a car approaching the barn, he had it, the front anyway, looking something like a working farm.

"You better get on to the house, boy. Mama's been waitin' supper on you fifteen years. She ain't gonna wait all night now!"

"Jimmy!" Ray called as he trotted to meet the voice coming through the dark behind bright headlights. He had never hugged his brother before, but now it came as natural as breathing. "How are you? Well," he commented after looking Jimmy over, "I guess I don't have to ask that. City life got the best of that wash board belly of yours, did it?"

"That's why I'm glad you're back, bro," Jim replied. "Diane and Mama have had this undeclared war over who can stuff me the most for years now. I didn't stand a chance. But, with your bottomless pit, at least you can help me with Mama. Take a fair warning, they are all working on you tonight, boy."

"There's a spread on the table, huh?"

"Boy is there!" a cracking voice said from within the car. "Hey, Uncle Ray!" the boy exclaimed as Ray bent to see whose mouth that sound had come from.

"Well, hello there, Nephew Wil," Ray said shaking the young teenager's hand.

The boy looked puzzled. "How did you know who I am?"

"Your grandmother has kept me well informed about all of you young'uns. There's no mistaking Wil Bennett. I'm glad to meet you. Where's your sister?"

"She's at Grandy's, helping with supper."

"Helpin' with supper," Ray said with surprise. "Why she must be quite a little . . . all grown up. I guess I expected her to still be just five years old."

"Hey! It amazes me," Jim said patting his brother's shoulder. "Let's go on home. Everybody's waiting."

"Yeah. You go ahead. I'll bring Pappy's truck. You wanna ride with me, Wil?"

"By the way, bro," Jim called as Ray and Wil turned toward the barn, "You've got the place looking pretty good already, and just so you'll know, we're all very glad that it's yours now. You two deserve each other."

"Thanks." Ray replied, "And you ain't seen nothin' yet, . . . bro."

At the house, Ray washed his hands as best as he could at the faucet by the old shed. The cold, crisp night air, the lights from the house, the laughter from inside . . . it all made him feel quite at home. "At home," he thought. His second greatest wish over the past fifteen years had come true. His greatest wish? Well, that one might have to wait a while longer.

The evening was a roller coaster of emotion for everyone at the Bennett home. Ray was reintroduced to neices and nephews who hardly remembered him, if at all. Gran was there again, looking tired, but happy. Aunt Mae was there, hoping Ray would ". . . work hard to restore the family name."

Pat, never one to be put off by his eternally depressed great aunt responded for Ray by saying, "Aunt Mae, Ray has enough troubles of his own without carrying the burden of our tarnished family name. You're just gon' have to live with it. Besides, anything you did happened so long ago that nobody can even remember it. And it ain't Ray's place to go around fixin' your reputation anyhow."

"Huh?" she hesitated for just a moment before protesting, "I didn't mean . . ."

"I know," Pat interrupted, "that you never meant any harm. I don't know what it is that has you worried so suddenly, but I'm sure today's society would find whatever it was to be quite acceptable. Ray, come in the kitchen and let me tell you where your horses are." Pat rushed Ray out of the room before Aunt Mae could respond directly to him. Ray and Pat both laughed, though, when they heard Aunt Mae go into a small tirade behind them.

"Thanks, Pop," Ray said. "I guess I have to play nice even to Aunt Mae, for a while anyway."

"Oh, don't pay her no mind, son. Before you became her black sheep of choice she gave Uncle Ed fits about his drinking."

Ray laughed, "Yeah, I remember. She used to tell everybody in the county what a disgrace Uncle Ed was to the Palmer name because he stayed drunk all the time. Nobody much would have known if it weren't for her, but everyone knew she was the reason for his drinking. Well, I'm glad I could take the heat off of him, rest his soul."

Gran had followed them into the kitchen and was all too ready to join the discussion. "That old biddy. Ed should have wired her jaws shut years ago. I swear, if I were ever to hear five pleasant words in one sitting come from her I would take it as a sign that the Second Coming was near."

Ray and Pat chuckled. Gran and Aunt Mae, while civil to each other face to face, had kept a behind-the-back feud going since Mary had married Pat which made Gran and Aunt Mae in-laws of a sort.

"I'm going home. Ray, I saw some of what you've done to the place already. You should have settled in for a day or two before you started, but I'm as proud as I can be. I know Joseph would be, too."

Ray could only nod. It indeed was an emotional time, and he was almost ready to cry at anything.

"These," Gran said, holding up two small vinyl folders, "are your bank books. I sold what cattle there was after Joe died. The money is in the savings account. I kept a little bit in the checking account. You'll . . . You will," she continued, when she saw Ray try to interrupt, "need to go in to the bank tomorrow and get your name on a signature card. You may want to move the money into completely new accounts. Do whatever you want to do. But, I have already done my part and Tom is expecting you. And, Stanley Neely's boy can finish up the paper work on the place for you."

"Gran, I can't . . ." Ray began.

Gran interrupted, "Ray, this is farm money. You would have had the cattle, but we didn't know when you would be coming home, so I just sold them off. You know you need some money to live on and get the business going again. You need to restock. The place is in no condition to produce any income right now and neither is the farming equipment for contracting. I didn't turn the place over to you just to watch you fall flat on your face and take it with you. I love you both too much for that!"

"Yeah, Gran, I know you do. Thanks . . . again," Ray replied.

Long into the night Ray lay awake staring into the darkness of his room. His room. It was much like he last saw it, only cleaner. The same pictures and posters decorated the walls. His rifle and shotgun hung on the rack. The very same table top radio he listened to as a boy sat on the nightstand and it still did not keep correct time. The bed was covered by the same spread. But this was not the same home he had left.

The more he dwelt upon it, the more he realized that nothing here was the same, save this shrine to the years they had all lost. Time had taken its toll on his parents. His grandmother, once strong and active, was now a frail old lady fighting to hold to her independence. His brother was a good forty pounds heavier, his sister tightly drawn and somewhat skeletal from too much dieting. Wil had not yet been born and Mandy had been a baby when he left. Had he really expected them to still be in training pants?

The drive home, through town and the surrounding countryside, had been a disappointment to Ray. The landmarks he had longed to see were either gone or deteriorating, abandoned and forgotten. Was it really any different for him or anyone else trying to go back to what was? Others may have witnessed the change. Some may have paid no attention until they looked up one day to wonder what had happened. Ray had been away for a long time. If there was nothing else to be held in common, none of them could go back to what used to be. Because that's all it was. On what should have been one of the happiest nights of his life, Ray found himself feeling rather sad.

Not sure which was more over whelming, what lay behind or what lie ahead, Ray's signature on the day was a simple three word prayer, "Thank you, Father."

2.

Staring at the ceiling, listening as the morning stirred, Ray suddenly realized that he was still there! He had not left Parchman after all! Why? What could he have done? It came back to him. So stupid! He had not been ready to go on time. He had to pack just one bag. How could his small cell hold all that stuff? Nine bags! But, he had only one more bag left. Why couldn't he just leave it behind? It was only trash! Why had he packed his trash? He had to leave by ten a.m. He was three minutes late. Three lousy minutes and they wouldn't let him go! "Maybe next year," they said. "Pack early." And they laughed. The echoes of their laughter bounced around the cramped cubicle and across the metal door. It became louder and louder. How could he stand another ye . . .

Ray was awakened by his own scream. Unsure as to whether he had yelled out only once or several times he sat and listened. He was not breathing heavy, but he was sitting up. And he was trembling. But . . . he was home! He looked around the room and chuckled slightly to himself. That was the first time he could remember dreaming that he was dreaming!

"Ray?" His mother's concerned voice lilted through the walls.

"It's alright, Mama. Go on back to sleep."

The sun had not yet begun its journey across the crisp Fall sky. Ray had not witnessed a single sunrise in sixteen years. He did not intend to miss this one. He always rose before dawn, but he could never watch as the sun peeked over the horizon to survey the day's work. This was his quiet time. He pulled his old, worn Bible from his knapsack. Ever since his life changing gift from Gran almost ten years earlier, his morning with the Bible had been a daily routine. And now he read from the book of Job, perhaps the last time for a while, feeling as if he had come through his own test. A tiny voice within him, though, whispered of unknown trials to face. Closing his Bible after several minutes, he said a short whispered prayer . . . thanks for his freedom, and promises of future days not to be wasted topped his list. His only request for today was that he not wake up to find that the past twenty four hours really had been a dream.

He lifted his head to see the sky, gray through his window. Dressing quickly, he tiptoed into the kitchen and put some water in the tea pot to heat for instant coffee. With some leftover ham and cheese and rolls, he put together four breakfast biscuits. With the biscuits wrapped in paper towels and a thermos filled with hot coffee, he went to his grandfather's truck . . . his truck, and headed for the barn. His first full day of freedom, and he didn't want to waste a minute of it.

Breakfast was gone before he reached the barn. About three bites each were all the biscuits stacked with ham and cheese had to offer. Sitting on the tailgate of his truck, he planned his morning while he sipped his coffee. The morning chill, a light fog covering the barnyard, the far away low of someone else's bull beginning his day, brought a great comfort to Ray. Some things don't change.

The peace . . . the freedom that this moment in the day had brought to him as a youth returned to him now, sweeter than ever before. "Thank you for this, Lord," he said softly. "Please help me make the most of it."

The tractors and implements, gray through the mist, took him again back to his boyhood when he and Jimmy would join Pappy here before the sun was up good to run cows from one pasture to another or do whatever task there was to do. The sting of cold air through his nostrils only heightened the cleanliness of this place. Ray reached with his senses to find old familiar smells, but they were gone. A living, working farm is filled with the character of its various functions. If it is a part of your life, you could be deaf and blind and still you would know just where you were by the smell of your location. Long years of bleaching in the summer sun and rinsing in the cold storms of winter had faded the character of this yard. But, the memories were there.

As many times as he had thought and dreamed of this place and his life before Parchman, he had never felt those memories as he had over the past two days. There would be more memories ahead, he was sure of that. For everywhere he would go, here, in Delta Hills and Coleman, in Jackson, there would be reminders of his youth. It was as if his time behind the walls of prison had been a completely different life. He had left his real life behind fifteen years ago. Now he was back to pick it up again. But everything had changed. He could not just pick up and go on. He had to come to terms with the present for it was here he must live. And that meant remembering less and living more. At that, he drained the last of the coffee from the mug and set off to find his horses.

"Hello?"

"Hi."

"Hi," came the reply after a moment's hesitation.

"He came home yesterday," Laura said.

Lorraine swallowed hard. "I know that! Have you seen him?"

"No. I'm sure it was a busy day for him."

"Then why are you telling me he's here?"

"Because I knew you would want to know. You love him don't you?"

More hesitation. "A lot of people love him, Laura."

"But, not like you," Laura explained.

"A lot of good it does. He's not gonna want to see me."

"If you think he won't remember, you're wrong. Of course he'll remember."

"He may remember your bratty fourteen year old sister, but I'm the last person he'll want to see."

"He'll remember. And even though he doesn't know it now, he will come to realize how much he needs you. You have been more loyal to him than anyone . . . other than his family."

Lorraine faked a chuckle. "You're blowin' an old junior high crush a little out of proportion, don't you think? He was with you back then. Hardly knew I existed. There's no reason to come lookin' for me. And I don't have any excuse to go see him other than to say 'Welcome home!'"

"That's a start. It'll work itself out, Lori."

Lorraine sighed. "It's all too complicated anyway. We both know it would just make things worse. And . . .

there's things you don't know, things that can't be worked out."

"I have to go. We'll talk more later?" Laura said.

There was silence from the other end of the phone.

"Bye," Laura offered.

Again, silence and the click that ended the conversation.

In the worn surroundings of her trailer, Lorraine Sullivan Parker wiped a tear from her cheek. What had been unreachable for so many years in Parchman Penitentiary now seemed even more distant. And the chasm that divided her family grew ever wider.

"You're looking very cheerful this morning," he said, his voice dripping with sarcasm from behind the newspaper. "I wonder what would be the cause of that."

"Well, I would think you'd be happy today, too, Clint," Laura replied. "After all, an old friend is home after a long time away. He was your best friend for years."

"Fifteen years in prison is not what I call "away". And we've not been "best friends" since long before he went in, if you will remember, and, if you will think a little harder you will remember the reason for that!" he snapped. "Even in a perfect world best friends don't often stay best friends forever. And our little world is nowhere near perfect, is it?"

Yes, she did remember the reason. No, the McKay world was not perfect. She had been reminded of it daily. But, today, like yesterday, she was happy. And the school girl stirring within her was responsible for this little spark of joy. It was silly, she kept telling herself, to think of

Ray's homecoming as some sort of long awaited date. After all, her last words to him had been less than kind, even if the conversation had been civil.

"You've ruined all our lives," she said, "Even if you didn't mean to, you've ruined us. This is the last thing you'll ever be able to do to make at least something right. Papa has agreed to everything you asked for. Will you keep your end of the deal?"

"You'll see to it?" he said softly.

Whether this had been a demand or a request she could not discern.

"Of course," she replied.

Ray nodded, simply, almost imperceptibly, and the bargain from which he personally benefited none in the least was sealed. But then, it wasn't about him, was it?

"Goodbye, Ray," Laura said tersely.

"Bye, Laura," and he was lead away to spend half of his life in confinement.

Her husband was in no mood for joy from anyone today, however. "Maybe you won't be so happy when you realize how much we stand to lose."

"Clint, he won't say anything! Lord knows, he deserves a chance at life."

"He got what he deserved, and if it were up to me, he would be getting more of it. Another fifteen years would not be long enough! He could come back here and . . . "

Laura sighed. "Clint, I thought we were past that long ago! Don't tell me we have all of that to get through again!" she cried. "What are you worried about? You and Papa have been plotting to grab the old Winstead place for years and you knew all along Mrs. Winstead would never sell it to you, not for any price!"

"Maybe you think there are a few other things around here that are rightfully his. Maybe a big piece of our future is not enough for him." He paused as he heard the sound of footsteps trotting down the stairs. "Maybe you want to give him what actually is his!" he spat.

"Clint, I am not . . ."

"Good morning," Emmy interrupted. "Mom. Daddy", she said as she gave each of her parents a peck of a kiss on the cheek. "Bad morning, Dad?"

Clint started to speak, but Laura interrupted. "Emmy, honey, there may be some talk at school today."

"Somebody is always talking about somebody down there, Mom," Emmy said cheerfully.

"Well, this talk will hit kind of close to home. Your brother left early to ride with Chad, so we've already told him."

Emmy's pretty face grew serious. "What is it, Mom?"

"We knew this was coming, honey, but we didn't know exactly when." She hesitated. "Ray Bennett came home from prison yesterday."

"He's here?" Emmy cried. "The man who paralyzed Papaw is here? How could they just let him go, Daddy? He's dangerous!"

"Well if it was up to me . . ." Clint started.

"If it was up to your father, they would throw away the key to every cell in America and no one would ever get another chance," Laura said. "Emmy, we talked about this. We told you that this could happen. And Ray Bennett is not dangerous. What happened was an accident."

"Mom, I'm old enough to know that they don't hand out forty year sentences to good ole boys that have accidents," Emmy protested.

Laura turned her head to fight back the tears suddenly coming into her eyes. "Sometimes the whole system breaks down, honey, and innocent people get all caught up in it. Ray never meant for anything like that to happen." She wiped her face and turned back around. "We just wanted you to be prepared. Now hurry up and finish your breakfast and I will drive you to school."

They rode in silence for several miles before Emmy spoke up. "I don't see how you can be so forgiving, Mom! Papaw almost died when Ray Bennett tried to kill him. He has been in a wheel chair since before I was born!"

"It was a terrible thing and Ray has paid no small price for it. And, for the last time, he didn't try to kill your grandfather. There is so much hostility toward him around here. Not many people are going to welcome him back. He can expect little or no help from anyone outside of his family. He is going to have a hard time making it. I'll be the first to admit that I had . . . harsh feelings for Ray for a long time. But, he wasn't the kind of person people have made him out to be. He has served his time and he deserves a fair chance at some kind of life."

"Well, he needn't look for any second chances out of me. I won't even give him the first one. I hope I never see him. Things would have been different with Papaw. Maybe he wouldn't be so bitter. Maybe he . . . maybe he could have loved me," Emmy said, her voice trembling.

Laura, fighting back powerful emotion, looked over at her daughter. "Sweetheart, Papaw does love you," she lied. "He just isn't good at showing it. He's in pain much of the time, you know."

"I know, but he sure doesn't have any trouble showing Jason." She was crying now. "Even Daddy loves Jason more."

Laura pulled the car to the side of the road and put her hand on Emmy's shoulder. "Honey, why would you say something like that? Your daddy has given you everything." She struggled for words that at least spoke half-truths.

Wiping the tears from her face Emmy said, "I think Daddy has always been mad at me because ya'll had to get married . . . because of me. It's obvious that he wanted Jason, he never wanted me," she sobbed.

"Emmy! Why would you say that? We had to get married?" Laura tried to sound incredulous. "I mean . . ."

"Mom! I'm not a kid anymore! I can count, you know." Emmy explained. "I know when you and Dad got married, and I know when I was born. And I wasn't premature. So, that can only mean that you were pregnant with me before you got married. Daddy blames me for messing up his life. It's that simple."

"How long have you felt this way, sweetheart? I had no idea," Laura asked deciding to table the matter of the timing of her marriage. Actually, Laura had always feared that Emmy might notice the difference with which she was treated. Now, she didn't know what to say. Her daughter was no longer that trusting little girl who would take her word for anything, accept any explanation she felt was best for her question or problem. The lies had always been meant to protect Emmy and to protect the Sullivan name. Laura's stomach churned at the thought that Emmy might someday learn the truth. How could she protect her daughter then? What destruction would be wrought by the revelation of the truth and the uncovering of a lifetime of lies?

"I've known for a long time, Mom. It started when Jason was born, and it has gotten worse over the years. Dad just can't get close to me. It's like he's not comfortable being around me anymore. And it hurts."

"Emmy, you're seeing things that aren't there. A new baby always gets more than its share of attention, honey, and it was hard to be fair no matter how hard we tried to treat you special, too. And, as for your father's relationship to Jason, things are different with men and their sons. It doesn't mean that you are loved any less."

Emmy was almost belligerent now. "I can see, Mom. Renee's dad and Corinne's dad are so cool. It's obvious they care. Even when they have those regular parent-kid fights, anyone can see how much their fathers care about them. They have brothers and there is no 'boy thing' in their families. Dad treats me like I'm some kind of unwanted stepchild or something."

"Boy! This is the time of life when kids want to pull away from their parents. And here you are complaining because your father is not involved enough in your life,"

Laura said, wishing she could come up with something more meaningful to calm her daughter.

"Most of us won't admit it, but even if we do want to pull away, we want to know that there is something there to fall back on. Where Dad is concerned, I've never been close. You know that, Mom. You must have to have seen it, too."

Laura felt the pall of guilt. She had seen it, but there was nothing she could do about it. And, she supposed she had known that Emmy saw it, too. Now the dreaded day had come when her daughter could hold it in no longer. Emmy had made known her feelings, and those feelings were not unfounded. Of all the things she could protect her daughter from, the truth was not one of them. What now? What now to rescue this precious life? At a loss to do anything else, Laura decided to change the subject entirely.

"Do you have any tests today, Honey?'

"No, ma'am, not any that are scheduled anyway."

"I'll tell you what. You skip school and I'll skip my Bible study and we'll go to Jackson. Spend the day together! How about that?" Laura asked. Hopefully she could get her daughter's mind off of her childhood. "We can do some early Christmas shopping. And then we'll go to Mamma's. She's looking for me around three thirty and you know she is always glad to see you."

"I don't feel much like school today anyway." She would get no answers from her mother today. An offer to skip school with your mother does not come your way every day, so Emmy decided she may as well take advantage of it.

"Do you ever?" Laura said smiling. The slight grin on her daughter's face eased her apprehension.

Clint left the house soon after Laura and Emmy. Anger still burned within him. How much would Ray take from him? Nothing if he could help it. He turned his pickup truck left to go up the dusty gravel road to Carl's tractor shed, the center of operations for the farm. Until he could figure out how to put a stop to things he would have to slow them down. His first plan of action would kill two birds with one stone. Ray Bennett would find out how things were, and his father-in-law may finally decide that he could trust Clint with more than just the foreman's job on the farm.

Walashabou Creek Farm and Livestock Company, or Washabow, as grammatically lazy locals had come to call it, was one of the largest farms in Winstead County. Carl's business interests went far beyond the productivity of his acreage. Oil leases, directorships, and some stock trading kept them all in Caddies, Lincolns, and Ford's best pickups. Of all of Washabow's loyal employees, a few were always willing to go the extra mile for Mr. Carl . . . or rather, for Mr. Carl's "bonuses". The biggest bonus of all might just be the farm itself to a deserving son-in-law. Ridding Carl of Ray Bennett, may just rate the big one.

Stopping his truck in the early morning shade of the big shed, Clint motioned to Buck Ammons, one of his own long time employees. Already covered with grease, Buck joined Clint away from the shed where the sun warmed them some on this cold morning.

"Buck, I want you to get Albert and Jessie, and meet me over at Carl's."

"But, Bob wanted me to get this picker in shape before noon." Buck replied. "And, while we're on the subject, Bob said Miss Emily didn't want anybody up to the house botherin' Mr. Carl today."

Clint snapped back, "Bob works for me, and Miss Emily has nothing to do with the running of Washabow. We'll see Carl when we need to. You keep in mind, Buck that you work for me, too. When I tell you to do something, I expect it to be done."

"Yes, sir. We'll git right on over there." Buck said sheepishly, "You'll git with Bob on this picker?"

"Yeah, I'll get with him," Clint grumbled. Bob Riley was yet another matter to take care of. Bob drew more respect from the men of Washabow than either Clint, or Carl himself. Why Carl had kept Bob around for all these years was a mystery to everyone. Bob did pretty much what he wanted without regard to anyone else's orders.

There was not much land left for Ray to search. Mounting interest and a couple of bad years once left Joseph Winstead with no choice but to sell off what acreage he must to pay his debts. That the land sold came to be in Carl Sullivan's possession left no doubt as to why banker Jordan had refused to offer another extension. Hard times in Winstead County often seemed to benefit the likes of Mr. Carl Sullivan.

Determined not to be defeated by his long time nemesis, Ray's grandfather decided that he could make a decent living contracting his labor and equipment for services to other farmers. He had the equipment. He kept enough land to support some livestock and upon which to grow hay and feed crops to sell to those who would buy. Winstead Farm Services had been started with a hay baling operation for spring and summer. Then Pappy expanded to pick cotton, and combine wheat, oats and soy beans. He kept his operation small, but he did well with it. He had made big plans to bring Ray on with him full time after high school. With his grandson to help, his small business would grow into big business. And one day, when he could no longer climb onto a tractor or could work no more in the humid Mississippi summer, he would turn it all over to his grandson. And he would sit on his front porch and sip iced tea . . . and be proud of his life's work.

The summer season of 1972, which was to see the beginning of this dream, however, saw the end of it. And, again, Carl Sullivan had managed to deal the cards. Ray was sentenced to a lengthy prison term. If he served his full sentence, Pappy would not live to see him alive and free again. The family was sure, though, that Ray would get whatever so-called good behavior reduction could be had, and that he would surely win parole. They underestimated the reach of Carl Sullivan's power, however. Joseph Winstead held on as long as he could. He died of a sudden stroke determined that someday Raymond Lee Bennett, his grandson, would carry on the family business . . . and spit in the face of Carl Sullivan.

Before noon, Ray had located his three horses, two of which he did not recognize, but then, he had not expected any of the horses he had once ridden to remain alive. And these were not young animals. Molly was four, maybe five years old when Ray had last seen her. A gelding he did not recognize had to be eight or ten years old at least. Ray was never a good judge of animal age. He only knew when certain ones were aging while others appeared to be in their youth. There was another mare that was probably no more than six or eight years old. Pappy must have brought her to the farm when she was just a colt.

Finding the horses had been the least of his problems with them. They had run loose for years and had grown rather wild. Even the old mare, Molly, lead Ray on a fair chase before he was able to get a rope and makeshift halter on her. He chased the gelding and the younger mare for hours. He had read in a western novel once that a man could walk any horse down given enough time and stamina. He had both, but he finally gave up on the idea of the chase when it dawned on him that the two loose horses might follow the mare, so he tied her to the draw bar on the tractor and slowly lead her across his pastures and overgrown fields to the ramshackle old corral beside the barn. He drove the tractor through the gate into the corral itself, but the two horses that had followed at a safe distance would not go through.

Hearing the high-pitched sound of a two-cycle engine, Ray walked around to the front of the barn to see Pat trimming weeds along the fence row. "Thought you might like some help."

"I appreciate it, Pop. How long you been here?"

"Two or three hours, I reckon. Long enough to get all this done and work up an appetite. Dinner'll be ready in about half an hour, by the way. Where have you been?"

"I went to get my horses," Ray said surveying his father's work. "I'll tell you what. I'm going to pen them up. Why don't you go on home and clean up. I'll be along in time to eat."

"Well, get along little doggies," he said to himself as he opened the tack room. There inside, he found four saddles, six bridles, five saddle blankets, and three old pairs of spurs. Most of the equipment he recognized as that he and his brother and his grandfather had used so many years ago. The newer tack, he had never seen, but since it was in generally good shape, he decided to use it. The leather was dry and cracking in places. He could try to recondition everything later.

After knocking the dust from the saddle and bridle, and beating the dust out of the blanket with a baseball bat he found in a corner of the room, Ray approached the old mare. She was skittish, but she was also old, so she was not very difficult to handle. Memories of human contact seemed to return to her and, when Ray mounted her, she offered no resistance. The old mare was not fast or agile, but, she was steady. Using the fence to hold the other horses to his right, they soon had herded them into the corral.

Noticing that it was getting to be lunch time, Ray turned the old mare into the corral with the gelding he had named Dan, and Lillie, the younger mare. Molly would be a good horse for his nieces and nephews to ride. Dan, too, probably. But he doubted that Lillie had ever been saddle broken. She would provide him with some fun.

Back at the house, Ray saw an unfamiliar car in the driveway. It dawned on him that every car he saw now was unfamiliar to him. He did think he caught some familiarity in the face of the elderly black man sitting behind the steering wheel. The man waved, and Ray smiled and waved back, but he still could not put a name with the face. This changed immediately though, for as he walked through the front door into the living room, his stomach leaped into his throat.

There, standing right before him in his own home, was the wife of the man responsible for his long, unjust imprisonment, if, indeed it was unjust. She probably had witnessed the whole thing. No one knew for sure, but, if she had seen anything, she had remained silent. Carl had testified at the trial that his wife had seen everything and could corroborate his story. But, ". . . no, she is still far too traumatized by it all to speak of it." It was a testimony in itself to Carl's power that she was never called as a witness for the prosecution . . . or the defense. But, then again, Carl was powerful enough on his own. He could get his way in the Winstead County Court House.

"Miss Emily," Ray said removing the cap from his head. "I see you have ole Phillip drivin' for you now."

"Ray. Oh, Ray!" Mrs. Carl Sullivan cried. She had been tearful since arriving at the Bennett house some twenty minutes earlier. But, at the sight of Ray, she began to sob uncontrollably. "I'm sorry, Ray," she managed to say. "I should have said something long ago . . . long ago. It's all my fault."

"Now, Miss Emily," Ray replied. He walked to her slowly and gently hugged her. Her body felt frail and weak to him. She had once been very active and robust. She clung to him, sobbing into his chest. "That's just it. It was all a long time ago. I got over all the anger and blame a while back. And I never blamed you. I told you that in my letter and I meant it. I don't know what you saw. It might have made it worse for me, it might have made it better. But, I know you had your reasons for keeping quiet. I've always trusted you, Miss Emily."

"Oh, Ray, you've lost so much. You were just a boy, and now you're a man, and everything between is gone. I should have made him tell the truth. I should have . . ."

"Then why didn't you?" Mary interrupted harshly. "Fifteen years! Fifteen years out of my boy's life. Out of all of our lives! And all for that . . . that animal of a husband of yours!"

"Mamma!" Ray scolded.

"She's right. You are right, Mary," Emily said. "But, I was so . . . so . . ."

"Hush, now, Miss Emily," Ray comforted. "We know. We know. It's just hard to deal with. It's been a hard time for all of us, and you, too. I know. There's healin' to do, and there's buildin' to do for all of us, you included."

Emily wiped at her eyes with a tissue. "You're a fine man Ray. You always were. I just can't believe that you can be so forgiving after all these years."

"There's nothing to forgive, at least not for you. The only person who could be forgiven ain't here. And he never asked anyway," Ray said matter-of-factly.

"He never will. And worse than that, he's bound and determined to run you out of here, Ray!" Miss Emily shook her head, shame on her face, "I can't stop him. I . . . I'm just too weak."

Ray took her hand, "I'm a free man now, Miss Emily. And Carl is my problem. If he don't want to get along, that's his decision. But, I'm stayin'. I never expected me and him to socialize much anyway."

"Be careful, Ray. He's still a powerful man. And he's raving mad about your parole."

Ray chuckled. "I figured he'd lost his hold on me when the parole board changed that last time. Nobody stuck in his grip, I suppose."

Miss Emily glanced nervously around the room. "I should go. I just wanted to see you."

"And I want you to know how much I appreciate it. I know it wasn't easy for you."

"Stop by, when the Cadillac is gone. I'd love to visit with you. That is, if you . . ."

"I'd love to myself. You still make that cake with the bananas all over it?"

For the first time, she smiled. "I'll have one in the morning."

Seeing that she was about to tear up again, Ray said, "Miss Emily, I hope you won't think any more of it. It's all any of us have thought about for the past fifteen years. I think we need to look ahead now. We can't do nothing about the past, so we need to do our best with today, and the future."

Emily nodded her head and turned to leave the house. She paused at the door as if there were more she wanted to say.

Reading her mind, Ray said, "I'll get around to seeing everybody soon. . . . Everybody."

Miss Emily nodded her thanks and closed the door behind her.

Pat put his hand on Ray's shoulder. "Since Emily brought it up, son, if you want . . ."

"Pop, I had plenty of time to get ready for most anything out here, but that conversation is not one that I am ready to have. Maybe in a few days."

The mood at the dinner table was getting to be too somber for Ray. He knew the visit from Miss Emily had upset his mother, and that she was dwelling over all that lost time. Pop, too. Ray had dealt with those feelings a long time ago. He had to. Otherwise, he would be dead or crazy now . . . or a crazy dead man. He had accepted what had happened to him. He controlled the anger and bitterness and disappointment by pushing thoughts of the outside world and the life that he was missing from his mind. He had learned to live with and through his unfortunate situation. Unfortunate, that is how he had come to term it. He took his parole as more of a reprieve than a wrong beginning to be made right. He considered that his life now actually would turn out much better than it would had he served his full sentence.

His parole was a good thing. As much as possible, he would think only of his life from that point on, no earlier. Sure, twinges of nostalgia, flashes of pain, rage and resentment, and bitterness would harass him from time to time as they always had. But, the past would not control his life. He was determined about that.

Ray explained these thoughts and feelings to his parents. Perhaps knowing that he was dealing with these same emotions and how he was doing it would help them.

"Now!" he said emphatically, "let me tell ya'll about the place."

Immediately after dinner, Ray went to make a phone call. Neither Pat nor Mary knew who he was talking too, but it was obvious that he was enjoying the conversation. Emerging from the hallway that had been the keeper of the phone from the beginning of time, Ray pecked his mother on the cheek and said, "I enjoyed my dinner, Mama."

"I'm glad you did," she said, as she always had as Ray raced for the door . . . as he always had.

Pat asked about the phone call.

"Good friend of mine", Ray replied. "He's going to come to work for me. I'll see ya'll later." With that, he was gone.

Pat grunted. "Here I am taking a few days off, he's been gone for near 'bout sixteen years, and he can't wait to get to work."

"Now, Pat," Mary said rubbing his shoulder, "do you remember when he was a teenager. He was in such a hurry to 'start my life', as he called it. He's waited a long time to get that life off to a start and now here he is trying to catch up with a world that didn't wait on him. We weren't being very realistic if we really expected him to sit around here reveling in his freedom."

"Yep," replied Pat. "I'm proud of him for jumpin' right in like he did." He took his wife's hand. "There's plenty of time for us to spend with him yet."

As he pulled out of his parents driveway, Ray turned south, rather than north. There were other holdings to check out, and he could put it off no longer. He had to know what shape the pride of the family was in. If it was anything like the old barn, his work was cut out for him.

Less than a mile down the road, he turned into a rough, overgrown graveled lot that lay before his grandfather's huge, rambling tractor shed. Having been added on to at both ends, several times, and built into an "L" shape it managed to hold two rather large tractors. Beneath the rusty tin roof were also his combine with its grain header and bean header in an adjoining stall, two cotton pickers, a corn puller, which had not been used since Ray was a boy, all of the hay baling equipment, a pto driven conveyor and various other farm implements. Others were standing in the midst of the tall weeds that had invaded the parts of the lot not covered by gravel, or more accurately, covered by hard packed dirt. Hardly anything to hold the title of "pride of the family" except for what lay beyond.

Past the tractor lot, across a narrow stretch of gently sloping over-grown pasture land, loomed the big two story structure that housed the Sullivan family. Ray stood staring at the second story window that appeared between the leafless branches of two tall oaks. Many times, from childhood through adolescence he had caught glimpses of Laura through that window. It was too far away for him to see the soft details of her face, but, it had been her. Her thick brown hair and dark complexion sometimes blended into the darkness of the room behind her. At other times, at dusk, sometimes even late at night when Ray could sneak down here, her form stood out, silhouetted against the light from her desk lamp.

He would sit hidden in the dark shadows of the shed, staring into that window as she, for what seemed like hours, stared out. He daydreamed of climbing over the barbed wire fence and crossing the field that separated them. There he would whisper her name and she would come down to him and they would walk the trails of his boyhood until just before dawn. They would part with a tender, passionate kiss and agree to meet again the next night. For a brief time, in the summer of his eighteenth year, this dream was something of a reality.

Ray walked to the backside of the lot, behind the shed. He peered down the long slope toward the lake where his life had been forever altered. He could see the trees which sheltered the south and west side of the lake, but he could not see the lake itself. It was hidden, much like the secret, known now to only a few. The tender secret . . . if only it could have stayed that way . . . that brought such everlasting turmoil and devastation to the few who did know . . . and one who didn't.

The sound of slamming car doors shook Ray out of his memories. As he rounded the front corner of the tractor shed, he was confronted with a scene he could not have imagined. It was like something out of a television show. A black Cadillac was parked inside the lot. A pickup truck was immediately behind it in the gateway. Two very large men flanked the car, their arms folded, their faces locked in what had to be their most threatening pose. 'Well practiced,' Ray thought. One more stood next to the passenger side door. Though he had not seen him for so many years, Ray immediately knew who he was. Before he even looked into the car, he knew who he would find there.

"Come over here, Bennett," the crusty voice of Carl Sullivan commanded. "I have something to say to you."

Standing his ground, Ray said, "Why don't you get out and come on over here, Carl?" It was a cruel statement, he knew, but years of conditioning kicked in. You don't back up in the face of such a threat as was being presented to him now. If you give an inch, you've lost. No sooner had these words left his mouth than the two men guarding the backside of the car advanced toward him. Instinctively, Ray threw off his denim jacket and took his stance.

"Back off, boys," Carl ordered. "We're not here to make trouble. We're just talkin' today."

The muscle stepped backwards to their former position. Ray stepped forward. He would make his moves on his own terms.

"Clint," he said, holding out his hand.

Laura's husband just stood there. His jaw clinched tight.

Ray withdrew his hand and hooked his thumb in a belt loop. "You've been a bad influence, Carl."

"Carl, is it now? It used to be Mr. Carl."

"Used to be I had some respect for you," Ray dead panned. "Clint used to be a friend. Best friend, in fact. Even after I stole his girl." He wanted to establish that he was not at all intimidated by the man and his entourage. He was, though, disappointed in Clint. He had hoped to come home to at least one friend.

"You have no friends around here, Bennett," Carl shot back. "You'll see that soon enough." He paused as if expecting a response of some kind. When Ray kept silent, he continued. "Life here won't be much easier for you than it was in Parchman. You'll find credit to be tight. Markets will be hard to find, as well as suppliers."

"You gittin' at something?"

"This whole county is not big enough for you and me both. And you have to know I won't have you working over here right next to my home!"

"I'm here, Carl."

"Well, not for long. You won't last! I'll end up with this place after all, and you'll be broke and homeless."

"You been wastin' your money callin' those physic phone lines, Carl?"

Sullivan sighed and shook his head. "I'm here to save us both a lot of pain and aggravation. You sell out to me now and you can go anywhere you want to and start over. You never have to come back here. And you never have to bother anybody around here again. Not my wife, my daughter, my son-in-law . . . or my granddaughter."

"Well, Carl, I want you to know how deeply I'm touched by your sincere concern for all our welfare. I also want you to know that you can take your offer and stuff it!"

The muscle moved again, but Carl raised his hand to stop them. "You better think it over, boy. Your future could end before it begins."

Ray slipped his jacket back on. "I reckon I'll stay. If my presence here bothers you, you might want to take the long way around. Otherwise, you'll be seein' a lot more of me than suits you." Ray turned to walk back to his work. "I will say this, Carl. I have no intention of making any trouble for you or anybody else. I just want to live my life and work my business. I doubt there will ever be any of that by-gones-be-by-gones stuff between you and me. I'm sorry about what happened. I truly am, even if I don't really know just exactly what happened. I don't know how many times I'm supposed to say that, but I ain't sayin' it no more. We're just gonna have to learn to live in the same community, 'cause I ain't goin' nowhere!"

"We'll see," Carl snapped. "You won't last. You might find it hard to do business in these parts." The heavily tinted window silently closed.

Ray turned his back and walked into the tractor shed, ignoring them as they left. By the time they were gone, Ray was almost shaking with rage. It was clear that Carl Sullivan was not yet through with him. The fear of a naive eighteen year old boy was gone, though. In its place was the anger and determination of a man. Carl Sullivan had taken all of Ray Bennett's life he was going to get.

3.

The old barn had been in bad enough shape, but this tractor lot was something else. The shed was already old before Pappy ever came into possession of the place. Except for a closed in room built onto the south end, it was walled on three sides. It had a tin roof, but everything else, including the pegs used to hold the original structure together, was of wood. Time and lack of maintenance had certainly taken its toll. Loose boards and loose tin, weeds growing among the equipment and junk piled into the empty stalls, pot holes throughout the lot created long ago by equipment moving across the sparsely graveled apron after a rain . . . all combined to make little more than an eyesore of the small piece of ground that had been at the root of the trouble between the Winsteads and the Sullivans for decades.

The shed had been added on to several times, which was painfully obvious by the difference in materials from one project to the next. Its beginnings were those of a shed to cover mule drawn wagons and farm implements. The height of the leaky tin roof had greatly restricted the use of the structure as the prosperity of the farm and advances in equipment allowed for more and larger rolling stock. More or less tacked on to the north end of the shed were stalls tall and wide enough to accommodate the combine and cotton pickers and additional tractors.

Of course, that was all before Pappy had come into possession of this particular section of land in a manner that burned in the pit of Carl Sullivan's stomach to this day. The small holdings of Winstead Farms had not immediately required the amount of equipment demanded by Washabow.

Washabow . . .

An old red and white truck protesting its decades long call to service fought its way onto the lot. The motor continued to churn as if in rebellion after the ignition was turned off.

A familiar figure seemed to unfold itself from within the aging Ford pickup truck. A small yellow dog bound out of the truck bed and fairly danced to Ray as if he were an old friend. Ray knelt to pet the dog and watched as the angled shape of an old acquaintance approached him.

"I reckon Miss Emily'll be pleased to see this grass get cut," Bob Riley said offering his hand. "Carl will, too. It just eats at him who's doin' the cuttin'. They'd prob'ly do better by a man givin' 'im a lawn mower when they let 'im out rather than a suit and fifty dollars. You can do more with a lawn mower than you can a suit and you can't buy nothin' worth havin' for fifty bucks anymore."

Bob had always walked a bit on the eccentric side of life, and the years had apparently kept him good at it. It didn't matter who he was approaching or who he was talking to. Life was kind of like one long conversation to him. There were few "hellos" and practically no "goodbyes". He just usually took up where he had left off, or, as in Ray's case, he started where he wanted to, beginning, middle, or end. His talk with Ray began in the middle because he had not come just to talk about weeds, and there was no need to waste a whole conversation when half of one would do.

"Mr. Bob," Ray replied shaking the older man's hand tentatively. "They do things a little different nowadays, but you might mention it to the governor or the warden next time you see them."

They stood looking at each other for a few moments. Bob Riley was about five feet seven inches tall. Ray didn't know just how old he was. In fact, Mr. Bob had seemed to be an old man for as long as Ray had known him. Perhaps it was the lines in his face and the slight stoop in his shoulders that had given him such an appearance for so long. He had always seemed to be gray headed, but, there was no doubt of that now. Ray calculated that this man had to be somewhere over seventy years old. Either Bob Riley himself didn't realize his age, or he ignored it. Apparently, he was as robust and able as ever. The glint that Ray had remembered as residing in Mr. Bob's eyes was there as well.

Finally, Ray broke the silence. "Speakin' of Carl, he's already been out knockin' at my door. He forget to tell me something?"

Bob spit tobacco juice between the dog's front legs. "Git on away from here," he scolded, "This conversation don't concern you." Dutifully, the dog trotted away to explore the shed. "I've been a lot of things and I've done a lot of things. One thing I ain't never been and that's Carl Sullivan's messenger boy. And one thing I ain't doin' now is deliverin' any message from him. I've always thought he would do well to hire him a spokesman, though." He hesitated and said, "I went up to your other place and when I didn't find you there, I thought I'd look here."

"I guess you found me."

"Ain't findin' you that's as important as how I find you."

Ray arched his eyebrows.

"What I mean is . . . is . . . Well, do you have any help workin' this place?"

Ray shuffled his right foot in the dirt. "I got a man comin' in a day or two. He'll be workin' as a mechanic to start." He looked Bob in the eye. "You know anybody willin' to come to work for a raggedy, worn out, broke down and just plain broke custom farmer? . . . who ain't got no custom farmin' to do?"

"Well, now that you make mention of it, I might be seekin' a new situation myself."

"Why? You've been with Washabow for as long as I can remember."

"I was workin' this particular piece of land before that. I went with Carl when he bought up everything he could get his hands on back after the war. I ain't never liked him, but I had my reasons for stickin' around. Still do, but, I can take care of that pretty well from right here."

Ray studied the weathered face for a moment before speaking again. "You never tried to go to work for my grandfather that I know of. Why me and why now?"

"For one thing, Joe Winstead was about the hardest workin' man I knew. And tight as a drum to boot. He only had one man workin' for him full time in all those years. Took on extry help whenever he needed it, but, 'cept for you, he might' near worked this place all by his lonesome. He didn't need me."

"And you think I do," Ray said completing the thought that Mr. Bob didn't want to.

"Ray, I'm glad you have the place now."

Ray cast a puzzled look at Bob.

"You may not know this; it's been so long ago. Before you were even a twinkle in your Daddy's eye. But, this partic'lar piece of land was part of the original Washabow holding. Except when Carl came by it, it was known as the Montana Miss. And he married into it."

"This place belonged to Miss Emily's father?" Ray asked.

"Been in the family for years. Some of it before the war even."

"That's a long time. I 'magine there was some Rebel and Yankee blood spilled over it."

"Yep. A few of Grant's boys wandered up here from Vicksburg. Got whupped, though."

"I suppose you were there," Ray prodded.

"I ain't quite that old yet, son. My granddaddy was though. A miniball took his life, and Miss Emily's great granddaddy took his land. It was part of the original Montana Miss holdings."

"Did Miss Emily inherit it?"

"Actually," Bob explained, "Miss Emily's parents did own the place, but they were both killed in a car wreck when Miss Emily was in her early teens. Her two older brothers, somewhere in their twenties, worked the place as best they could. It suffered some while they were in the army in the other war. The older boy was killed at Normandy, the younger brother lived through the war, but couldn't handle the place on his own. He was always kind of wild, and a big drinker. Well, the worse things got with the place here, the worse he drank. He was found one morning, drowned down in Washabow Creek."

"So that left everything with Miss Emily."

"Yep. But, she was just a young girl, and there was no way she could handle the place. She was a pretty thing, though," Bob said wistfully. "Along comes a big talking ladies' man name of Carl Sullivan, who knew how to farm but didn't have a single dirt clod to call his own. He had been an officer in the war. He had him some money and some bankin' connections. Well, he fell in love with this place before he fell in love with Miss Emily, if he ever did love her." There was a hint of bitterness in Bob's voice. "It didn't take much convincing for her to marry him. When more land came available he convinced Miss Emily that he couldn't borrow any money to expand unless the land was all in his name, so he got half title to the Montana Miss, made his first acquisition, and changed the name of the place to Walashabou Farm and Cattle Company. You folks have been a burr under his saddle ever since he lost this parcel to Joe over a horse race back around fifty-eight."

"He wants it back," Ray said. "and I get the feeling he don't much care how that comes about."

"Ray, I worked for Carl Sullivan for a long time, and I was loyal to him, even if I didn't never like 'im. But, I know him as a hard man and I know there was a lot more to what happened between you and him than what we all heard about. And I saw Em . . . Miss Emily suffer terribly in those years after you went to prison. The truth was something she couldn't tell for some reason. It is no secret that Carl was rough on her. He may even be the reason she has that limp. He almost died a young man over that, I'll tell you. But, after your trial, it was like nothing he could say or do could hurt her any more. It was like he, or she, had done worse to herself than anybody else could ever do to her again." He paused. "I hope this won't go no further."

"Of course not."

"Folks're already talkin', sayin' you'll never make it. And here you are, determined to do it in spite of it all. I'd give what's left of my virility to be in on it! And, if that ain't enough, any burr under Carl's saddle is a friend of mine."

"You serious, Mr. Bob?" Ray queried.

Bob chuckled as if he were embarrassed. "I'm sorry, Ray. I . . . I guess I kind of got caught up in the excitement for a minute there. You don't need an old coot like me slowin' you down. I guess I'd better just count my days with Carl."

"I am gonna need some help, Mr. Bob," Ray said. "On the way over here I got scared to death about all this. I know how to farm, but, gittin' people to trust me enough to do business with me is gon' be tough. It may take awhile. But, I'm gon' need the best help I can get. I can't think of none better'n you, particularly around here. I hadn't thought about it 'til now, but, maybe some folks'll do business with me because they trust you."

Bob lowered his head in a rare moment of humility; his battered old cowboy hat was turning in his hands.

"I can't pay much to start, but I'll be better than most when we turn a crop. Until then, I'll pay you as good as I can and you can keep your . . . your . . . virility, as you say."

"Ray, I don't care what you pay me," Bob cried. "And I've got some fire left in me yet, boy. We'll show 'em all. You don't know what it would mean to be back where I feel like I belong. Where I feel like I count for something."

"Yeah, Mr. Bob, I do know. I know exactly what you mean." Ray extended his hand again. "Welcome to . . . to . . . Winstead Farm Services." (He had only now thought about what he might name his business.)

Bob took Ray's outstretched hand into his own. "You might fire me before we get started good, but, I got a small piece of advice for you, if you'll listen. Do what you want with it."

Curious, Ray replied, "Let's hear it."

"You got a good name, Ray. It's as good now as it was fifteen years ago. I can understand that you might think you'll do better without the Bennett name attached right up front of your business. But, if you want folks to trust you, it seems to me that you'd want 'em to know what kind of man you are, who you are, and how proud you are to be who you are when you walk in the door. I understand you wantin' to honor your granddaddy by keepin' his name on the business. I think he'll be honored plenty by the work you do and the kind of man you are. But this place is yours now. And it's gon' try to do you in. If you really want to own this place, you gotta take this place."

Ray looked down and stomped the dust from his shoes. He looked at Bob, then turned slowly and surveyed what amounted to the ruins of a once thriving business. In order to rebuild the ruins of his life, he had to rebuild the ruins of this business. He had to repair or replace virtually every piece of equipment his grandfather had owned and once kept in prime condition. He had to start from scratch in a hostile community and find local growers willing to give him a chance. And he had to overcome as yet unseen obstacles and traps no doubt laid by Carl Sullivan. Above all, when all was said and done, win or lose, he had to be Ray Bennett.

"Like I said," he grinned, "Welcome to Bennett Farm Services!"

Bob's eyes glistened at the sound of those words. "I'll have to give Clint some notice. Right thing to do. Here he is, been tryin' to run me off since Carl turned most everything over to 'im. Won't he be surprised to hear where I'm headin'?"

"You come on over as soon as he cuts you loose."

Mary had been trying to talk Ray into a shopping trip to Jackson. She had already bought a couple of pairs of jeans and some shirts for him. But, he needed much more. He wanted to have something other than the shoes he had been given in prison, for work. He needed a coat, more work clothes, something dressy enough for church or a funeral (although he was rather apprehensive about going to church anytime soon.) "I've been saving and waiting for this for years," she insisted. "I want to fix you up just like I did when you were in school."

There was no fighting it. Mary was determined to make the trip with Ray in tow. He decided that he should give in and let his mother take him shopping, and that now was as good a time as any. He closed the gate to the tractor lot and headed for home.

"Home," he said to himself. "There's something else to take care of."

4.

His third day of freedom began much as the second one had. Ray awoke, loudly, from the same nightmare that had plagued him the night before. He read from his Bible, the Book of James this time. Then he donned new clothes from head to toe. He preferred a cowboy hat and cowboy boots, and he had purchased two of each, again at Mary's insistence, but, he did not think they would be practical for the day's work, so he grabbed one of several new caps his father had given him, which had been given to Pat. (The popular notion being that you should never purchase a cap for your own use. Taken as a gift or as a promotion of some kind a man could accumulate quite a collection of fine new caps over a lifetime.) His new lace-up work boots were comfortable and functional. And they would be warm on these cold Fall mornings. The stiffness of the new jeans he would have to live with for a while.

Two eggs, a healthy serving of grits, two pieces of toast and three cups of coffee later, Ray was out the door and on the short drive to the tractor shed. The reddish orange face of the sun peeked at him just over the far tree tops as he pulled in and opened the gate. It was a crisp, cold morning. And Ray had never felt better.

By seven o'clock, Ray had used his father's gasoline powered trimmer to clear the tall dry weeds from around the fence posts and beneath the fence that surrounded the tractor lot. Pausing to decide on his next project, he was surprised to see Pat drive up with his big Yazoo lawn mower in the back of his truck.

"I thought you might need some help cleanin' things up down here, too," Pat said. "I can get up close to the fence with this mower and you can catch the rest with your bush hog."

"Well, Pop, I appreciate it," replied Ray, "but, you don't need to come down here and work."

"I've about decided that if I'm gonna spend any time to amount to anything with you before I go back to my job, I'm gonna have to go to work with you. Besides, I've been looking forward to just this thing for a long time."

Ray grinned. "In that case, let me help you unload that mower, and if you'll run me up to the old barn, I'll bring the little tractor and bush hog down here."

Working straight through to dinner time, Ray and Pat had cut all of the grass, or rather the weeds, along the fence line. Towering weeds had been cleared from most of the stalls and new light bulbs in the dark recesses of the tractor shed awaited the power that would bring them to life.

After surveying the needs of the structure and the lot, Pat insisted on being allowed to go to town and order a couple of loads of gravel for the lot, some rough lumber and a few pieces of new tin roofing to make some much needed repairs. Ray suppressed his independent streak with the knowledge that his parents, who had done more for him through his years in prison than they would ever know, felt a great need to do for him now. He also knew that his homecoming had opened a lot of old wounds and placed his family back on the forefront of the gossip mill. His success here, now, was important to his family for more than just his own happiness and well being. It could put the Bennett name, the Bennett family, back into the normalcy and acceptance they all desired so much.

Ray wanted to let Miss Emily know that he would get the tractor lot and shed back in better shape as soon as possible. He was sure it had been a disturbing sight to her as it deteriorated over the years. The family may have been able to have it kept up some better, but, they had no inclination to make things pleasant for any of the Sullivans. They only had this one place to use as a constant reminder of the demise the Sullivans had brought to the Bennetts. The message probably fell on blinded eyes, but it was there.

A plump black woman wearing the face of serenity answered his knock at the door. "May I help you, sir?" she asked.

"I'm Ray Bennett. I wanted to see Miss Emily for just a minute if I could."

Rona studied Ray for a brief moment. "I remember you now, Mister Ray. You growed a bit, but you are still a handsome white man."

"Yes, ma'am, if you say so," Ray replied.

"Come on in," Rona said. "I'll go tell Miss Emily you're here. She's got company."

Ray threw up his hand. "No, don't bother her if she has company. I can come back later."

"No, sir. You best wait. Miss Emily would be some kind of perturbed at me if I was to let you go. 'Sides," she said studying Ray's face, "you might want to see her company, too." Rona disappeared toward the kitchen.

Ray wandered into the large den that once was so familiar to him. The feel of this great house was much the same as it had been so many years ago. He swung open the double doors that led to the raised deck and walked out into a cold October wind.

Again, memories flooded into his consciousness faster than he could sort them, much less handle them. Gazing over the rail at the far side of the deck to the low rock retainer wall below, Ray was suddenly transported back over sixteen years in time to a rainy night in July. The musty smell of hot wet concrete filled his nostrils. The sound of rain falling on the roof above and behind him, and the splashing of water to the ground below as it tumbled off of the deck drummed in his ears. There, lying with his legs twisted oddly behind him and blood washing from the gash in his head, with rain pelting his unconscious face laid Carl Sullivan. A scream welling up inside him . . .

"Ray," the voice was little more than a whisper. "Ray, oh, Ray! I can't believe it's you," the unmistakable voice of Laura Sullivan wafted across the deck.

Ray turned to see Laura rushing across the few steps between them, her arms flung wide.

"Laura!"

He grabbed her and twirled her around twice before setting her down. He was embarrassed to have to stop himself from kissing her. He had so dreamed of such a kiss, but he knew it could not happen. No matter how much he wanted it, and even if Laura did as well, it could not happen.

"Laura," he said softly before letting her go. "As pretty as ever."

"Oh, Ray," she said wiping the tears from her eyes. Shaking her head in frustration she said, "I don't know what to say. I've wanted to see you and talk to you for so many years. And now I can't think of a thing to say! It is so good to see you."

"Good to see you, too."

They stood there awkwardly for a moment.

"Mama will be here in a minute. She has a cake in the oven." After another long pause, Laura spoke out, "Ray, I want you to know that I don't hold anything against you. Papa still blames you for everything, but I realized long ago that it was all a tragic accident." She paused. "I said some horrible things to you, and I've regretted every word for years."

"He never told you the truth?" Ray asked in surprise.

"Yes, he said . . ."

"He told you what he hoped would be a believable story," Emily interrupted. "So few know the real truth. And, God help me, I'm one of them."

"What do you mean, Mama? Papa said Ray didn't mean to knock him off of the deck, but that he . . . he did attack him."

"I mean it's time you knew the truth," Emily said bitterly.

"Miss Emily, I would like to know that truth more than anybody. But, I think things should be left as they are for now," Ray pleaded.

"No, Ray," she responded, "you were cheated out of half of your lifetime. You were jailed unjustly for fifteen years while life here went on and the lies were told and lives have been altered and manipulated in ways they never should have been. People here still think of you as a criminal. Some of them are afraid of having you around. And it's all my fault."

"No, Miss Emily. Don't go on. It's ok. People are going to think what they will. And it's not your fault."

"Oh, Ray," Emily continued, "so much of your life was taken from you, I won't allow you to sacrifice the rest of it to cover my lies."

"Mama!" Laura exclaimed. "What are you talking about?"

"Nothing," Ray blurted. "She ain't talking about nothing." Turning to face Laura's mother, Ray said, "Miss Emily, it doesn't matter what people think. And there are others involved besides you and me."

"Of course there are," Emily almost shouted. "One is my daughter, and the other is my granddaughter! Oh, the misery I've caused! If I could only go back," she sobbed.

"What misery, Mama?" Laura asked, fright in her voice. "What do you mean?"

"Your mother has caused no misery," Ray said. "Miss Emily, we've been over this. Nobody blames you. You didn't do anything. What happened happened. That's all there is to it. And it wasn't your lie. If there was one, it was Carl's. And those lies hurt. What is the truth going to do now but just cause more hurt. It ain't necessary."

"Oh, but it is, Ray. I can't live with it any longer. I thought that when you were paroled it would be easier. And I thought when you took over your grandfather's place everything would be alright. But it isn't. You are a fine man. You should be respected in the community, not feared. And my silence, silence as damaging as any lie my husband ever told is responsible for it. You cannot continue to sacrifice yourself! Don't you see? Carl won't set things straight. I'm the only one that can do it. And that makes me solely responsible."

"Will someone please tell me what is going on?" Laura shouted with anger in her voice.

"I'm going to right now, darling," Emily said holding her hand up to silence Ray. "You've not been told the truth about your father's accident."

"What truth?" Laura shouted in frustration.

Ray spoke before Miss Emily had a chance to start. "The truth that Miss Emily thinks would have kept me out of prison. She just feels responsible because she didn't testify, that's all. Your daddy wouldn't let her appear in court because she saw things differently and he wanted me put away. Your mama feels responsible."

"Mama, that is ridiculous," Laura said. "You can't blame yourself for what happened. We all feel bad now about the way things went, but you couldn't have changed anything."

"Honey, you just don't know," Miss Emily said.

Ray turned and walked slowly to Emily. "It was not your fault," he repeated slowly, evenly. "Nobody blames you. I have never blamed you. We were all victims of Carl Sullivan. Miss Emily, you're a dear lady, and I so regret what all this has done to you."

"You have every right to hate Carl. God forgive me, I have hated him just as I have loved him," Emily sobbed. "With the baby coming, he knew he had to get rid of you. You were never in his plans for Laura. The marriage of Walashabou and McKay Farms was almost an obsession with him. That's why he pushed Ben Corman to charge you with attempted murder. Statutory rape . . . well . . . it . . . soiled . . . " she winced at the vulgar connotation of the word, "the family name. You had just turned eighteen years old, Laura's eighteenth birthday just months away. And he didn't need that to put you away. No, attempted murder affected only you . . . and your family. And . . . there was the . . . problem . . . of everyone knowing that Laura was carrying your child, not Clint McKay's."

Laura gasped.

Ray drew a deep breath and exhaled slowly. He hadn't expected it to come up in open conversation. Precious few people knew this secret. He had thought of his daughter, day dreamed about her constantly, but seen her only in the few pictures his parents were able to bring to him down through the years. There had been little discussion of her, though. He feared now, as he had then, what the truth would do to her. This great lie protected her from him, or rather what the knowledge of him could do to her. It provided for her in a way that he never could have. And it grieved him more than anything else that ever happened to him in his life.

"Oh, honey!" Emily said in horror. "I forgot you were there!" She hurried to hold her sobbing daughter.

"Papa made a deal with Clint? He paid Clint to marry me?" Laura cried. "I thought he loved me!"

"Honey, Clint did love you," Emily said. She placed her hand on Laura's shoulder. "During those few months after you and Clint broke up and you were going with Ray you know he kept calling trying to get back together with you. Your father just accelerated things somewhat. Clint gave up a college education, Carl gave up some land right then and promised the rest through inheritance. Emmy was raised as Emily McKay, Clint's daughter. You both, Ray as well, agreed that it was for the best."

"For the best?" Laura exclaimed. "It was for a lie! For Papa's own selfish reasons! Sure, Clint was willing. I thought it was because he had changed into this super great guy who could love me and love another man's child as his own. Ray was going to be in prison. He would be fifty eight! Fifty eight years old when he got out because I'm sure that the mighty Carl Sullivan had removed any chance of parole. I didn't want that baby to come into this world facing that. I wanted her to have the best life she could have. And Ray! Ray wanted that, too."

Turning back to Ray she continued, "You were so kind, so . . . so wonderful those last few times we talked. You agreed that Emily should be born as a McKay. You wanted her to have a father she could be proud of, not one who was a convict. This wasn't supposed to be some kind of a business deal orchestrated by my father! And all along you knew the truth. Mama could have kept you out of prison, couldn't she? You tried to tell me, but I wouldn't believe you. I wouldn't even listen to you. Emmy should know you. She should know such love from her father!"

"She cannot know it," Ray said reading the thoughts behind Laura's eyes. "Miss Emily, we've all suffered some through all this. We've lived through it, and we still have lives to live. If you need to hear it from me, I forgive you. But, I will say it again. As far as I am or have ever been concerned, you were blameless. There is nothing to forgive. And, no, Laura, your mother could not have stopped Carl." Ray wondered if those words he was speaking really were truthful when it came to Miss Emily's ability to keep him out of prison. "Nobody could. We all just did the best we could for Emmy back then, and we have to now."

Emily started crying again. Laura hugged Ray and quietly, simply, whispered, "Thank you."

Just then a door closed inside the house and a young voice yelled, "I'm back. I have your bananas, Mamaw!" As she came into view of the strange scene on the patio, Emmy drew up short. "What's happening? Why are you crying, Mamaw? Mama? You've been crying, too!"

Ray stood in shocked silence. Trying not to stare, yet unable to turn away. He was afraid to move, afraid to speak lest anything he did might give away the secrecy of the moment. And he could not process the thoughts and emotions attacking him at this, his first glimpse of his daughter. He wanted to reach out to her. Run to her and hug her and tell her . . . Tell her what? He was pulled from his thoughts by Laura's voice.

Laura wiped her eyes and took her daughter's arm. "Emmy, I want you to meet somebody. This . . ."

"I'm Ray Bennett," Ray interrupted afraid of what Laura might say in such a state of high emotion. He feared that his own thoughts would be betrayed somehow. His stomach churned, his voice quivered a bit. The eyes that he looked into, growing angry though they were, were those of his own. He extended his hand, even as it trembled.

His daughter was beautiful. He saw much of her mother in her dark complexion and her soft features. Her dark hair matched his own and fell over her shoulders much as Laura's had at that age. Those eyes, a pretty brown unlike his hazel color, were his, though. He wondered if she recognized the same thing, but knew that she had no reason even to consider who this man in front of her resembled. Her five feet four inch frame was set in an aggressive pose. Her stare unwelcoming. She did not like anything about this Ray Bennett fellow. She had no reason to.

"You're him!" Emmy said after staring for half a minute, ignoring his outstretched hand. "What have you done to my Mama and my Mamaw?"

Laura pulled her advancing daughter back. "Ray has done nothing wrong here, Emmy. In fact, he has just done a great kindness to your grandmother . . . and to me."

"Yeah, I'll bet. He's out of prison and just wants to fool everybody into liking him." She directed those hard eyes at Ray, "Well, Mister, you can just go on back to prison where you belong. Don't you come around here bothering my Mamaw. She has suffered enough because of you!"

"Emmy!" her mother scolded. "You've no reason to speak to Ray in such a manner."

Ray held his hands up in surrender before Emmy could say anything else. "I only meant to stay for a few minutes. I'll be going." Turning to Emily, he said, "Miss Emily, I stopped by to tell you that I'll have all that junk next door cleaned up just as soon as I can. I'll be operating my business from there, but, I'll keep the place up, I promise."

Miss Emily's bottom lip quivered. "I'm glad you're going to be there. It's a big job. I know you are up to it."

"Me and my new top hand, Bob Riley, can handle it o.k. I have another man coming and we'll have the place in top shape before you know it."

A sparkle came into Emily's eye. Ray wondered whether it was at the mention of cleaning up the eyesore next door or the sound of Bob Riley's name. Perhaps it was a little of both. "I can think of nothing finer, Ray. Nothing at all." A sudden calmness enveloped her as she returned in her mind to those happy days as a child on the Montana Miss. She reached to hug Ray once again and whispered, "I know the truth, Ray. The whole truth. You must let me tell it, for your own sake. Laura should know. Everyone should know."

Ray shook his head and replied softly, "We have other people to consider. And there's enough old wounds to heal, Miss Emily. There ain't no need in openin' new ones."

"I'll walk you to the door," Laura offered.

Ray looked at Emmy, who was still glaring at him, and managed to say, "It was nice to meet you, Emmy."

"I wish I could say the same," she retorted.

"I'm sorry, Ray," Laura said quietly when they reached the front porch. "She's a very sweet girl. But, she is very protective of family. It's not what I had hoped your introduction to her would be."

"Well, it's not what I've dreamed about for years either," Ray said. "But, I'm proud of her for standing up for you and Miss Emily. She's got fire in 'er." He paused for a brief moment, reluctant to leave. "I better go. Good to see you, Laura."

"You too, Ray. We should get together soon. There is so much we need to talk about," Laura replied wistfully.

"She's beautiful," Ray said. "You and Clint have done a good job." He turned and walked a few steps beyond the porch before he looked back to see her still gazing after him.

"I've got a lot to sort out. We'll talk soon, Laura, real soon."

Laura stood still in the doorway, watching as his truck turned out of the drive and disappeared from sight.

5.

Ray worked the remainder of the afternoon and evening at the old barn. He wanted to get away from the sight of the Sullivan house for a while. Out of sight did not, however, equal out of mind. Images of Emmy clouded his thoughts throughout the day. He had not been prepared to see her although it had been an event he had longed for, for fifteen years. In his dreams, Emmy had instantly recognized him for who he really was to her. She had rushed into his arms and whispered, "I've waited so long for this, Daddy!" The pain of the knowledge that this scene would never play itself out as a joyful celebration would not fade into the work Ray now threw himself into. She despised him.

With the line trimmer and the lawn mower, he soon had the lot around the barn looking good. With the tractor shed serving as his present base of operations, the barn was of little practical use to him at the moment, but he wanted to get it back into good shape, and it would be put to use soon enough when the hay and grain season came.

"Looks like you've had a long day, son," Pat said as Ray joined his mother and father for supper.

"Yes, sir. Quite a day," Ray replied after a moment. Buttering a roll, he said, "I got me quite a place to look after now. I appreciate your help, Pop."

"By the way," his father said, "Four loads of gravel will be delivered tomorrow, and your lumber and tin for the shed should be out tomorrow or the next day."

"Bob Riley stopped by and I ended up hiring him. You know, I think he's as excited as I am. I know he's glad to be getting away from Clint.

Pat smiled, "I've got to get back to the plant and you're gonna need more help than Bob can give you to start. Have you given any thought to that?"

"I have, and I need to make another phone call, now that you've reminded me," Ray replied. He walked to the hall where the phone was located. Before he closed the door behind him he said, "I saw Emmy today. She's a fine girl." He paused and looked into the searching eyes of his mother and father. "I doubt she'd say anything near the same about me . . ., but, maybe it's for the best."

Despite the cold, Pat went out and sat on the front porch. The only light out there was the glow from his cigar, the only sound the creak of his rocking chair against the wood plank floor of the porch. Mary cleared the table silently except for a muted sniffle from time to time as she fought back her tears.

The morning fog had not yet cleared and Ray had just backed the little Massey Ferguson up to the rusty box blade. He hoped for an early delivery of the gravel and he wanted the box blade on the tractor so he could begin spreading the gravel over the lot as soon as possible. Gazing up over the blade when he detected movement in the corner of his eye, he found himself looking at the slim frame of a teenage boy. The boy waved shyly.

"Mornin'" Ray greeted. He left the tractor idling and climbed down to shake the outstretched hand. "Ray Bennett."

"I know, I mean I'm Matthew Warren, Mr. Bennett."

"Glad to meet you, Matthew. What can I do for you?"

"Well, sir, I was wondering . . . I mean everybody has . . . I heard that you got yourself a place to run all of a sudden," the boy stammered. "I like doing farm work a lot, and if you need some help, I'd like to . . . I wanted to see if you needed some . . . help."

"You know all about farmin', do you?" Ray asked amused at the boy's nervousness.

"Yes, sir . . . I mean I . . .uh . . . have a lot to learn, but I can drive a tractor, and run cows, and fix fence, and I'll do just about anything you need me to. What I don't know I'll learn real fast."

"I see," Ray said. "How old are you? You still in school?"

"I just turned sixteen, and I'm a sophomore at Coleman. But I can work for you after school, and on weekends and holidays. I can even work before school some, Mr. Bennett. I can get up real early when I have to . . . I mean I like to and all, so I'll put in a good day for you."

Ray looked beyond Matthew toward the road. "You walkin'?" It was then that he noticed the boy's worn cowboy boots, and patched jeans. He wore a nice enough jacket that was obviously not enough for this very cold morning. The boy was shivering despite his best efforts to control the shaking of his body.

"Yes, sir. I live just about a mile and a half over between here and Little Bridge." Matthew pointed toward his home as if Ray could see it and approve. "I thought I'd walk on down this mornin' and find you. I was gonna go on over to your other barn. I'm glad you're here, though. I can catch the bus when it comes through around twenty 'til."

Before Ray could speak, Matthew burst out, "Hey! I could catch this bus from school and get off here in the afternoon! I could put in more time for you then. Uh . . . that is if you need me."

"Well, anybody that will work this hard to get a job is bound to work hard at it. Six bucks an hour, at least two hours a day after school, and we'll just have to see what goes on around here on Saturday. Sundays off, unless something special comes along." Ray reached to shake Matthew's hand again. "Glad to have you, Matt. When can you start?"

"Today, if you want me to," Matthew responded grinning.

"I'll see you after school, then."

"What all are you going to need to do around here?"

"You eat supper with me and my folks tonight and I'll tell you all about it."

Matthew shuffled his feet nervously. "Well, I appreciate the offer and all, but, I got to take care of my little sister most nights."

"Oh?" Ray mused. "Well, I like a man that takes care of his responsibilities. You'll find out what's going on soon enough anyway. See you after school."

Matthew turned to walk to the road to wait for the school bus. The scuffed and worn heels on his boots reminded Ray of the way he had always worn his own boots long past their normal life.

Four truckloads of gravel arrived soon after eight o'clock. Ray spent the morning spreading the gravel as best he could with the small box blade on his smallest tractor. It was slow going, but the place was really taking shape. Viewing his progress, Ray realized that he very soon would be in a position to start the second most important job he had to do; that of getting his equipment in working order. The most important job was going out and finding work to do. He also had cattle to buy and crops of his own to plan.

Just before he stopped for lunch, Bob drove up. "I'm not real sure whether I quit or got fired," Bob said. "I caught up with Clint about twenty minutes ago and told him I was signin' on with you and he blew his top. You'd of thought he wanted to keep me or somethin'. He ranted and raved about me bein' a traitor and you stealin' everything he has. Anyway, the long and short of it is he don't want no notice from me, so he paid me off and here I am," Bob said slapping the tall rear tire of the tractor. "I figured since I went to the trouble to get out of bed this mornin', I might as well put in a full day's work. I'll take my vacation when you're payin' me for it."

"Well, I was just on the way home to eat dinner," Ray said. "Why don't you come on with me and you can fill me in on what all really needs to be done on this place while Mama fills you up."

Bob exclaimed, "I knew I would like workin' for you, Ray! Carl ain't fed me a meal in longer'n I can remember."

Matthew was so excited that his day at school was almost wasted. A generally good student, he could always be counted on to get his assignment done, mostly right, and he was not a trouble maker. He was, however, a source of jokes and ridicule by many of his peers. His clothes were not what anyone would call stylish, even by the mostly rural standards of his public school classmates. The kids that attended any of the three private schools that this part of Winstead County offered were unmerciful.

To some extent, Matt, endured taunts from one sector of teen society or another on a daily basis. His boots, which he wore year round, were badly scuffed and had holes in the soles. He had two pairs of jeans and usually alternated them every other week rather than every other day. He dressed as neatly as he could, though, and the pride, to him at least, of his wardrobe was his 'Future Farmers of America' jacket. He had worked hard for the money to buy it and he took the best of care of it. Normally, he wouldn't have worn it to school on such a cold day as this, but he wanted to look his best when he asked Mr. Bennett for a job. His heavy coat had seen its better days a year or two ago and his long skinny wrists reached far beyond the ends of the sleeves. His father said he looked like something out of a Frankenstein movie in that old coat. It would have been alright if he had been joking, but he hadn't. Felix Warren was not one to carry on with his children.

The main reason for Matthew's distance from others his age, though, was his father, Felix. His mother had run off with a door to door cancer insurance salesman when Matthew was seven. Felix Warren was a rather unpleasant character. And, truth be known, he would just as soon his wife had taken the children with her when she left. His alcoholism and his brusque, abusive manner had kept him in poverty. He had started more than his share of brawls in beer joints and even at school sporting events. He was just plain mean, drunk or not, but more so when he was drunk. If he couldn't find anyone else to beat on, Matthew was there to satisfy his brutal impulses.

Somehow Matthew had always managed to protect his younger sister, Billie Rose, from their father's tirades. Billie Rose, who was four years younger than her brother, had many of the same problems at school as Matthew. As a young girl in elementary school, she had had many friends. The paradox of small children is that while they can be so mean to one another, they can also be quite accepting. However, as they grew older, when status and group acceptance became so much more important than friendship, most of Billie Rose's friends abandoned her.

Still, Billie Rose was a fine student, in no small way because of her brother. Following the departure of their mother, the children bonded closely together, at first in fear of their father. When the bad times came, Matthew would hurry Billie Rose off to her special hiding place while he stood and took whatever amount of punishment Felix was handing out at the time. Matthew always saw to it that his sister had something to eat, even if he had to go without. Felix was not much of a provider. As for school work, Matthew was a hard task master and patient teacher to Billie Rose. As a result, she was among the brightest of students in the sixth grade at Coleman Attendance Center.

Today, as on most days, Matthew ate his lunch by himself. Lofton Freeman, the closest of Matthew's few friends, was not in school today, probably having skipped as he was prone to do. He received the usual requisite stares. It was strange how the other kids would ostracize Matthew and at the same time think him strange for being such a loner. Today, though, nothing could bother Matt . . . almost nothing.

One of the ways Matt earned his money was by working at the school. During the growing seasons, he cut grass on campus and he helped the custodian, Mr. Saxton, during the colder months, or whenever he was needed. On this particular day he was needed for an important errand.

Coleman's principal, Garland Hinton, had a nephew, Robert Carter, who was the head football coach at Winstead Academy, which was the private school over between the wee town of Coleman and Little Bridge, which was nothing more than a small grocery store at a cross roads. A wheel had fallen off of WA's field marker the previous Friday as they prepared for their upcoming football game. As Coleman's game was away that night, Uncle Garland was accommodating enough to send Coleman's field marker with a load of Winstead County lime in it so young Robert would be able to hold his game on a well defined field.

The field marker had not yet been returned and Coleman's Coach Harris was getting rather antsy. Besides, he didn't know who this honky principal thought he was sending public school equipment over to the private school. His silence, however, had been assured by the reciprocal promise of the use of Winstead's fine new outdoor heater for the all important Friday night game with Holly Bluff. His boys might freeze next week, but, tonight, they would keep their feet warm compliments of the Winstead Academy Booster Club!

Matt's errand was to take the ancient sixty-nine Ford pickup truck over to WA and pick up both the field marker and the heater . . . by all means, the heater. Arriving at Winstead Academy during their lunch period, he searched for the person unknown to him, but most likely to be Coach Carter. Told that the coach was down at the field house fueling up the heater, Ray began to make his way there. Winstead Academy did not have a cafeteria or a lunch room of any kind.

The kids brought their lunch, the boys in paper sacks and the girls in cute lunch boxes and bags, and each day, weather permitting, they went to their group's respective territory around the campus and stood, sat, or squatted to eat their turkey and ham and cheese and bologna sandwiches.

Matt passed near one of these groups eating on the tailgate of a fully customized, daddy-paid pickup. He recognized most of the faces there, and sought frantically for a way to reverse his course before he was spotted. The conversation being held there at the tail end of the truck, however, pulled him in closer to this group of privies he would much rather avoid.

"That Ray Bennett guy was at my grandmother's yesterday," he heard Emmy McKay say.

"You mean the one that was in prison so long? You actually saw him?" Allison asked.

"What was he like?" two other girls asked in unison.

Emmy shrugged. "I don't know. He just introduced himself to me and left. My mother and grandmother were both crying when I got there."

"Crying? What did he do to them? What did you do?" Carol asked.

"My mom said he was nice to them, but something weird happened. I don't know what. They said they didn't want to talk about it and I couldn't get anything out of them. I know that he and my mom were friends in high school. She even went out with him. I think my dad was friends with him, too. I guess I was kind of rude to him, but, so far, he seems pretty nice."

"Yeah, he was nice enough to break Mr. Carl's back," Bo Hopson interjected. "He ain't nothing but a convict. Probably turned sissy in jail. Hey, Emmy, you think he's nice? Mr. Carl will have him where he wants him soon enough."

"You plannin' on marryin' Emmy and gettin' that land for yourself, Bo?" his buddy, Tim, laughed.

Above the laughs of the others around him, Bo replied, "I'm not planning to marry anybody. I just hate to see some low down convict get it, that's all. You just wait. Mr. Carl will send him crawling out of the county like the jail bird slug he is."

This was more than Matt could stand. He had only met Ray Bennett this very morning and he had received not one dollar from him, but he had read enough Louis L'amour books to know that a man defends the brand he rides for. It did not matter that he had not yet lifted a finger in labor for Bennett Farm Services, as Mr. Bennett had called it. He was part of the outfit.

"What do you know about Mr. Bennett?" Matthew asked Bo. "You've never met him. I have and I think he's an o.k. guy."

"Oh right, Warren," Bo retorted. "Like any of us care what you think. What business is it of yours anyway?"

"He's my boss, and I won't have him talked about like that!" Matthew said tensing his muscles.

A sudden hush swept the area.

"Is there something you want to do about it, hayseed?" Bo taunted.

"I'll do what I have to," Matthew responded.

As the two boys maneuvered closer together Mr. Peyton, the school headmaster stepped between them and diffused the situation. Before he walked away, Matthew cast a quick glance at Emmy and gave a barely perceptible nod. Those who did notice it giggled. Emmy blushed and averted her eyes. She had always felt sorry for Matt. He was quiet. He was cute . . . once you looked at him. And he was probably very lonely. She felt for him. But, she could do no more than speak to him in hushed tones on the few times they came that close together. To do more might hurt her social standing around school. First things first.

As he loaded the field marker and heater into the back of the truck, Matthew felt more cold stares and endured more whispers than usual. He was undaunted, though. He had stood up for his boss, for his outfit. Anyway, he was no more alone now than before.

Perhaps that was what attracted Matthew to farm work. Much of one's time on a farm was spent alone. There was no group of jerks hanging around to kid and laugh and make jokes about every move he made. His clothing didn't matter. Only his work mattered. And at the end of the day he could look back with great satisfaction and see what he alone had done. In a world where Matthew Warren got little satisfaction and less praise, farming, for him, was its own reward.

By mid-afternoon, Bob and Ray had looked over much of Ray's holdings. They were on their way to the pasture where he planned to hold his cattle once they were bought. They had to drive past the tractor shed to get there, and as they approached it, they both noticed a cloud of dust rising from the wide gravel drive that lead to the lot. "Who do you reckon that is?" Ray asked Bob.

Ray turned into the lot and was surprised to see his little Massey Ferguson pulling a rusty four row planter across the newly graveled lot. At the wheel sat his newest employee.

"I forgot about my new man," Ray chuckled. "Matthew Warren. You know anything about him?"

Bob rubbed his chin. "I know you got yourself a worker there. He's a good boy. Had 'im a rough time though. His mama run off when he was just a little fella. His daddy is horse crap, pure and simple."

"He seems to be a good kid. How did he turn out that way with the life he's had?" Ray asked.

"It's hard to say. I don't think he has many friends and, other than school, he don't get to see much of them anyway. He has a little sister. He's more of a father and mother to her than Felix is." Bob sighed. "You know sometimes no matter how well a kid is raised there's always a bad seed? Well, Matt there is just a good one. I'm glad you put him on. Maybe he will last longer with you than he did with Clint."

"Huh?"

"Oh, he came by Clint's place every other day until Clint finally put him on. He went right to work, too. Do anything you asked him to." Bob laughed, "Clint saw 'im makin' eyes at that Emmy one day and fired 'im on the spot."

"Sounds to me like Clint was over reacting," Ray said.

"Oh, well, that's what Clint is best at," Bob answered. "As a matter of fact, he is really out there over you bein' back and workin' this place and all. Laura don't know how bad he is and Miss Emily sure don't. I expect Carl will be pushin' him to push you. I 'magine you'll be hearin' from Mr. Clint McKay."

By this time, Matthew had made his way back across the lot. He left the tractor running and trotted over to greet Ray and Bob.

"I hope you don't mind me movin' this stuff around. I kinda figured out what you were doin' and I hated to just sit around until you came to tell me what to do. I thought I would move as much as I can and then cut the grass that's been growin' up through that old equipment."

"You're doin' fine," Ray said. "I think you know Bob here."

Bob and Matt nodded at each other and shook hands.

"You just keep going like you are. I want things as neat as possible. I don't want to throw anything away just yet. We'll spend the next few days figurin' out what all can be salvaged. We'll be back before time for you to go. Five thirty or six o.k. with you?"

"I'm here 'til you let me go, Mr. Bennett," Matthew said matter of factly.

Ray and Bob spent the next hour looking over the pasture land. He wanted to make sure water and shelter were still where he had remembered them as being. They went to the old barn to see what was needed to put the feed room back in shape. The floor was rotten in places. There were a few loose wall boards. Nothing that could not be fixed easily enough.

It was just after five thirty when Ray and Bob returned to the tractor shed to find Matt still hard at work. Ray was pleased to see that the weeds had been clipped. The assorted implements, broken down and rusty though they be, were lined neatly along the fence line, spaced perfectly. Two sections of the shed had been cleared of junk and it was easy to see that it would soon be of practical use to him.

Bob got out of the truck and walked over to inspect Matt's work. "None of this stuff might be worth a poot," he said grabbing Matt's shoulder, "but, it sure does look purty!"

Ray agreed to meet Bob at the old barn early in the morning. They were going to saddle up the horses and check out the fences on his back pasture land. He was anxious to get a few calves on the place. He would have to feed them through the winter, but he could turn a profit on them come spring. When he told Matthew to call it a day, the boy parked the small tractor in its place in the shed and started for the road.

"I'll see you tomorrow, Mr. Bennett," he called.

Bob chuckled. "I'd about forgot about that boy walkin' everywhere he goes."

"Hey, Matt, wait up. I'll drive you home," Ray shouted.

It was clear that Matt appreciated the ride, but his manners made him protest. "That's alright, Mr. Bennett. I don't mind the walk. Besides, I better get used to it. Oh! I almost forgot." He ran back to the shed and came back carrying his school books. "Got homework to do."

"Hop in," Ray said. "I can't have one of my top hands freezing to death or failing high school either one."

As they drove up Dover Road toward Matthew's home Ray could see that the boy was going to be short on conversation. He gave him instructions for work to do to keep him busy over the next few days. Matt would simply nod and say "Yes, sir," or "That's fine," or "Great!"

The Warren home sat on an embankment just off of the road. It was in bad need of paint and repair. One porch step was missing altogether. A beat-up Rambler American sat in the yard. Smoke was wafting up through the crumbling chimney.

"Looks like Billie has a fire going," Matthew said. "Well, I'll see you tomorrow. Thanks for the ride, Mr. Bennett."

"One other thing, Matthew," Ray said seriously.

"Sir?"

"This 'Mr. Bennett' stuff ain't cuttin' it. Why don't you just call me Ray?"

"Oh, I can't do that. It ain't right," he quickly replied.

"O.K., then. Let's compromise. 'Mr. Ray' works for me, how 'bout you?"

"Alright, Mr. Ray," Matthew beamed. "See you tomorrow."

As Matthew was walking away, a thought struck Ray. "Hey, kid!" he called.

Matt came trotting back to the truck. "I almost forgot. I have a kind of a . . . sign on bonus. You're supposed to get it when you finish your first day," he fibbed.

Straining to reach into the front pocket of his jeans he pulled out a small wad of folded bills. Counting out fifty dollars, that would leave him ten for gas, he handed the money through the window to Matthew.

The boy started to speak, but Ray held up his hand. "Part of the deal. You work for the Bennett place now. This ain't no rinky dink outfit." Backing out of the drive way he called, "See you tomorrow!"

Matt waved enthusiastically.

"Maybe he'll buy himself a coat . . . or some boots one," Ray said to himself as he turned for home.

6.

"Ray, come on up to the house," Pat yelled from the cab of his truck. "Your mama's about got dinner fixed for you and your friend."

Ray stopped his work on the cotton picker. "Pop, I don't think Mama or you are ready to sit down and eat with Thomas. He's . . ."

"We know he's one of your old buddies from prison, Ray. That won't bother us a bit. I've got to get on home. They'll be there soon." With that Pat sped away before Ray could object further.

Cleaning his hands as quickly as he could, Ray jumped into his truck and hurried home. Things had changed a lot here, but he didn't think they had changed quite that much. Thomas wasn't expecting a meal; he was just going to meet Ray at his home so Ray could take them to the house he had found for them to rent. If he could get Thomas and his family away quickly, an embarrassing situation for everyone would be averted.

As he trotted up the steps and through the door Mary called, "Is that you, Ray? How many extra plates do we need to set?"

"I don't think you want to put any extra plates down, Mama," Ray said. "These are not . . ."

"Nonsense, son. I'm sure this Thomas is very nice and his family, too. He would have to be since he is such a good friend to you. What's the matter, does he have bad table manners or something?"

"He is a good friend and he has great manners, but I don't think ya'll are ready for . . ."

"We'll decide what we are ready for, Raymond Lee," his mother interrupted again. "How many plates?"

"Five, they have three kids," Ray said resignedly. He moved to the bathroom where his father was washing his hands. "Look, Pop, I'm not sure this is such a great idea."

"What do you mean, son?" Pat queried. "Here this Thomas fellow has up and moved his whole family down here to help you out on short notice. It seems to me that the least your mother and I can do is feed them dinner. What is the problem with that?"

Ray drew a deep breath. "Thomas is one of the finest people I know. It's just that I'm not sure that you and Mama are ready to sit down and eat at your table with a . . ."

"Here they are!" Pat blurted at the sound of tires crunching on the gravel driveway. Walking to the front door he said, "The way Sport is barking you would think they were . . . oh, Lord!"

"Well don't just stand there, Pat, go out and greet our guests," Mary fussed.

"Hon, maybe you better . . ."

"I'll be along in a minute, now scat!" Mary ordered.

Ray, who had followed his father to the door, was wearing a wide grin when Pat turned to look at him. "Times a-wastin', Pop," he said. With that he led his father through the door and skipped down the three steps to greet his old friend.

Ray and Thomas gave each other the manly version of a hug, slapping each other on the back as if it were supposed to hurt or something. Thomas introduced his wife and children. Ray introduced his father, who shook hands with each of his visitors. When it looked like Pat was not going to extend the invitation, Ray said, "Well, ya'll come on in. Mama's been cookin' all morning."

"Oh, we don't want to impose," Thomas' wife said.

"She's been workin' hard to make ya'll feel at home," Ray replied. "It would be more of an imposition not to stay for dinner. I'll take you to that house I found for you after we eat."

"You all . . . come on in, and have a seat," Pat said hesitatingly. "Dinner will be on the . . . table . . . in just a minute."

Thomas and Linda cast nervous glances at each other. This was a new experience to them as well.

"I hope you don't think we bein' rude, showing' up right at dinner time like this," Thomas apologized. "We wuzn't expectin' to set an' eat, but we thank you jus' the same."

At that instant Mary was carrying a tray filled with glasses of tea to the dining room table. When she heard the unmistakable inflections in Thomas's voice she realized what Ray had been trying to tell her. In her shock, she dropped the tray in a great crash of ice and glass, much like the bomb that had just dropped on her.

"Oh, my! Let me help you with that," she heard a clear friendly voice say. She looked up into the pretty, smiling, black face of Linda Washington.

In the living room Ray could see that Pat was not sufficiently over his shock to bring up any engaging small talk. He sat there with a smile of sorts locked on his face but astonishment in his eyes. History was being made in the Bennett home today. Their first inter-racial meal was about to be served. As a matter of fact, this was surely a historical moment in all of Dover . . . Coleman as well, and possibly the whole of Winstead County. Neither Pat nor Mary had ever seen the movie 'Guess Who's Coming To Dinner' mostly because they rarely went to the movies, but also because the theme of the picture clashed with their social upbringing.

Social upbringing was the reason Matt Warren was, for the most part, shunned at school. It had been the reason Carl Sullivan did not want his daughter nor his grandchild to be a Bennett. It was the reason white folks and black folks did not invite each other to tea. "Social upbringing" was the condensed version of "that's just the way things are".

Ray had come to realize that the way things were minus the way things are did not always equal the way things ought to be. But they were closer, and continuing to grow closer. Evidence of this was the fact that the Washington family was still in the Bennett home, and even more so that Pat now seemed to be having a good time carrying on with Thomas' four year old daughter Vanessa. And there was Mary, apologizing for the mess and chatting with Linda. The talk was forced, but it was talk nonetheless.

When the spill had been cleaned and fresh glasses of tea were poured for the adults and milk for the kids, Mary called everyone to the dinner table. Pat, before going into the dining room, went to the front door to peer out. Maybe he was going to make family history today. The neighbors didn't have to know about it just yet, though.

When everyone was seated at the table, Pat noticed that everyone, which meant the Washington's, sat very politely waiting for some signal to start eating. "We'll . . . uh . . . we'll just ask the blessing," he said bowing his head. "Our most gracious Heavenly Father, we thank you for this day and all of the blessings of this day, we thank you for this food and the hands that prepared and brought this food to this table, we ask you to bless it to the nourishment of our bodies, in Je . . ., and, Father, we . . . we want to thank you for Ray's friends, who have joined us here today and have come to help our son, and we pray for your blessings upon this family that their life here will be a good one. In Jesus' name, Amen."

"Amen!" the Washington's echoed.

"Thank you for that fine prayer, Mr. Bennett," Thomas said. "We been thankin' the Lord a lot for Ray ever since he called me. Things ain't been . . . well, they gonna be better here, for sure."

"Ray didn't tell me everything about you, Thomas," Pat said casting a glance at Ray, who now wore a grin of his own, "but he did say that you are a first rate mechanic."

"Yessir, I work on everything . . ."

The dinner conversation went well. Ray was pleased that Pat and Mary, having accepted a situation they would have resisted had they known the Washington's were black before hand, loosened up and talked normally, not guardedly or merely politely. Everyone seemed to enjoy the meal. Thomas' children ate quietly and carried their plates to the kitchen when the meal was finished. Linda insisted on helping Mary with the dishes, and Mary accepted that help. In the living room, Ray could not tell what the conversation in the kitchen was about, but, Linda was obviously confiding in Mary. The kids went outside to play with Sport and roam around the Bennett place. The men sat in the living room talking about Ray's plans. Mary and Linda joined the men after clearing the table.

"Thomas, those are some well behaved children you have there," Pat commented.

"Thank you, sir," Thomas replied. "Life was hard enough for them before I . . . messed up. Because of me, it has been even harder and may be harder still. A child needs someone to look up to, and they have that in their mother," Thomas said patting Linda's knee. "I done told them that people that know about me, won't respect me, and won't respect them because of me. I'm tryin' with all I have to be a man that they can look up to and respect, but I teach them that as long as they live their own lives good, and in a way that they can truly look up to theyselves, then anybody, and I mean anybody, that don't respect them is wrong. It's just that simple."

Pat and Mary glanced at each other. Pat cleared his throat. "Well, you've obviously done right by them. I know from personal experience that it is not easy to raise children to be noticeably good. I always try to compliment the people behind that raisin'."

After a short visit Ray led the Washington's to the house he had found for them to rent. J.V. Carter, their landlord, had accepted the first month's rent from Ray and given him the key. When they arrived at the small white frame house, Ray laughed as the two small children ran inside followed by Marcus, the fourteen year old. Thomas and Linda stood arm in arm, gazing at the house and the neat yard that surrounded it.

This new home was very important to the Washington family. It represented the new start that they had all but lost hope for. Thomas had been released from Parchman about a year prior to Ray's parole. He had served four years of his sentence for armed robbery.

He had committed the crime while drunk, after being fired from his job as a mechanic at a busy service station in Itta Bena. Vanessa was on the way. He had no insurance to help with the doctor and hospital bills, and his anger at the owner of the station for letting him go to hire his white high school dropout nephew increased with each gulp from his quart jar of bootleg whiskey. Finally, he went immediately before closing time, and at gunpoint, robbed the very station, the very man, he had been working for on the previous day.

He went to his sister's home where he passed out. He awoke around four the next morning. Finding the small wad of money in his pocket, he immediately remembered what he had done and cried in shame and fear. A few hours later he was in his car, headed back to the station to return the money and beg forgiveness. He would not make it back to the station, however. A deputy sheriff stopped and arrested him two miles from his destination.

The court had little mercy on Thomas. The station owner had less. By the time Thomas had been paroled, the crime had not been forgotten. Thomas had not been forgiven. Work was hard to come by in LeFlore County at that time, harder still for an ex-con. The Washington family had struggled while Thomas was in prison. They seemed to struggle more when he was released. He had resolved, though, that his one crime would be his only crime. He was proud of the positive changes he had made in his life. He could not overcome his own shame, however, in the problems he had caused and left with his wife and children. His children, whom he wanted so to grow up with pride and integrity, had an ex-con for a father. To make bad times worse, steady work for Thomas was non-existent. He took whatever odd jobs came his way. He earned some money, but not enough, as a shade tree mechanic. His old wrecker, which was now his only mode of transportation, hardly paid for itself. Thomas was in despair and hardly able to look his family in the eye when Ray called him and offered steady work on his place. Thomas had explained that he knew little about farming, but Ray had insisted that there was plenty of mechanical repair to be done on the place and that he would teach his friend everything he needed to know to be an able hand.

Here was the new start. Thomas Washington was not known in Winstead County. He had a good, steady job. The house he was to rent was no mansion by any standard, but it was much nicer than the shack his family had occupied for so long.

"Thank you, Lord," Thomas said quietly.

"Amen," Linda repeated as she took her husband's hand and led him through the front door.

Ray helped unload the small U-Haul trailer. "You can take my truck if you need to make another load, Thomas," he said as the last box of clothing was taken inside.

"Ain't no more, Ray. This is it," Thomas replied. "Thanks anyway. We left a few pieces of furniture that was junkier than what you see here and a couple of wore out mattresses. There ain't nothin' there worth goin' back for. When you gon' be wantin' me to come to work? I'm ready now!"

"Well, you take tomorrow and the next day if you need it to get settled in here. I expect ya'll will want to get the kids enrolled in school."

"We'll be settled in tonight. Linda can take the kids on to school in the mornin'. I'll get her to drop me off on your place if you'll tell me where. Will I be needin' my truck?"

"I guess if you're so all fired up about goin' to work, Thomas, I'm ready for you. Just go back up here and take the same turn off we just did, go past my Mama and Daddy's place and you'll see the tractor shed on the left down yonder. You still know right from left, I hope," Ray joked, "I'd hate to see you get started at the wrong barn for the wrong farmer."

"Linda tells me all that complicated stuff, Ray, but I'll make it there."

Ray said his goodbyes to Linda and the children and shook Thomas' hand before leaving to check on Matt. It was now past five thirty and he was sure the boy would work past dark if he was not there to tell him to go home.

The lot was about as neat and clean as it could get! There was not a dry weed left standing in or around the shed. Ray found Matt in the tool room sorting through the tools that he had gathered from various pieces of equipment and shelves and bins throughout the shed.

"You'll have plenty of tools, Mr. Ray," Matt said, "soon as I get the rust cleaned off and all. With everything you have here, it will take me a day or two, though."

The boy was a fast worker. And good too! Despite his age, he would make a good hand . . . one that could be trusted. And that was what Ray needed most.

"Day after tomorrow's payday, Matt," Ray said as he drove the boy home. "You been thinkin' up good stuff to do with your money?"

"Yes sir," Matt responded. "I got me some shoppin' to do soon as I get the chance."

"Well, I figure we'll quit at dinner time Saturday. That lot is comin' along pretty good. Me and Thomas, the new man, you'll meet him tomorrow, will be workin' on those pickers, but not much else will be goin' on," Ray said. "You might as well take the afternoon and do what you want with it."

"Son," Pat greeted, "did you get your friends settled in all right, or do we have to entertain them again tomorrow?"

"You know it wasn't that bad," Ray responded. "I think you enjoyed the visit as much as they did."

"Well, it was an experience, and I'd have thought we'd never see the day," Pat said. "But, I guess it was not much different from any other dinner company we've had." After a pause he added, "Except those Washington children were better behaved than most."

"I carried some groceries and a cake over to their house late this afternoon," Mary said as she entered the living room.

"A little insurance against having to feed them again, I suppose," Ray joked.

"Raymond Lee," his mother scolded. "I doubt that they had any time, if they had any money, to go pick up anything from the store. They seem like a nice family and anyone can see they need just a little help right now."

Ray put his arm around his mother's shoulder and turned her into the dining room where supper was waiting. "Mama, you'd feed the world if you could."

"You should talk," Mary replied. "We'll see the thirty first of April before we'll see J.V. furnish one of his rental houses with a nice new ice making refrigerator and gas stove like the ones that are sitting over there right now. The refrigerator loaded up as well, I might add."

Pat cast a concerned look toward his son. "You got a long winter ahead, Ray. You better take it easy."

"I'm alright, Pop. They just need some help is all. Besides, a well fed hand is a good investment." Ray took a deep breath and let it out slowly. "I've been thinkin' about something over the past few days, and I made up my mind this evening." He paused, looking each of his parents in the eye. "I can't live here forever. It's time I found a place of my own to move into. Thought I might buy me a camper and put it over by the old barn. Then, when I'm able, I can work on buildin' me a place on that old lot on the far side where the old family place used to be."

"That could take a lot of money, Ray," Mary protested. "You don't have to be thinking about leaving home so soon."

"Mama, the last time I left home I moved up to Sunflower County and stayed there for fifteen years. I'll be thirty four soon. I'd have been in my own place a long time ago if I hadn't been . . . up there."

"You're welcome here for as long as you like, son," Pat suggested.

"I know that, Pop, and I appreciate it. But, I ought to be takin' care of myself. Besides, it's not like I'm moving fifty miles away! I'll be just up the road, across from . . ."

"Across from your place," Pat smiled. "I know, son. It's where you belong. Count on me for help."

"Thanks, Pop."

"You needn't think I'll be helping you get away from here," Mary said half fussing, half crying.

"I wouldn't have it any other way," Ray said bending across to plant a kiss on his mother's cheek. Already she was sorting through her mind to decide what furniture they could do without and give to Ray in his new home.

7.

Thomas was waiting for Ray when he arrived at the shed at five-thirty the next morning. In the crisp cold dark of the early morning, he had wandered around the equipment now neatly placed around the lot and under the shed. He had found the tools in the only enclosed part of the shed, but was glad he had taken much of his own large assortment off his wrecker before he allowed Linda to take it back home. One thing he had was good tools. He hoped his first assignment was not going to be cleaning and reconditioning those little piles of rust that passed for tools in Ray's shed! He had been out of prison for almost two years, and he was ready to get down to some real mechanic's work!

As soon as Ray arrived they shared a cup of coffee from the thermos Thomas had brought with him. By the time their first cup was gone, it was light enough to start working. Bob arrived at about seven. He was riding Pappy's Ford Eight Thousand, the larger of the two tractors that had been kept at the old barn, and was pulling an eight row disc.

Ray introduced Bob and Thomas to each other. The two men shook hands. "I don't guess they gave you a lawn mower either," Bob commented.

Thomas looked at Ray.

"You'll catch on," Ray said smiling.

" 'thought I'd go on over and disk up the firebreaks in that pasture you want to burn off," Bob said.

Ray nodded his approval, and Bob was on his way.

"So this is the place you used to bend my ear about?" Thomas said as he looked around appraisingly. "Don't get me wrong, it's a great place, but it's not quite the way you described it."

"There ain't much anywhere around that looks like I remembered it."

"What about that little girl of yours?" Thomas was the only person outside of family he had ever told about Emmy.

Ray sighed. "All she knows about me is that I'm the man who put her grandfather in a wheel chair. She, uh, she sees me in something less than a favorable light. We can't tell her who I am. It goes without saying that our families are not close, so I don't see that there's much of a chance for us to have any kind of a relationship."

Knowing how much Emmy meant to Ray, Thomas felt for his friend. "Give it time. You never know what might happen."

Ray forced a grin and nodded.

Thomas rubbed his hands together and said, "So, boss, where do we start?"

"That cotton picker right there," Ray replied pointing. "There is still some cotton in the fields. Maybe I can rustle us up a job or two if you can fix me up something to work with."

Circling the aging John Deere cotton picker, Thomas tugged at belts and squeezed hoses. He felt the brake and clutch pedals and pulled the gear levers. He inspected the hydraulic system. Finally, he issued his declaration. "She's been sittin' up a while, but, I can have her checked out and goin' in two days if I work straight on."

Ray grinned. "That's one reason I brought you here, my man. I want you to fix anything that can be fixed. Use whatever spare parts and used parts you can scrounge. I'll set up a line of credit for whatever you have to buy. I figure a man with your talents can get this business rolling as well with old equipment as it would with new. All of this so called junk once turned a crop on this land. Maybe, with your help, it can do it again."

Thomas turned in a circle gazing at what he considered to be paradise. "I don't know, Ray," he said, "but if I can do what I think I can, you'll have all the operatin' equipment you will need."

"Good. I plan to need it all and then some!"

Just about that time the school bus passed by. Ray decided that it was time to tend to a very personal matter. "Thomas, I'm gonna go make a phone call." He paused, "As a matter of fact, I'm gonna make two calls and one of them is to get some phones installed in these two barns of mine. This here is supposed to be a modern operation, man." Walking to his truck, he turned and called back, "While I'm gone I'm also goin' to town and set up some charge accounts so you and Bob can go in and pick up what you need without me."

Thomas chuckled, "You sure are gettin' industrious on me of a sudden. Which town is town?"

"Delta Hills!"

Ray had a busy morning. He went to the telephone company and made arrangements for phones to be installed at both barns. He also went by the Rural Electric Association office and arranged to get electricity hooked back up to both places. The morning went smoothly but developed a few wrinkles after these two successful transactions.

"I can't extend credit to you, Mr. Bennett," Ellis Hodges stated. "You haven't been in business long enough."

"You know what my situation is, Mr. Hodges," Ray protested. "I just need for a couple of my hands to be able to come in and sign a ticket for my farm supplies. I'll settle up with you once a month, Just like everbody else does."

"Everybody else doesn't do that anymore," Hodges said sarcastically. He gave special emphasis to the "everybody" part. "I'm sorry, Mr. Bennett. We'll have to do cash business."

The story was the same at the auto parts house and the tractor and implements dealer Ray went to, only less polite. "Carl Sullivan is a good customer and a good friend," Walter Hinton spat. "Hell will freeze over before I give credit to the likes of you, Bennett."

These were problems he had not expected to encounter. He had thought the fact that he was on the place ready to do business and his family's reputation would earn him some startup short term credit. While eating lunch, Ray decided to take Highway Sixteen to Benville and try the farm supply store there. He wasn't quite as well known there and Carl Sullivan nor Clint McKay carried as much weight because they did not do business there. Finishing his sandwich, he could find no other reason to put off the phone call he had been intending to make when he left the tractor shed earlier in the morning.

He held the small Winstead County phone book open and dialed the number with the same hand. "Hello?" It was amazing how Laura's voice still sounded the same after all these years. "Hello?" she said louder.

"Hi," Ray said.

"Ray?" Laura said plaintively.

"I . . . uh . . . thought it was time we had that talk."

"Yeah, . . . I guess so," Laura replied slowly. "Today is probably not good, though."

"For me neither," Ray said. "Lots to do."

"I've seen how hard you're working. The place is shaping up. Listen," Laura said suddenly, "I can get away for a few minutes tonight. There's a big pep rally at the school for tomorrow night's game. Everybody will be there. Can we get together then?"

"Sure," Ray replied quickly. "Down by the old iron bridge? Seven?"

"The old iron bridge," Laura repeated almost sadly. "I haven't been over there in years! But we better make it seven thirty. There will be a lot of . . . of traffic between here and the school."

"Yeah, sure," Ray said. "I'll see you then."

"Bye."

The phone clicked and went dead.

The trip to Benville turned out to be worth the detour. One of Ray's old friends, Lamar Majors, was the owner of the small seed and feed store there.

"I heard that some folks might be less than accommodating to you," Lamar said after the 'Good to see you's' and 'You're looking goods' had been exchanged. "Some want to hold a grudge, others, I think are just jealous. They don't like to see anybody get anything good out of life. I don't understand folks, Ray. I don't know what all went on between you and Carl, but I do know what kind of person you were. Accident or no, I just can't see you pushing Mr. Sullivan off that deck. Whatever happened, in my opinion, I think you more than paid for it."

"Thanks, Lamar," Ray said. "I appreciate you saying that."

"Well, your credit is good here! Just tell me who will be signing your tickets and you get whatever you need. And if I don't have what you need, I'll get it until the bigger shops in town loosen up on you."

"Lamar, the big shops in town can loosen up all they want. My business will be comin' to you. There'll be me, of course, Bob Riley, Matt Warren, a sixteen year old kid, and Thomas Washington, new to the area, a good man."

Lamar took down the names. "We'll be looking for you, Ray."

"Thanks, Lamar," Ray said. "I can't tell you how much I appreciate it. I didn't think I had any friends left around here." They shook hands and Ray returned to the tractor shed.

Thomas had the engine torn down to the block by the time Ray made his way back. Ray was relieved to learn that no major motor components would require replacement to get the picker back to work, but, there were some necessities.

"Check everything, hoses, hydraulics, electrical . . . Make a list. My credit is tight on this kind of stuff, so we'll need to use salvaged parts wherever we can. If we can make it through this season, we'll do 'er up right before next year."

Matt arrived at his usual time and went straight to work on the tools after introducing himself to Thomas. He had a big job before him, but he was sure that he would finish sometime tomorrow. The idea of moving on to more important work for Bennett Farm Services excited him. Maybe Mr. Ray would put him on that picker. Especially if he helped fix it.

Ray had been tinkering with an old 1967 Dodge pickup that had long been known as "the farm truck". It had actually been Pappy's favorite truck from long ago. When Jimmy and then Ray became old enough to drive, he decided to keep the truck on the farm rather than trade it in. It would be there for whomever needed it around the place. Ray had his own ideas about the truck and was anxious to get it cranked. He had found a cigar box full of keys. Some had tags attached to identify the hole they went into. Most did not. The key to this truck, however, was not difficult to locate. It was still on the same "Delta Motor Company" key ring it had always been on.

After a lot of tinkering around which included transferring the battery from his good truck to this one and pouring an inordinate amount of gasoline down the carburetor, the engine actually fired up and ran. If it could be called running. It was more of a bump, pop, shutter, sigh . . . in rhythm. Turning the most important knob in the vehicle, Ray smiled when the am radio warmed to life and bid its static filled hello after a decade of silence.

Matt came trotting over to the truck when he heard it sputter to life.

"I think we've got us a farm truck here, Matt," Ray said as the boy approached. "It's old and just about wore out, but it will run, and I think that big Chevy bob truck will, too."

"I bet Thomas can get them going just like new," Matt said, proud to be part of an outfit on the move.

Ray motioned toward the passenger side. "Hop in. Let's see what this baby can do flat out!"

Overcoming every objection the old truck put forth, Ray pulled it down into first gear and managed to get it through the open gate into the pasture behind the shed. He drove slowly across the smooth ground of the pasture turning left and right, making full circles, stopping and starting. Satisfied that the truck would perform the most basic requirements of operation, starting, stopping and turning, he drove back through the gate to the pasture and on through the gate that led to the road. Thomas laughed and waved at the sight of Ray and Matt playing in the truck.

Matt found a strong am signal for a country music station out of Jackson. Ray frowned at the noise coming from the obviously cracked speaker. "We'll have to do something about that," he yelled over the static.

When the truck made its way back into the lot, Thomas noticed that Matt was now at the wheel. His smile shone through the cracked, dirty windshield. Ray was talking to Matt as they left the truck parked in its place under the shed.

"Yep. I'm gonna get 'im on this truck as soon as he's through with that cotton picker. I don't imagine it'll take him long to have 'er purring like a kitten." After a pause he added, "I'll tell you what. If you would go ahead and check all the fluid levels and check the lights and turn signals, you can drive that Dodge home tonight."

Matt's mouth dropped. "Sir? Are you kidding?" he asked.

"Nope. As a matter of fact," Ray said conjuring up a serious look, "that farm truck is your responsibility. You can, and should, so you can get out here quicker, take it to school, (Matt could hardly contain his excitement) take it anywhere you need to go, and pray that she gets you there and back. You just be careful, and . . . well, I doubt she'll work up enough speed to earn a ticket."

"Thanks, Mr. Ray," Matt beamed, "I'll take good care of her. She's a fine truck!"

"Well, you might want to take a closer look before you make any rash judgments," Ray replied. "But, I believe she'll get you around. I want to get away from here early today, so as soon as you get through with that little assignment, I'll give you your check, and some cash for gas, and you can go. Just don't get caught on the highway before we get a tag and inspection sticker. I don't imagine you'll get into any trouble between here and home and school."

Matt walked around the truck looking at it as if it were a new sports car. "Do you mind if I drive it to the game tomorrow tonight?"

"I already said you can drive it anywhere you need to go, and that includes any where you want to go," Ray fussed. "I trust you, Matt. Just check 'er out good. Make sure those tires will hold up, test your brakes, you know. You might want to drive it around some this evening to be sure it's gonna keep running. She may not even make it up that hill over yonder before you get to your house."

"She'll make it!" Matt said. This truck thing was now a matter of personal pride for him. The dull, faded paint didn't matter. Neither did the few dents and the badly scratched interior of the truck bed. A three dollar beach towel would do for a cover over the dried and cracked vinyl upholstery. His new boss trusted him. That was all that mattered to Matthew Warren today.

By five o'clock, Matt was gone, the old Dodge jumping and sputtering but showing signs of life after all. Ray was ready to leave and offered Thomas a ride home. On the way there, Ray offered the Chevrolet to Thomas for his use.

"Look, with the kind of work you're going to be doing for a while, you might do better bringing your wrecker and letting your family use that big one ton Chevy until we can find them a car. Whatever you need, you just do it."

Thomas thanked Ray, but kept to himself how nice it was to think of his family going shopping, going visiting, going to church, going anywhere, in anything other than the beat-up wrecker. A full ton flat bed dual wheeled truck is not what anyone would call a family vehicle. But it would do until . . . wait! Until "we" find a car? What Ray had in mind, Thomas didn't even have to guess at. The man's generosity was sometimes his biggest fault. Well, the bob truck would be made ready for duty. Maybe Ray could wait until next week, but Thomas was going to work late Saturday and on Sunday, if need be, to get that Chevrolet running.

Ray dropped Thomas off at his house and paid him for his first day's work, and gave him the "sign-up" bonus, for which cash poor Thomas was grateful. Ray also told Thomas to get the old Dodge truck in shape to pass inspection as soon as he could.

"Won't be nothing' hard about gittin' that truck to pass inspection," Thomas replied. "Gittin' it to pass anything else on the road, that's the problem."

From Thomas' house Ray went directly to the old barn. It was quite dark out, but there was now sufficient light around the old place. He had been spending some time every day with the three horses held there. The gelding, Dan, came to him to get the sugar cube that he knew was there just for him. Ray clipped a rope to the horse's halter and led him through the gate and tied him just inside the barn. The horse fought the bit as Ray attempted to put a bridle on him. Finally, he gave in. He danced away from the saddle blanket but Ray continued to speak softly and was able to lay the blanket over Dan's back. Ray expected a nervous reaction to the saddle, but Dan stood remarkably still while Ray swung it gently as possible into place and tightened the girth.

Now Ray grew a bit nervous. So far the horse had reacted pretty well, but how would he feel about having a human on his back?

Dan didn't take to the idea at all. As Ray swung into the saddle, Dan was off and bucking. A few jolts and a quick spin sent Ray sprawling to the ground. Once rid of his rider, Dan stood still, confident that he could continue his lazy routine in the holding pen. Dan was wrong.

Ray again swung into the saddle, but this time, try as he may, Dan was unable to roust the intruder from his back. As soon as the bucking and rearing stopped, Ray spurred the horse into a good run. It was time to show Dan who was boss. Working with Dan in the pasture, Ray soon had him under control. With some training, he would make a fine pleasure horse. Out through the entrance gate and up the road toward home they went. Ray sensed that Dan was enjoying the run. After a few minutes, he reined the horse in to a fast walk.

Sport met them before they drew to within sight of the lights of the Bennett home. Dan was skittish at first, but soon became bored with Sport's attempt to assert authority. The dog grew tired of barking and nipping at the horse's fetlocks and fell in to join horse and rider for the brief remainder of the trip.

Ray picked at his supper. His stomach was knotting as he grew more and more nervous.

"If that's the way you're going to be eating, you better find yourself a line of work that does more for the appetite," Pat said pointing his fork at Ray's plate. "I hate to have to give all this good food to the dog 'cause you don't eat it. Spoils 'im. He gets fat and he won't chase nobody off."

"Pat!" Mary scolded. "What's wrong, Ray?"

"Nothin', Mama. Linda gave me a piece of chocolate cake she made when I took Thomas home," Ray said. "I guess I'm not that hungry any more. It sure was good, though, what I ate. I think I'll go get cleaned up and take that horse out for a while. I miss ridin' at night. Ya'll have a good evening." Ray rose from the table and gave his mother a quick kiss on the cheek.

After showering and dressing in clean clothes, Ray put on his "good" cowboy hat and "good" boots. The crisp feel of new denim, the department store smell of his shirt and the stiffness of new cowhide boots brought Ray to a momentary halt as he was reminded of the excitement new clothing brought to him in his youth. He tried to fight the notion that he was going on a date. After all, they were only going to talk. But that's the way it had been that first time they were alone together at night. They were just going to meet and talk, to comfort each other, companion souls, so to speak. And they did. They met over by that old iron bridge on that piece of abandoned road. And they talked for hours about the boyfriend and girlfriend they had just broken up with. And they talked for an hour about how nice it was to have someone to talk to that understood such things, such feelings.

They began to feel better about being with each other than they felt bad about being estranged from their former steadies. But they did not voice these feelings until after that kiss took them both by surprise.

They talked for another hour, between kisses, about how fate had brought them together. Fate. Was it the same fate that brought them together that four months later took away almost sixteen years of Ray's life?

Ray didn't worry about fate anymore. He had defeated fate, with faith. He had come to believe that fate was merely falling into the devil's plans for us. Perhaps it had been his fate to grow old in prison. It was faith, on the parts of a lot of people that got him out. If fate did exist it was far too fickle for him. Anyway, he had lost enough to fate. He had his faith to act upon, and he would not wait for "the fickle finger of fate" to point him any where he did not want to go ever again!

"Bye! Nice night for a ride," Ray said as he walked through the living room and out the door.

"He has a date," Mary said quietly. "Either that, or he's going to meet somebody."

Pat looked at her quizzically. "Now what makes you say that?"

"He always acted that way before his first few dates with a girl. So queasy he couldn't eat. He always said he wasn't hungry, but I knew better."

"Well now, if you didn't notice, he's ridin' that horse!" Pat retorted. "He's liable to freeze his own butt off ridin' around out there in the cold. I doubt he'd risk that happenin' to his first date in sixteen years. Besides, who is he going to go out on a date with on a horse?"

Mary caught her breath, "There was one," she mused. "Oh, dear! There could be more trouble!"

"Aw, honey, don't go gettin' all upset," Pat said walking to the television. "If it's who I think you're thinkin' it is, those two have a lot to talk about. I wouldn't read no more into it. It's time for 'Family Matters'."

"You don't get all fixed up for a talk," Mary replied, but Pat was intently watching Erkle destroy Carl's living room.

Laura drove the red Blazer slowly through the tall weeds that now grew where the old road once was. Tractors and pickup trucks had made a good path to follow for a short distance, but the remainder of the brief trip to the bridge was pretty much guess work as far as the road was concerned.

She had seen no other tracks and no other vehicle, so she determined that she must have arrived before Ray. She drew a deep, nervous breath. What was she doing here? What did she and Ray have to talk about? It wasn't so much that she needed to see him; it was more like she felt that she should. Although she had never believed that Ray had intentionally hurt Carl, she had thought, no, known, for years that the accident was his doing. She had been bitter and angry at Ray for the change the accident had brought to her father and the way he treated her. Was it the injury that brought out the cruelty in Carl Sullivan or was it the fact that his grandchild was actually a Bennett, a descendant of the Winsteads?

Laura had spent the past few days immersed in that question. As a seventeen year old girl, she had not questioned her father's version of the accident beyond her own assertion that Ray did not intend to hurt him. In the years following her father's confinement to a wheel chair, and Ray's incarceration, she had struggled within herself to forgive Ray for those unseen actions which brought so much pain and anger and resentment to her life. She had worked so hard to forgive Ray when it should have been him forgiving her! Would he forgive her? Should she ask?

The unmistakable sound of hooves on hard dirt warned Laura that someone was coming. Frightened, she considered a run to the Blazer to speed away. It wouldn't do for her to be caught out here at this time of the evening. And what was she doing sneaking out here like some kind of school girl or, worse, a cheating wife, anyway? It wasn't like she had anything to hide.

"It's me," Ray said quietly through the mist rising from the creek. He emerged from the shroud of gray, dismounted and tied Dan to a low hanging limb. He walked slowly, but purposefully toward Laura. He hugged her tightly. Would he? Would she? No. It didn't matter.

"Oh, Ray," she whispered.

"You know, I've played this scene out in my mind a thousand times. I would take you in my arms. We'd kiss. You'd melt. You'd leave Clint and bring Emmy to live with me." Ray stared into Laura's eyes. "But, it ain't there, is it?"

"No, Ray. Not like it was."

"Not for me either. I hope you don't take that as an insult . . . that it's different."

"It is different, Ray. A lot of time has passed."

"Not to mention you're a married woman. I'm sorry."

"Don't be, Ray," Laura replied. "It's just that I . . . well, I am married. It's been years. I have feelings for you, but . . ."

"It's alright, Laura. In a way it's what I wanted. It's what we both needed for Emmy's sake. But, I didn't try to get over you. I used you, and your memory, and some built up hopes about our little family to get me through. There's people in there who had nothing when they went in, and nothing waiting for them when they get out. If they don't find something within themselves to get them through, they might as well walk on over to the chamber and get themselves gassed because they ain't good for nothing and never will be, for themselves or anybody else."

Laura crossed her arms to keep herself from trembling.

"I was on a downhill slide myself until Gran reminded me of something. So anyway, I made up this life that me and you and Emmy were going to have. I thought about it every day. I even imagined I was there all the while she was growin' up. I heard her cryin' at night. I held her and walked her when her stomach hurt. I saw her take her first steps."

Ray gave Laura his handkerchief to wipe the tears streaming down her face.

"It was hard, Laura. Sometimes I wanted to be here so bad I couldn't stand it. I thought I would go crazy."

"She missed a lot not having you around," Laura said. "She should know you now."

"Well, we've met, and I don't think I made such a great impression. I'd like nothing better than to be a father to her, but, that can't be. No more than you and I can be what we were."

"We can't be what we were, Ray. With Emmy and everything, we'd probably have gotten married. We may have had a happy life together," Laura pondered. "But, what if I hadn't been pregnant. Who can say what would have happened. I loved you at the time, Ray, I really did. We had something special. Very special. He has never said so, but I'm sure Clint has always resented the fact that you and I . . . well . . . we did . . . what we did, and he and I never . . . " her voice trailed off. "We were so young, Ray. Do you think we would have stayed together?"

"I don't know," Ray sighed. "I never really thought about it that way. I do know that what I felt for you was strong. And it was special. That was not just fooling around, that night we were together. It was a special thing. It shouldn't have happened. We shouldn't have been off ridin' horses at midnight, and we shouldn't have let that ole moon shinin' on your daddy's lake pull you in for that swim. And we shouldn't of had that bottle of wine. It wasn't right. But it was something special. It meant something to me. I just want you to know that. And I'm sorry for what it did to your life."

"Hey, Ray!" Laura cried. "Quit apologizing! There were two of us there. You didn't force anything on me. It just happened. And it was wonderful for me, too. And with all the pain and hurt and everything else bad that came from it, one good precious thing came from it."

"You are right about that," Ray replied. "Emmy's a wonderful girl, I know. And I'm proud to be her father. She'll never know but, . . ." Ray choked back tears of his own now.

"Maybe she should know, Ray," Laura said. "I don't know how, but she has to be told. You deserve it and she deserves the truth."

"Whoa, now," Ray interjected. "This truth now could hurt her. It could near 'bout destroy her. Her whole life has been built on the basis that Clint is her father. It could be bad enough for her to find out that an ex-con is her real father, but think of everything else she will learn along with that." He paused. "I feel so guilty about all the lies."

"I know. Her whole life has been built on lies and pictures of people that just aren't true. But, she's hurting, Ray. She knows something is up. Clint doesn't . . ."

"Clint doesn't what?" Ray said angrily. "If he's not treatin' her right I'll take 'im out yonder and plow up the cotton patch with him!"

"He tries," Laura explained. "It's just that ever since word of your parole came, Daddy has been scheming to get your place. And now they know that you intend to stay. Well, Clint has been . . . distracted." She chose her words carefully. "He has never mistreated Emmy in anyway. It's just that he has been reminded, in a big way lately, of where she came from. And I think he's afraid."

"Of what?"

"Of losing everything. Other than the acreage his father gave him, most of what he has is what Daddy throws to him as foreman of Washabow. And he has that because of you. Now that you're back, he feels threatened."

"Well, if he's worried about me takin' it, he can rest easy. I don't want anything he has . . . except to be left alone to run my business and work my place. Otherwise, I've got plenty to give him and Carl both enough to worry about!"

Laura sighed. As different as all men are, they are still so much the same.

"I'm going to talk to Clint about telling Emmy," Laura said as if she had not yet sealed her decision. "I don't know how or when, but she has to know."

"What's to be gained from it, Laura? She'll be hurt and confused. Her life, a life built on lies, but still the only life she knows will be shattered. I don't like lying, but we started it. How can we end it without destroying her? Besides, I'll never be a father to her. She hates me. And I hate to think of her finding out about all this while she despises me so."

"Her opinion of you is undergoing some changes, Mr. Ray," Laura said.

"Oh?"

"Well, first there is me and Mama. She can't understand how we can be so forgiving. And then there is this Matt Warren boy."

"How does Matt figure into all this?"

"We were in town this afternoon. There was Matt, whom I've never met, and his little sister. I don't know her either, but she's a cute little girl. Anyway, they came walking out of K Mart carrying all these bags. We were in that little entrance way waiting for someone to get off of the pay phone. Well, Billie, that's what he called her anyway, stopped and started tearing into this big bag and she was saying,"'I want to wear it now! I want to wear it now!'" So Matt stops and takes this cute little coat out of the bag. He takes all the tags off and helps her put it on. She was just beaming! Then she sat down on one of the benches and started taking off her shoes, which were in pretty bad shape. Matt just grins at her and pulls a shoe box out of another bag and Billie puts on these nice new sneakers, socks and all!

Matt says,"'I suppose you want to put your new outfit on, too." Well, little Billie, she just laughs and then, Ray, I thought I would cry. She reached up and hugged her brother right there in front of everybody and thanked him. Him, Ray! I guess he used his own money to buy her those new clothes, and him standing there in old worn out boots, and a thread bare coat, and, well, everything he had on was just worn out!"

"Anything in those bags for him?" Ray asked.

"Billie told him he shouldn't have used all his money on her."

Ray shook his head.

"He did say that he would save up some more money and next time she could help him pick out something new." Laura laughed then and said, "Oh, yeah. He pulled a new cowboy hat out and put it on. He said, "This hat'll do for a while. A Bennett man ought to have a good hat. I don't want Mr. Ray to start thinkin' he's hired himself a slob."

"Um!" Ray grunted. "I was hopin' he would get himself a few things. He sure needs 'em."

"Emmy and I were both almost in tears by then. From what Emmy tells me they don't have a mother and not much of a father," Laura said. "Apparently, Matt has at least partly taken over those roles. But, that's not what I wanted to tell you," she added quickly.

"There's more?"

"We went over to Hank's Hamburgers for a shake and Matt and his sister were in there. I swear, Ray, you'd think the child never got to eat out in her life. She was carrying on and thanking Matt and he was just eating it all up. You know how men are," she teased. "But, it was a special thing he was doing. He had bought her one of those magazines the teenagers like and she found a hair style in it that she liked, and Matt promised her he would take her back to town Saturday afternoon so she could get hers fixed like that. He's some boy."

Ray was reminded then of Laura's attention to detail.

"Anyway," she continued, "in comes that Bo Hopson, he's been dating Emmy some, but I don't think I like him anymore. Well, Emmy said, '"Uh oh"' when she saw Bo going over to Matt's table. I guess he hadn't seen us yet. Bo starts in chiding Matt and making fun of his hat. Matt just sat there and took it, like you would have, until Bo made some remark about him being a . . . a manure shoveler, he didn't use that word, though, for a thief. Then Bo knocked Matt's new hat off of the table, turned his drink over and it spilled all over the hat. You know, that boy has manners. Most of them won't even turn their old caps around right much less take them off inside! But, anyway, Matt just reached down and picked up his hat and wiped it off with a napkin. Then he pushed back his chair and stood up and said, '"Bo, say what you want to about me. You've never said a kind word to me. You don't know me or much of anything about me, so I can over look your ignorance where I'm concerned."'

Bo started to say something then, but Matt just held up his hand to keep him quiet, then he said, '"Your opinion about me don't matter none to me, but I won't have you talkin' about a fine man like Mr. Ray like that."'

Ray lifted his eyebrows. "What happened then?" he asked.

Laura took a deep breath. "Bo asked him what he was going to do about it. Matt says, '"I reckon I'll do what it takes to change your mind or shut your mouth one."' Well, Bo bristled up and said, '"Don't you threaten me, boy,"' and before Matt could say anything else the manager jumped in between them and started to throw Matt out!"

"Throw Matt out!" Ray said incredulously.

"Of all things!" Laura replied. "I just got myself up and told that manager he was throwing the wrong people out and that he well knew it. He backed off then and just told them that there would be no fighting anywhere around his place.

"Bo turned white as a sheet when he saw me," she laughed. "Bo and his friends left, and that was about all there was to that. But, he sure thinks the world of you, Ray. And I believe it has Emmy thinking, too. She'll come around."

"I sure hope so," Ray sighed. "I guess somewhere deep inside I've always known that you and I wouldn't . . . well, we'll be friends. I have an ache, an empty spot, where there ought to be a daughter. But, the last thing I want to do is hurt her. Maybe I ought to talk to Clint, try to bury the hatchet. It just might be better for Emmy if things stay the way they are, that is if Clint can get his head straight and love her like he should."

"And you keep that ache buried inside you along with all the rest?" Laura said taking Ray's hand. "It's not fair."

"No, it's just life."

The cold began to get to them so they sat in Laura's Blazer and talked and listened to the radio. As nine o'clock approached Laura decided that she should start for home so she could be there before the rest of the family arrived.

"Well! So much for our big date," Ray joked.

"We share a child. And you will always hold a special place in my heart," Laura said softly. They hugged.

Neither had an inclination to take it any farther than that. And so, it was done. And so it would be.

Hesitating for just a moment Laura blurted, "Lori works some nights at the Bodock Bar and Grill in town. I know she would like to see you. Life has been hard for her."

Ray nodded and replied, "We'll see you, Laura."

Laura watched Ray walk away. Feelings of sadness for Ray and guilt over this clandestine meeting, as innocent as it was, brought her to the edge of tears.

Ray climbed into the saddle and reined Dan into the night. He was numbed less by the cold November night air than by the loneliness that embraced him. He was in no mood to go home and explain to Pat and Mary where he had been and why. He wanted to be alone. Behind him, there was the sound of Laura's Blazer easing out onto the blacktop.

8.

Riding aimlessly in the moonlight over the rolling hills of the pastures and fields that lay behind the tractor shed, Ray tried to sort through the events and conversations of the past few days since his return home. Everyone who cared about him was trying their best to make things seem normal when they all knew that normal for Ray Bennett had yet to be defined.

He had inherited a business with no business. And if he were successful in developing new business, it would have to be done with very old, outdated equipment. Farming with old equipment was in no way a novel idea. Garden plots and farmlands of various sizes throughout the country were worked regularly with aging tractors and implements. Old Ford and Farmall tricycle tractors had for decades broken the ground, planted the seed and brought in the harvest on the same land that new plexi-glass enclosed air-conditioned four-wheel driven monsters now worked. Another difference was that Ray's equipment had sat idle and rusting for so long. As able a mechanic as Thomas was, and as certain as he was that Thomas would put everything he had as right as possible, Ray wondered if the combine and cotton pickers that had long ago given their best had just a few more seasons left in them. If he was to build a business at all, it would have to rest on his reliability, and he could be no more reliable than the equipment he depended on to do the work his farmer customers needed for their livelihoods.

The fragile bubble he had built where he and Laura and Emmy would live happily ever after had burst. It had been unrealistic, he knew, to dwell on this notion, but, as he had told Laura, it had gotten him through fifteen years of incarceration. He didn't even love Laura. Not in the same way he had as an eighteen year old starry-eyed youth. The fantasy, though, had required them to be together, with Emmy, as a loving family. This dream had played itself out in many scenarios over the years, but Ray had never been able to imagine himself as a father to Emmy apart from Laura.

And then there was Emmy. As many ways as he had plotted their first meeting to occur, Ray had never expected it to go as it had. He had never once pictured himself as meeting with such hostility and disdain in the heart of his daughter. And did he even have the right to call her daughter, likewise in his own private thoughts? Hadn't he given her up, and in doing so given up any hope he might have of ever being a father to her? Perhaps, but he'd not given up the love he had felt for her from the moment he first learned of her existence in Laura's young womb.

As he pondered these things, Ray found himself facing the lake where he and Laura had created Emmy. It was in this way that he had come to think of that night. For only a short while after it had happened had he been able to think of the late hours of that May night as a young man remembers his first time. It was not how he had planned to lose his virginity. And it was not how Laura had planned to give herself up to a man either. Since junior high school when he first began to recognize the stirrings that girls caused to rise within him, Ray had held fast to the idea that he would lay with no one until his wedding night. After all, if he wanted this in the girl he married she had every right to expect it from him in return.

Despite the locker room talk and crude suggestions that emanated from the pack he ran with, he saw it simply as a matter of respect. Ray knew, or thought he knew, which girls were likely to be free with themselves. Some were not so particular who with, others were probably very particular, but none gained his respect. He did find himself feeling sorry for those who did, or were thought to, give themselves away easily. Why would a girl lessen herself like that? And the boys? Some said it was different with boys. The urge was greater for certain. But, how can it be ok, even expected, with boys at the same time it is degrading to girls?

Laughing to himself, Ray wondered at how things had changed. How easy it had been to cast stones until he had made himself a target of his own harsh judgment. Where could he point his finger other than at himself? His own sin made no one else's sin right. It just placed him within the ranks of those he thought himself above. He realized that he had only his own sinful nature to rise above, not anyone else's. But, oh, the price of that lesson!

High school graduation, sixteen years ago.
It was a warm night, a good moonlit May night.
The graduation parties had bored him and Laura.
The parties were designed by frightened parents
to keep their newly released children out of the

kind of trouble they were likely to find themselves in.

Reveling in their new found freedom, Ray and Laura desired to be alone. Sneaking into Carl's barn, they quietly saddled two horses and led them out into the night. Deciding that the moon shining over the lake would set the mood for some serious making out, Ray led the way. He knew just how far they would go, where they would stop, and that he would go home after a while with a frustrated body, but a contented mind.

The water was dark and still. A full moon hung overhead, its eyes reflected in the blackness of the water below. The sound of the horses chomping the grass trying to chew and swallow with the bits in their mouths was the only sound to be heard as the young couple sat on the bank that gently sloped to the edge of the lake. The cheap strawberry wine Ray had procured to toast the evening baited these novice drinkers, bolstering their courage and dulling their inhibitions. Ray reached to kiss Laura full on the lips. She responded likewise but pulled back suddenly.

"My feet are killing me," she said. "I feel like I've been standing for hours."

With that she took off her shoes planning to wade into the shallow water that waited only a few feet away. Realizing that she was still wearing her hose she hesitated for a moment, but nothing would do except for the midnight wade she suddenly craved. Turning her back to Ray she quickly dropped her jeans right there on the grass and wriggled out of the hose. 'No big deal,' she thought, 'Ray has seen more of me in my bikini.'

Indeed, that was true, for her shirt tail covered her bottom quite nicely. But, there was a big difference in just how things got covered that she ignored.

"Laura!" Ray gasped.

"Oh, hush! You can't see anything!" Laura scolded as she stepped off into the cool water not quite oblivious now to the fact that it was still what kept one from seeing that determined how much was revealed.

"Come on in, Ray, this feels great," she implored.

No sooner had these words left her mouth than she slipped off of a small embankment beneath the water. It was less than a foot deeper than she expected, but it caught her off guard and she tumbled into the lake falling to her knees which brought the water level to just below her neck. She instinctively jumped up and lunged forward falling again and having to catch herself with her hands.

By now Ray was rolling in laughter on the bank.

Laura stood carefully to exit the water, but realized that her white shirt was clinging to her body and was now quite invisible. Ray had stopped laughing, and sat staring, wide eyed, with his mouth gaped open.

Embarrassed she shrieked and retreated into slightly deeper water. She had also seen that her scramble to stand had left her body as well as the white shirt smeared liberally with mud from the soft bottom of the lake.

"You ought to be ashamed, Ray Bennett, staring at me like that! Mama's gonna kill me!" she wailed.

"I . . . I'm sorry, Laura. I couldn't help . . . it's just that . . . I never . . . I mean you . . . .," Ray stammered. "Are you alright out there?"

"You're gonna have to go home, Ray so I can come out of here!" Laura scolded.

"I can't leave you out here by yourself."

"Of course you can. I've been here by myself plenty of times and I did just fine without you gawking at me!"

"Well, you've never been out here half drunk and half naked at midnight before!"

"How do you know?" Laura cooed. "I bet I've been skinny dipping in this lake more times than you have."

"Yeah, I bet," Ray retorted. "And how do you know I've been skinny dippin' out here?"

"Proper young Southern ladies got eyes, too, sir!"

Ray was glad it was too dark for Laura to see his face turn blood red with embarrassment of his own.

"You mean you've seen . . .," his voice trailed off.

"More than you'll ever see of me," she chuckled, her teeth beginning to chatter from the still cold water.

Drawing deeply from the wine bottle, Ray muttered, "Don't seem fair to me." After a moment he said, "Come on out, before you catch pneumonia. I'll turn around." He scooted on the blanket they had laid on the ground until he faced away from the lake. He resisted the strong temptation to turn and look when he heard the water swirling and dripping as Laura stood and walked onto shore.

"Here. I'll give you my shirt," he said over his shoulder. The snaps on his western style shirt gave way as he pulled at them. He held his breath as he heard the soft sounds of Laura slipping out of her clingy wet garments. Her breath, quick and choppy through her shivering lips.

"I'm so cold," Laura said reaching for the shirt Ray held over his shoulder.

"Take a big swig of this. It'll take the chill off." He reached down and behind himself to get the wine bottle. As he did, he stumbled slightly and knocked the bottle over. Instinctively, he turned to grab the wine before it spilled out. He raised up and caught himself gazing intently into the eyes of the most beautiful girl in the world.

Laura quickly clutched the shirt closed, her cold fingers unable to negotiate the snaps. "I'm so cold," she said shivering.

Ray wrapped his arms around her and pulled her close trying to warm her body with his. The trembling slowed as the gentle spring breeze dried Laura.

"I'll get your jeans," Ray said softly, reluctantly. The thought of turning loose of his nearly naked girlfriend caused his muscles to rebel against his words. It all felt just too good to let go just yet.

"Just hold me," was Laura's reply. "I could stay this way forever."

Their lips met. Perhaps it was the moon, the wine, the situation . . . or maybe this was all a convenient excuse. But, as the moon moved across the clear Mississippi sky and as Laura's clothes dried on the bank of her father's great lake, as the horses watched in unconcerned boredom, Ray Bennett and Laura Sullivan made love . . . and a life was created.

"This is not quite the ending I had planned to our graduation night," Ray said again. After several minutes of silence he added, "I'm sorry."

"Don't be," Laura said softly. "It was . . . all I hoped it would be . . . just sooner."

"I didn't plan it this way," Ray said as if in defense of himself. "I love you, Laura. And I respect you. I want you to know that."

"I do know, Ray."

"If this is the only time we . . . well, that'll be alright."

"Yes, Ray. That would be alright." Laura stroked Ray's cheek.

"Trespassing is against the law. Or don't you care?"

So deep in thought had he been that Ray did not hear the approach of another horse. He jerked around to find himself staring into the eyes of his daughter. She was beautiful. In the moonlight, Emmy resembled Laura at a younger age. In fact, it was almost like gazing into the past. Long dark brown hair, a proud, almost defiant, posture. Though he could not clearly see them in detail in the subdued light of the night, Ray knew that a pair of brown eyes was trying hard to burn holes right through him. Her dark complexion seemed to blend into the shadows of her hair wafting across her face in the cold breeze. She sat her horse well, comfortable, confident.

"I didn't hear you coming," he said softly.

"What are you doing here?" Emmy demanded. "This is my grandfather's land, in case you didn't know."

"Yeah, I know. I was just thinking' . . . rememberin'." Ray looked around at the lake. "I don't mean no harm. Didn't expect nobody to be out here this time of night."

Emmy stiffened. "I guess I can come out here any time I like!"

"I reckon so," Ray chuckled. "As long as your Mama don't catch you sneakin' out by yourself."

"That's none of your business."

Shaking his head, Ray replied almost sadly, "Nope, I reckon it's not." After an awkward moment of silence Ray said, "This used to be one of my favorite places, too."

"What makes you think it's mine?"

Ray shrugged, "Because you're here."

"Don't start thinking you know anything about me or that we have anything in common," Emmy said angrily. "Since you've been back, everything has been messed up. Papaw is meaner than ever, Mamaw is nervous all the time, Daddy doesn't talk. Even Mama acts different! I guess you think you're going to get back in with everybody and make big friends again and go on like nothing ever happened. Well, we have to live with what you did, what you caused. I wish you'd never come back! I wish you would just go away and leave us alone."

Ray stared into Emmy's eyes and then looked away. Of course, she was right. They all probably would be better off if he had never come home.

"I'm sorry, Emmy, that you've been affected by all this. I don't know what all has been goin' on in your life and I won't ask. It ain't none of my business. But, if there was any chance I could fix it, I would."

Ray walked to Dan. The horse was green and shied away as Ray reached for the bridle. He was embarrassed for Emmy to see him having trouble with his horse.

"Have you forgotten how to ride a horse?" she taunted.

Without replying, Ray tightened his grip on the saddle horn and swung onto the animal's back. "I truly wish it was different for you. I know all the 'I'm sorry's' I can muster won't help you none. But, I truly am."

"What do you care?"

"I just care, dar. . ." Ray turned Dan toward his own land. "I just care." He moved to nudge Dan into a trot, but stopped. "Look," he sighed taking off his hat, "I gather that everything in life has not been so great and easy for you. Well, that's tough. It really is. But, it's your life, so live it!"

Emmy's glare hardened.

Ray continued, "One thing I've learned is that it's not the troubles you encounter in life that define you. It's the way you deal with them, or the way you let them deal with you. It's gon' be one way or the other. There's been a lot of sufferin' over an accident that happened a long time ago, the least of which has been felt by your grandfather. I know it's been hard on you and I'm sorry for that and I wish I could change it."

Ray looked squarely into Emmy's eyes. He hurt for her. He ached to put his arms around her and tell her that he would make everything alright and make all the hurt go away. He would give all he had for a kind word from her. Her steely gaze told him that even that was far too much to expect.

"But, I can't," he said softly. "I'm probably the last person on earth you want to get advice from, but I know what I'm talkin' about. Blaming me for your problems might make you feel better, and that's alright, I can take it. But, it won't make you any better. It won't make you any stronger. It'll just fuel a fire that will burn you up from inside out. Change it now, Emmy. You're young, and you can have a wonderful life. You can be happy with yourself, and that's what counts at the end of the day. You don't have to like me. You don't even have to acknowledge my existence! But, you've got to let go of all this hate, or whatever it is. It'll eat you up. I've seen it happen. And you're too good to spend your life that way."

Emmy sat defiantly, resolutely, but she could no longer look Ray in the eye. She fought to hold the tears in. He might have been right in what he said, but she didn't have to let him know that. Why didn't he just leave?

"Well," Ray said when Emmy gave no response, "I've said too much, I reckon."

Suddenly a piece of advice he had been given long ago came back to him. Perhaps it would help his daughter now. "Go on home, Emmy. And when you get there take a good long look in the mirror. Leave everybody else out of it. Carl, your mama, your . . . your daddy, . . . me. Just you and that mirror. See how you feel about what looks back at you." He drew a deep breath and let it out slowly. He didn't want to leave, but he knew he must. "You just trust in the Lord, and live your life like He made you to live it." He paused. "Nice talkin' to you."

Ray touched the brim of his hat and loped away.

Watching the shadowy form of Ray Bennett and his horse blend into the darkness Emmy sat her horse shaking and crying. She hoped he could not hear. Was he right? Was she hurting herself more than him? And how much blame did Ray Bennett carry in the sad turns of her life? That her grandfather hated Ray Bennett and held an obsessive grudge against him was understandable, but why should that affect her so? Whatever had happened took place a long time ago. Her Mom was willing to give Ray Bennett a second chance. Perhaps . . . well, maybe she would try to go a little easier on him if ever they met again. In the meantime, she would go home and take a look in that mirror.

The pickup truck that pulled up alongside of Ray carried a familiar rattle. "You want to go with me?" Bob Riley said hanging his head out of the window.

"Where you goin' this time of night?"

"Thought I'd drive to Jackson and eat some breakfast."

Ray stared blankly at Bob for a moment. "Ain't it a little late for that? Or early one?"

"A western omelet goes good this time of night. Stretch your wings, son, try something new. You'd be surprised how many people eat breakfast at midnight these days. Then they go home and go to bed so they can get up and eat breakfast again. 'Sides, I'd like the company and you look like you could use some."

Just over an hour later, Ray and Bob were sitting in a booth at one of the four "Pancake Palaces" in Jackson. No sooner than they had given the waitress their order than she turned around and repeated it to the cook for all to hear. "Two westerns, both with grits and toast, one large hash brown scattered, smothered, covered, and swimming." The cook repeated the order back to her.

"I might have been too hard on her," Ray said relating his conversation with Emmy. "She's just a kid. She has a lot to deal with and I'm tellin' 'er to just handle it."

Bob grinned slightly and replied, "It's high time somebody told her that, Pop!"

Trying, but failing, to hide his surprise, Ray asked, "What do you mean, Pop?"

"I mean I know who that girl is!" Bob's eyes sparkled and his face betrayed his longtime knowledge of Emmy's parentage. "Know'd it for years." Noting the concern in Ray's eyes he added, "Don't worry, I ain't told nobody, and there ain't nobody else knows that I know of."

"Two eggs over hard, bacon, and hash browns, one steak platter, extra fries," the waitress shouted.

"Two eggs over hard, bacon, hash browns, steak platter, extra fries," the cook shouted back.

"I hope you're right about that," Ray answered. "The last thing Emmy needs is to find out the truth about me."

Bob shook his head. "She could do a lot worse than to know what kind of man her real father really is."

"Patty melt, hash browns scattered and smothered."

The portly short order cook never looked up from the huge griddle which held eggs, omelets, and hamburger meat all in various stages of preparedness.

"Patty melt, hash browns scattered and smothered," he repeated.

Bob looked around at the waitress and the cook who stood only a few feet apart behind the long serving counter. "You know? They run this place kind of like a submarine."

9.

Friday was largely uneventful, at least during the daylight hours. Ray, Thomas, and Bob worked on the cotton picker. Thomas took some time away from the picker to get Matt's truck in shape to pass state inspection. Of course, since Mississippi state automobile inspections are done by "authorized" privately owned service stations and repair shops, there are those who would place an inspection sticker on the windshield of any wreck that could be driven into and out of their facility. But, Ray wanted to be sure that the vehicle was safe for Matt to drive. He had grown fond of the boy in a short period of time and wanted to do good by him.

By the time the sun descended over the tree tops, the Bennett Farm Services crew had put in a good day's work. The cotton picker was not yet operational, but close to it. An older picker felt to present a greater challenge to Thomas' mechanical abilities was next in line. Then the combine would follow. The area in and around the tractor shed was shaping up nicely, even if the shed itself was pretty much an eyesore. And the outfit was coming together. The men were bonding well, enjoying working together. There was a sense of belonging together, the men and the Bennett place. All they needed now was some work to do that would bring Bennett Farm Services into its purpose. They needed cotton to pick, beans to harvest.

"Friday night. Time to howl." That's what the boys back at Parchman used to say as they recalled their own raucous weekends. Whether from the country or the city, they were all pretty much the same come Friday and Saturday night. Beer joints, loud juke boxes, wild women. The stories changed little and over the years Ray had heard them all. He had heard them, but never lived them himself.

He had driven past many of the bars and clubs with bright neon beer signs hanging in the windows and over the doors. There were always a few people loitering outside, drinking beer from cans or bottles poorly disguised by small brown paper bags, cigarettes dangling loosely from their lips, bouncing as they spoke their tough guy talk. The music and din from inside the buildings rising and fading whenever the door opened briefly to allow a new comer in or to release some unsteady patron into the night to try his luck elsewhere. "There ain't no women in there tonight," most could be heard to mumble.

Curiosity had never compelled Ray to overcome his conscience or his fear, whichever was ruling him at the time, to make his own way into such establishments to see firsthand just what went on in there. He should wait until he was a little older, he convinced himself. He never saw himself the same as these people. He would stand out too much. And he did not at all wish to stand out in a crowd such as these.

Maybe now, thirty three was too old to go out "jukin'". Well, he had never been before, and he may never go again, but tonight, he would just see what it was like behind those painted glass doors where young women went looking for love and men of all ages hoped they would settle for something less. Beside that, the horses were poor company, so Ray decided to head for town.

None of his old friends had bothered to contact him yet. Perhaps he would run into someone he knew at one of those beer joints he had passed while driving through Delta Hills.

Ray drove past two bars that were doing a brisk business. The third one he came to had only two trucks and a rather beat-up foreign car parked in front. Not quite up to confronting a crowd, Ray parked near the front door before he noticed that he had happened upon the Bodock Bar and Grill.

"This is where Lori works," he said to himself as he remembered what Laura had told him. As most beer joints are, the Bodock was dark and pulsated with country music blaring from a strange looking juke box. Upon closer inspection, Ray saw that it played cd's. Would wonders never cease! It was all new to Ray, though. Two pool tables and three pinball machines were there to draw the sporting crowd to the far end of the small building. Two side by side doors, one with a big red "L" splashed across it, the other with similar elegance displaying a somewhat crooked "M", obviously directed the more literate patrons to the correct restrooms.

There was no one tending the bar at the moment. Probably they would emerge from behind the "M" or the "L" soon. Two young men were playing pool while another sat on the other pool table watching them. They glanced up at Ray as he entered the bar, but immediately went back to their game. The juke box played the last notes of an Alan Jackson tune and shut down, the fifty cents spent. Ray sat down at one of three small round tables near the bar.

He settled into the chair and propped his elbows on the table before him. Recalling the events of the night before, he fell into a stare with nothing particular in sight. Strangely, he realized that he was not particularly disappointed that Laura had not spent the past fifteen years pining away for him. His dream, one of the few things that kept him going all these years was that a remorseful Laura, who held the key to making everything alright, would do just that. He had envisioned the three of them, Emmy, Laura, and himself, making up for lost time. Picnics, long horseback rides, working the place together. All happy to be together.

As much as he still wanted a place in Emmy's life he knew now that his great dream would not come true. It had served its purpose. And now it was time to build a real life. His relationship to Laura was now one that would always be special to him, and he sensed a bond there holding them together. Perhaps it was a bond named Emmy. Reconciling his feelings for Laura did nothing to ease the loneliness Ray felt. A false hope was still hope, and now even that was gone.

"Starin' at walls is a bad habit to get into, Mister," a vaguely familiar voice said.

"Well," he replied, "With me it's more like a hard habit to brea . . . Lo!" Ray exclaimed turning to see who he was talking to. "Lorraine Sullivan!" he repeated.

Lorraine Parker, two marriages had passed since she had been a Sullivan, stood with her mouth open. In her jeans, white shirt and vest she looked good, Ray thought. Bright eyed and full of spirit despite the troubles she had known, Lorraine was the kind of woman every single man fell in love with, and every married man wished he had married, but was glad his wife was not like.

"You better stand up and give me a hug, Ray Bennett," she said through moist glistening eyes. "I'm so glad to see you," she said still holding him tightly.

"I'd of come around sooner if I'd known the clientele here got such a fine welcome," Ray said.

"Oh, hush! They don't all get this," she said wiping her eyes.

Ray was puzzled by her reaction to seeing him.

"You look good, Ray, real good. I just can't get over you bein' here."

"Well, you look mighty fine yourself, Lorraine," Ray replied. "'Course," he said grinning, "I always did think you was a good lookin' girl!"

"You thought no such a thing, Ray Bennett," Lorraine slapped him on the arm. "Your eyes were glued to my sister and her prissy little self. You didn't have no time to cast even a look toward little sister Lori!"

"I said it, and I'll stand by it," Ray defended himself, "and the way you turned out, I believe I was right."

"Yeah, 'turned out' describes my life to a "T"," she said. "But we don't want to talk about all that depressing old stuff now anyway, do we?"

"Not me," Ray said. "I've had all the depression I can stand for one night. Findin' a friendly face has kinda turned things around. There's too few of them around."

"Well, I imagine there's more than you know, Ray."

"How 'bout three more beers, Lori?" one of the pool players yelled from the back.

"What can I get you, Ray?"

"How long you been workin' here?" Ray asked.

Lorraine hesitated. "It's just part time. I've got three kids to feed and to get through Christmas. Anything wrong with that?" Her tone of voice changed slightly.

"No. No," Ray said. "I admire it. In fact, I'm glad you do. I wouldn't of seen you if you didn't."

Her eyes brightened. "Maybe that's the real reason I'm here!"

"Whatever they're havin'," Ray gestured. "It's been a while. I don't know what's good."

Lorraine gave Ray a sympathizing look and turned to go behind the bar. Retrieving five bottles of beer from the cooler, she took three to the boys in the pool room and sat down at Ray's table. "Do you mind if I join you before the football crowd gets here?"

"I'm glad to have the company," Ray replied. "You're a sight prettier than my horse and a much better conversationalist."

Lori laughed. "So, you're back on those horses!"

Small talk passed between the two while empty beer bottles took up more and more space on the table as Ray felt more and more of the effect. He couldn't help but notice how he would catch Lori gazing at him strangely from time to time.

"You're gettin' less particular about what you drink with every day, Lorraine," a rough voice said from behind her. "It's bad enough you swipin' my beer to drink with regular customers, but I won't tolerate it with the likes of him!"

Ray stared into the cold, hard eyes of Buster Pritchard. Flanked by several equally dissatisfied faces, some familiar, others unknown to Ray, Buster stood out as a leader of sorts. But that was probably because most regular patrons of such establishments find it to be a social coup of some kind to be considered friends with the owner.

"I'll drink with who I want to, and I ain't stole none of your beer, Mister Pritchard," Lori retorted, placing special sarcasm on the 'Mister".

"I don't want you in here, jail bird," Buster said to Ray.

"Well, it's good to see you, too, Busted," Ray grinned. "Larry, Wayne," he said looking to two of the men behind Buster, "How ya'll doin'?" Ray could see Buster growing red faced. He didn't like being called "Busted".

It was a nick name he had acquired while in the fourth grade after falling out of a window at school. He was standing in the window sill showing off his muscles, such as they were, when he lost his footing and fell outside. His fall was broken by the Home Economics Class hand stitched apron display which preceded Buster into a shallow, but sufficiently muddy, ditch. It could be said that Buster was then busted in more ways than one, so the name Busted became attached to him in a secretive sort of way since he was prone to beat up anyone he happened to overhear uttering it. Even though Ray had only been a second grader at the time, he had always thought of Buster Pritchard, the bully, as Busted . . ., the bully. In his fear of the older and much larger boy, Ray found unrevealed courage in that whispered nickname. Now, the events he had dwelled upon, or maybe it was the beer that he was unaccustomed to drinking, had him feeling less than gracious towards such characters as Buster Pritchard.

"Nobody calls me that," Buster snarled.

"Do you get mad at him, too?" Ray asked.

"Who?" Buster snapped.

"Nobody," Ray said.

"What is it you're talkin' about?" Buster shot back.

"Never mind, Busted," Ray replied. "I didn't mean to take the conversation over your head. Now, if you boys ain't gonna sit down and tell me how glad you are to see me, I'd just as soon finish my beer with Lori here." Ray turned to face Lorraine as if dismissing the men hovering over him. He was well aware of where they were, though, and how they were postured. He had played this game many times before.

"You ain't finishin' nothin' with her," Buster snapped, "she's got work to do." Turning to Lorraine, Buster said, "Git to it!"

She made a sound much like a grunt and rolled her eyes at Buster. "I don't think I like the tone of your voice. You never have a problem with me sharin' a beer with anybody else in here."

"Well, he ain't stayin' long enough to finish his. Move on, Bennett," Buster gestured toward the door. "Your kind ain't welcome here."

Ray didn't move. He didn't respond. This was shaping up to be an interesting night.

"I think he's scared," Wayne said. "He always was a scaredy cat!"

Ray cast a sideways glance at Wayne. "I'm glad you haven't let adulthood corrupt your vocabulary, Wayne," he said. "You're right, though. I wet my pants at the sound of your voice."

Larry chimed in now chuckling, "Yeah, I bet you wet your pants over another man, prison boy. I know what goes on in there."

"Prison boy?" Ray mused. "I'd have to say you fellows don't watch enough TV. And of course you know all about what goes on in there, Larry," Ray replied, "your name and phone number is scratched on every bathroom wall in Parchman."

"Why you . . . !" Larry screamed charging toward Ray.

Ray, who had calmly remained seated throughout this exchange with Buster and his cronies, sprang up shoving his chair against the wall behind him. Unfortunately, he had been seated closer to the wall than he thought and the chair bounced back into the crook of his knee interrupting his balance. He was able to duck beneath Larry's swing at his head, and he came up with a blow to Larry's chin that sent him and the man standing right behind him sprawling to the floor.

"I got you now, jail bird," Buster said moving around the table to get closer to Ray.

At that moment Ray sensed more than saw movement on his right side and turned to see a fist coming into his jaw. The punch knocked him sideways, but he held to his feet. Buster knocked a glancing blow to his ribcage which spun him to his right. He found himself facing the person who had just hit him in the jaw. Ray's right arm shot out catching the man full in the chest and taking his breath. The man doubled over so Ray used his left in an upper cut to the man's jaw which reversed his momentum and sent him to the floor on his back.

Buster waded in and caught Ray in the stomach, almost taking his breath. Ray threw up his left and deflected what would have been a vicious blow to his eye. Buster drove a right into Ray's right side causing him to double over gasping for breath. By this time, the three pool players had trotted to the front of the room to watch the fight. When Ray bent forward with Buster's blow to his side, one of the youths, caught up in the excitement of the moment swung down over Ray's shoulders with his pool cue. Ray fell to his knees.

Struggling to get up, the next thing Ray felt was Buster's knee lifting hard into his face. He heard a strange almost distant shuffle of feet, he heard a woman scream, and he felt the blows all over his body from the small mob. Still gasping for breath and woozy from the knee to his face, he knew this was a fight he could not win. He could only try to protect himself as best as he could, but that was not enough.

This was not to be a stellar night for the BFS boys.

After the football game, a large crowd of high school kids, and what middle schoolers were allowed to be out, gathered, as they usually did, at "the coke machines". "The coke machines" was a small store that housed a limited supply of grocery items, and a large supply of beer, soft drinks and fishing supplies. The owner, Tiny Wiggins, closed at six thirty on game nights and didn't mind the kids congregating on his large gravel lot.

In the old days, ten or fifteen years ago, the crowd stayed right there on his lot until midnight or later. Jackson was too far away just to go for a regular night out, and there was little or nothing to do in Delta Hills. So the kids stayed there pouring money into his two soft drink machines, often to mix drinks, or drinking the beer he had sold to them illegally earlier in the day. Now, they merely seemed to meet there to decide where their next stop would be. Forty-nine was four laned now so Jackson was much closer. The kids still poured money into his drink machines though, but he also had more trash to clear from his lot come Saturday morning, even with fewer and fewer visitors the night before. Each Saturday morning he reflected that juvenile delinquents were not nearly as respectful as they used to be.

Matt had taken Billie Rose to the football game in his "new" farm truck. She had wanted a chance to show off her new clothes and he couldn't resist her pleadings to go. Once there, Billie Rose took off with her friends and Matt noticed that as time passed more and more of her classmates joined the small group that Billie Rose was with. Matt thought it sad that Billie Rose was no different from before, but her new clothes made her acceptable to kids who would not otherwise give her the time of day. He knew that his own worn and shabby wardrobe contributed to his lack of friends. And he couldn't help but wonder if a new outfit would make him not only welcome, but wanted in any of the social circles in Coleman High. He knew more about loneliness than he cared to, but he was beginning to feel that he belonged with the odd crew of

Bennett Farm Services. And belonging was something that he wanted to know more about.

None of the few people in school that would talk to him were at the game, except for Bill and Glen who were on the football team. It was always so awkward and embarrassing to be left standing alone among a crowd. Matt considered going over to the opposing team's side of the field. At least no one over there would know who he was as he sat alone in the stands. He could go sit in his truck and listen to the radio, but am radio did not appeal to him. Going to the concession stand, he bought a hot dog and a drink. From there he spotted a small group of men huddled on the sidelines near the end zone. Taking up a place just beyond these men, Matt was far from the end of the bleachers most of the students occupied, and by pretending to be intently interested in the game, he hoped to appear unconcerned with the frivolities of the football night social scene.

At half time, Emmy and two of her friends, Robin and Leigh, were walking to the restroom. Their path took them right past Matt, who was busy planning what he was going to do during half time. He couldn't just stand there staring at an empty field and neither team had a band, so there would be no half time show. He decided to check up on Billie Rose, which could be good for ten or fifteen minutes, and then he would head for the restroom where he could probably dawdle until the game resumed for the second half. Turning to go find his sister, he found himself staring into the beautiful eyes of Emmy McKay! Actually, he almost walked right into her.

"Hi, Matt," Emmy said cheerfully as the three girls walked by him without stopping.

Stunned, Matt was hardly able to respond, but he did manage a weak, "How ya doin'?" The girls were almost past him at this point.

"I'm fine," Emmy replied. "See ya."

"Yeah," Matt smiled, "see ya." Then he added under his breath, "And you are some kind of fine!"

"Why did you do that?" Leigh asked Emmy. "He's so weird."

"He's not weird," Emmy replied. "He's just a loner and I feel kind of sorry for him. He's sweet to his little sister."

"I wouldn't doubt if he were sweet on his sister," Robin laughed. "He just doesn't fit in."

"Maybe that is only because nobody will let him in," Emmy said.

Matt fairly glowed for the rest of the game. 'Emmy McKay spoke to me!' he thought to himself. To get attention from a girl was a new experience to Matt. He knew it was probably a meaningless gesture for her, but to him it meant the possibility of acceptance. Maybe she didn't think of him as such a hick after all.

Still reveling in his eleven word conversation with Emmy, Matt impulsively turned his truck into Tiny's parking lot after the game. Maybe Emmy would be there and maybe she would speak to him again! It was more than he could hope for, but at least he might get to take another look at her.

"I'm thirsty. You want something to drink?" he asked Billie Rose.

"Sure," she responded enthusiastically. She wasn't really thirsty and she thought it was too cold to be drinking soft drinks while standing outside, but there was the possibility of hanging out with some of the big kids. And she could brag to her new friends that she had actually been to the coke machines. It had been a good night for her, too.

They weaved through the cars and trucks that had drawn them there to get to the two drink machines. Matt gave Billie Rose some change and tried to casually scan the crowd while she made her selection. Just at the moment he spotted Emmy, Bo spotted him.

"Hey, cowboy," Bo shouted, "what are you doin' here? This is a private party. Invited guests only! I don't think you two are on the invitation list!"

Matt immediately realized that he had made a mistake by stopping here. After all, Bo was standing there with his arm around the girl he had come to . . . well . . . to look at. Now, he was in a tight spot. In those few seconds, there was no way he could think of to get out of this without looking like a fool or a coward or both.

The girl that had spoken so nicely to him, and had made the whole evening worthwhile, would soon be laughing at him along with all of the others there at Tiny's.

"I'm just gittin' a drink," Matt said evenly.

"Well, get it someplace else," Bo snarled. "I've seen enough of you for one day." He took a few steps toward Matt.

"Bo!" Emmy whispered, but he acted as if he didn't hear her.

Matt dug into his pocket for more change. "I'm here," he said. "I reckon I'll go ahead and get what I came for."

"I reckon," Bo mocked, "you'll get it somewhere else or do without. We don't want you here. Does anybody want this hayseed at our party?" he shouted turning to look at everyone else around him.

No one said anything.

"See, cowboy," he snarled, "nobody wants you here."

Emmy stood with her arms crossed tightly across her chest and glared at Bo.

"Didn't come to stay, I just came for something to drink," Matt said, his cheeks burning. 'I just came to make a fool out of myself,' is what he was thinking. "You go on back to the truck," he said to Billie. Pulling some change from his pocket, he turned toward the drink machine.

Bo was now very close to Matt. He threw his hand up under Matt's knocking the change from his hand. As Matt bent to retrieve his money, Bo knocked Matt's hat from his head.

"You quit messin' with my hat," Matt said straightening up with a jerk.

"Or what?" Bo taunted.

"Or since your head's too dern big for any hat to fit, I'll just have to knock it off!" Matt retorted. "Or at least let some of that hot air out of it!" He was surprised to hear a few chuckles emanate from the crowd intently watching them.

"Sure you will," Bo snarled as he pushed Matt's left shoulder.

Matt immediately thrust out his right arm catching Bo by surprise and knocking him to the ground. He did not immediately get up, so Matt turned to pick up his cowboy hat. Bo, seeing the opportunity he was waiting for, sprang forward placing his shoulder under Matt's ribs and drove him back against one of the drink machines. Matt shoved Bo back with his right arm and hit him in the jaw with a left jab that stunned Bo.

"I've about had it with you, Bo," Matt shouted. "I don't want to fight you or nobody else, but you keep pushin'."

Bo said not a word, but shook his head as if trying to clear the cloud Matt's fist had put there. He swung at Matt, but missed as Matt ducked back. Matt, however, placed another left on Bo's jaw knocking him back to the ground. Sounds of surprise rose from the small crowd which had been, and still was, in support of Bo.

Matt did not attack Bo, but stood his ground. Bo came up quickly, swinging wild glancing blows at Matt. A couple of Bo's swings connected with Matt's torso, but only served to push him back a couple of steps. Bo circled around Matt which put Matt's back to everyone else. After exchanging a few blows that connected but did little damage, Matt caught Bo squarely in the stomach, knocking the wind from him. He immediately followed with a swing to Bo's head sending him to the ground yet again. Growing weary, and off balance from the punch he had just delivered, Matt staggered back and was caught and held from behind by Tyler Bates and Neal Franklin, two of Bo's friends.

"Git 'im, Bo," Tyler cried as they pushed Matt back toward the wobbling Bo. With Neal and Tyler still holding him from behind, Bo hit Matt twice in the stomach and then in the face. This brought on a few muffled squeals from the girls in the crowd. The boys were cheering them on. Emmy shouted for Bo to stop, but he did not hear, nor did he care to stop.

As Bo drew back to deliver a hard blow to Matt's jaw, Billie ran up and grabbed his elbow just as he began the swing. "Leave my brother alone, you bully," she cried. Her actions slowed the force of the blow, but got her thrown up against Tyler. Tyler promptly shoved her away sending her crashing hard to the ground and half into a small mud puddle.

By now, Emmy had pushed her way through the crowd of teenagers and was shoving against Bo herself. "Stop it, Bo!" she shouted. "You just stop it!"

Bo backed away, looked at Matt sagging in the grips of Tyler and Neal, and said, "O.K. He's had enough." With that, the two boys simply let Matt fall wheezing and gasping to the ground.

Billie struggled to her knees and crawled crying to her brother. "Matt! Matt! Are you all right?" she cried.

"He'll be alright, honey," Bo said. "He just learned a hard lesson, that's all," Bo laughed.

"Yeah. He learned what cowards you three are," Billie shouted as she threw a small rock at Bo.

"Come on, let's go," Bo said to Emmy.

Emmy looked at her boyfriend with disgust. "I'm not going anywhere with you, Bo Hopson. And I'll find another ride home. Why don't you just go on!" It was more of a demand than a request.

Bo looked around and chuckled nervously. "O.K. Be that way. Come on, guys," he said to Neal and Tyler,

"Let's go find something to do." He started walking toward his car, but stopped and trotted over to Matt's hat lying upside down on the ground in front of the drink machines. His last step landed squarely on the crown of the hat, flattening one side. He picked it up and tossed it toward Matt who was on his knees trying to regain his breath. "Here's your hat, Matt. Looks like it got stepped on or something."

Tyler and Neal and a few others laughed. Bo and his friends got into his car and were backing out of the lot when Neal said, "Would you look at that?"

The three boy's eyes, as did everyone else's, followed Matt as he struggled to his feet and staggered to the drink machines. Billie had picked up what she could find of the change Bo had knocked out of Matt's hand and gave it to him. He dropped four quarters into the slot, pushed a button, (at this point he didn't care what came out) and took the canned drink and his sister to his truck.

"I'm sorry, Matt," Emmy said weakly as he passed her.

"It's not your fault he's a jerk," Matt grunted. He stopped and turned to face Emmy, and was surprised to hear himself say, "But, you deserve better."

Emmy watched as he slowly climbed behind the wheel of the truck. In contrast to Bo's exit, which had included spraying gravel and squealing his tires on the pavement, Matt left slowly, safely, in control.

'What must he be thinking?' Emmy thought. 'How alone he must feel! And why didn't I do more?'

10.

"You should be moanin' and groanin' and everything else, Ray, this stuff is supposed to burn," Lorraine said as she dabbed the cuts above Ray's left eye and the corner of his mouth with a cotton ball soaked in alcohol.

"It does," Ray replied. "I learned a long time ago to keep my moanin' and groanin' to myself." He grimaced slightly as Lori rubbed harder, obviously with the knowledge that rubbing alcohol could do no good unless some kind of pain were associated with its application.

Lori lifted her eyebrows. "It strikes me that it would be a lot less painful to learn to keep your opinion to yourself."

"Not in the long run, Lo. Not in the long run," Ray sighed.

"I hope you ain't plannin' to start in callin' me Lo again," she scolded. "I don't like it no more now than I did when I was your girlfriend's bratty kid sister."

"It's just a term of endearment, Lo," Ray said turning slightly to face his private nurse. "Just like it always was."

Lori pursed her lips and smiled. She dared not admit to Ray how she felt at the moment he called her "Lo", or even how she felt when she first saw him sitting at that table at Buster's place. How could she tell him anyway? She had not yet been able to describe the feelings to herself. It was probably just a wave of nostalgia anyway. She had fallen in love with Ray Bennett even before her sister, Laura, supposedly did.

It was an unrequited lifelong love. Even as a young girl in grammar school, Lori had always liked that Ray Bennett. As she grew older and into her teens it was more than just a junior high crush on her sister's boyfriend. The feeling had never changed. For years, just the thought of Ray and the time and distance between them would bring tears to her eyes. He had never done anything to encourage Lori, except maybe pay polite attention to her when he visited the Sullivan house. He even offered to take her along on a few of his and Laura's dates. It was just him. He was the boy she wanted as a school girl, and he was the man she still wanted to this day. But, having gotten little she ever really wanted out of life, Lorraine Sullivan's love for a man she never expected to be with had not kept her from marrying . . . twice.

Now, here he was, in the flesh, on her couch, exchanging attention with her . . . just her!

"Those boys really worked you over," she said. "I was just fixin' to hit Buster with a pool cue when he decided you'd had enough."

"He quit too soon," Ray grunted as Lori touched his rib. "I just about had 'em tired out. He could prob'ly see I was gettin' ready to make my move."

"Men!" Lori huffed. "You get yourselves beat half senseless and you still can't admit defeat. You . . ."

"Where's my truck?" Ray asked hoping to change the subject.

"It's still up at Buster's. I couldn't talk anybody in to drivin' it here for you. I thought them Thompson boys would, but Billy was the one that hit you across the back with his cue stick and I think he was scared you might try to kill him if you was to come to while he was out here with just his brother. His brother ain't much of a fighter. Neither one is for that matter."

"Well, at least they have some sense," Ray said. "Still, I can't blame a boy for takin' a whack at a known criminal when he gets the chance. Busted'll probably give him a free beer just for that." He picked up a picture that was on the end table. "These your kids?"

"My pride and joy," Lori smiled. "About the only three things I've done right since I was a junior in high school."

"Don't knock yourself, Lori. Why would you say something like that anyway?"

"Don't ask me, ask my Daddy," she sighed. "Or better yet, go ask Laura. She can do no wrong in his eyes!"

"You still fightin' with your big sister?"

"No. We get along o.k. In fact she's keepin' the kids this weekend." Lori fidgeted with a loose thread on the couch. "It's just that she's mostly made all the right decisions in her life . . . except for breakin' up with you. Everything just falls right into place for her and Clint. And Daddy rewards that by helpin' them out with money and all, even when they don't need it. Me. . . . well, ever since . . . that summer . . . I barely got by in school. I was in trouble a lot. Then I took up with Tim in the eleventh grade. . . . Daddy's been on my case my whole life. I didn't turn out like he wanted." Her voice trailed off.

Lori's life in the shadow of her straight A, correctly dressed, well mannered sister, who broke up with Ray on the promise of a secure future from her father, had been difficult, to say the least. Carl had even forgiven Laura for bearing Ray's baby. But, raising the child as a McKay was the price for that forgiveness.

Lorraine did not carry as much favor in her father's eye. She became pregnant by Tim the summer before her senior year in high school was to begin. Carl Sullivan had no forgiveness and no bright promises for her. Consequently, she never went back to school, and never finished. Her marriage to Tim ended even before their daughter, Susanna, was born.

Her parents took her and the baby back into their home. Up until then, Lori and Tim had been living with his aunt. After six months of beratement and overbearing interference, Lori rented a small apartment in town and went to work checking groceries. The manager there assumed she was loose, thought she was dumb, and committed sexual harassment against her before it was decided that there was such a thing as sexual harassment. Lori got fired when she poured chlorine bleach down his britches.

From the grocery store, she went straight to the bag plant to apply for work, but could not be hired because she had no high school diploma. While waiting tables at the truck stop, she met a young truck driver from Tupelo named Davey Turnage. After a three month courtship, they were married, and Davey promptly took Lorraine and Susanna to Tupelo where they spent most of their time in a rundown rental house waiting for him to come home from driving all over the south.

Between Susanna, Davey Jr., and Priscilla Marie (Lori had become mildly obsessed with Elvis while in Tupelo) Lori studied for and obtained her GED. At the age of twenty four, newly educated, and with a six year old, a four year old and a two year old, Lori found herself also to be newly alone. Davey Sr. had met another waitress, a college girl this time, in Tuscaloosa and felt that his horizon would stretch farther with a more sophisticated mate. Lori doubted that it was his horizon that was being stretched. She would only let him take his clothes and a few cassette tapes. She doubted that she would get anymore child support from Davey than she had from Tim, so she kept their furniture and household goods, for all their worth, to have something to sell if need be.

Her mother had called at least once each month while she had been gone, and they had exchanged visits a few times over the years. Lori, for her part, tried to call home when she knew her father would not be there. She could no longer stand to hear what a fine life her older and wiser sister had made for herself while she apparently just rambled along with no plan and no ambition, taking up with whomever would have her.

Laura had called often and was always supportive of Lori. She had long ago recognized the distinction her father had made between the two of them, and she realized in time that it was partially because she had always given in or compromised on her father's wishes. She was afraid to stand up to him. Hers had been a life of compliance and conformity. Lorraine, on the other hand, had lived in rebellion and independence. Each was, however, driven by their father and thus, held by him, controlled by him in a strange sort of way. It was mostly from guilt that Laura supplied what support she could to her younger sister.

When Laura learned that Davey had left Lorraine and the children, she and Clint went immediately up to Tupelo and moved the little family and their meager belongings back to Winstead County. Clint, more from obedience to Laura than sympathy or generosity for Lorraine, went to his deer camp and towed back the old dilapidated trailer that his grandmother had occupied in the lonely years prior to her death. The trailer house was set up on the back side of a small piece of land that Clint owned, and was located around the corner and up a gravel road from the fine four bedroom brick home he and Laura occupied.

This "temporary" arrangement had existed now for almost four years. The bag plant wasn't hiring at the time and she had no secretarial or business skills of any kind, so she went back to waiting tables. Pretty and perky despite life's wear and tear, Lori was much in demand by the men folk, single and married, in the area. She had received proposals of marriage, and even a few proposals from well to do businessmen and travelers of "upkeep". At first, she had been somewhat taken in by the poor misunderstood young married men until she realized that this was probably the same line Davey had used on his Tuscaloosa college girl. Too, a bit of observation revealed in almost every case that most of what these men wanted understanding about were not the kind of things that any wife should be expected to understand. Oh, there were a few who probably would have been better off married to someone else or alone, but Lori was not in the "life fixin'" business where other people were concerned. Her own life was "still broke" and she reckoned that "a broken down man and a broken down woman had little to offer each other in the way of something to build a life on."

The would-be sugar daddies got a nice turn down, with a wink and a smile designed to keep the big tips coming.

Lori and Carl rarely spoke. He seemed to be more angry and embarrassed by his daughter's circumstances and lifestyle than sympathetic to it. If only Lori were more like Laura. Not only financial help, but love and support would flow her way. If only she would do something to deserve it. For her part, Lori knew that she was a disappointment and embarrassment to her mother. But, for the time being, she was helpless to do anything about it, short of collapsing and crawling back as a seventeen year old girl with no other ambition than to please her father, pliant and obedient to every wish and whim. And, she took enjoyment from the fact that her predicament was a source of humiliation to Carl. It was a not so subtle message to Winstead County that Carl Sullivan was not all he presented himself to be.

She never said it to his face, but Lori knew what kind of man her father was. And she despised him for it and for the evil things he did to people who got in his way.

So, here she was, living in an old worn out mobile home, with old worn out furniture, fighting to keep herself from becoming old and worn out before her time.

"Well, I guess he'd really get on your case if he knew you were here consorting with a shirtless ex-con," Ray joked.

Lori chuckled and then gasped. "Where did you get those scars?" A long scar across Ray's abdomen, another on his chest just above his heart, and one more, as yet unseen by Lori on his back, were barely visible in the pale light from the small table lamp.

"Souvenirs from the Mississippi Delta," Ray replied reaching for his tee shirt. He had never been comfortable around girls without his shirt on and he suddenly felt very self conscious.

"I'm sorry for what my father has put you through just because you got his daughter pregnant!" Lori said angrily.

"What?" Ray said. "Why would you say that?"

"Now, Raymond Lee Bennett, don't you go tryin' to tell me no stories!" Lori shot back. "Anybody who would look could see that that girl is your daughter! She's yours and you can't tell me she ain't!"

Ray was speechless. Had anyone else noticed the resemblance? He had thought his own such feelings were merely the wishful thinking of any normal father.

As if reading his thoughts Lori said, "I doubt anyone has bothered to make the connection. Everybody was so glad to see Laura and Clint get back together that they never stopped to consider that Emmy might not be his flesh and blood."

"But, I did," she added. "I know . . ." Lori caught herself before she said too much, "that whatever it was that happened to Carl Sullivan that night was his own doin'. I know he was probably drunk and got fightin' mad when you and Laura told him about the baby bein' on its way, and . . . well, what happened just happened. It was nobody's fault, Ray, least of all yours. You should never have gone to prison. I've always believed in you." Lori started to say more, but stopped herself.

"Well," Ray hesitated, "you have the gist of it, alright. And don't worry about me goin' to prison. There's nothin' you or anybody else could have done about it. "

At that Lori caught her breath. She struggled to keep tears from filling her eyes. "But, Ray, I . . . I . . ." She could say no more.

"This thing about Emmy is complicated," Ray continued. "Things have gone on like they are for so long that . . . well . . . I don't see how she can be told any different. It could hurt her. It could hurt her real bad. Her not knowin', well, it hurts me worse than any beating I've ever taken, but, I can take it better than she can. Sometimes I think I should have just stayed in prison. By the time I got out, she would be all grown up, with a family of her own, livin' who knows where, and . . ."

"And you'd still be hurtin'," Lori interrupted, "because you own daughter never knew you for the man you really were."

"I love her, Lori. I always have. Even though I'd never laid eyes on her until the other day."

"I know, Ray. I know," Lori said with a tear in her eye. She reached out to hug him.

"I really always did," Ray whispered into her ear after a long moment in Lori's arms.

"Always did what?" she asked, sniffing.

"I always did think you were every bit as pretty as Laura."

Lori drew back to look into Ray's eyes. His face was swollen and bruised and cut, but she could see the honesty and sincerity there. Their lips came together in a long passionate kiss. Though neither spoke of it, they each felt a strange sense of rightness, of closeness and comfort neither had felt for a long, long time. And even though his lips were beyond sore, Ray had never felt so good.

11.

For the first time he could remember, the morning sun caught Raymond Bennett asleep under the covers. He was stiff and sore, and his face hurt like crazy. He just had not been able to answer the call of the alarm clock that he rarely needed. He had hoped to leave the house before his parents awoke. The familiar sounds and smells of his mother's kitchen told him that he was much too late for that.

"You were out late," Mary said when she heard his door creak open. She was facing the sink with her back to Ray, however, so he was able to slip by her without being seen.

"Yep," he replied when he was safely away from her line of vision. "I'm not used to keepin' late hours, though."

"That is probably an old habit best left alone," his mother remarked.

"Yes'm. I expect you're right. I don't think it's the time so much, though, as where and how you spend it," he grunted bending over to pick his cap up from the floor.

Mary did not respond.

"Get back out of the way!" Ray heard Pat scolding Sport out back. 'Good!' he thought. 'I'll just take off out the front right quick." He shook his head at the wonder of a man his age still worrying about his parent's reaction to such matters as the previous night.

"I've got to meet Bob over at the barn, Mama," Ray called. "Runnin' late. I'll see you later." If he could just get out now without being seen perhaps he would not look so bad by the time he returned late in the evening.

"Nonsense!" Mary shouted back. "You bolt out of here every morning and we don't see you all day. It's time you had breakfast with us. Beside that, I cooked plenty for you, and I won't have it wasted."

"Really, Mama, I have to . . ."

"Boy what in the world happened to you?" Pat gasped as he entered through the front door.

"Pop! I thought you were out back."

"Never mind where I was," Pat snapped. "Where were you and how did this happen?"

Mary, hearing the exchange in the living room, hurried in and drew a deep breath throwing her hands to her mouth. "Raymond, what happened?"

"Nothing, Mama, really. A few of the boys just gave me a welcome home party is all. It's not as bad as it looks." He winced slightly as she touched his face tenderly. "I'm just a . . . heavy bruiser. It's all right."

Coerced into telling the story, he did so over breakfast. It hurt to chew, but the food was good. Ray decided that he would breakfast with his parents more often.

"So that's why that tractor is out front," Pat said.

"Yes, sir, I got my friend to drive me over to the barn and I came on home on the tractor. Me and Bob can go get my truck later."

"I hope it's still there to get," Pat mumbled.

"What friend?" Mary quizzed.

Ray hesitated. "I doubt you'd know her."

Mary was half the way back to the kitchen with the dirty dishes before she realized what she had heard. "Her?"

Ray and Matt arrived at the barn at the same time. Bob took one look at the both of them and said, "Ya'll look like you went to a gang fight and your gang didn't show up."

Matt and Ray just nodded.

"Well, I ain't hittin' a lick until I hear 'bout it."

"Me neither," Thomas added, wiping grease from his hands as he walked from the cotton picker he had been working on. "I'd like to hear 'bout white folks gittin' beat up for a change."

"Age before beauty, Matt," Ray offered. "Let's hear it."

By the time both stories were told, Matt and Ray had gotten in a few more punches and their adversaries had known beyond any shadow of a doubt that they had lucked out, pure and simple.

"Mighty poor showin' for the outfit," Bob droned before turning to climb on his tractor. "Fire breaks'll be done today, I reckon." He throttled up the engine and yelled as he drove past the others, "Don't you gals forgit your appointment at the beauty parlor this afternoon."

Ray tipped his cap. Matt looked away to hide his grin.

"Matt, if you're up to it, I need you to go over to the old barn and clean out the stalls. Put some new hay down, too. I might want to bring in the horses," Ray said.

"I'm up to it, sure enough, Mr. Ray. It might hurt more than usual today, but I work for you and I'll do whatever you need me to," the boy said seriously.

Ray slapped Matt on the shoulder. "You're a good man, Matt. I'm glad to have you with me. Be back by noon."

"Yes, sir."

"Well, Thomas, you think we'll get that cotton pickin' cotton picker pickin' cotton today?"

"Ought to," Thomas replied. "Depends on how fast you can move. Most white boys I know don't get around so good for a few days after a good whuppin'."

"You just lead the way. This white boy will keep up," Ray chuckled.

As he worked, Ray's thoughts continued to stray to Lori. Her smile, easy and warm, her hair, sandy blonde, shining in the harsh light of her little trailer, her eyes bright and clear. It was as if she was unable to hide the fact that she was happy just to be with him. 'Just to see me,' Ray thought to himself. But, that was all it was, just a thought. A silly day dream. No one had ever been so happy just to be around him. Not even Laura. 'Nope! She's just a happy person,' Ray thought. 'I reckon there's still a few of them left on this world.' But, that face, prettier than ever. . .

The sound of tires crunching on gravel brought Ray out of his trance. It was Matt returning from the old barn. Looking at his watch, he confirmed that it was a few minutes past twelve noon.

"If you'll hold this while I tighten down on that nut, I think we'll be through," Thomas remarked.

Ray started to move around beside Thomas, but called Matt over instead. "Help Tom out with that lever," he said. As Matt turned his back, Ray picked up a small oil can and squirted Matt with oil, from his old coat down to his boots.

"Aw, man! Look at me!" Ray cried.

Matt turned quickly startled by the tone of Ray's voice.

"I'm sorry, man. I thought the spout was pointed the other way. I've ruined your clothes, Matt. I'm sorry."

Matt shrugged. "It's o.k., Mr. Ray. I 'magine I can wash that oil right out. Don't worry about it."

"No, no," Ray repeated. "that stuff won't come clean. I've ruined your clothes and there's only one thing to do. I'm gonna take you to town and git you some more."

"No, Mr. Ray," Matt protested, "you don't have to do that. It'll be fine, really."

"I won't have it any other way, partner," Ray replied. "I messed it up and I fix what I mess up. Thomas can tell you that. And besides, I'm the boss. It's my responsibility to keep the BFS men lookin' good at all times. Ain't that right, Thomas?"

"Well, Matt, I know he gon' fix what he screws up. Keepin' us lookin' good, well, that might be too tall of a order. But, that don't mean he can't try," Thomas laughed.

"Well, I . . . uh. . . I kinda promised my sister I would take her to town today," Matt said weakly.

"Bring 'er along," Ray commanded. "I need to meet her anyway. And you can take me by to get my truck. You go on and change into something less oily and pick me up at my house around two, o.k.?"

"Yes, sir. Two o'clock. We'll see you, Thomas," Matt waved.

"See ya Monday, Matt," Thomas called after him.

"You done taken a likin' to that boy, ain't you?" Thomas asked when Matt had left.

"He's a good boy. And it's a wonder with the life he's had. There he is doin' the lookin' after and the providin', and he needs lookin' after and providin' for himself. I can't do it all, but I can help." Ray turned to examine the big machine before him. "Let's crank this baby up and see how she does. Maybe we can put 'er to work next week."

He and Thomas laughed and yelled triumphantly as the engine roared to life. Working levers and gears, Thomas soon assured himself that this piece of worthless farm equipment would now do everything it was designed to do. Repairing sick machinery was one thing; bringing it back to life after a long sleep had a satisfaction all its own. "I'm ready for the next one," Thomas yelled over the noise of the engine. Ray gave his friend a thumbs up and a satisfied smile.

12.

"Well, I hope this will serve as a lesson for the both of you," Ray sighed wearily. "Don't be hangin' 'round no broken down old beer joints. They'll bring you nothin' but misery."

He and Matt grunted and groaned as their damaged bodies protested their movements in bending and kneeling to examine Ray's truck. There it sat in Buster's parking lot, but not quite in the same condition as the night before. Every piece of glass on the truck had been shattered. All four tires flat, slashed. The spare had been stolen. "Jail Bird" had been scratched into the paint across the hood. "Parchman Peach" was scratched down the driver's side door. The passenger side was just scarred from one end to the other, the vandals vocabulary obviously exhausted.

In the door of the Bodock Bar and Grill stood Buster and a few of his companions, snickering at Ray and Matt.

"I'll stand with you, Mr. Ray," Matt said. His voice was trembling slightly. He had not looked forward to the confrontation of the previous night; he certainly wanted no part of these men today. But, he was a hand. He would fight for his boss.

"I appreciate that, Matt," Ray replied, "but this is not the time. We got Billie Rose to think about." Matt turned to look at his sister standing by his own truck. Tears were forming in her eyes. The last thing she wanted was a repeat of last night. And she feared for herself as well.

"Ya'll wait here," Ray ordered. "I'm gon' call Thomas." He walked briskly toward the bar. Buster and his friends showed no sign of moving. "You'd best git out of my way," he snapped.

"You ain't welcome here, Bennett. I thought we made that clear last night," Buster growled.

"The only thing you made clear last night was that you're too much a coward to take me on one-on-one and that you all fight like a bunch of girls," Ray smirked.

"I'll show you who fights like a girl," Buster snorted angrily.

"You already did, Busted," Ray said coolly.

"I guess you're lookin' for another beatin', boy!" Buster shot back in frustration. He knew numbers and a pool cue had worked in his favor before. This was a dangerous man he was facing.

"Nope, I'm lookin' for a telephone and something to drink for me and those kids over there. But, I'll tell you this, Buster, if you think you want to jump on me, come on ahead. There won't be no sucker punches, and there won't be no pool stick across my back. There will be just me and you."

Buster hesitated. Looking from Ray to his friends, he finally spoke up. "Come on and make your call and get out. I won't have it said that I kicked the same dirt clod two days in a row."

"You and Wayne must spend an exceptional amount of time together," Ray chuckled as he stepped through the door. "Ya'll kind of talk alike."

"You sorry ..."

Ray turned quickly to see Wayne advancing with his clenched fist drawn back. Before Wayne could swing his big arm, Ray planted a right jab to his chin sending Wayne down . . . and out. A gasp from the direction of the bar caught his attention. Glancing that way his eyes found Lori's. Her hands covered her mouth and her eyes betrayed her fright.

Pivoting to make eye contact with everyone else in the room, Ray said, "That the way you boys want it?"

All eyes turned to Buster. Some of them had seen Ray the night before and knew what shape he was in. For him to take Wayne so easily, in obvious pain, took more than they had thought he had in him. The cold piercing stare was much like that of an animal ready for the attack. It spoke of a man none of them wanted to push farther.

"Go on. Make your call," Buster said.

"You never were one to push things before," Lori commented quietly when Ray moved behind the bar to get the phone.

"I still ain't," replied Ray. "I just don't take bein' pushed around like I used to. You let folks like that start pushin' and they'll never stop. Where I spent the last fifteen years you learned that when anyone pushes, you better push back right then, only harder." Giving attention to the telephone in his hand Ray's demeanor suddenly changed. "Hey, Linda," Ray said. "How you doin'? . . . Is there anything ya'll need over at the house? . . . You know all you have to do is let me know. Look, is Thomas there?"

After Ray had asked Thomas to bring the wrecker and a couple of tires, he asked Lori for two Cokes and a root beer.

"Don't you serve him nothin!" Buster clamored. "I told him to make his call and get out."

"I guess I can serve the man a few drinks," Lori protested.

"If you will remember I let you get away with that last night. I even let you leave early to take care of 'im. But, I won't have no employee of mine servin' the likes of him!"

Scowling at her boss, Lori reached into the drink cooler anyway.

"Lori, I done told you . . ."

"Don't you start on me, Buster," Lori shot back.

"You put them drinks up or go get yourself another job, missy," Buster said curtly.

Lori put the soft drinks on the counter and pulled a second root beer, for herself, from the cooler all the while engaged in a stare down with Buster. She took off the little apron she was wearing and threw it on the counter. Ray smiled as she picked up her purse and the drinks and walked out the door without saying a word. He left three dollars on the counter, certain that it was more than enough to cover the cost of the drinks.

"Keep the change, Busted," he said smiling as he followed Lori outside.

"Lori, you get back in here!" Buster screamed after her. "You got work to do, and I ain't told you you could go nowhere."

"You just fired me," Lori shouted back.

"I didn't say nuthin' 'bout you bein' fired," Buster protested. "Now come on back in here."

"Well, Buster, I'm going to consider your offer to come back to work for you. But, you might have to come up with a raise," Lori said matter-of-factly.

"Well, you can forgit that," Buster snapped. "You're more trouble than you're worth now. Sassin' me all the time!"

"Well . . . bye!" Lori replied crisply.

"I'm sorry about your job," Ray said walking Lori to her car. "I hate to see you lose it over me."

"O-o-o-h, I'm sorry about your truck," she replied, "and I'm well rid of that place. I was just tryin' to make a little extra money. You know, school and Christmas and all. I'll find another job. I would do better pullin' double shifts over at the cafe anyway."

Ray remembered Matt and Billie were waiting for him. "Come on and meet my friends here," he said taking her arm. "Matt and Billie Rose Warren, this is Lorraine Sullivan."

"Parker," Lori corrected holding out her hand. "But, you can call me Lori."

"Matt here is one of my top hands," Ray said as the boy's face reddened. "Billie Rose gets by on her looks," he joked.

"What I want to know is what these two young'uns are doin' standin' around outside this den of iniquity," Lori queried.

Ray thrust his hands into his pockets and shrugged sheepishly. "This was 'sposed to be a quick stop to pick up my truck. I wasn't expectin' all this." He nodded toward his grounded pickup.

"We was gonna do some shoppin' after we got Mr. Ray's truck," Matt offered in hopes of getting Ray off the hook. "Billie has an appointment to get her hair fixed."

"I swear I still can't tell where it's broke," Ray said looking the giggling girl's head over as if closely inspecting it.

"Do you want to see a picture?" Billie Rose asked. She was pleased to have some grown-up female attention other than her teacher's. Apart from school, she had no social life, and no women to talk to.

"Sure, honey! Oh, my! You'll have those boys followin' you around everywhere with that one," Lori carried on. She glanced at Ray and back at Billie. "You know what? I just happen to have some free time. What would you think if I took you to the hair stylist and we let Matt and Ray go do man stuff?"

"That would be great!" Billie clasped her hands together in delight. "Can I, Matt?"

"I don't know," her brother said pensively.

Ray slapped Matt's shoulder. "It's o.k., pard, I can vouch for Lori here. Billie Rose will be in good hands, and they'll have a good time. Besides, those beauty parlor fumes are toxic to men. You wouldn't last five minutes in that place."

Drawing closer to the boy, Ray added in a near whisper, "This here sure ain't the place for her."

"O.K.," Matt said somewhat reluctantly. Ray admired Matt's sense of responsibility for his sister.

As Ray opened the car door for Lori, he slipped her a fifty dollar bill. "She would probably enjoy a little shopping trip, if you have time," he whispered.

"We'll make time. As a matter of fact, why don't I just take her home with me and you bring Matt out? I'll fix supper for us all."

"Sounds like a done deal to me. I'll have to clear it with Matt. He's awful protective of her, you know."

"Well, I've seen their daddy in here plenty of times. And from what I've heard, they could both use some protectin'."

Ray reached over and kissed her quickly on the lips. It seemed a natural thing to do, but he was embarrassed by his impulsiveness. He cleared his throat. "See ya later," he said before turning and trotting over to his truck as if some pressing business was waiting for him those few yards away.

Lori smiled.

Thomas arrived a few minutes after Lori and Billie left. He circled Ray's pickup three times, whistling all the while. "Fixed you up good, didn't they?" he said.

Ray frowned and nodded.

"I can fix her up, though. The glass won't be hard to replace, but it will be expensive. I got me a spray rig, so I can paint her up real good. The tires, . . . well, tires're tires. I got some old ones with me. They'll get 'er home."

Thomas went about the task of changing Ray's slashed tires. Matt jumped in to help. Ray paced back and forth across the parking lot. With each turn his emotions grew. From frustration to aggravation to anger to fury . . . one more trip would surely result in rage. Step, step, step, turn . . .

"You tryin' to wear a path over there?" Thomas shouted.

Ray glanced toward the door of the bar. "Gittin' thirsty is what I'm doin'!" he replied too sharply to mask his notion.

"If you'll hold your horses for a minute I'll be thirsty, too. 'Sides, me and Matt need to wash our hands." Thomas chuckled. "I swear, Ray, I think all this freedom is makin' a soft man outta you. Never thought I'd see you stand around watchin' somebody else get dirty changin' your tires."

"I'm savin' myself for that root beer," Ray replied glaring at the door of The Bodock as if it were an enemy in itself.

A few minutes later, Ray sauntered into the Bodock Bar and Grill with Matt and Thomas in tow. As soon as they entered the darkness of the room, Ray pointed toward the door with the huge, crooked "M" dripping down it. The two moved toward the door, but Buster, flanked by the ever present Larry, and a wobbly Wayne moved to block their path.

"This boy's too young to be in here," Buster said gesturing toward Matt. "And this boy," he said looking at Thomas, "we don't serve such as him in here."

Thomas opened his mouth to speak, but Ray held his hand up. "They are going to wash their hands, and we are going to get something to drink, and then we will go. I'll send you a bill for my truck."

"Hold on there," Buster snapped. "I guess I can decide who will and who won't be usin' my bathrooms. And I ain't payin' nuthin' on your truck. You was the one that left it here in the first place. Anybody could have messed with it."

Ray sighed, "You're right, Busted, anybody could have done it, but, anybody didn't do it. You, or some of your entourage here did it, and we all know it."

"Yeah, but you can't prove nuthin'. Now ya'll git your butts out of my place. You boys can wash up at the hose outside."

Thomas took a step forward. Matt swallowed hard, but stepped with him. He figured he really couldn't hurt much more than he already did, although he did hate to be reminded of the pain.

Buster, Wayne and Larry inched forward. Two other men in the bar rose from their table, their chairs squealing loud against the floor in the silence of the room.

Thomas stopped short and glanced at Matt. The last thing he wanted to do was to get the boy into a fight with these men. He dropped his head and relaxed his fists.

"Ya'll wait right there," Ray said. "I'll be back in a minute. I think we can settle this matter." He darted out the door. Inside, the sound of his boots trotting across the gravel parking lot could be heard. The sound moved away, stopped momentarily, and then grew slightly louder on the return trip.

The door had closed behind Ray when he went out. Buster and his friends flashed a wicked grin at Thomas. "Looks like you're on your own, boy," Larry snarled. "You," he pointed at Matt, "back over there in that corner over there."

Matt set his jaw and did not move.

At that moment the door seemed to disintegrate. Ray limped in, the kick to the door having injured his foot. Immediately, he swung the axe he now carried and toppled one of Buster's tables with a single blow. Everyone jumped back, startled by the noise and unsure of Ray's next target.

"Now," Ray shouted, "these two men are going to go in that nasty bathroom of yours and make liberal use of your dirty soap. Then we're going to get something to drink and be on our way."

"They can't go in there, it's closed for repairs," Buster smirked.

Ray strode to the door and removed it in three blows with the axe. "Now it's open."

Thomas laughed as he strode through the sagging frame of the restroom door. Matt followed in awe.

"You out of paper towels, man," Thomas scolded Buster as he walked back out of the cramped restroom. "We havin' to use your cheap old toilet paper to dry our hands."

"If he wasn't holdin' that axe I'd dry you out," Buster said to Thomas.

"Matt," Ray said, "take this axe on back out to Thomas' wrecker and wait for us."

He handed the axe to Matt. Matt hesitated at the door, not wanting to leave his buddies. "Go on," Ray said motioning toward the wrecker. "We'll be there in a minute."

"I'm 'mon take those doors out of your hide," Buster growled.

"Good," Ray replied, "I guess that means I can take my truck out of yours."

"I thought you said you was thirsty," Thomas said to Ray.

"Didn't say what for."

Thomas slowly backed to Ray's side. The odds were not great.

Five to two. And if the other three bar patrons that had stayed outside the fracas until now decided to join in, the BFS crew would be a sight for sure.

Buster and his group moved slowly forward, flexing and releasing their fists. Even Wayne, still unsteady from Ray's previous punch, seemed to be up for another round.

"What's goin' on here?" a commanding voice yelled from the doorway. Deputy Sheriff Leon Pitts stepped over the debris that once was a door. "Who's that boy with the axe out there? Did he do this?"

Nobody said anything.

"Well?" Leon demanded.

"I know you," Leon said studying Ray. "You're Ray Bennett." Turning to Buster he asked, "Is he responsible for this?"

"Destructive ain't he?" Buster replied. "It must be some of that there repressed rage or something."

"Well, Mr. Ray Bennett, you are under arrest, and your friend, too."

"What's the charge?" Ray asked, as if he didn't already know.

"Breaking and entering, destruction of private property." The deputy pursed his lips. "I bet we can even add contributing to the delinquency of a minor to all this. Looks like a violation of your parole to me," he said happily.

"I didn't break and enter," Ray sighed, "the place was open for business. And I ain't violated no parole."

"Oh, it'll all be the same when you end up back in jail," Pitts snorted. "You boys goin' peaceable like or do I have to get rough?"

"I didn't know they taught procedure out of paperback westerns these days," Ray said.

"Don't go gettin' smart with me!"

"I reckon it'll be peaceful . . . I mean peaceable like," Ray mocked. "I doubt you could get rough enough."

"Are you threatenin' a officer of the law, boy?" Leon snapped reaching for his billy club.

Ray remembered Leon Pitts well. He had run with Buster for most of his high school days. Leon was never quite the bully that Buster was. He just didn't have the knack for it. He used Buster's ferocity to supplement his own. He was a friend of Buster Pritchard; therefore he could push people around because no one wanted to answer to Buster for taking on Leon. Leon's mettle had never really been tested. He always had something larger than himself to stand behind. Before, it was Buster, now it was the law, or rather his badge. The law actually had little to do with the way Leon Pitts used his badge.

"I'm not one to threaten," Ray replied.

"Ya'll walk real slow out to the car," Leon ordered. "My extra cuffs are out there."

"Bye, Busted," Ray called. "You get off the hook again." He turned to leave.

"Hold up a minute, Leon," Buster cried. "Just what do you mean by that, Bennett?"

Ray turned to face him. "Just that there is always somebody there to protect you. Last night it was your friends here. Today, here they are again, but they ain't enough. Now you got your deputy friend here to haul me off to jail. And ever body here thinks you're such a big man. Well, you and me know different, don't we?" Ray spun on his heel and stepped through the hole he had left in the doorway. "You ain't near 'bout the bully you used to be," he shouted behind him.

Before they reached the deputy's car, Buster caught up with them. "Let 'em go, Leon," he said.

"What?"

"Let 'em go. They ain't done so much more than anybody else. Besides, this thing is gittin' personal."

Leon blew hard and stammered around for a moment. "O.K. You two are free to go. But stay out of trouble. I'll have my eyes on you."

"I don't want you comin' back in here, Ray," Buster said coldly. "If you do it'll be me and you."

"I don't plan to be back, Buster," Ray replied. "But, if you have it in you to bother me or any of my friends again, I'll be around to take you up on that offer."

13.

The sun had long since left the Mississippi sky and was making an impressive showing off the west coast by the time Ray and Matt drove up to Lori's trailer. Behind the shade covering the big front window little heads could be seen bobbing around inside. Matt parked his truck beside Lori's old rattle trap of a car and glanced apprehensively at Ray before climbing out into the cold night air.

The outside light came on and they made their way to the narrow steps that would take them inside. Just as Matt was reaching to knock on the door, it flew open! There, standing proudly, and pretty, he had to admit, was Billie Rose. Her hair was just about like that girl's in the magazine picture that she had been carrying around. And she wore new clothes. A denim skirt and brightly colored sweater. Her face shone in a way he had not seen for a long time.

"Aw, you look real pretty, Billie!" Matt said. "Where'd you get that outfit?"

"Miss Lori bought them for me," she replied with a hint of guilt in her eyes. "I tried to stop her, but she just insisted!" she explained.

"Well, ya'll did a good job all around," Ray said. "I wish I was about twenty years younger."

"Don't you two make a handsome pair, bruises and all!" Lori exclaimed. "Did I miss the announcement that this was Beautify Winstead County Day or something?"

Ray and Matt both had haircuts. And Matt was decked out in one of the new outfits Ray had purchased for him. For a country boy from Mississippi he looked to be the perfect Western man. His own pride was impossible to conceal. Ray had told him that discount store clothes were fine for work or where ever else he might want to wear them, but, sometimes a man needed to get all decked out in something extra nice of a Saturday night. So here he was, in some of Crenshaw Clothing Company's best, from head to toe. Compliments of Ray Bennett. Except for the scene at the Bodock, it had been a great afternoon for him as well. Mr. Ray had treated him more like a son in that one day than his own father ever had. He fit in. Maybe life was changing . . . maybe.

For the remainder of that Saturday evening in Lori's cramped little trailer, everyone there experienced such a happiness that none had felt in a long, long time. Between the grilled hot dogs and card games and jokes, there was a feeling of normalcy. Just a normal Saturday night, doing normal things with normal people. Each gathered here thinking it was the others who made them feel normal for a change.

As ten o'clock approached, Matt told Billie Rose that they had better head for home. The carefree, happy smile she had worn for most of the night instantly left her face to be replaced by a look of something between dread and resignation.

Lori put her arm around Billie Rose's shoulder and said, "I'd love for you to stay the night, honey. I know the kids hate to see you leave. I'll get you home tomorrow."

"Oh, can I, Matt?" she begged.

"We could call your dad," Lori suggested.

"I . . . I don't think . . ." Billie Rose began.

"I don't think he would mind," Matt said. "You stay, sis. It'll be alright."

"But, what about you?" Billie Rose whispered, concern in her voice. "It's Saturday night!"

"It's fine, Billie. You stay and have a good time. Everything will be alright." Turning to reach out and shake Lori's hand Matt added, "I sure enjoyed the visit, Miss Lori."

Matt was anxious to leave, this being Saturday. His father might stay out all night, but he was just as apt to show up at home at any time. Wherever he was, he would be drunk. Saturday offered the opportunity for a full day's drinking, which he was compelled to take advantage of. Consequently, he lost all track of time and might come home at nine o'clock drunk and mean, or he may stumble in at three or four in the morning and pass out for a good twelve hours.

It wasn't the pass out drunk that worried Matt; indeed that is what he hoped for. It was the mean drunk where the slightest of infractions, like eye contact, was likely as not to trigger a cursing and a beating. The fear of their father, shared by he and Billie Rose, was accompanied by a suppressed hate that both felt guilty about and neither shared with the other.

For the most part, Matt had kept the worst of their father's drunken rages from hurting his sister physically. He was always the first target and took whatever beating Felix had in him. Billie Rose had suffered a few slaps from time to time, but Matt doubted that their father had ever gone beyond that where his daughter was concerned. Protecting her as best he could, Matt always sent Billie Rose to her special hiding place when Felix became riled. Usually Felix would wear himself out wearing out Matt and fall asleep in a stupor making it safe enough for Billie Rose to return to her room to where she slept cold in the winter and hot in the sweltering Mississippi summer night.

A few miles up the road, Matt dropped Ray off and headed toward his own home. It had been a good day. The best he and his sister had known. Maybe it would end good. Maybe.

Sunday morning was spent lazing on the couch browsing through the newspaper. Ray had slept late again. It was the best night's sleep he had experienced in many years. No thick metal doors clanging in the night, no incoherent shouts from adjoining cells. No nightmares. He found an advertisement for some building material he needed. Twenty percent off. He made a mental note to go get a load on Monday. Just before twelve, Pat and Mary came in from church.

"Everybody's asking about you," Mary said with some disapproval in her voice. "They would like to see you in church."

Ray grinned tightly and nodded.

"So would I." Mary continued.

Ray remained silent.

Mary pressed on. "I know it must be hard to get started back after so long . . ."

"Mama," Ray smiled as he set the paper aside, "I went just about every Sunday up in Parchman. There was always somebody comin' up to tend to all those lost souls. But, I'll tell you something. There's fewer Hell bound men up there than you might think. We had a Bible study. We had a prayer group. I'll get back to church soon as somebody else comes along that's worth more gossip than me. In the meantime, you don't have to worry about my soul. I'm as saved as I ever was. I at least ought to get shed of some of these lumps and bruises before I show up over there."

"Everybody is anxious to see you is all," Mary said meekly.

"I'll get seen, Mama, in all the right places."

After dinner, Ray decided to ride up to the old barn and maybe take one of the horses out. Thomas still had his truck to repair, so he borrowed Pat's. He smiled when he saw that Matt was there. "The boy must be proud of those new duds," he said to himself, "he put 'em back on this morning."

"Afternoon, cowboy," Ray said.

"Mr. Ray," Matt replied somewhat subdued.

Ray noticed that Matt had not turned to look at him with that friendly smile of his.

"One of these nags got the best of you?"

"No, sir. They're all fine horses if you ask me. Even that old one." He kept his back turned and fiddled with a saddle stirrup.

"What's got your goat then? I can tell you ain't happy about something."

Matt hesitated and shook his head. "Ain't nothin' wrong. I guess maybe I'm tired."

"Well, you ought to be. You put in a hard week."

Matt still kept his back turned. "Thank you. I thought as long as I'm workin' these horses I might as well ride some fence. If you're gon' put some cows in the back pasture, that fence might need some fixin' up."

Recognizing that the clothes Matt wore had been slept in, Ray moved slightly to Matt's right side. He stood staring, not wanting to believe what he saw.

"Did you go on home after you dropped me off last night?"

With his head dropped Matt replied, "Yes, sir."

"Have any company when you got there?"

"No, sir."

Ray swallowed hard. "Was your daddy home?"

His mouth opened, but the words wouldn't come. Matt nodded slightly.

Ray took the few remaining steps to Matt's side. The boy turned away, but then looked Ray square in the eye, almost defiantly.

"Did he do this to you?" Ray asked tenderly feeling the swollen bruise on Matt's cheek and the fresh cut at the corner of his lip. He grit his teeth and fought back a shiver.

Matt shrugged "Gittin' beat up is gittin' beat up. Don't much matter who's doin' the beatin'."

"It matters when it's your own daddy!"

"He wanted to take your truck. I tried to stop 'im. It ain't such a big thing, Mr. Ray. He's done worse."

It was then that Ray realized that Matt's truck was nowhere in sight. "He ever hurt Billie Rose?" Ray asked, almost afraid to hear the answer.

"No, sir. Not much anyway. I usually get her out to the car or something. He's always too drunk to go lookin' much. I guess he wears himself out beatin' on me. Anyway, he ain't never hit her hard that I know of."

A rage thought defeated long ago rose within Ray. His greatest urge was to find Felix Warren and beat the very life from him. There had come a time, before his second year at Parchman was up, when he had known that he could kill under the right circumstances. Until this moment, the circumstances had never occurred. And were Felix Warren standing before him at this moment, his life would end . . . here . . . now . . . in front of his abused son.

"You want me to ride along with you, Matt?"

Matt looked at his feet for a moment or two. "It's not that I don't want you to go with me . . ."

"I understand. A man needs his solitude at times."

Matt remained silent and nodded.

"My folks' house is not exactly the Ritz, but there's plenty of room for you, and I would be glad to have the company if you want to come stay with us for a while."

Matt shook his head. "I appreciate it and all, but I've got to look after Billie."

"We'll look after Billie Rose," Ray explained. "You take some time to yourself and think it over. I just thought of something I have to do anyway."

Less than five minutes later Ray arrived at Thomas' house. After a quick explanation, the two men were on the road toward Little Bridge. They had to park out by the road when they reached the Warren home. Matt's truck was blocking the drive way, one front tire in the ditch. The door on the driver's side was open and the radio was blaring. Thomas turned it off.

The front door was cracked open. Ray and Thomas entered the house without knocking. They had expected the interior of the house to be somewhat warmer than the cold November air outside, but there was no heat and there was no discernible difference in the temperature between inside and outside.

Felix Warren lay sprawled across a bed in what apparently was Billie's room. A tattered quilt covered one leg and his lower back. He still wore all of his clothes including a ragged heavy coat.

"It's too bad he don't sleep nekkid," Tom said. "He might of froze to death."

"That wouldn't hurt enough," Ray said. He turned and went to the kitchen. He came back carrying a pitcher of water he had found in the refrigerator. Without hesitation he dumped the entire contents onto Felix's snoring face.

Sputtering and coughing, Felix sprang up. "What the . . ."

Ray backhanded Felix sending him back down onto the bed again. "I didn't tell you to get up!" he barked.

"Who are you? What are you doin' in my house?" Felix demanded shaking the cobwebs from his head. "And what's he doin' in my house?" he added gesturing toward Thomas.

Grabbing a handful of hair and ear, Ray jerked the confused man to his feet. "Be careful how you talk to my friend here. As a matter of fact, you better just shut up and listen, 'cause you are just about this far," he held his thumb and forefinger an inch apart, "from meetin' your maker!"

"What 'chu want?"

Ray violently shoved Felix to the cold floor. "Your children are movin' out, and you ain't gonna come lookin' for 'em."

"What do you mean? You ain't takin' my kids!" Felix started to get up, but Thomas pushed down on his shoulders holding him in place.

"Me and Tom here don't hold to child beatin'. It's what they call a zero tolerance situation. Hear me good! I'm only gon' tell you once. You leave them alone. Don't look for them; don't try to contact them in anyway."

"Or what?" Felix said defiantly.

"Or a shriveled up drunk like you could disappear real easy, Felix. The Walashabou's deep enough in places to swallow you up from now on. Matter of fact, a man could wander into the swamps over by Big Black and never find his way out. 'Course, on short notice, a fellow could be plowed under real good on the backside of my place. Trouble with that is, I don't know whether you'd make good fertilizer or poison my land."

Thomas laughed, "I got kinfolk'll haul him up north."

Felix looked around nervously. "I'll get the law after you two!"

Ray sighed and shook his head slowly. "Tom, if he was to call the law that might knock us out of that good citizenship award we were lookin' forward to."

Tom smiled. "We can't have that. Maybe we just ought to take care of this honky, . . . no offense, Ray, right now."

"Ray?" Felix sputtered, "Why, you're . . . you're that convict feller!"

"Yep," Ray replied. "So you think it's gon' bother me to do in the likes of you?"

Felix' eyes were darting back and forth, searching for options. He was in a haze. Clear thought was foreign to him even when he was sober. There were no options. "O.K., O.K., I get the picture. Take 'em. They're yours. They're more trouble than they're worth anyways."

It took only a few minutes to gather Matt and Billie Rose's belongings. Unable to find anything resembling luggage and no plastic garbage bags, Ray and Tom resorted to bundling the few clothing items the kids had into tattered bed sheets. In less than ten minutes everything that they thought belonged to Matt or Billie was piled in the back of Pat's truck. It was a meager assemblage at best. All the while, Felix sat quietly on the floor in a corner of Billie's room.

Taking a quick sweep around the house, Tom spotted a naked doll under the girl's bed. He reached to pull it out, and saw that it was missing one leg. He kept it anyway. He was moved to see white folks with so little. He knew what it was like to grow up in one of the poorest families in the area. And, where he came from, that status usually did not include even the poorest of white families. It struck him that a lot of folks were wrong about a lot of things. It was not a life he would wish upon anyone. He turned a cold gaze toward Felix. "You done seen all the mercy you gonna get from us, you hear?"

Felix nodded weakly.

With Thomas pushing, Ray was able to back Matt's truck out of the ditch.

Mary shook her head as she went through the clothing piled on Ray's bed. "I'll wash and iron these later," she said as she separated the clothes into very small piles on the floor. She took all of the under garments and threw them in the trash can. "Right now I'm going to town. They don't have a decent piece of underwear between them. Do you suppose they still wear these sizes in everything? I can't get much, but anything will beat what they have here."

Ray grinned as he reached into his billfold and pulled out a small scrap of paper. "Here you go, Mama. I just happen to have their sizes. A little subtle research can bring in all sorts of useful information. Only thing is, how in world are you ever gonna live down the great sin of shopping on Sunday?"

With a stern look in her eye, Mary replied, "It's the Lord's own work I'm about today, Raymond Lee. I'll be back by five. You have those children here. Lord knows they must need a good meal." Before she walked away, she said softly, "I'm not sure about your methods, but I think you've done a bit of the Lord's work yourself today. I don't think we've heard the last of it, though."

"Yeah, well, I let my temper get the best of me on this one. Main thing is that those kids needed to be out of that house. The man needs help, that's plain. I know of a program I can get him into. I'll let things settle for a day or two and then I'll go see if he's interested."

Ray drove to Lorraine's and told her about the events of the day. Lori insisted that Matt and Billie Rose stay with her until it could be decided just what they would do now. Ray agreed that Billie Rose should stay with Lori, but he wanted Matt to spend a few days with him.

"You just want to be somebody's daddy, don't you?" Lori said.

"I doubt that I will ever be anybody's daddy," Ray replied. "Not even to my own daughter. That chance is gone just like Matt and Billie's chance for a decent childhood. All any of us can do is take what we have and make the most of it, and what we have is today."

"Well, I don't think those kids need to be separated right now!" she argued.

"They can spend some time together at Mama's tonight. They both have a lot of junk to sort out. Billie Rose needs the company and the comfort . . . and the distraction you and your kids can provide." Ray scratched his head. "Matt, now, he's a different story. Likes to be alone at times. I just think he can do that better on my place. Safe and alone with his thoughts, and I'll be close by. Face it, Lori, there ain't much room for solitude in that crowd at your house."

"That crowd? That's how you think of us? That crowd at my house?" Lorraine said, hurt in her voice. "That "crowd" happens to be my family in case you forgot!"

"Lori, I didn't mean . . ."

"Don't try to back out now Ray Bennett! Maybe you've had too much solitude of your own in your life, but you have no right to go referrin' to my family as a "crowd"! They are all I have. We are all each other has. You just go on back home and get away from this crowd! But don't you dare turn that boy into what you've become. I can just see him runnin' around threatenin' to kill people to get his way!"

"Lori, I . . ."

"Just go, Ray! I'll send Billie out!"

Lorraine turned and disappeared into the trailer. Several minutes later she and Billie Rose emerged. Tears streamed down the girl's face. Ray figured Lorraine had already delivered the news. "Better from her than from me," he thought to himself. Lori hugged Billie tightly and turned her toward Ray. Without a word, or even a glance into Ray's eyes, Lori went back inside.

The ride to the old barn was a mostly quiet one. Ray apologized for the situation, and tried to comfort her as best he could. He told her that everything was going to be all right, but he didn't think she believed him. As they pulled into the barnyard, Billie Rose asked, "Are you in love with, Miss Lori?"

Ray felt his face flush. "What makes you ask that?"

"Because, I know she loves you."

"Well, I . . . uh . . . You see, Billie Rose, . . . uh . . . Hey, you like to ride horses?"

Without waiting for an answer Ray caught old Bessie and saddled her. In just a few minutes, Billie was on her own, guiding Bessie around the old farm equipment on the back lot. For the time being at least, she had her mind occupied by something other than her abusive father and her presently homeless situation.

Supper time at the Bennett house was unusually quiet. Mary tried to get some conversation from Billie Rose as they cleared the table, but all she said was "Yes, ma'am" and "No, ma'am."

Matt pitched in to help with the dishes. Ray and Pat spoke in hushed tones in the den.

"How 'bout we run Billie Rose on back over to Miss Lori's, Matt?" Ray said as the last dish was dried and put away.

"Sure, Mr. Ray. I enjoyed my supper, Mrs. Bennett," Matt said.

"I'm real glad you, did. Ya'll wait just a minute. I have some things for you," she said cheerfully as she disappeared into Ray's room. She came back out carrying three big shopping bags. "K Mart is about the only thing open in town on Sunday where you can get any clothes. If there is anything you don't like, we can take it back, o.k.?"

Matt forced a slight grin. Billie's eyes lit up. If nothing else, the past few days had been something like Christmas to her. Actually, better than any Christmas she had known. She had never had so many new things at one time in her life. These folks seemed like rich people to her. And she never knew that rich people could be so nice.

"Mrs. Bennett, you shouldn't have done this," Matt managed to say.

"Nonsense! I enjoyed every minute of it. And there were some things you two just really needed anyway."

Billie was busily unfolding the few tops and jeans Mary had bought for her and holding them up to her to test the fit and the look. For the first time that evening, she broke into a smile. "Can I try them on?"

Ray and Matt stayed for the fashion show. Billie Rose lost some of her shyness as she pranced in and out of the bedroom in her new outfits. She hugged and thanked both Mary and Pat. Aside from that of her brother, she probably could remember no other time in her life when she had felt such love. She craved it.

Before they finally left, Ray went into his room and emerged with a fleece lined denim jacket. "Here, Matt. I figure this is better to work in than your new coat. And certainly better than your old one. I got it the Fall before I . . .", he paused. "It was my favorite and it still has plenty of wear left in it."

"Gee, thanks, Mr. Ray," Matt said. He took the jacket and seemed to Ray to handle it as though it was something Elvis or somebody had worn at one time. Shedding the new coat Ray had just bought him, he tried the jacket on. It was slightly on the large side, but not so much as to make a big difference. And Matt seemed to hold more pride in that old jacket than in anything else he had been given over the past two days.

14.

Just before six am, Matt emerged from the guest room to find Ray sitting at the kitchen table reading a book. When he came closer he saw that it was not just a book that Ray was reading. It was the Bible. He hadn't thought about it, but it didn't surprise him to find Mr. Ray reading the Bible. And just after sunrise, at the kitchen table, in his sock feet, no less.

"Mornin', Matt," Ray said without looking up. "You'll have to oil that door if you expect to be sneakin' up on me any time soon."

"I . . . uh . . . I wasn't sneakin', I just . . ."

"I know. You didn't want to interrupt my readin' here."

"Yes, sir," Matt hastily agreed.

"Well, son, you wouldn't want to interrupt a man while he was prayin' or kissin' his girlfriend or anything like that that's private, you know. But, it's probably alright to interrupt somebody while they're readin', if you need to. 'Course, I never liked to interrupt anybody in the middle of anything. You never know what might put a bad taste in their mouth. I admire manners in a person, though. That's one thing I like about you, Matt. I don't know where you got 'em, but you do have good manners."

"Thank you."

"See what I mean?"

"I reckon," Matt answered weakly.

Ray opened his mouth to say more, but stopped and chuckled. "I reckon I've been hanging around Bob too long. We talk so much nonsense I forget to turn it off sometimes."

"Yes, sir."

"But not that part about your manners," Ray added quickly.

"Yes, sir. Thank you."

"You always this talkative in the morning?"

Before Matt could answer, Ray jumped up and reached across to the heating vent in the floor to pick up his boots. "I like a good pair of warm boots on a cold morning. Stickin' a cold foot in a cold boot ain't no way to start the day."

Matt just stood there.

"Come on over here and warm yours up while I fix us some breakfast. I think I'll do the cookin' this morning. I can light up that griddle and we'll have us some bacon, eggs, sausage and toast. It's a good breakfast! You'll be surprised how well I can fix it. As a matter of fact, as soon as a few more people hear about it, my big griddle breakfast will be world famous." Ray stood and stepped to the refrigerator and looked over his shoulder. "How 'bout spreadin' the word around school if you get the chance?"

Matt chuckled. "Sure."

After retrieving the needed items Ray began his task. "I wish you'd think up something to say. I'm havin' a hard time holdin' up this conversation by myself if you haven't noticed." He glanced sideways at Matt.

After a moment, Matt said, "I didn't want to mention it, but I did notice. Anyway, I was just listening. I figured maybe if I can keep you talkin' that nonsense of yours, maybe I can finally understand some of those talks you and Mr. Bob have!"

Ray laughed. "Well, Matt, I hope you'll aim your aspirations a little higher than that, because once you figure out what me and Mr. Bob are talkin' about, you'll find out that there's nothin' to be learned by listenin' to us carry on."

Matt kept quiet this time. He felt that there was truly much to be learned from these two men. And he could hardly wait for the school day to end so he could spend his time with them. He felt relieved, strangely so, not to have to face his father anytime soon. He didn't know how long his present arrangement could last, but, he was set to get the most of it, however long it was.

"I thought I'd get Thomas to check your truck out today, so bring it on to the shed as soon as you and Billie Rose get back from school. I hope to rustle us up some real farm work to do before long, so everything needs to be ready to roll."

Before he left for school, Matt asked if he had any special work assignment for the afternoon. He was elated to learn that he was to help Thomas with the equipment repairs.

By eight thirty a.m., Ray had learned from Bob of the local farmers who used contract services to harvest their cotton and soybean crops. It was late in a late season, so there was not much left to do and they all had someone lined up to handle their harvests. But, Bob had heard that Glen Melton, the big contractor from over near Satartia who had most of the Winstead County business sewed up, had suddenly gotten three big contracts from further up in the delta, and had left two or three of the smaller farmers in the community waiting for their cotton to be picked and ginned.

"They're in a hurry, and they're desperate. They might just deal with us," Bob said.

"Well, if we're gonna have to depend on desperate farmers to make our livin' we might as well quit now," Ray replied. "But, they'll make us a start, I reckon."

Just before nine, they drove up the long gravel driveway that led to William Perry's home. Bob knew Perry well enough. Mr. Perry, nearing seventy years old, was in no mood to do business with a convict. He had trusted Glen Melton to honor his contract, and he saw no reason to expect better of a man fresh out of prison. Especially when he was using extremely old equipment that was being rigged together by another convict. And a black one at that!

Ray returned no part of the argument except to say that Thomas Washington was a fine mechanic and that any equipment that he worked on would be in the best of condition. "If you change your mind, Mr. Perry, give me or Bob a call. You'll find you can trust us."

Things went even worse at Fred Tipler's place. As soon as he realized who he was talking to, he ordered Ray and Bob off his land. Ray tossed one of his new business cards through the open window of Tipler's truck as he walked past.

"Bing Russell has a small place up in the north end of the county. Good delta land, as a matter of fact," Bob said as he pulled away from Fred Tipler's nice steel shed. "Nice yield this year. We can go on up there, git run off again, and be back home by dinner time."

Ray sighed heavily. "Sounds like a plan to me."

Dan Russell was a big red-headed bear of a man. Sometime during his adolescence he had won the nickname "Bing", and most people that knew him had forgotten what his given name was. Living on the "delta side" of Winstead County, he owned a small plot of flat, fertile farmland. His money went into the land rather than equipment, so he was known to contract for most of his labor and equipment needs. His methods had proven successful, and he was the envy of some of the much larger farmers for his profitability.

"You say you just have one old two row picker?" he asked Ray.

"Another one will be on line before the week's out," replied Ray. "I reckon we'd have your cotton pretty much in by then."

"And you'd supply the trailers?"

"Got five of 'em rollin'. Four more on the way. You set things up at the gin, and we'll haul it for you."

Bing was thinking hard. Ray could sense his mind racing.

"Well, you know I'm contracted to Glen Melton," Bing said as if it were his final defense.

"I don't know Glen Melton," Ray said. "I'm sure he is a fine man. But, if he's contracted to you, he ought to be here pickin' that cotton of yours. He should have taken care of you and a few others who already had agreements before jumping to those bigger jobs. Any contract you might have had was violated when the other party failed to perform as promised."

Bob picked at the pure white cotton fibers he held in his left hand. "Glen's alright. Does a good job. The thing is, Dan, he won't be here in the mornin'. We will."

Bing looked at the open field before him. His cotton was ready for picking. The weather wouldn't hold forever. Damaging rain was sure to come before Glen got back around to him. And, if Glen had a chance at another larger job, he was sure to take it.

"I doubt I'll see Melton anytime soon. So," he said extending his hand to Ray and then Bob, "I guess I'll see ya'll bright and early in the mornin'!"

Ray was glad that he had made plans to eat dinner with Gran today. She had been asking about his progress, and she would be proud to know that he had his first job lined up in just over a week since his release. She should be the first to know. He felt confident that as soon as he proved himself on Dan Russell's job, others would follow. They had to. Cotton season was almost over, the bolls were open, and damaging rain would be coming.

After dropping Bob off at the shed, Ray headed over to Gran's house. He had been looking forward to this time. His grandmother was really too old to be worrying about feeding him, but, she had insisted. She would have all of his favorites ready, and the two of them would enjoy their time together.

With his truck parked out front, Ray walked around to the back door. As soon as he reached the porch, he could hear the pots boiling, and something frying in the pan. He was surprised to find the back door closed. Gran had once had a habit of leaving the back door, which lead directly into her kitchen, open whenever she cooked. "If you can't stand the heat, get the heat out of the kitchen" was one of her many mottos.

Ray rapped lightly on the door before letting himself in. He was expected, and this was his grandparent's house, his old home away from home.

Gran was not in the kitchen. He immediately caught the odor of fried corn scorching in the pan. "Something's burning, Gran, he called. I'll get it." He then smelled gas and saw that the juices from the black-eyed peas had boiled over enough to extinguish the gas flame beneath it. This was definitely not like Gran. She would never leave her stove unattended in such a way. He turned the burner off and looked around the room.

Moving through the dining room, Ray could see into the living room. Gran's feet and legs were visible through the wide doorway. She was sitting in her rocker.

"There you are!" Ray said teasingly. "Did cooking me this dinner wear you out?"

There was no reply. No sound. And Ray realized that the chair, which should be rocking if Gran was in it, was not.

"Gran?"

The funeral was held the next morning. In the crisp November air, Gran was laid to rest beside her beloved husband. The double tombstone that had been waiting for her held all of the pertinent information already. Even the epitaph was there . . .

"Troubled though these fields may be,
good harvest has been made.
For as my dear Lord died for me,
my troubled soul was saved."

As soon as Mary remembered to make the call, the engraver would be out to place the date on the stone. Then the family would come and gather round the grave and read the date as if that small change to what they had been looking at for years brought closure to the life and death of Cornelia Barnes Winstead.

Gran had no family left, except for the Bennetts. The community's huge outpouring of sympathy and support came as no surprise to anyone. Ray, as did each member of the family, young and old, shook a lot of hands, heard the "I'm sorry's" and the "Let me know if there is anything I can do's". Most of Dover and surrounding areas seemed to have declared a temporary truce of sorts where he was concerned. The people were as polite to him as they had to be, no more.

Then there were Gran's closest friends, what few were left, and his mother's closest friends. They each offered a special word of support or encouragement to him as they passed. "We're so glad you are home now", and "Your grandmother always believed in you", and "She lived to see her greatest prayer come to be." There were even a couple of "Give that Carl Sullivan what for's!"

Lorraine was at the funeral, and visited the Bennett home afterwards. She had shown up at the funeral home the night before and apologized to Ray. "I was wrong, Ray. I don't know why I acted like I did. It's just that, well, those children are my life. I took it wrong, I know you didn't mean anything. Will you forgive me?"

Ray said, "It's me who should be askin' forgiveness. I guess I'm a little rough around the edges when it comes to sayin' things right."

Without making a show of it, they were seen arm in arm by enough people to get some serious gossip started. A funeral is not just an occasion to get the living through the passing of a loved one. It is almost as much a social occasion as a wedding. The tones may be more hushed and reverent, but the words are much the same.

Ray was near exhaustion. He'd not slept at all. Yesterday morning, when he and Bob had finally succeeded in lining up a job, seemed like days ago. Finding Gran there in her rocking chair, and leaving her there to go break the sad, totally unexpected news to his mother were all events recalled now in a haze.

Ray had stayed with Mary until Pat could get back home from work. He spent a couple of hours at the shed working on one of the cotton trailers, while Thomas labored over the older and much more needful cotton picker. Some would call it disrespectful, but Ray felt that meeting his obligation to Dan Russell was the best way he could honor his grandmother. She knew that farmers lived by beating the deadlines of nature and creditors, and that her late husband, and now her grandson, were vital to their customers' survival as farmers.

"Never look at what you do as just business," she had said recently, "Working the land, bringing in the harvest.

You are part of feeding and clothing the world. It's a huge responsibility, yes, but it is also a blessing and an honor. Crops fail, crops succeed, crops barely make it. And when they do make it, it's up to you to bring them in."

Arriving back home shortly before his parents came in from finalizing the funeral arrangements, Ray cleaned up and put on his new suit for the first time. He had bought it for church and funerals. It saddened him to think that his own grandmother's funeral would be his first occasion to wear it. She was supposed to have seen him in it and carried on a bit. ". . . handsome as your Great Uncle James!"

The Bennett Farm Services crew had made a fine showing at the funeral home that night. And again at the funeral. Bob had a suit he kept hung in plastic for such occasions. Matt had no suit, but he dressed in his best new clothes. The Washington family received more than a few curious stares, but they were welcomed as friends by the Bennetts.

"Thomas here works for my son," Pat would say as a prelude to his introductions.

"Must be a convict, too," Ralph Smith sneered. "Nobody decent would work for him."

"Ralph," Pat sighed hiking his pants, "you'd best shut up and go on home. Otherwise everybody here will have to come back tomorrow for your funeral."

"You threatening me?" Ralph said drawing close to Pat's face.

"No," Pat replied evenly. "There's no need for threats. I won't tolerate this kind of behavior at my mother-in-law's buryin'. It's that simple." After a moment of staring at each other Pat added, "You ought not to show up at places like this when you've been drinkin', Ralph. Now, are you leaving, or do you want more than a hangover when you wake up?"

Ralph's eyes darted around the parlor as if he were looking for a graceful way out. Even in his present condition he knew there was no way he could walk away on the top-side of this confrontation. "Just wanted to pay my respects," he said sharply, and then he turned to leave.

"I'll tell Mary."

Pat turned to Thomas. "I'm sorry about that, Thomas. He's drunk. Shoot, he's even more obnoxious when he's sober!"

Thomas laughed. "That's alright, Mr. Pat. Folks like me hear a lot of that kind of stuff."

Bob and Matt stood awkwardly, their backs to the wall in the narrow hallway as visitors ebbed in and out of the small parlor where the body of Ray's grandmother was on display. Matt's constant attempts to find a place to rest his hands were almost comical. A wealth of advice, good or bad, for any situation, Bob leaned slightly toward the shifting teenager and offered, "Always bring your hat to a funeral. Gives ya somethin' to hold on to."

Matt drew a deep nervous breath. "I don't much know what to say to folks when somebody dies."

"Neither do these folks doin' all the talkin', son. The family of the deceased would be a lot better off if most of 'em would just keep their mouths shut and stand by and keep quiet . . . like you."

Bing's cotton weighed heavy on Ray's mind throughout the morning. He had waited until Mary was in bed last night, and then he went back to the shed. Bob and Matt were finishing up on the second big cotton trailer as he rolled into the lot. Axles had been greased. New wheel bearings and used tires had been mounted. Nuts and bolts were tightened. Thomas was hard at work on the two ton Chevrolet that would be used to pull the trailer that was to haul the cotton pickers, one at a time, to Bing's Holly Bluff acreage.

Upon sending Matt to the house for the night, Ray and Bob turned their attention to the long trailer that had to carry the cotton pickers. Thomas had hurriedly gathered everything that was needed to put all of the trailers in shape including a large supply of used tires. Tires were always in demand on any farming operation, and Ray, though glad to have the used ones, looked forward to the day when he could meet his needs with new tires and parts. It would take days, Thomas had speculated to get that older cotton picker operational. Used parts would be harder to find. And there was a lot of work to be done.

Bob left the tractor shed a little past one thirty that morning. Ray did not want all of them to be so long without sleep. By four am, he and Thomas had the old Chevrolet running and in good enough shape to make it to Holly Bluff and back. Thomas went home to sleep until time for the funeral.

Ray went home and showered in an attempt to refresh himself.

By five, he and Bob were back at the shed loading the picker onto the trailer. With Ray pulling the picker in the two ton, and Bob pulling the best of the cotton trailers with his truck, they made it to Bing's place by seven. They returned to Dover in both trucks with plans to haul two more cotton trailers up to Bing's after the funeral.

Having paid his respects, Bob left for Holly Bluff for the second time that day. He would get started on Bing's cotton. Thomas would go back to work on the other picker. Matt could handle most of what was needed to get the final two trailers ready. He had stayed out of school to go to Gran's funeral. Ray had decided to take a nap that afternoon, and drive up to Bing's before dark. He would relieve Bob and operate the picker into the night. All night perhaps.

He ruled out the nap, however. He had to see how his machine was working. After everyone but the immediate family had left the Bennett home, Ray took his mother aside. "Mama, I'm gonna go on up to Holly Bluff. I hate to leave you, and I know we just buried Gran and all, but I have to."

"I understand, son," Mary said patting Ray's arm. "And it's what Mama would want. Don't worry about me. Pat's here, and all of my other children and grandchildren are here."

"I just hate to go."

"We all know how important this job is to you. You made a commitment to be there this morning, and you've already had to go back on that. This could well be the most important job you ever have. A lot of eyes will be on you now. And that means they are on all of us. You go on for Gran. You go on for all of us."

"O.K., Mama," Ray kissed his mother on the cheek.

15.

The sight of his lone cotton picker floating through a sea of white swept the gloom from Ray's consciousness. It was thrilling! Long spindles pulled the huge white boles into the two headers where they were ripped from the stalk and sucked through rubber and metal ducts to be deposited into the great mesh bin that sat atop the machine. The engine droned smoothly, monotonously, just as it should.

Bob sat at the controls on the open deck. Huddled against the cold he held a cigarette tight in his lips as if warming himself from the inside out. A trailer sat at the far end of the field. Almost full, Ray reckoned. One more dump from the picker and Mr. Dan Russell would have cotton on its way to the gin. Bennett Farm Services was at work!

"Thank you, Lord. Thank you. And, if you would, tell Pappy and Gran we got our start."

By the time Bob turned the lumbering machine toward the trailer; Ray had backed his truck into place and connected the hitch. Sitting in his truck, the door open, his foot resting through the open window, he recalled that there was a lot of waiting involved in farm work. You are always waiting for the weather to do something that it is not. You wait for rain, you wait for everything to dry out, you wait for it to warm up, you wait for cooler temperatures. You wait for the crop to grow, you wait for harvest time. You wait for machines such as cotton pickers to do their jobs and bring in the harvest. You wait in line at market for your contribution to the feeding and clothing of the world to be removed from its container so you can get back to waiting for that machine in the field to fill up once more. Then you wait for the next planting season, and you start waiting on the same things all over again.

The roar of the cotton picker passing by his door woke Ray from his realization of just how much work was involved in all this waiting. Bob put the hydraulics in motion that lifted the bin teeming with cotton and poured its contents into the trailer. Once the bin was back in place, he left the engine idling and climbed down to greet Ray. "I 'spected you'd be up some time or another."

"How's she doin'?" Ray asked handing Bob a cup of hot coffee from his thermos.

"Complains a bit on a left turn, rides like it has square wheels," Bob replied. "Other than that, she does as good as an old picker can do. If ol' Thomas can do as good on that other rust bucket of yours as he did on this one, we'll finish out the season just fine!"

Anxious to get to work himself, Ray rushed past Bob. "I'm gon' take 'er out. Why don't you haul that cotton in? It'll give you a chance to warm up."

"You don't have to ask me twice," Bob said sliding into the cab of the truck. Ray didn't hear him, though. He had already scaled the steps to the deck of the picker and was throttling the engine. Bob smiled as the cotton picker bounced its way back across the end row to return to its duty. "Welcome home, son," he said tipping his cap.

The ecstasy wore off after five runs up and down the rows of prime delta white. Once the cold had seeped through the excitement and the energy it generated, Ray quickly recalled that there were actually unpleasantries involved in farm work. Still, he knew he would rather have spent the past fifteen years freezing his tail off atop a bouncing lumbering near-obsolete cotton picker than behind the cold block walls of Parchman Penitentiary. Steeling himself against the bone chilling wind Ray determined to return to the methods he had used as a boy to ward off the cold, or the heat, or the boredom often associated with his work. This was just after he promised himself a picker with one of those heated cabs next year.

The controls of large self propelled farm implements do not always receive the operator's total concentration. In fact, one who is prone to thinking a considerable amount of time tends to do just that. And there was much thinking to be done atop this machine. There was the next job . . . and where to find it. There was the bean season, already upon the land. What to harvest them with and where to find the jobs. There was the hay season coming in the spring. What to bring it in with . . . and where to find the jobs. There was . . . Lori. A pleasant thought indeed!

Lorraine Sullivan, he would never think of her as Parker, had flowed into Ray's life as smoothly and as naturally as the Mississippi River flowed past Natchez. Dropping into place much like a tumbler in a combination lock, she had immediately become a necessary, no, the most important component in the mechanism that would open the gate which led to Ray Bennett's life. And perhaps, Ray thought, he would be the same to her. They fit together. They belonged together. And, in a way, Ray mourned for all the years they had not been together. But they had come through all the tragedies and disappointments in their separate lives to find each other now. There must be a reason for it. There must be a plan set in motion from God on high. They fit. They were. They just were.

Matt arrived at the field pulling another trailer just after four thirty. With less than an hour of daylight left, Ray invited the boy onto the deck of the cotton picker.

One trip down and one trip back and Matt had been shown and told everything he needed to know in order to operate the ungainly machine in the field. One trip down and one trip back, Matt at the controls and Ray standing by, and Ray was satisfied that all his youngest hand needed now was experience.

For the next forty-five minutes Ray and Bob sat in the warm cab of his truck chatting about how well Matt was doing, how well Thomas was doing, and how poorly Bennett Farm Services was doing with just one job to its credit.

"It's a start, Ray," Bob said. "Most folks take to you once you've been around 'em long enough. The only jobs you get this season may well be from farmers who need you just because it's late in the season and they've got to get the crop in. When they know they can depend on you for that, they'll be back and more will follow. Your granddaddy had to convince folks he could do all this better and cheaper than they could themselves back when he first started. Now, you just have to show 'em they are better off usin' you than any other custom farmer. Be there for 'em. They'll remember."

Deep in the dusk when objects twenty yards away seem almost invisible, the two headlights on the cotton picker turned toward the waiting trailer. As he approached, Matt could be seen shivering from the cold but grinning widely.

"I wish I could work up that kind of enthusiasm for freezin' my butt off while my insides are gittin' pureed into mush," Bob mused.

By dawn of the next day, Ray was standing in the tractor lot grinning as Thomas steered the reanimated International Harvester cotton picker toward the trailer that would carry it to Bing Russell's land. The engine carried a deep throaty sound. It reverberated off the walls of the shed as Thomas slowly approached the long ramp attached to the trailer. Suddenly, it died. The motor sputtered to a tense silence.

The wheels ceased to roll. The sound of the engine turning over as Thomas worked to bring it back to life evoked no hope of resurgence.

"Fuel?" Ray questioned.

"Acts like it," Thomas replied climbing down, already checking connections as he moved. Reaching the ground, he immediately began tracing the fuel line. "There she is," he announced pointing, "cut, clean as a whistle."

"How'd that happen?" Ray asked. "Is there something rubbin' against it?"

"Yeah, somethin's been rubbin' against it," Thomas declared. "Something like a knife blade or a hacksaw!"

Ray shook his head in frustration. The effort to ruin him had taken a new turn. He had no doubt as to who was involved in damaging his equipment, but proving it was beyond him. He didn't have the time, and he simply didn't have the proof. "How long to fix it?"

"Replacing the line won't be no problem. Finding it will." Thomas quickly eliminated a patch or splint of any kind. A quick fix would not hold up in the fields. "I'll get to lookin' and I'll bring 'er up yonder soon as I have it runnin' again."

By seven, Bennett Farm Services was back on the job at Holly Bluff. The picker was greased and refueled, the steel and cast iron cold even through the cotton gloves worn by Ray and Bob as they worked their way around the machine. Four trailers were now on site. One more would be brought up later in the day. Two trailers were filled and ready for transport to the gin by the time Bing Russell arrived to check the progress of the harvest.

"I'm sorry to hear about your grandmother," Bing said by way of greeting Ray.

Nodding slightly, Ray replied, "Thank you, Bing. We ought to be caught up tonight."

"Oh, I'm not worried about that. I can see ya'll are going all out. The fact is, I didn't come by yesterday because I didn't expect you to be here. A friend of mine called me last night and told me he saw ya'll working. I just wanted you to know I appreciate it, but, I can understand if you need some time."

"I gave you my word I would be here to bring your crop in. My grandmother would expect me to hold to that."

"Well, I'll let you get back to it. The grocery store in town has a good plate lunch if ya'll need a place to eat later on."

"Thanks. We'll give it a try."

Just after lunch, Ray and Bob were surprised to see Thomas drive up pulling the old International Harvester on a trailer behind his wrecker.

"Where did you find that part so fast?" Ray yelled over the din caused by the big machine.

"Don't ask," Thomas yelled back. "Jus' let it go that there's a lot of old cotton pickers sittin' around rustin'. Ripe for the pickin', so to speak."

"I thought your days of wanton thievery were behind you."

"Didn't' say nothing' 'bout stealing' anything, did I? Made a deal, that's all."

Although he was anxious to try the older machine out himself he slapped Thomas on the shoulder and told him to give her a trial run. "You deserve the pleasure," he said.

"This one," Bob interjected gesturing toward Ray, "has a warped sense of pleasure. I ain't been able to sit down on both sides at once ever since I climbed up on that John Deere."

Thomas laughed as he took to the deck and started the engine on his latest conquest. Ray's patience lasted about twenty minutes. He had to drive that International. Maneuvering the John Deere so that he finally met up with Thomas in the end row he yelled, "You ought to try this one out. I'll switch if you want to!"

For the next several hours Ray stayed at the controls of the old International. He decided that this was "his" machine. It rode rough, it had most of a full turn's play in the steering wheel, and the transmission was contrary. But, he loved operating it. The picker did what it was supposed to because he made it do it!

The sun loitered on the low side of the western sky when Ray noticed an old pickup moving gingerly across the end row of Bing Russell's field. In the evening light, he could not make out the face behind the steering wheel, but a vaguely familiar form emerged from the truck as it came to a halt.

Before Ray could reach the end of the row to hop down from the idling cotton picker yet another truck, a much newer one, turned into the field and moved toward them. William Perry stood beside the old Chevrolet with his hands in his pockets and embarrassment on his face.

"Mr. Perry," Ray said nodding and extending his hand.

"Mr. Bennett," Perry replied taking Ray's outstretched hand.

"I reckon I need you to bring in my cotton," Perry said almost defensively.

"Something change?" Ray asked.

Bill Perry looked embarrassed. "Not really. Russell here swears by you. Melton ain't coming' no time soon."

Saying nothing, Ray turned to watch as Thomas maneuvered the cotton picker he was driving across the far end of Dan Russell's remaining cotton.

"Look, Ray," Perry said plaintively, "maybe you don't like having to prove yourself to other people. But that's just the way it is. The fact is, you've got more to prove than most folks starting up a new business." He paused searching for a reaction. The other pickup had reached them and the driver was approaching them purposely. "For what it's worth, you've proved yourself to me. I'm in a scrape, for sure, but, I feel like you'll do a good job for me."

Before Ray could respond, the man from the other truck introduced himself with an out-stretched hand. "Nathan Carter."

"Ray Bennett. This here's," Ray said gesturing, "Mr. William Perry. What can I do for you?"

"You can pick my cotton. The rain is coming before Glen Melton does and it is ready now."

A sick, sinking feeling hit Bill Perry in his stomach. His own crop was nowhere near as large as Nathan Carter's. And the way he had treated Ray Bennett just a few days ago deserved no favors.

Ray shook his head. "I'm committed to Mr. Perry, here for my next job."

Bill audibly chuckled but checked himself when Ray and Nathan glanced his way.

"It'll be a good job for you. I carry more acreage in cotton than even Bing did this year."

"I need the job, for sure," Ray replied. "But, I need my reputation more. One thing you'll find about me, Mr. Carter, I'm a man of my word. If you'll give me a chance, I'll bring your cotton in. Just as soon as I finish with Mr. Perry."

Carter shook his head and took a deep breath. "I don't see as I have any choice. I trust you to be there. I don't much trust the rain to hold off, though." Shaking his new customer's hand Ray said, "We'll beat the rain."

"I'm glad things are looking up for you, son," Pat said as he handed Ray a bowl of gravy. "More people will come around, you'll see."

"Could you stand some more good news?" Mary asked.

"I can stand all of the good news I can get, Mama," Ray replied. "Lay it on me."

"I've talked to everyone in the family, your brother and sisters, that is, and we all agree."

"Agree on what, Mama? That secrets are a good thing to keep from me?"

"No-o-o!" Mary laughed. "We all agree that you should have Mama's house!"

"Ma'am?"

"I want you to have Mama's house. It's the logical thing to do."

"I'll be glad to rent it from you. Works for me!"

"No, son, I don't mean to rent. I mean to have .. . to own!"

"Mama, I can't just take the house. I already got the rest of the place. What about you? It's rightfully yours. You should sell it or rent it and take the money and you and Pop go on a nice trip somewhere. Lord knows you deserve it."

"What I deserve is seeing my son who has had so much bad happen in his life have some good happen. And what I deserve after almost sixteen years is to give that son whatever I want to," Mary said as she began to cry. "You deserve to be happy and I deserve to see you being happy. And I deserve to see that house that has sheltered generations of my family be home to yet another. Now! Is that enough deserving for you?"

"You'd best give up, son," Pat advised. "I know that tone of voice. She'll have her way and that's about it!"

"Pat!" Mary scolded.

"Just want the boy to understand the gravity of the situation is all," Pat droned.

"I thought you had something to show me, Clint," Carl growled. "Ray Bennett is up and running and you haven't been able to do a thing about it! I want him ruined! I want him down! I want him out of this county, crawling or carried! Now do I have to tell you every move to make?"

"No, sir. We'll get him. It's just going to take some time."

"I don't have time! He's got Emily all stirred up and he'll be back in your wife's britches before you know it."

"That's a fine way to talk about your daughter, Carl!" Clint said meekly.

"You let it happen once before and look where it got us all. I don't intend to let it happen again. And when you lose your wife, you'll lose your daughter. And when that happens you'll lose any chance you ever had of running my place . . . much less owning it."

Clint sighed. "He may be your son-in-law yet, but it won't be with Laura. Maybe you should keep up with your other daughter a little better. Lorraine? You remember her?"

"You mean he's after her now?" Carl asked incredulously.

"Or the other way around," Clint smirked.

Carl was seething. "You stop him," he ordered, his voice barely under control. "You stop him and I mean it!"

16.

"Ray, why are we sittin' out here in your truck freezin' while my nice warm trailer is just over there?" Lorraine asked.

Ray didn't respond.

"Is something wrong? Did something happen?"

Ray cleared his throat. "Lori," he began, "sittin' in prison gives a man a lot of time to think. Not that it's a good thing to be locked up, but I reckon a person ought to make the best of it."

"I suppose so."

"Well, one thing I guess I was able to figure out is how I feel about things. I don't mean just how I feel at the moment, but that I know what I feel. I know what's real and lastin'. You know what I mean?"

"Not yet."

"Well, . . . Lori, . . . Well, I . . . uh . . . I know for a fact that I . . . I . . . love . . . you." "Love" came out more like a sigh than a real word having taken all of Ray's vocal energy just to force the breath that carried it from his throat.

Lorraine's eyes glistened. "How did you make it, Ray?" she asked after a few moments of silence.

"Huh?" That was not the response Ray had hoped for.

"In prison. How did you make it through all those years?"

Ray swallowed. "Well, I day dreamed about havin' a family when I got out. Me and Emmy . . . and Laura. But, that's all it was. I won't ever be nothin' to Emmy, And Laura, well, it was just a dream to help me get through."

"That's not what I mean, Ray. I'm not jealous of my sister. Is that all that got you by? A dream?"

"No," Ray replied, "mostly, it was my faith. I knew God was with me. And I knew He would give me the strength I needed to get through anything. My family was behind me. I had just about all I needed . . . except my freedom. And now I have that. There's one more thing, and that's you."

Lori began to cry softly. "You can't love me, Ray. I'm not . . . I'm not . . . worthy of you."

"Lo, you're . . . Worthy? If anything it's me who is not worthy!"

"You had every reason to turn against everything you were raised to be. But, you kept your integrity. You were a good person then, and you are a good person now. You held onto yourself." Lori hesitated. "Ray, I lost myself . . ., no . . . I gave myself away at the moment you were convicted."

Lori continued. "I felt so worthless. And that's how I've lived, Ray. Like a worthless tramp. That's about the only thing me and my dad agree on. I'm not what you want. I'm not what you need. You can't love me."

"Life is awful hard on people sometimes. What happened, Lo? I know all this had to be tough on someone your age at the time, but, why did it affect you so much?"

Lorraine drew a deep breath. Her voice quivered as she revealed the secret she had carried like a weight for almost sixteen years. "Ray, my daddy hates you. He hated you before the . . . the accident, and he hated you after it. I never thought it would be possible, but he hates you even more now. He really thought he had gotten rid of you. And here you are. All up in his face down at that tractor shed every mornin', workin' off of that little piece of land that he would do anything for. And I think that's what he did, Ray! I don't know what happened that night out on the deck, but I never thought you hurt him. I knew you couldn't do what he accused you of, and I never said anything. I said nothing, Ray! And I'm so ashamed!" she sobbed. "Oh, Ray, I'm so sorry."

"Lori, Lori," Ray whispered, holding her head tight against his chest. "You were just a kid. There was nothing you could have done. You didn't see anything. You didn't know what did happen or what didn't happen. And Carl would never have let you testify anyway. You know that!"

"I could have told them that I saw it! I should have. I should have told them that you never touched my daddy, Ray, because I never thought you did!"

"If Carl had thought you saw anything, there ain't no tellin' what he might have done, Lori. And you couldn't lie in court."

Lori cried, "You and your truth! It wouldn't have been the worse lie told in that courtroom, Ray. And I do know what Daddy would have done, because he did it!"

"What do you mean, Lori?"

"I told him that I saw everything. I was there, upstairs in my room, and if I had gone to the window when I heard all the noise instead of running downstairs I would have seen. But, I told him that I saw it all. Those were my words, "I saw it all, Daddy!" And all you got to do is look around to see what he did. This and worse." She began to cry again. "I should have lied for you, Ray. I loved you, but I betrayed you."

Ray continued to hold Lori tightly as if that would squeeze all the guilt and pain from her.

"But, there is so much more, Ray. If you knew the truth you would hate me."

"Shhhh, . . . hush, now," he sighed after a few moments. "Don't you think no more about all that. It's in the past. Let's leave it there. And don't even think about askin' me to forgive you. You didn't do nothing wrong. You didn't do nothing wrong," he repeated. I'm here now. I'm fine. I got by all that, and I'll help you. We already talked about this, Lori, and we don't need to talk about it no more."

Ray kissed Lori's forehead. "I love you, Lo. I know that as well as I know anything. Ain't nothing gonna change that."

"I love you, Ray," she returned. "I think I have since I used to watch you ride up and down the road on that red bicycle of yours when you were just a boy. I told Gracie, Gracie was my horse, that I was gonna marry you some day."

They kissed.

"That marryin' part," Ray continued, "I'm glad you stuck that in there."

Lori looked questioningly into his eyes.

"Things have been movin' pretty fast for me ever since I got paroled. And that's alright. The way I see it, it's helpin' me make up for lost time. I know I won't ever get all my time back, and I can't change anything that's happened. But when folks know how they really feel about something, there ain't no use in puttin' off what should have already happened, is there?"

"What do you mean by that?"

"I mean I should have let myself fall in love with you a long time ago." Taking her hand, Ray looked deeply into Lori's eyes. "We were meant to be. I believe that more than anything. You and me, Lori, we could . . . I ain't got much to offer. A business that ain't doin' much in the way of business. Every piece of equipment I have is wore out. Pasture with no cattle. A house that was here when Grant rode through. I have few friends but the ones I do have are good ones. Most of the county don't care whether I live or die much less whether I make anything out of myself. There's a rough road ahead. I've got a lot I want to do but none of it I want to do alone. You'd be crazy to want to, but I promise I'll spend ever day the rest of my life tryin' to make you and your children happy if you'll be my wife."

Lorraine wiped tears from her eyes.

"Will you marry me, Lori?" Then he quickly added, "I won't blame you if you don't."

"Are you trying to back out of this already?" Lori asked.

Ray didn't catch the jest. "No!" he said. "I ain't never gon' back out of nuthin' with you, Lori Sullivan!"

"And you think we were meant to be?"

"I do," Ray said. "You know how the Bible says God has plans for all of us? Well, I think you and me are in each other's plan. It just took a while to come around where we could be together."

Lori replied sheepishly, "I don't know much about the Bible. I do see what you have, and I want that for myself, and for my kids."

"Well, you can have it, Lori. I'll show you how, and it'll be the best thing you ever did. All these burdens you carry, all that weight, you can just give it away! That's just for openers, and then there's Heaven!

"I know it's sudden and all, but I know it's real. I'll ask one more time and then I'll shut up. Will you marry me, Lorraine Sullivan?"

"Of course I'll marry you, Raymond Lee Bennett!" Lori said reaching to hold Ray tightly to her. "I've waited for this moment all my life."

"Your mama and daddy are so nice," Lori said following Ray into the darkness of his grandmother's home. "They treat me like family already. Better really . . . than my own does."

"You are family, darlin'. Just wait. Thanksgiving and Christmas are going to be something this year. Who knows? Maybe even your daddy will take to the idea of me and you. At least the two people he don't never want to see will be in the same place. Now your mama, I think she'll be real happy. I think the world of your mama.

"This," Ray announced finding a light switch, "is gonna be home."

Lori drew a deep breath. The house was old and spacious. It smelled of home and family and love. And even though the heat was off, it had a warmth that beckoned her. She had to go no further than one step into the large living room to feel at home. "It's wonderful! I can't wait!" She hugged Ray tightly. Even their affection felt as though it belonged here. "It's like we've been here all along."

"I keep tellin' you we were meant to be."

"And I keep tellin' you, I've known it longer than you have!"

Ray smiled. "How long are you going to keep rubbing that in?"

"For as long as it works to my advantage. You can expect me to be usin' that one when we're old and gray," she laughed.

"I'll be done out loved you by then," Ray challenged.

"I don't know what's involved in being out loved, but it sounds like fun. When does it start?"

"It already did!"

Ray began the tour of the house. The front porch was much as it had been since the beginning of time. The passage of time was chronicled throughout the house by add-ons and remodeling materials. Hardwood flooring in the living room was covered by cream colored loop carpet, the latest addition. That same original flooring was still exposed in the dining room lending an echo of sorts to the special occasions for which it was used.

The "new" wood kitchen cabinets had been built when Ray was in grade school. The beige and blue linoleum floor covering that was installed at the same time now had a well worn path along the sink to the stove and the refrigerator. As the years passed Gran had refused to replace that worn flooring. "Walking the paths all over this place is like a stroll down memory lane," she had said. "They'll help me remember when I get old and decrepit."

Shag carpet from the sixties adorned a small hallway that had been converted into a sitting room. Dark paneling from the seventies was in two of the four bedrooms as well as the ceiling fans that hung in most rooms where large ornate light fixtures had once been. Flowered wall paper and chair rail left the mark of the eighties on the "master" bedroom.

The attic was filled with items dating back to the Civil War. Ray related stories from his childhood about sneaking up here to rifle through the trunks and boxes. As a boy he had been sure there was treasure stowed away here somewhere. His grandfather's tales of Confederate gold hidden on the place were always a great motivator for bored boys. "There's enough space up here to make another bedroom or two if we need it," Ray commented.

"We forgot to look in one of the rooms," Lorraine said as they descended the attic stairs.

Ray sighed. "Not really. I wanted to save that one for last. It was my Uncle Jimmy's room. He was killed in Viet Nam. Gran hadn't changed anything in the room since he left for boot camp. When word came that he had been killed, she closed the door and declared the room off limits. She used to go in there sometimes and just sit. I was always kind of scared of it, I guess. Like there might be a ghost or something in there." Pausing with his hand around the door knob Ray added, "I feel like I'm violating something just by openin' the door."

It was obvious that Gran had not come to this room in a long time. Everything was neat and orderly. The bedspread was wrinkled where she might have sat and wept the last time she visited this shrine to her only son.

But the dust was thick. The single twin size bed was one of those old wagon wheel types. The dresser and chest were of cheap brown laminate. An orange plastic cone shaped lamp sat atop the small night stand where old automotive and motorcycle magazines were stacked as if waiting suspended in time for their reader to return and take them up where he had left off. Model airplanes dangled from the ceiling, held there by thread tacked to the sheetrock above.

"Mama's prob'ly gonna want to do something with this stuff," Ray said reverently. "One of the kids will bring life back to this room soon enough."

Cuddled together on the porch swing, Ray broke the long silence, using his sleeve to wipe a tear from his cheek. "I'm blessed to have you, Lori. Maybe it's your real love that got me through all the years in prison, not my made up one. There's more hard times ahead I'm sure. But, me and you are gon' make it. We're gon' make it just fine."

After a moment, Ray said, "I wish you'd of been gone somewhere else that night."

"Why's that?"

"Because you might be closer to your family if you hadn't been there and didn't have these notions of yours about what happened."

"That's a sweet thing to say, Ray Bennett, but, my daddy lied. I know that. I've always known that you could never do such a horrible thing. Whether I was there or not, I would never believe his side of the story."

"Maybe not back then, babe. But, now, well . . . you've seen a little of what I'm capable of."

"My daddy did that to you, too. And for that, I'll never forgive him." Lori squeezed Ray's arm.

"Yep. I'm real blessed to have you. I wish you wouldn't be so hard on your mama, though. She couldn't do no more back then than you could. And all this has taken a toll on her. She blames herself, you know. I think she's been tortured for years. Maybe if ya'll will just sit down and talk, you can work things out."

Several more minutes of silence passed. "Yessir! I'm a blessed man!"

It was a surreal scene; or maybe an enigma. Since Ray was unsure of the meaning of either word, he settled for weird. In neither his favorite dream nor his worst nightmare in all of his adult life had he ever pictured himself having Sunday dinner in the home of one Carl Sullivan. But, here he was and almost as nervous as his bride to be at his side. Well, Lori had been reacquainted with his family. Just because he already knew hers was no good excuse to turn down Miss Emily's invitation. And if it caused Carl to suffer any degree of irritation, Ray was up for it. And, it may bring about a truce of sorts.

But, most of all, it meant a lot to Lori.

The atmosphere was strained to say the least. Arriving shortly before dinner was served had saved Ray the agony of prolonged small talk with Carl or Clint. In fact, there was no talk. Carl barely grunted when he and Lori entered the house.

"I've got work to do. Call me when dinner's ready." And off he rolled to hide elsewhere in the house. Clint pretended to be engrossed in a football game on television. Emmy hugged her Aunt Lori and hurried to the kitchen to help with dinner. Laura gave Ray one of those hugs where you never really touch. She sat for a few minutes and smiled pleasantly . . . nervously, but pleasantly, before seeking refuge in the kitchen herself. Jason helped his father be interested in the game. He ignored his cousins, Susannah, Davey, and Priscilla Marie, who sat quietly with their hands folded across their laps. Ray was glad that Matt and Billie Rose were dining with his parents.

Ray still felt like an underling of sorts in this great house. It was big, old, and elegant. Furnishings that he merely thought were old so long ago, he now recognized as antique. He sat nervously on the edge of the couch, unable to bring himself to the full comfort of sitting back in a more relaxed position.

Now, at the table, Carl held his traditional place at the head, with Jason, Laura and Clint on one side, Lori and Ray on the other, with Miss Emily at the other end. Emmy opted to eat at the small dinette in the kitchen with her cousins.

Judging from the noise, all the fun was being had around the kids table.

"I hear you ran into trouble at some beer joint in town," Carl remarked between bites of roast beef.

"That was a good one, Daddy," Lorraine said before Ray could respond, "you got us both with one shot!"

"Didn't go lookin' for it," Ray answered. "Walked in the door after I got there."

"I hate to know I have a daughter of mine working in that kind of place. It's too dangerous when people attract trouble."

"Yes, sir," Ray said, still chewing, "I know you'd feel better if she was to get a job in the higher class kind of establishment that a man like yourself might frequent."

Ray felt a sharp kick from Lori.

"What do you mean by that?" Carl snapped.

Laura jumped into the conversation before Ray could answer. "So, Ray, Lorraine tells me that your business is doing well?"

"We did get a good start to be so late in the season. I don't have any cotton jobs lined up after next week, but I will be harvesting some beans."

"If you don't mind my asking," Clint said, "where are you getting the equipment?"

"I have a real good mechanic, best I've seen. He's fixin' up my grandfather's rolling stock. Got those cotton pickers running strong. I'm sure he can do the same for the combine."

Carl still had the disturbed look on his face from Ray's comment to him. He opened his mouth to speak again when Jason asked where Ray had found such a good mechanic.

Ray wiped his mouth and hesitated, then answered saying, "I met 'im up where I used to live."

"I thought it was against the law for people like you to associate," Carl said smugly.

"Daddy!" Lori admonished.

"Well, it might be at that, Carl," Ray knew it grated on the man for him to use his first name, "but, if it is, it's the first law I've ever broken . . . that I know of!"

"I'm proof that's a lie!" Carl declared.

Ray put his fork down. "There were a few of us. In any case, I've served my time, right or wrong. I'm sorry if you have a problem with that!"

"I do, as a matter-of-fact, have a problem with that! Lorraine has made less than . . . intelligent decisions in very important matters in the past. She has been this way all of her life."

"And as soon as I make the right decisions, I'm back in your good graces, is that right?" Lorraine said evenly.

"Look, Carl, Miss Emily," Ray looked at each of them in turn, "I'm sure you know that Lori and I are getting married. And we're getting married very soon. And I know it seems sudden to you, and there's no denyin' it happened fast. But, we love each other very much. And we are sure of what we're doing. We can both use a better life, and there's no need to put off for months what can happen sooner."

"And you think you can give her a better life?" Carl asked sarcastically. "There are people taking bets over whether or not you'll last until the end of the year. And you won't if I have anything to do with it."

"That's uncalled for, Daddy," Lorraine said.

Ray lifted his hand. "The past fifteen years of my life are irrelevant here, we all know that."

Carl asked, "What do you mean by that?"

"I mean, that in your eyes, I could never be good enough to marry your daughter, no matter what." He shrugged. "I'll even agree with you about that. As for making a better life for her, you bet your pompous butt I can."

"Raaayyy", Lori said through clinched teeth.

"For one thing, she won't be livin' in some deer camp reject. She'll have a house to call her own. She won't be stuck drivin' some rattle-trap of a car, either. And for another thing, she'll have a whole family full of people who will care for her and about her, and welcome her in . . . just like she is, Carl!" Ray's voice was rising now. "She won't have to prove herself to anybody in my family. She won't have to dance on the end of a string for the love and attention she deserves. It's all there for her. And it's more than she's ever gotten from you!"

"Now see here . . ." Carl started.

"No, sir, *you* see here!" Ray said pushing his chair back and standing, "Lorraine and I are engaged. And it's gon' be a short engagement at that! You may not like it, but it is going to happen. And I intend to do my dead-level best to do better by your daughter and your grandchildren than you ever did. If I can't do anything else, I can love 'em unconditionally! Now, you might try to buy her off. But, I expect it'll take a sight more than a shiny red sports car to get it done!"

Laura and Clint, as well as the kids in the kitchen, had been sitting closed mouth throughout the entire fray.

Ray turned to them and said, "I'm really sorry to mess up ya'll's Sunday dinner."

To Emily he said, "The conversation might have been lacking, but it was a truly good meal, ma'am. I hope you can accept me and I'll try to be a good son-in-law." He reached to hug her.

"You'll be my favorite," Miss Emily whispered out of Clint's earshot.

Lori laughed and said, "I enjoyed it, too. We should have done this sooner! Call me, Laura. Mama, I'm sorry I can't stay and help with the dishes." She hugged her mother tightly and held her for several moments. They hadn't touched that way in years. "I'm sorry, Mama. We should get together and talk. I think we have some things to share."

"Oh, darling, I'd like nothing more," Emily said through her tears. "I'm so happy for you."

"Daddy, I got me a real man here, don't you think?" She took Ray's arm and walked toward the door, the kids in tow.

"You got yourself trouble there," Carl shouted back. "More than you or him, either one knows!"

Before leaving, Ray added, "Hey, Clint, now you can drag your ol' trailer back to deer camp while the season is still open!"

As they walked to the car, Ray and Lorraine looked at each other. Ray shrugged. "That went better that I thought it would, actually!" They were still laughing as they pulled out of the driveway.

17.

With Lori back at home, Ray phoned Nathan Carter to inform him that Bennett Farm Services should start transporting equipment to his fields late the following afternoon. They would begin the harvest Tuesday morning. Carter was still worried about beating the rain, but Ray assured him that his two pickers would run from "can to can't". "If the rain holds off 'til the end of the week, we'll have it beat," he had promised.

Bob and Thomas had operated the two pickers Sunday morning. Ray and Matt took over in the middle of the afternoon. By seven o'clock, it was past cold, and Ray saw that they would finish by noon or shortly after the next day. It would be a school day, so he needed to get Matt in. They emptied their hoppers into the waiting trailer and parked their machines about twenty feet apart. Ray sent Matt home in his truck, and he used the big Chevrolet to pull the trailer to the gin. He brought an empty trailer back as far as home, intending to pull it to Bill Perry's place the next morning.

In his brief conversation with Lorraine, he informed her that Mary had made all the necessary calls and, indeed, everything was out of Gran's house that would be coming out. And, yes, he had brought up the subject of Uncle Jimmy's room. It turned out that the shrine had always bothered Mary and she would be glad to see someone get some use of the room and the furniture. Ray had invited her to go into the room and take whatever mementoes she wanted. She would do that early the next morning.

"I was thinking," Ray said, "it would be nice if you and the kids went ahead and moved in. I'll stay here at Mama's and Pop's until the wedding."

Lori was quiet on the other end of the line. Finally she said, "You don't think it will bring us bad luck?"

"Luck ain't got nothin' to do with us, babe. I just can't stand to see ya'll livin' over there like sardines when you don't have to. I mentioned it to Mama. It's fine with her. As a matter of fact, she'll be able to help if you want to start tomorrow."

"Let me sleep on it."

"Sure."

"Son! Wake up!" Pat was jostling Ray's shoulder. "You got problems at the Perry place!"

"Wha . . . What?" Ray asked groggily.

"Bill just called. Your pickers're on fire!"

At that Ray practically leapt from his bed. Shoving his feet into a pair of uncooperative jeans, he asked, "What time is it?"

"Close to two. Steve May's boy saw it from the highway. He's the one that went up and told Perry."

Sliding his bare feet into his work boots and grabbing a shirt and coat, Ray was on his way out of the door. "Pop, call Thomas for me, o.k.?"

By this time, the commotion had awakened Matt. Mary, who had heard the phone ring, was in the kitchen fixing coffee that no one was to have time to drink.

"Mr. Ray, what's the matter?" Matt asked.

Pat told the boy what he knew.

"I'm going with you," Matt insisted.

Ray replied, "I can't wait for you to get dressed, bud."

"You go on, I'll bring 'im after I call Thomas," Pat offered.

As Ray was pulling away, Matt suggested that Pat call Mr. Bob as well. "He'd want to know."

In just over ten minutes, Ray was running from his truck to join Bill Perry and Jerry May in fighting the fire that was spreading across the dry weeds at the end of the cotton rows. Mrs. Perry was ferrying wet crocker sacks from their barn up by the house.

Fire was blazing up under the older cotton picker, but the picker itself was not on fire. Ray jumped up on the deck and brought the machine to life on his third try. Bill was yelling that it was "gonna go!", but Ray drove it a safe distance from the remaining fire.

It was then that he saw the John Deere picker silhouetted against the moon above and the fire below. The scraps of cotton that were trapped in the wire mesh of the hopper still burned. In the darkness, they looked like little balls of fire hanging in the sky. The front tires smoldered, the flames from the larger rear tires made standing rings of fire. Ray's heart fell. There was no hope for this one. The better of his two cotton pickers, though not his favorite, was lost. As much as he enjoyed operating the old International Harvester he wasn't sure she still had it in her to carry Bennett Farm Services alone. And . . . one picker was not enough anyway.

Taking two of the heavy wet sacks in his hands Ray waded out into the edge of the cotton rows themselves. He beat furiously at the knee high flames lapping at the dried cotton stalks. Pat, Mary, and Matt arrived just before Thomas and Marcus.

No pleasantries were exchanged among the men. They went immediately to work on the fire. Mary and Mrs. Perry stood together arm in arm. Except for smoldering ashes, the six men soon had the fire under control. By the time Bob arrived, the fire was out.

"First chance for any excitement I've had in years and I missed it," he said meandering up to the group of tired, soot covered men. "At least I don't look like I been barbequed," he added betraying his regret in not being among them.

"We're goin' up to the house," Mrs. Perry shouted as she led Mary toward Bill's pickup. "Breakfast'll be on the table by the time ya'll get there."

"I like my breakfast steak tender and on the medium rare side," Bob yelled back.

"Bacon and sausage are the closest you'll get to steak on my breakfast table, Bob Riley," Mrs. Perry laughed.

"I thought you said your equipment was in good shape," Perry said harshly.

"It was," Thomas answered. "I checked both them pickers out real good."

"Well, it came near to burning me out! Weren't for this boy here, it would have."

Turning to Jerry May, Ray introduced himself and thanked him for his help. "You saved us both from a big loss. Losing that one picker is gon' hurt enough. Both of 'em would of done me in for sure!" He reached into his pocket and brought out a twenty dollar bill. "It's not much, but . . ."

"No, sir," the young man interrupted. "I can't take nuthin' for that. I'm glad I could help. If that other fellow hadn't of nearly run me off the road, I might not have even seen the fire!"

"What other feller?" Bob asked.

Jerry told them how he was on his way home from a date in Jackson. He was drowsy and hadn't been paying attention, but, he suddenly realized that a pair of headlights was swerving on the road just ahead of him. He had to leave the road and bounce into Mr. Perry's cotton field to avoid being hit. When asked where the other vehicle came from, he couldn't be sure, but the way it was veering all over the road it looked like it had just swerved onto the highway, coming out of Mr. Perry's field, " . . . come to think of it!"

Thomas moved his wrecker closer to the burned picker and turned the rack of spotlights toward it. He whistled long and low and sniffed at the air. He then took his flashlight and went to the other picker. He walked around it sniffing at the air as well. "Time I shined my lights on that cotton picker I knew this wasn't no electrical fire. Gas done been poured all over both of these pickers."

"Are you saying that somebody did this on purpose?" Bill Perry exclaimed.

"Yes, sir, that's what I'm sayin'. I know that picker didn't catch fire all by itself. Ray, you just lucky. I figure they used most all of their gas on that one. They didn't have enough to soak the old one down good. Look at the way them tires burned," Thomas said pointing to the remains of the first picker. "I don't think they would catch and burn like that 'cause of no electrical fire."

Ray walked closer to the badly burned picker. "They must have lit a match to this one and then tore on out of here thinkin' the fire would spread to the other one. Mr. Perry, do you mind if I use your phone. I want to get the sheriff in on this. I don't know what good it'll do, but, we need to report this."

The sound of gravel crunching beneath slow moving tires on the driveway woke Emmy from a light sleep. Her clock showed the time to be three thirteen a.m.. Peeking nervously out her window her stomach jumped. Coasting under the greenish hue cast by a security light, a truck crept up the drive with no headlights on. She did not realize that she had been holding her breath until her father appeared from the side door and walked to meet the truck in the dark shadows of a large cedar tree near the back of the house. Relieved that this obviously was not a burglary attempt unfolding right before her eyes, she released her breath in a long, heavy sigh. She thought she recognized the truck as belonging to Buck Ammons, her father's right hand man. 'So it's farm business,' she thought. Then she realized the time, and began to wonder just what would be happening at this time of the night. Quietly, she raised her window just a bit to see whether she could hear what was being said.

". . . know we got one." "had to. . ." She could make out a word or two here and there. ". . . seen." This brought a curse from her father. He put his hands on his hips and walked in a small circle beside the truck. "Don't worry . . . ."

After a moment, her father handed something to the driver of the truck. She was almost sure it was Buck. She couldn't see the other man with him, and he had said nothing that she could hear. The engine started, and the truck pulled away slowly, circling the drive and idling out to the road. Even there it was driven away slowly and quietly. Clint stood in the yard staring after it for several minutes and then went back inside the house.

Lying awake in the darkness, Emmy considered her life. Her father had done well enough, thanks in no small part to his father-in-law. Being Carl Sullivan's granddaughter had its perks and benefits. She was popular at school. She was able to dress well. She would have a new car at sixteen and funds for her college education were in the bank. Forty acres of her grandfather's land were even recorded in her name.

Someday they would be hers to do with as she pleased. These three provisions, she learned, had been set in motion before she was even born. The college education was understandable, the car and the land, though, puzzled her whenever she gave it much thought.

All of this she would trade, however, for genuine love and acceptance from the two most important men in her life, her father and her grandfather. Carl often did not offer even the pretense of love. At least Clint tried, or pretended. Her mother could make all of the excuses in the world. Emmy was old enough to see what was real and what was false. She sensed at times that her father wanted to love her, he just couldn't for whatever reason. Maybe he did blame her for coming to her mother's womb when she did. Maybe she had interfered with some grand plan that he had for his life. Maybe this plan didn't include her or Chad or her mother!

Her thoughts wandered to Matt Warren. No matter how bad she thought her own life was, she knew his was not one for which she would trade. She regretted all the times she had done nothing while her friends mercilessly badgered him. To be ostracized by everyone around was horrible enough. But, to be scorned and abused by your own father, abandoned by your mother, how could he be as . . . nice as he was. She couldn't pity him, though. He was too proud for that. He was strong. He deserved better than life had handed him. If there was anything good about that Ray Bennett guy, it was that he had taken Matt under his wing and was doing good by Matt and his little sister. But, there was nothing good about Ray Bennett. Somehow, he was responsible for all of her own troubles.

Footsteps moved across the carpet down the hall in front of Emmy's door. She heard the gentle click of her parents' bedroom door closing. She lay on her back wide awake now. Bo drifted into her thoughts. She felt differently about him after his fight with Matt. She had dated him to begin with because he was somewhat of a heartthrob among all the girls at school. He had asked her out, she went, and they were together. Considering her feelings, as she was now, there really was nothing of substance between them. They were together because the society of their peers thought they fit together. A cute couple, each one popular, each well off financially. It was an arranged relationship, not by old world tradition, but by teenage peer pressure.

Emmy swung her feet to the floor and got out of bed. "This is ridiculous," she whispered, "I've got to get out of here." She dressed quickly in jeans and a sweatshirt. Thick socks, boots, and her down filled jacket, and she was ready for the cold night air. Raising her window more, she slipped out and trotted down the sloping hill to the barn behind the house.

A soft whistle and whisper brought Montana Miss, her Appaloosa mare named after her grandmother's stories of the old ranch, from the darkness. The horse took the bit readily. Emmy placed a saddle blanket on the mare's back and swung her right foot over, pulling herself up into position. A quiet "cluck" from Emmy's cheek was all Montana, or Miss as she was sometimes called, needed to strike out at a lope across the pasture. Taking the back trails she would soon be at her grandmother's lake, the same one that lay behind Ray Bennett's place.

Pat and Mary had already left the Perry place, and now Matt was on his way back "home" in Ray's truck. Ray, Thomas and Bob were going to wait for the sheriff to come. Matt drove slowly in the silence of early morning. He passed Emmy's grandmother's house, all dark except for the big security light out front. He turned off the highway, driving past the north side of the Sullivan's house and was nearing Mr. Ray's tractor shed.

Suddenly, from the corner of Carl Sullivan's land where it met Mr. Ray's, just as Matt reached this spot, a horse veered into the road and then seemed to shy immediately to the right. The horse twisted violently. The rider slid off backwards falling to the hard asphalt surface of the road. Matt braked hard and ran to see about the rider.

"I'm sorry, I didn't mean to . . ." It was Emmy McKay! "Hi." He knew it was a dumb thing to say at a time like this, but it was all he could think of.

Emmy took Matt's hand and pulled herself upright. "My horse spooked. It's not your fault." She finished dusting herself off and finally looked at Matt. "What happened to you?"

Matt remembered that his face was still streaked with soot. His clothes were permeated with the musky odor of smoke. "Somebody burned one of Mr. Ray's cotton pickers a little over an hour ago. We all had to go put out the fire. I must look like something."

Emmy appraised the boy standing before her. "You do look like something," she said staring into his eyes. Catching herself, she looked away. "My horse ran off."

"Don't worry," Matt said in his best take charge voice, "We'll find her."

"How do you know it's a her?" Emmy asked.

"Oh . . . I . . . I just like horses," Matt said hoping that would explain well enough. He couldn't tell her that he had watched her ride that horse many times, and that he himself had once sneaked a short bareback ride on the animal himself. He thought patting and talking to that horse unseen on the backside of the pasture was as close as he would ever get to Emmy McKay.

"Oh," Emmy said nodding and smiling slightly to herself. As they drove slowly up the road they talked about the fire. "And you don't think Ray Bennett set it himself?"

"Mr. Ray would never do anything like that!" Matt retorted. After a moment he said, "You don't like him much, do you?"

"My grandfather is very bitter. And he takes it out on other people. If Ray Bennett had not broken his back he might be different."

Matt had seen and heard enough about Carl Sullivan to know that he was a hard man before Mr. Ray was even born. It wasn't right, though, for him to say any of this to Emmy.

"Look, Emmy, I know . . . Well, things didn't happen the way most folks say they did. Not even the way Mr. Sullivan . . . remembers it."

"Were you there?" Emmy argued. "Or do you believe everything Ray Bennett tells you?"

"Mr. Ray hasn't told me anything. And I haven't asked. It's just . . . he's just a good man, Emmy."

"Sure, he is . . . now," she said caustically.

"He took me and Billie Rose in. He gives me these so-called bonuses so I'll have some money. He found Thomas Washington and his family this great house to rent. And he paid the deposits and first rent. And he bought them a new stove and refrigerator, and filled the refrigerator with food, to boot! And he's marryin' Miss Lori and movin' her and her kids into his grandmother's house and he wants me and Billie . . ."

"I know he's marrying my aunt!" she said insidiously. "He's just using her to get at my grandfather. He can't love her. He's been home less than a month!"

"It don't take forever for Mr. Ray to make up his mind about much. And from what I hear, Miss Lori has been in love with him most of her life. I wish you'd get to know him. You'd probably like him," Matt implored.

"I'm glad he's good to you and all, but, I don't want to get to know him. And I don't want to like him!"

"So if he didn't set the fire, who did?" Emmy asked after a minute of silence.

"There's plenty of people that would love to see 'im gone," Matt replied.

Emmy was suddenly reminded of that strange scene at her house just a short while ago. Could her father be a part of something like that? 'Of course not,' she assured herself, 'that was just some very important farm business.'

"There she is," Matt said excitedly.

The horse had finally stopped less than a mile away. She shied away at first, but Emmy's familiar voice brought her to a halt.

"Thanks . . . for the help," Emmy said taking the dangling reins into her hands.

"You want me to drive behind you to make sure you get home alright?" Matt asked hopefully.

"No. I'll make it alright."

"You know, Mr. Ray has a horse I can use. Maybe we can ride together . . . sometime."

"I would like that," Emmy said softly.

Matt felt faint.

Emmy reached quickly and kissed him on his cheek. "Thanks again," she said.

There was a black smudge on the tip of her nose when she drew away. Matt smiled sheepishly and pointed to his own nose. Emmy took the hint and chuckled as she wiped it off with her hand.

"You're rubbing off on me," she said. "Give me a boost?"

Matt entwined his fingers and stooped slightly as Emmy stepped lightly into his hands and mounted the horse. He grabbed her hand to steady her. That girl sitting on the big Appaloosa in the moonlight was about the prettiest thing he had ever seen. He couldn't move his eyes from the sight.

Emmy found herself staring back.

Almost unconsciously they pulled toward each other. Emmy leaned until their lips met. It was a brief kiss, Matt's first real one. They parted. Emmy backed the horse up a step or two. Finally, she said, "Good night, Matt."

"Yeah . . . uh, g . . . good night...Emmy."

18.

Dawn found Ray Bennett, soot and all, atop the older cotton picker. With an early start he may yet finish the Perry job and get to Nathan Carter's before dark. He was worried though. Even with all the work Thomas had done on her, he wondered if the old machine would stand the wear and tear of round the clock operation. It would surely take such hard work if he hoped to keep his promise to Carter.

There was a ray of hope. Bill Perry, as it turned out, found himself to be quite impressed with Ray Bennett. Whatever he might have done in his youth, he was now a good, hard working man. One to be trusted. One to "ride the river with" as his favorite western author might put it. Two years ago, when Perry decided to contract out what farm work he could, he had sold two of his three cotton pickers. The remaining one, a red and white International, still sat at the far end of his own shed where he had towed it three years before that.

"She quit on me. I towed 'er in, and there she sits," Bill said as he and the remaining BFS crew inspected the hulking machine it the dimly lit shed. "You say Thomas here can fix anything?"

"If it rolls, I'll figure it out," Thomas said.

"I'll tell you what. This old picker ain't worth much as she sits. How 'bout you take 'er like she is, and cut your price for bringing in my cotton by . . . say a third."

Ray cast a glance at Thomas who nodded. "It's a done deal then at a quarter off?" He held out his hand.

Mr. Perry chuckled and shook Ray's hand replying, "She'll probably make the best one you've had yet."

Before daylight, the old International had been loaded and Thomas, with Bob and Marcus' help, had hauled it back to the tractor shed to begin the repairs.

The events of the night troubled Ray. Someone was after him in a bad way and he did not have to guess twice at who it was. From cutting a fuel line to arson was a bold step. What would they try next? He was going to have to figure a way to protect his equipment from future attacks.

Little help was expected from the Winstead County Sheriff's Department. It happened that Deputy Leon Pitts showed up to handle the investigation. He scowled at Ray when he heard the story. "Arson, you think?"

"Arson, I know," Ray replied.

"Maybe," Leon said poking at charred wiring with a ball point pen. "Possible insurance fraud if you ask me," he added smiling wryly.

All of the men gathered around exchanged glances.

"Yeah, you check that theory out real good, Leon. You may be on to something," Ray said sarcastically.

Leon had his pad up now, ready to write. "Who is your insurance with?" he demanded.

Ray remained silent.

"You may as well tell me," he said snidely, "we have ways of finding out. Have you notified your agent yet?"

"Why don't you go ahead and find out, Leon? And let my agent know when you do."

"I'll do just that." Leon slapped his notepad closed. "We'll be watching you."

Ray smiled. "Somehow I feel safer just knowin' that!"

Bill Perry shook his head as Leon drove away. "The fire was on my land, I'll call the sheriff myself," he said. "Darryl Hogue owes me more than sending that doofus out here. They may have been gunning for you, Bennett, but they hurt me in the process."

The sheriff did show up shortly before ten that morning. Ray and Bill met him by the burned out picker. Darryl Hogue grunted a time or two as he circled the machine himself. Finally he said, "I'll have to agree. It sure looks like somebody torched it. Not too discreet about it, but effective. Amateurs, I'd say."

Ray kicked at the charred ground beneath his feet. "Well, you know, Sheriff, your assessment may interfere with Deputy Pitts' insurance fraud investigation."

He bit his lip to keep himself from laughing. Bill Perry had turned away from the sheriff to hide the grin on his face.

Sheriff Darryl Hogue moaned and rubbed his chin, rough with whiskers. "I wish you folks wouldn't take so much fun in making a jack-ass out of my deputies. Why didn't you tell him you just carried liability on this old piece of junk?"

Ray chuckled, "He pretty much made it clear that he would do all the askin'. And he didn't ask what kind of insurance I carried. Had his heart set on insurance fraud and I hated to disappoint 'im. Ain't that about right, Mr. Bill?"

Bill Perry grinned. "Yeah, Darryl, that's right. He looked to me to have his mind made up."

"I'll steer Deputy Pitts' investigation in the right direction," the sheriff said weakly before leaving.

Sitting atop a piece of farm equipment, going back and forth across a cotton field for hours on end, leaves room for deep thought on a number of subjects. All that was happening in Ray's life occupied his thoughts at one time or another that day. The cut fuel line, the fire, the law, his "new" International cotton picker with an enclosed cab and everything, Lori, the kids, the move, and Emmy. His daydreams included his daughter in his new family.

How could he ever have any kind of relationship with her? Should she be told the truth about him and about who she really was? Should he try to reconcile himself to the fact that they would live close together in this small community as virtual strangers? And could he do that? In the short time he had been here so near to her, catching glimpses of her here and there, the ache that had tormented him so for years at Parchman now tore at the very soul of him.

"She's alright," he kept telling himself. "She has a good life, a better life than I could have given her." But, Clint could never love her like he did. Maybe missing out on his love was a small price for Emmy to pay. But, for Ray, not being able to share his love for her was something like slow dull torture.

At dinner time, Ray stopped to call Nathan Carter and deliver the news of his problems. He was surprised to learn that he already knew of the fire. "Melton came by and tried to get me to sign him up for next week. I told him to kiss my butt! He needn't think he's gonna burn you out and get my business back."

Ray thanked Nathan for the sentiment, and tried to assure him that Glen Melton had not even crossed his mind as the arsonist. He had no reason to believe and did not believe that the man had anything to do with the loss of his picker.

"I wouldn't put it past him," Carter said. "He's been ranting all over the place up this way about you getting his business. Myself, I reminded him in a hurry that you wouldn't have gotten it if he hadn't lost it first! Now, what about my cotton?"

"We'll be there late this evenin' or early in the mornin'," Ray answered. "And we'll work round the clock. I told you we'd get your cotton crop in, and that's just what I intend to do."

"I'm counting on you."

When Ray arrived back at Bill Perry's cotton field, he was surprised to see a new bright red Dodge Ram pickup truck parked next to the remains of his old John Deere cotton picker.

"Glen Melton," the man said with an outstretched hand.

"Ray Bennett."

"I heard about your picker, here. Bad break."

"Yeah, well, we're workin' around it."

"So I see," Melton said casting a doubtful glance at the older operational International. Thomas was furiously working his way around the machine making sure that it could go on for another day.

The man's visit puzzled Ray. It didn't seem that he was here to gloat.

"It looks like you're about through here," Glen said.

"We'll finish up by dark."

Glen Melton nervously shoved his hands in his neatly pressed khakis. "Look, I guess you're wondering why I'm here."

"You could say that."

"I . . . uh, I guess I need to do us both a favor."

"Oh?" Ray queried.

"Yeah, well, I've had a few calls this morning. Word of something like this moves pretty fast sometimes."

"Obviously," Ray said.

"Anyway, I want you to know that even though I was upset that you are getting some of my business, I had nothing at all to do with this." His eyes were wide, like a kid trying his best to look as innocent as possible.

Ray smiled. "Glen, I never considered that you would. I don't know you, but, you're nowhere on my short list."

Glen let out a heavy deflating breath that seemed to shrink him by several sizes right before Ray's eyes. "I'm glad to hear that. But," he continued, "it seems that a lot of people think that I did. I've had a few customers threaten to pull out on me because of it. And this late in the season, there are not that many customers left. You'll probably get some calls."

"I'll tell 'em we're sure that you had absolutely nothing to do with this."

"I appreciate that."

"Well, if you're gon' lose business to me, I want it to be under fair competition," Ray said laughing.

Melton laughed along. Turning serious he said, "It's a bad rumor that could hit me hard next year. The only thing I can think of to turn it around is to loan you one of my pickers."

"That's nice of you, but . . ."

"I wish you'd take it, Ray. I've made more than a few good farmers mad by putting them off for bigger jobs. It's my fault, but I've hurt my reputation. I've no doubt that you'll pick up business that I've lost, and I'm o.k. with that now. The thing is, we're both in a bit of a pickle here. Come next year, folks will remember if you didn't get their cotton in this year. They won't necessarily remember why. Then they'll turn around and quit me because they think that I was somehow involved in you losing a picker!

Let me loan you one of my four-rows, and you'll bring Nathan Carter's crop in sooner than anybody expects and I'll get some good publicity for helping to keep you in business. We might both survive that way."

Ray could now understand where Glen Melton's reputation as a big time wheeler-dealer had come from.

"Looks like I've made two good deals today," Ray said.

Matthew Warren, dirty, smudged, and a little bit shabby, lay heavy upon Emmy's mind. His strength, his manners, his kindness . . . his good looks, had placed him there. A growing affection, a longing to know more of him, held him there. Both pleased and disturbed at the same time, Emmy almost wished their encounter of the night before had not happened. Why should she have feelings for this boy so different from herself? How could she reconcile him to her life? To her friends? And should she? Clearly he belonged to another class, perhaps one somewhere above her own and that of her friends. Proud, she could handle. Lonely, she could change. Poor. . . . Poor? What could she do with this, and should it matter as much as it did? He was working to make his own way and taking care of his sister at the same time. Loyalty, courage, and morals made him a better person than any amount of money could.

He would be good for her, and maybe she for him. But, what would her father say? And her grandfather? They would never accept the idea of Emmy McKay dating Felix Warren's son. Poor Matt. So much going for him and so much against him. Which side would win? And could she stay on the side against him? Or could she do just what he would do and stand with him? The prospects intrigued Emmy and she decided that another "accidental" encounter with Matthew Warren might be in order.

"But, Lori, are you sure?" Laura asked.

Emily smiled. "Of course she's sure! It's different this time."

"Mother!" Laura snapped. "Don't you think . . ."

"Let me, Mama," Lori interrupted. Turning, she locked eyes with her sister. "I've made bad choices, I know. And I am sorry for that. Not, sorry for you or Daddy, but sorry for myself and my children."

Laura opened her mouth to speak, but Lori placed her fingers over her lips."I also know that you've never been pleased by anything I ever did. And maybe you think I never tried, but I did, Laura, I did! I just could not live my life the way you wanted me to. I could not let Daddy run my life, and I could not make the decisions for myself that you would have made for me. And that used to bother me. It used to bother me a lot, because I never felt . . . adequate. I never felt that I had it in me to measure up to you. So I gave up trying, and for a long time I felt inferior. I felt that I was not quite as good as anyone else. And it was all because I couldn't please you and Daddy."

"If you would just listen . . ." Laura pleaded.

"Be quiet, Laura," Emily hissed.

Laura and Lori looked at Emily, their mouths open.

"Lori is trying to tell you something, dear."

"Laura," Lori began, "you've been supportive of me in so many ways. There were times when you were there for me when I had no one else and I'll never forget that. And because of some of the things I've done, I really can't blame you for doubting my decision to marry Ray. Maybe it seems sudden. But, you've forgotten something. I made that decision a long time ago. That dream has finally come true, and I never thought it would. I'm going to live it. It's the best decision I ever made."

Laura reached to hug Lori. "I just want you to be happy. Ray is a good man, I know that. But it won't be easy. Daddy, and I'm afraid Clint, too, will see to that. They are both so blinded by their hate for Ray that they won't see they're hurting you, too."

Lori knew her sister's words were true. But, it all had to stop sometime. The one thing that everyone else seemed to be forgetting was that the two people who had stood strongest against Carl Sullivan now stood together!

19.

The conclusion was drawn that God smiled upon Bennett Farm Services for the remainder of the week. Tuesday morning, work started on Nathan Carter's acreage with Glen Melton's borrowed four-row John Deere cotton picker and Ray Bennett's somewhat ancient two-row International Harvester. Even though Ray handled the controls of the borrowed picker, after each of his crew had a turn at it, he found himself longing to be on the older one. Still, he felt responsible for Glen's picker and wanted to operate it himself, just in case something went wrong.

Bob arrived at Nathan Carter's place Tuesday afternoon pulling Ray's latest purchase behind his truck. In the Sunday paper, which he had dug out of Pat's garbage, Ray found a small camper trailer for sale in Pocohontas, just north of Jackson. As with so much of what he had, it was old, and it was used, but it was cheap. It was also small, but would sleep three as comfortably as such a thing could. The only thing about that was that two of the three had to occupy the same bed, so Ray doubted that the "three sleeper feature" as he jokingly came to call it, would be used by his crew. The camper would, though, allow him to stay with his equipment, wherever it was. He hoped this would discourage any further attacks by his saboteurs.

Wednesday morning, by eleven o'clock, Thomas drove up in the big Chevrolet truck pulling Bill Perry's old four-row International cotton picker behind him. Ray and Bob ran to meet him and marveled over the machine as if a brand new four-row picker of their own had been delivered. Within minutes Thomas sat at the wheel enjoying the results of two long days' work.

From his perch within the cabin of the four-row John Deere, Ray wished that he could stand back and witness the sight of those three cotton pickers moving synchronously through the white fields one beside and behind the other. It was a spectacle he had witnessed many times before, but this time it was his spectacle.

Just as Matt arrived, having come straight from school, a reporter from the Winstead County Clarion bounced across the end row in her dusty early eighties Volvo. Word of Ray's problem with the fire, and of Glen Melton's subsequent generosity in helping his competitor with the loan of one of his best machines had reached her at the paper and she thought the story and a couple of pictures would make an interesting feature. When Glen just happened by at that same time, Ray ceased to wonder where Miss Deborah Leister had procured her information.

A picture of Matt, Thomas, and Bob standing by as Ray and Glen shook hands would be the centerpiece of the article. A smaller photo of the three machines working in the field along with one of Ray's burnt up John Deere, which Deb had taken at her liberty when she first went looking for Ray at his shed, would support the article. It would be a great piece, she assured them all.

"Your own story intrigues me, Mr. Bennett. I'd like to do an interview with you soon."

"Thanks for the interest," Ray replied, "but, I don't think so."

"I get the feeling there is more to it than we all know. Maybe your side should be told," she insisted.

"Most of the people that really count know the truth," Ray smiled slightly and nodded. "The rest are just gonna believe what they want to."

"Well, I'll call again," Deborah said as if to put Ray on notice that she was not through with him.

By dusk it was apparent that all of Nathan Carter's cotton would be off the stalk before noon Thursday. Thomas and Matt ferried the five full trailers to the gin and headed for home. Ray and Bob stayed behind to work further into the night. The cab on Melton's fine new John Deere was heated. The cab on the older International was really just a shelter from wind and rain and dust. Ray worried about Bob huddled in the cold air that made its way into the enclosure. He switched machines, insisting that he had been wanting to drive the International all afternoon and he was tired of Thomas and Matt and Bob hogging it!

Later that night, sipping coffee and eating sandwiches in the slight warmth of the camper, they talked. It was not their everyday "skirt the edges, but never get personal" kind of conversation. Perhaps it was the close quarters of the camper or the weariness of a good day's work that left them unguarded, but they soon found themselves on very personal territory.

"How're the wedding plans coming?" Bob asked.

"I don't know," Ray laughed. "She could have run off with some pastry chef since I last talked to 'er."

"Ya'll like to move fast, do you?"

"It's one of those things, Mr. Bob. When you know, you know. And we know."

"Did you think you knew with Laura?"

Ray cast a puzzled glance at Bob. Waving his hand, Bob said, "I know all about it, son. I've known for a long time. I already told you that."

How Bob knew did not matter much to Ray. He obviously had kept the confidence over the years. That he knew was somehow a comfort of sorts. The understanding in his eyes was touching.

"We were kids, Mr. Bob. And we messed up. Something that should not have happened did, and look at us today. Our lives are all something short of what they should be. Everything that has happened to us since then is based on lies, and the one person in this whole thing that counts the most don't understand, probably don't even know, what all kinds of deception revolves around her."

"You know it's for her own good."

"Yes, sir, I know. But that line was a lot easier to live with when I was in prison."

"I know it's rough. Believe me, I know how it is not to be able to be with somebody you love. It bites on you ever day, if you let it. But, you're strong, Ray. You'll get through it. It won't be nuthin' pleasant about it, but you'll make it through." Bob sipped from his coffee cup. "Besides, you're gittin' yourself a new bride to help!"

"Yeah. Yeah, I sure am," Ray smiled. "How about you, Mr. Bob? If you don't mind me askin', why didn't you ever get married?"

"Got real close to it once," Bob sighed. "I was back from the war. There was this little girl who had grown up while I was gone. I kinda watched out for 'er, you might say, when she was little. I had a good eight or ten years on 'er, I forget now. But, she always tugged at the inside of me. It's hard to say why, but, we were just real close. Well, I marched around all over France and Germany and I missed that girl somethin' fierce. Close like we was, I figured maybe she was missin' me the same way."

Ray sat spellbound by the tale.

"The war ended. I mustered out and came on back home. The first place I went was to her house. There she was, prettier than anything I'd seen in England, France or Germany. She ran to meet me at the end of the walk and she hugged me like . . . well, like she'd missed me the way I'd missed her."

In Bob's eyes, Ray saw the wistful look he'd seen on so many lonesome faces at Parchman. Bob was wandering back to the best days of his life.

"It was a good homecomin', huh?" Ray said softly.

"We pretty much got together after that. It was down to her and her brother by then. I'd worked on their place before the war, and I went right back to what I was doin' soon as I got home. She'd bring picnic dinners out to where I was workin', whether I was plowin' with the mules or workin' the cows. We'd find us some shade and talk for a while. We went to town once or twice to the picture show, but folks stared a lot, me being a good bit older'n her and workin' for 'er and all. So we stayed mostly to ourselves. We had more fun that way anyhow."

"You ever ask 'er to marry you?"

"I did, and she said yes!" Bob grinned. "That was the happiest time of my life."

"What happened?" Ray asked cautiously as if not to intrude on his friend's good memories.

"Wasn't much to her brother. He couldn't farm, wouldn't work. He got to drinkin' and turned mean. Treated his sister awful, and them livin' up in the same house. Me and him had more than a few words over the way he treated 'er. He tried to think that I was marryin' his sister to git my hands on their place. He knew better, or at least he should of."

"Well, this drifter come through lookin' for work. Just somethin' to get 'im enough money to move on further west. The brother put 'im on more to irritate me than anything else. This drifter was a drinker of sorts so they got along good."

"That feller took a shine to . . . my girl." Ray noticed that Bob was trying hard to keep any names out of the story. "I was out of town over night one time; up in Greenville lookin' at a tractor I thought might be good for the place. Well . . ." Bob's fists clenched and his voice trembled slightly as he said this, "that drifter was up at the house drinkin' with the brother. It was stormin' pretty good and the lights went out like they often did in those days. The drifter said he'd like to get to know little sister. Brother says he better go on ahead since there wouldn't be much of a chance for it when I got back."

"That low down snake went up the stairs and found her in her room." His voice was gruff, hoarse sounding. Bob bit at his lip and shook his head.

Ray reached and touched his arm. "You don't have to go on," he said.

Bob threw up his right hand and continued. "The long and short of it is . . . he had his way with 'er." Emotion ran strong in his voice. "She fought, and screamed, and cried. That no 'count piece of a brother of hers could hear her, but he didn't do nuthin'. He sat down there and listened to the whole thing . . . and drank."

"That feller passed out after . . . when he was done. She got up and ran out. Her night gown was torn, she didn't have no shoes on or nuthin', and it was rainin' hard. It was late mornin' 'fore I got back. I went on to the house to talk about buyin' that tractor for the farm. The car and truck was there, but nobody answered when I knocked on the door. I walked around back to see if maybe somebody was outside. It had quit rainin', but it was muddy as all git out, and soon as I stepped up to the back porch I saw those bare foot prints leadin' out toward the pasture.

I found the brother layin' on the living room floor passed out. I called for 'er, but she didn't answer. I tell you, Ray, I got scared then. I knew somethin' bad had happened. I just didn't know what. 'Time I got to her room, I had no doubt.

That drifter feller was sprawled across her bed. He was half nekkid, his britches around his ankles . . . and him stinkin' . . . There was blood on the bed, too. I turned him over and he had some scratches, but it wasn't his blood on those sheets. I yanked 'im up off that bed and slapped him awake. He wouldn't say where she was.

He finally come to enough to recognize me. I asked 'im what he did with her. He said I was gittin' a good one. He knew 'cause he'd broke her in for me. And he laughed.

I slapped 'im again and asked where she was. . . . said he didn't know and he didn't care; he'd got what he come for.

Well, I threw 'im through that window. The roof over the back porch broke his fall, but he still fell hard enough to break his leg and probably a few ribs. I just looked at 'im down there moanin', and left 'im there."

"Her brother was in a stupor, I couldn't wake him up to save my life, so I took off followin' those tracks as best I could. She wasn't too hard to follow across the pasture. I'd lose her trail when the horses or cows milled across it, but she had made a pretty straight trail. I finally found 'er. She was squattin' down, leanin' against a tree up by a little pond out there. Just starin' off into space somewhere. She didn't . . ." Bob wiped tears from his eyes as he spoke, "she didn't hardly have no clothes on. Her night gown was just tore all to pieces. Soakin' wet from head to toe. I don't know if she recognized me or not at the time. All she would say was that she had tried to wash 'im off."

Bob's voice cracked and he paused for almost a minute. Ray kept his silence.

"Well, I put my shirt on 'er and carried 'er back to the house. She had come to herself enough to change into a clean gown. I put 'er in her mama's room, and left 'er to sleep. I woke her brother up so I could beat the hell out of 'im, but he wasn't up to it and I wanted him to be well aware of what was happenin' when I did it."

"What about that drifter?" Ray asked.

"He . . . disappeared," Bob said grimly. "Far as anybody around knew, he just took off. Nobody cared anyway."

"You didn't get the law after 'im?"

"It wasn't for the law to take care of. My lady there would of been hurt more by the gossip and the stigma of what happened than she would have been helped by bringin' the law in. It was a different time, then. They didn't have no counselin' or anything back then to help her either. She got justice, though. That's about all I can say."

"And her brother?"

"He finally sobered up enough to realize what had happened. I told 'im as soon as he was over his drunk I was gon' kill 'im. I don't think I've been so mad for so long before or since. I come close a time or two, but not like that."

"A man that would let something like that happen to his own sister don't deserve to live," Ray observed.

"Well, I don't know if I really would of killed 'im, but I didn't git to anyway. He stayed drunk for days after that. He left the house late one night and apparently took off walkin' down the road. Lookin' for a full bottle I reckon. He was killed when he fell off a bridge. I don't know if the fall killed 'im or he drowned. And that brings me to why we didn't git married.

"That darlin' girl was scared to death that drifter feller was gon' come back and have at 'er again. She knew, though, when I told 'er that he wouldn't never hurt her again, that . . . that he wouldn't. She had heard me threaten to kill her brother. And she knew I blamed him as much as anybody for what happened.

Well, when he turned up dead, she was convinced that I had something to do with it. I don't know, maybe she still wasn't thinkin' clearly, or she just felt too guilty because we both wanted him gone. Anyway, she said she loved me, but she couldn't marry the man who had killed her brother.

"It was crazy. She said she knew I would never lie to 'er except maybe to protect 'er in some way. And that I would lie if I thought it would keep her from seein' her brother's killer ever time she looked at me! She wasn't mad at me for killin' 'im. In her mind, she knew I did it for her. But, she couldn't marry me. The thing is, I didn't kill the man, and I don't know if I ever convinced 'er of that."

"That's some story!" Ray sighed.

"Not long after her brother died, some slick from over in Alabama came sniffin' around. They ended up marryin' but, that's too long of a story to start now. Me and her, now, we've remained close over the years. I reckon I'd marry 'er tomorrow if I could." Bob wiped at his eyes again.

"In all these years, there's never been anyone else?"

"Nothin' close to serious. I ain't a monk. But, it's like you said about yourself, son, when you know, you know."

They sat silently for a few moments until Bob finally reached to turn off the lantern sitting on the table between them. "Well, tomorrow's comin' early." After another moment he spoke through the darkness. "Most of what I just told you, Ray, there ain't but three people alive that know it. You're one of 'em."

"Sure, Mr. Bob," Ray said settling into the thin, lumpy mattress. "It ain't mine to repeat."

Through the darkness in the little camper Bob said quietly, "Ray, you're a good young friend. Yessir, a good friend indeed."

Thursday morning arrived behind an overcast sky. Ray and Bob said little over breakfast that did not concern the job before them. "Maybe Thomas will change his mind about workin' on that combine and come on back up here when he sees those clouds," Bob remarked. "Me and you might make it o.k., but I'd feel better with three pickers runnin' this mornin'."

Ray was glad that they had worked later last night than he originally planned. The skies were threatening. No sooner had he and Bob picked their first rows of cotton and turned to make the return trip up the row than they saw the old International Harvester moving across the turn row with Thomas at the wheel. A simple wave of acknowledgment and they all continued their work. By ten thirty, the field was picked as clean as it was going to get. One of Nathan's farms hands had been helping to get the cotton to the gin, so he, Thomas and Bob, each pulled a trailer when the picking was done ensuring that Nathan Carter's cotton got to the gin before the rain fell.

"Ray," Nathan said extending his hand, "it's been a pleasure doing business with you. Can you get my beans as soon as the fields dry up enough?"

"Tuesday . . . Wednesday at the latest," Ray replied.

The past two weeks had moved at a dizzying pace. It was good to have money banked from the work he had done. Though Ray had kept high hopes since leaving the gates of Parchman, he had not really thought he would actually be working his business so soon. He was tired; bone weary. But it was a good tired, a satisfied tired. With all that had happened to him, he was still moving forward.

A strange pickup truck was parked at the tractor shed when Ray arrived. He pulled into the lot with the faded red and white International in tow. The solitary figure that had been waiting there walked hesitatingly toward him when he climbed down from the truck. It was Fred Tipler! 'Another reluctant convert,' thought Ray.

"Mr. Bennett," Tipler said nervously rotating his hat in his hands, "I know you got no call to help me with the way I treated you and Bob the other week. But, I . . . uh . . . I still got cotton to pick."

"Rain's liable to get to it before I can," Ray said matter-of-factly.

"I know, and it's my own fault if it does, that's for sure!" Tipler said in a trembling voice. "But, I'm here asking if you'll do your best and bring in what you can. Maybe the rain'll hold off. If it don't maybe it won't ruin my crop and you can finish when it dries up enough. I'll pay you extra if you'll try."

Ray walked back and looked up at the cotton picking machine waiting there on the trailer. The temptation was great to leave this man in the problem of his own making. Make him squirm, make him crawl a little! He deserved it.

"I treated you badly, Mr. Bennett. I know I did. And I apologize."

Ray turned and saw fear in the man's eyes; not fear of him, but fear of losing his crop. For a lost crop in these times could well mean loss of everything.

"I doubt we'll beat that rain, Mr. Tipler, but we'll do our best. And my price for you is the same as it is for anyone else. I won't take advantage of a man in trouble."

He surveyed the ever darkening sky. "I'm afraid there's a truckload of it headed your way."

Ray worked alone for two hours before Thomas could get to Nathan Carter's place and back with the other picker. Glen Melton had picked up his four row machine. Fred Tipler had gone begging to neighboring farmers for the use of another picker or two. Because of insurance and outstanding loans and other hastily conceived excuses, he was unsuccessful. He finally paid Earl Jones two hundred dollars cash for the use of a badly kept two row picker. Thomas and Matt hauled it to the field and Thomas operated it while Matt and Tipler hauled cotton to the gin.

By late afternoon, when the first drops of rain began to fall, they had made more progress than any of them thought possible. In a light drizzle all three pickers headed for the trailers to dump what cotton they had in their hoppers at the moment. With the trailers covered with tarps, they returned to the white rows and resumed their work. Each driver was anxiously urging their machine to move just a bit faster, take in just a little more fiber. It was as much the thrill of fighting the elements as it was the attempt to keep another small farmer in business that drove them.

With almost one and a half more rows behind them, the down-pour came. It was sudden and swift. And it was a hard, wind driven rain that could ruin a crop. The rows quickly ran with water, and both of Ray's pickers were too far out in the field to make it to the end row. Ray and Bob scrambled to cover the hoppers of their machines with tarps where they stood bogged almost to the axles in the middle of Fred Tipler's make-it-or-break-it cotton crop.

Thomas was able to drive Earl Jones' picker to an empty trailer and dumped his load there to be covered and taken to the gin.

Matt had returned and pulled the first trailer out of the field before the rain made it impossible to do so. Ray waved to signal him to take it on to the gin. Ray stood along with Bob and Thomas watching Fred Tipler stare into the gray sheet of water that was destroying the remainder of his crop. It was not the kind of rain that would lower the grade of the cotton. It was the kind of rain that beat everything Fred had worked for all of his life into the ground, irretrievable and rendered useless.

"I wonder what he's thinkin'?" Thomas mused.

"He's thinkin' he should of been more open minded a week and a half ago," Bob answered. "He's thinkin' that if he weren't such a jackass this fine crop of cotton would already be ginned and at the compress and he'd of made it by for another year. . . . He's thinkin' 'bout what he's gon' tell his wife." Bob shook his head and began the walk to his truck. "We'd best git on outta here ourselves if we can."

Ray stepped out into the downpour but instead of running to his truck, he moved in Tipler's direction.

"Where you goin'?" Thomas asked.

"This is no time for a man to have to stand alone," he replied.

Thomas and Bob looked at each other. Without a word they walked through the rain and the mud until they stood to the other side of the defeated man.

A hard rain continued to fall as the four men stood side by side helplessly watching what was sure to be the end of Fred Tipler's life as a farmer.

20.

Lorraine stroked Ray's arm. "Are you still worrying about that Fred Tipler guy?"

"If he'd of let me know he wanted me out there sooner, we could of hauled one of our pickers down here last night and one of us could of got started on his crop early this mornin'. We wouldn't of brought it all in, but maybe enough to make a difference to 'im."

"He made his bed, Ray," Lori said. "What happened to him is bad, but it's not your fault. You did all you could for him."

"I'm in this business to help farmers make it. Lori! . . . can't help but feel some responsibility when it's my equipment sittin' out there stuck in the mud. I just hope he don't lose his place is all," Ray said.

"Well, can't neither one of us do anything about that. Now, can we talk about something else?"

"What in the world do we have to talk about?" Ray said before turning to her with a wide grin.

"Do you know what's happenin' next week?"

"I sure do! Something I've been looking forward to for a long time."

"Oh?"

"Mama's Thanksgiving dinner!"

"You!" Lorraine shouted hitting Ray with a pillow from the couch.

"Well, it is Thanksgiving ain't it?"

"O.K. O.K. What happens after that?"

"You mean dessert or later?"

Faking a sigh, Lorraine said, "Later!"

"How much later?"

"Two days!"

"O-o-o-h-h! Oh, yeah! I remember now!" Ray said casting his eyes sideways at Lori. "That Andy Williams Christmas special comes on doesn't it?"

Lori could take no more. She pounced on Ray and pushed him off the couch to the floor. "You been smokin' cotton lint, or what?" she said straddling him and tickling him.

"You must mean the wedding!" Ray said through his laughter. "You thought I forgot that? You insult me!" With this he grabbed Lori's arm and pushed her over and he followed rolling over on to her.

Meeting eye to eye, their mood deepened.

"It's the most important day of my life," Ray whispered. "The day I've waited for. The day I marry the one. Before I even knew that you were the one, I longed for that day to come." He kissed her, tenderly at first, but then passionately.

"Ray," Lorraine said softly, "I've been wondering. Why haven't you ever tried to . . . you know." She rolled her eyes and looked away shyly.

"Don't think it ain't temptin'! You know about the only time I ever . . . well . . . was with a girl. I've been away from female company for almost sixteen years now! It's ah . . . um . . . I've wanted to get you into bed since I first laid eyes on you at Buster's that night." He sat up and leaned against the couch. "It's hard to explain. You see, I made a mistake . . . well, Laura and I did. We were kids, and we put ourselves into a situation that resulted in a pregnancy. And, other than that precious child, the results of that one time, that one night, were disastrous."

Lori reached for Ray's hand and entwined her fingers with his.

"I mean, who knows. I think you and I were meant for each other. Maybe we were supposed to get together a long time ago and live our lives and have our family. Maybe my mistake is the cause of your two bad marriages."

"Ray, I have to take responsibility for that," Lorraine protested. "I made my decisions. Maybe I should have just waited for you."

"Well, that's the point, Lori. We've made plans to go and have ourselves a little church wedding and join together in Holy Matrimony. That means something. God has blessed us with each other and we want him to bless our marriage, not our mistakes. The past is past. But if God in his great wisdom intended for us to wait for each other, I think we should now. Wait, that is."

Tears were falling from Lorraine's eyes and rolling down her cheeks. "I love you, Ray Bennett," she managed to say. "I never thought about it that way. I've made plenty mistakes of my own in . . . where that kind of thing is concerned. But, I feel different now. All of a sudden! I feel new like! I feel like I can present myself to you as your bride and it's . . . it's . . . so new and fresh feeling! And it wouldn't be if we didn't wait." Then she chuckled, "Thank God for short engagements."

Nodding, Ray replied, "It's the way to go alright."

They sat quietly for several moments, there on the floor, Lorraine leaning against Ray.

"I haven't thought about that for a long time. You know, what a wedding really means. How special the day is. And how special the night is. I wish I would have waited for you, Ray. I really do. But, it feels right; us waiting for each other . . . now."

"Some people would think we're off our rocker," Ray commented, "That it shouldn't matter at our age."

"But, it does," Lorraine doesn't it?" whispered. "It means everything,

The rain fell late into the night. There was no way that the two cotton pickers were coming out of Fred Tipler's field for days yet. Ray, Thomas, and Bob moved Lori's family into Gran's house on Friday. Lori and Mary, with Pat's help after work, had painted the window trim and the kitchen cabinets. The paneling had been cleaned and new curtains and blinds went up over the windows. The floors and carpets were cleaned. New bathroom flooring and a new kitchen floor would have to wait. Mary did point out that it was Lorraine's turn to make her own worn paths through the house. It was to be her home now.

When what little furniture of Lorraine's that could be used was in place, and all of the furniture left behind had been cleaned and parceled out among the rooms, Mary announced that a house warming was scheduled for Sunday afternoon. She said she had invited Lorraine's family, which brought a temporary halt to the festivities as Lori fumbled and dropped a vase, shattering it into tiny pieces. A tear etched her cheek. "Thank you," she whispered.

"We're all going to be family," Mary said. "How can we become one, if we don't act like it from the beginning? Besides," she chuckled, "it's time us in-laws got together."

"I'm sorry, but don't expect my father."

"When he sees how excited the Bennett clan is about this marriage, maybe some of it will rub off on him!" She reached to hug Lorraine. "And if he never accepts your marriage, honey, it's just too bad for him. There's love enough for you and your children with us. And I'm looking forward to getting to know my new grandchildren!"

Dover Baptist Church had visitors Sunday morning. Almost a whole pew full. Ray, who was still considered a member there, sat on the aisle end. Beside him were Lorraine, then Priscilla Marie, Billie Rose, Susannah, Matt, Davey Jr., and Mary and Pat completed the row. When visitors were recognized ". . . by an upraised hand," Ray nervously stuck his hand into the air and then jerked it down, not knowing just what his status was considered to be. Lorraine held her hand only slightly above her shoulder, but the kids all reached for the vaulted ceiling. It wasn't, however, as though this pew had gone unnoticed by the gathered assemblage.

Brother David Schilling, pastor of the church, stood beside the pulpit and joyously greeted the visitors to his flock, all of which were on the Bennett's row. "Though I've met you only briefly at your grandmother's funeral, I know who you are, Brother Ray Bennett. And I want to welcome you back into the fellowship of God's people here at Dover. You've been away for a very long time and I'm anxious to get to spend some time with you and get to know you," the preacher said seriously, but then broke into a grin, "and find out just how you fill a pew as finely as you've done this morning!"

The congregation joined their pastor in laughing at his joke. Some things never change, Ray thought. Preacher's jokes always get a laugh, no matter how lame they may be. He grinned and nodded sheepishly.

Later, young Brother Schilling along with his wife and four year old daughter joined the Bennett family for Sunday dinner. Ray had taken an instant liking to the man. He was easy going, good company, and apparently did not feel the need to be in "preacher mode" all the time.

Conversation around the table was light. Brother Schilling surprised Ray with his knowledge of their family and his familiarity with Ray's life since his homecoming.

"Your mother has not been gossiping about you all that much, Ray," David chuckled, "It's just that you are quite a conversation starter in the community."

"Folks around here never had much of anything to talk about," replied Ray. "I guess I'm as good a subject as anything when you need somebody to say something bad about."

"Oh, there's talk on both sides of that aisle. I will say this; no matter how people feel about you, they are impressed with the way you've gone about your work." The preacher chewed on a slice of roast. "You are building a reputation as a man who will do what he says he will, and will get the job done. You hang in there. Folks will come around."

After dinner, Lorraine and Ray cornered the preacher and told him of their approaching wedding. "We know it's kind of short notice, but we'd like for you to marry us, if you can."

"It would be my great pleasure," David said squeezing Ray's hand and hugging Lorraine. "I like to have a little talk with the bride and groom before I perform a wedding, though. When would be a good time for that?"

"Well, bein' as how the wedding is this coming Saturday, it better be soon. But, if you're gon' try to talk us out of it or into waitin' longer, you can save your breath," Ray commented.

"Oh, no! No, I wouldn't make that mistake! Why don't you two meet me over at the church at four o'clock."

The session with the pastor went well. David Schilling was a good person, Ray had already decided, but he was also an up and coming young preacher. He knew the Word well, and understood Its message. He spoke of the Biblical roles of husband and wife and how scriptural texts had been misused and misapplied to create false conceptions of marriage to suit the agendas of different groups and individuals. He emphasized that marriage between husband and wife was designed to be a living portrait of Jesus' relationship to the church.

"I've known you two for only a few hours," the pastor said, "and it is obvious to me that you belong together. No one on this earth knows what the future holds, but, God has blessed you with each other, and, if you are strong and diligent, He will keep you together."

"I guess I need to start goin' to church again," Lori remarked as they drove home. "I always took the kids to

Bible School and all, but, we haven't exactly worn out the hinges on the church doors, if you know what I mean."

"Well, there's no better time to start than now," replied Ray. "It'll be good for us and the kids. I have to admit, I was kind of afraid to go back. I didn't know what folks would say or how they would treat me. Maybe in time, we can win them all over."

The house warming was a small affair. Family mostly, and Ray's family at that. Lorraine's mother and sister attended, but largely kept to themselves. They seemed to be somewhat overwhelmed by the closeness of the Bennett family, nieces, nephews and all, and their acceptance of Lorraine as "one of them".

Jealously, Emily wished her own family held this kind of closeness. It was not to be, she knew. There were walls and chasms all through her small family and she hurt for them all. But, if the Bennetts could overcome the terrible ordeal they had all been through why couldn't the Sullivans and the McKays? Two reasons came immediately to mind. The Sullivans and McKays had each suffered separately while the Bennetts endured together. Then there was Carl.

Laura was noticeably uncomfortable. They all had to know, the adults, at least. Still she envied the life that lay before her sister. Ray, she knew, was steady. He would be there for Lorraine. Always. And Lorraine for him. And this big family would be there for them both. Good times and bad. This was the best place Lorraine could ever have been. And she, Laura, could have had it. Staring into the large diamond on her left hand she wondered if that kind of life would have been enough.

Ray was standing in the kitchen gazing out the window at nothing in particular when he felt another presence in the room. He turned to face Laura.

"I didn't get much of a chance to talk to you at mother's the other day."

Ray grinned. "Well, I guess we left rather abruptly. I'm sorry I was so rude."

"Oh," Laura waved her hand, "you weren't rude, you were truthful. You said things they needed to hear. I rather enjoyed it myself."

"Well . . ."

"That's a deep subject," Laura chided. After an awkward moment of silence she said, "For the first time in my life, I'm jealous of my little sister!"

"This has nothing to do with you," Ray said.

"I know, I know. I wonder sometimes, though. How different would all of our lives be had you and I stayed together?"

Chuckling, Ray replied, "I wouldn't be an ex-con, but I would be your ex-husband, probably. If we had gotten that far. I couldn't have given you the kinds of things you wanted. You'd find someone who could. That would be that."

"You could always give me what I needed, Ray. I just didn't know it at the time. And I suppose I did want more." Laura sighed. "You know, I still can't get enough. But, I'm actually very happy for the both of you. It's sudden. Very sudden. And Lorraine doesn't always know what she wants. But, I think she has found it this time. I hope she never forgets that."

"Thanks. If nothin' else, family get togethers at the Sullivan house will be something to see, won't they?"

The affair ended much as it had begun. The house emptied almost as quickly as it had filled. Ray and Lori sat with the kids, Matt and Billie Rose included, and went through the gifts again.

Towels, sheets, dishes, gadgets, utensils. "I can't believe all this new stuff so close to Christmas," Davey, Jr. exclaimed.

"You just wait, son," Ray thought he should start trying "the son thing" out, "We'll have us a big ol' Christmas tree standin' right in that corner there before you know it. And ol' Santa Claus will slide down that chimney and there's no tellin' what he might leave up under that tree for all of you!"

The children squealed in delight.

Susannah crawled up beside her mother on the couch. "It's so nice here, ain't it, Mama?"

"Yes, darlin'," Lorraine said putting her arm around the girl's small shoulder, "it's real nice. It's home."

21.

Thomas cursed as he banged his knuckles against the cold hard iron of the hydraulic housing on the combine. "My knuckles ain't bled this bad since I tried to whup you up at Parchman that time," he groaned. "I didn't know there was anything existed that was as hard as your head!"

"Nothing ever changes," Ray mused. "If you'd watch what you're doin' you wouldn't be bangin' up your hands. Just like if you'd of been watchin' where you were goin', we wouldn't of got into that fight."

"Yeah, and we woulda never met, and you wouldn't have a match's chance in a snowstorm of using any of this ol' junk you got here fo' nuthin' but rust factories. Ain't everybody gits to beat up a master mechanic like me and then git this kind of work out of 'im!" Thomas adjusted his wrench slightly to get a better grip on the large rusty nut that was keeping him from getting to some of the important inner workings of the red Case combine. "And I ain't takin' odds on just how much you gon' git out of this one here just yet either. It's been lonely too long, I'd say."

"Well, Mr. Master Mechanic, we got two farmers dependin' on us to show up before the weeks' out. This thing used to work. There's no reason it can't now."

"No reason 'cept maybe what ain't rusted is rotten or wore out."

"There's a place up at Cleveland that ought to have plenty of parts to fit 'er," Ray protested.

Thomas chuckled, "Yeah, plenty of rusted and rotten and wore out parts."

Ray shook his head. "Do the best you can. If we can get a good week's work out of 'er, we'll replace what we can with new and rebuilt parts for next year."

Thomas opened his mouth to say more, but was stopped by the sound of tires on gravel. He and Ray both turned to watch the powder blue Lincoln Town Car roll onto the tractor lot. From their position beneath the big combine they could see no more than waist high of the individual who walked around the front of the car. Shiny wingtips and pin striped pants jutted out from under a tan overcoat. Hands were shoved as deeply as possible into the pockets of the oversized coat.

"Mr. Bennett?" a nervous sounding voice called.

"Lawyer?" Thomas asked quietly.

"Could be," Ray said climbing out from under the machine. "I guess I better find out. If it turns out to be a parole officer, you stay hidden. I don't want it to get around that you and me are breakin' the law by associatin'."

"How you doin'?" Ray said wiping the grease from his hands. "Excuse me for not shakin', but I'm a little on the greasy side this morning."

"No worry at all," the stranger said. "I'm Willard Holmes with the Delta State Bank."

Things had changed, Ray thought. He'd never paid that much attention as a youth, but, bankers making house calls had to be something new. This one was young and obviously on his way up. Judging from the car he drove and the clothes he wore, perhaps he was there already.

"What can I do for you, Mr. Holmes?"

The tall, pale man looked at his surroundings with a critical eye. Finally, he turned his gaze back to Ray and said, "I was hoping I could do something for you, Mr. Bennett." He smiled broadly.

"I'm wonderin' what that would be," replied Ray.

"Your recent exploits, if I may call it that, are giving you the name of a man who is going places, Mr. Bennett. You've proven yourself to be an aggressive businessman, one who will stick to his word and get the job done, no matter what." He looked into Ray's bewildered eyes. "I think you're a good risk," he said briskly.

Not knowing where the banker was going with all this, Ray could only think to offer a weak, "Well, . . . thank you."

"I understand you've lost some equipment," Willard Holmes continued. "And I know that what you do have is old and, like your combine there, requires a lot of repair and maintenance to get it going and keep it on the job."

Ray turned to admire the old combine. Like all of his equipment, he was quite proud of it and knew he could handle whatever job was to be done with it, old or not. "It gets the job done," he said defensively.

"Even so, there is only so much you can do with one combine and two cotton pickers. And what about the hay crop this summer? There is still a market for the square bales your existing baler produces, but most livestock people have turned to round bales. And there is talk that you may well see a big increase in business next year. You are going to have to expand to meet the demands on your services, Mr. Bennett. And you are going to need funding to back that expansion. My bank has funding available to you, Mr. Bennett, and I am here to offer our services to you." Holmes finished his presentation as if he were handing over a check right then and there.

Ray took his cap off and smoothed his hair. Sighing, he said, "I've not had much need for credit over the past few years, Mr. Holmes. In fact, I've never borrowed a penny from anybody. But, I do know that banks don't just hand out money on a promise and a handshake."

"You are right about that, Mr. Bennett. Collateral is always necessary. But, you do have some land and a house. And, while we are not necessarily interested in loaning on used equipment, we have some very attractive plans that will get you most of the new equipment you need. Further along, you can get a construction loan with permanent financing to follow for a first rate facility here, if you like."

The man seemed to be rather free with his employer's money. Immediately a thought slammed into Ray's mind. It almost angered him.

"Does Carl Sullivan have anything to do with this?" Ray queried.

Holmes' confused expression surprised Ray. It was as if the man was trying to think what answer would win him over. As if the perfect solution had been found, Willard Holmes regained his confidence and replied, "Mr. Sullivan", he thought an air of familiarity would be helpful, "if what I hear is correct, has been somewhat of a hindrance to your credit needs."

"Somewhat," Ray echoed.

"Why, then, would he be involved in such an opportunity as this for you to acquire the things you need most?" Phrasing the lie as a question seemed easier if not more truthful. In fact, Carl Sullivan was more involved in the transaction than any of Holmes' fellow bank officers. Debt was to be his newest weapon against Ray. With enough pressure and enough debt, Bennett Farm Services would fold. Carl would simply buy the paper or he would be the highest bidder at the foreclosure sale. Either way, he got what he wanted . . . everything he wanted.

"It's an interesting proposition," Ray said after a few moments of silence. "It's a sudden one, too. I'll have to think on it."

"Of course," Holmes said handing Ray a business card. "Just don't take too long. There are those on our lending committee who disagree with our assessment of your . . ., well, your credit worthiness. At least to the extent that I am ready to offer. Indecisiveness may tend to strengthen their position. You understand."

Ray nodded. "Yes, sir, I do. I won't keep you waitin'. You'll hear from me one way or another within a day or two."

They exchanged "It's been a pleasure's", and parted; Banker Holmes to his Lincoln and Ray to the underside of his combine.

Thomas asked what that conversation had been all about. Ray merely replied that it was no parole officer, ". . . just a banker."

The offer was appealing, though. For years, Ray had dreamed of how his business would grow. He knew just how he would go about it, depending on the time of year and what crops were expected to thrive from one season to the next. A mortgage on his home and land scared him, though. But, it was no different from the way most farmers he had known operated. And, like some he had known, it was no different from the way they lost everything they had.

At least one more cotton picker, and another combine, there was no doubt about that, and a big round baler. Trucks to pull them with and trailers to haul them on. This could get out of hand in a hurry! The end of the season was a bad time to go borrowing money. There would be no way to even begin paying it back until the hay season. But, it was a good time to make the best deals on equipment.

Looking at Thomas, Ray realized that his business had a lot of mouths to feed. Debt would take badly needed money out of his pocket. On the other hand, he knew that he would make a poor showing with the equipment he had on hand. He just couldn't produce what he needed to without more equipment to carry a heavier load. Maybe a new combine, a big truck and a trailer to haul it with, would be a good start. After all, he could make use of the combine to a small extent right away and all of next season. There was grain to harvest in the summer as well. He could arrange financing for haying equipment in the spring . . . maybe.

Thomas' tirade as a spring valve assembly fell apart in his hand closed the matter for Ray.

The familiar sound of a Ford pickup entering the lot barely caught the two men's attention. They didn't take their eyes from their work as the driver's door creaked open and slammed shut . . . twice.

"If you girls can tear yourselves away from that combine, we might get them pickers out of old man Tipler's field this afternoon," Bob said. "In the meantime, I thought I might go ahead and burn off that back field."

Ray crawled from beneath the rusty bean header he was working on. "Go ahead, if your firebreaks're wide enough. I don't want to burn up the whole county!"

"I was cuttin' firebreaks before you were born. Most folks around here don't use 'em anyway."

"Well, I appreciate your vast knowledge on the subject," Ray replied. "I'll send Matt over to disk up a break in the old hay field as soon as he gets in from school. There ain't no partic'lar hurry in burnin' any of this stuff, but we might as well get it done now. Keep an eye on 'im."

"I'll make sure he keeps the break well back from the creek," Bob said. "If that fire was to get up into them dry trees along the bank and over into Carl's dried up corn field, folk's might think poorly of you. Those that lived through the fire, that is."

Instead of going home for dinner, Ray went into town. Delta Hills served her surrounding farming communities well. Equipment and implement dealers generally kept a good stock of the things "their farmers" needed. If it was not on their lots, Winstead County farmers, and adjoining county farmers as well, didn't need it. Ray found what he was looking for at two of the four dealers he shopped. If all went well he would be in the big time combining business soon.

Willard Holmes sounded surprised, and somewhat nervous, to be hearing from Ray so soon after his visit. "No, no," he assured Ray, "the funding you need is available. It's not necessary for you to come by the bank today. In fact, as soon as we have the documentation ready I'll bring it out to you." Then he hastily added, "With a certified check, of course!"

Refusing to believe his luck, Ray asked, "Don't you need surveys of my land and such?"

Seeming to grope for words, Holmes finally replied, "Certainly, we do, Mr. Bennett. But, we obviously need to fast track your loan. The documentation I bring will include agreements from you to allow surveys and inventories to be done at a later date. And although it has already been approved, I'll take a short application just for our records. Auditors, you know."

"Yeah, I guess so," Ray lied. In fact, he knew nothing of auditors nor the lending process. It all seemed so much more simple than he had imagined it would be. "Good then! I'll see you in the morning, and then you can arrange to have your equipment delivered."

"Great!" Ray said. He smiled as he hung up the phone. "Now to make a few more calls. Bennett Farm Services is on the way!"

Keeping the news of his latest triumph to himself was difficult, but Ray was determined that the delivery of a shiny new combine atop a shiny new trailer pulled by a shiny new truck would be a surprise to his crew. Their reactions had already played themselves out in his mind. Thomas would try to invent a reason to take it apart and see what it looked like inside. Matt would be having a silent fit to drive it, but would be too shy to ask. And Bob . . . well, Bob was a hard man to impress. And Lori. She would be so proud. Perhaps she might even see a better future in the reflection of the bright red paint. The kids would climb all over it. His parents would marvel at their son's ability to acquire such an expensive piece of machinery so soon. If Gran could only be there to see it all! What would she think? Would she approve? And Emmy. Would she even notice? And if she did, would she begin to think that maybe there is something to this sorry ex-con after all?

Suddenly, a new thought struck Ray. If he could not be known by Emmy as her father or even a family friend, maybe . . . just maybe she would come to know him as a person worthy of some respect. As much as he wanted his daughter to be proud of him, there would never be any reason on her part for that. Respect was the next best thing. It was all he could hope for.

"You girls went a little heavy on the make-up, didn't you?" Ray chided as the blackened faces of Bob and Matt hurried for the water hose.

"Wind shifted on us," Bob replied. "We had to beat the fire out with feed sacks."

"Purt' near got into the pines on the far fence line," Matt said as Bob scowled at him.

Ray couldn't resist the opportunity. "It couldn't of happened, Matt," he said, "Mr. Bob here has been cuttin' fire breaks since before I was born. There's nuthin' I can tell him about containin' fire. No, sir. This man is a pyro pro!"

Matt was obviously confused as to what it was that Ray and Thomas found so funny that would make Bob stomp off muttering to himself about the lack of respect the younger generation had these days.

"Matt," Ray said, "as soon as you get cleaned up a little, I need you to get dirty again cleaning out a couple of these stalls." He pointed to the tractor shed. How 'bout gittin' everything out of that wide stall yonder and that other one where the big tractor is parked. Find something to park that tractor under, though, will you?"

"Yes, sir," the boy replied. Only Thomas and Bob thought to question this move by the looks on their faces.

"He needs something to do," was Ray's only answer. "Let's go see if we can get those pickers out of Mr. Tipler's field. I reckon he'd like to gin what cotton there is in the bins before it closes down."

The arrival of the new combine had been almost as Ray had imagined. Almost! As soon as it was unloaded from the big trailer, Thomas was probing all over it checking fluid levels, testing gauges and levers. Matt, who had just come in from school, climbed into the cab and gazed longingly at the controls. Bob took a brief walk around the big machine and pronounced her a "beaut" and then muttered something about "borrowing us down the river" as he headed out to disk up more fire breaks.

Ray sent Matt to get Lorraine and the kids. Pat and Mary came down as soon as Pat got in from work. The kids climbed all over it. Pat and Mary, sure enough, beamed with pride at their son's resourcefulness. It was almost as he had imagined.

Lori slowly circled the combine. Without a word she studied the two headers that had come in on a separate trailer. She stood in front of the shiny new truck and trailer that would haul the equipment of Bennett Farm Services and stared into its grill as if facing down a competitor for her fiancée's affections.

Ray, somewhat puzzled by Lori's response, or lack of, swaggered a bit as he strode to her side. He stood for a moment, admiring the scene, as he was sure Lori was also doing. Finally, he said, "You haven't said anything."

Keeping her eyes planted on the front end of the big truck, Lori replied, "Your parents are here."

"Yeah," Ray said, "Yeah." When Lorraine didn't respond, Ray asked, "So what's that got to do with it?"

He almost reflexively took a step back as his wife-to-be turned to face him with a pair of cold, rock hard eyes. "They think I'm some kind of a lady. And the children do not need to hear what I have on my mind. So, I'm saving my comments for when I won't be overheard by any unknowing, innocent ears, Raymond Lee!"

Her words had a biting quality. Ray was not sure that it was possible to speak so softly and so harshly at the same time, but, Lori had done it perfectly.

"You don't . . . like it?" he said innocently.

She stood in stony silence.

"It's not really the top of the line, but it's close," he said. "She'll do fine for us."

"Us?" Lorraine mocked. "She'll do fine for us? Or will she do fine for you?"

"Us, of course, darlin'!" Ray said having no idea as to what was going on. "A big part of our future is tied up in that baby! It's for you and me and the kids. It's for Matt and Billie Rose and Thomas and Bob. Sure it's for us!"

"Just what else is tied up in it, Ray?"

"What 'chu mean?"

"I mean how much of our future have you given to this machine? Our house? Our land? Everything we own?"

"Machinery is what provides for us," Ray responded, still bewildered.

"How could you make this kind of a decision without discussing it with me?" Lorraine countered. "You said we would be partners."

"Well, I wanted to surprise you. And . . . we will be partners. In a few days." Before the words left his mouth Ray Somehow knew this was not the thing to say.

"Just not yet! Is that what you mean?" Lorraine turned to walk to her car calling the children as she went.

"No, that's not really what I meant, Lori," Ray said weakly. "I just thought it was my decision to make is all."

Lori glared at him. "Well, you made it didn't you?"

"I might could of gone about it better, but it was the right decision. You'll see," Ray said defensively.

"Maybe I will, maybe I won't!"

Before Ray could think of anything else to say, Lorraine was driving through the gate. The kids were staring back through the rear windshield of the small car waving happily.

By supper time the new combine had been loaded back on the new trailer and the bean header had been loaded onto an old flatbed trailer for the trip to Holly Bluff and Bing Russell's soybeans. All four of the Bennett crew had worked hard to rebuild the wooden flooring and sides on two grain box trailers. Everything was ready, Bing had been called, and the outfit was prepared for an early start to a long day. Matt had talked Ray into letting him skip Wednesday's half day of school. Although an early bedtime was on Ray's mind, he couldn't wait another day to straighten things out with Lori.

A timid knock on the door brought Davey Jr's face between a crack in the blinds.
"Ray's here," he called.
Lori opened the door and stood silhouetted against the light pouring from within the living room. After a moment she said, "Do you feel like you have to knock to get into your own house?"
Fumbling with his gray felt cowboy hat Ray replied, "Well, I was kind of at a loss for just what I should do. I think . . . I know I messed up, Lori. It ain't much of an excuse that I've been away for so long and I don't know just what the right thing is all the time. But, I did figure out two things. I'll catch on to more as we go along and hopefully before I mess up again. But, anyway, I don't ever want to let the night pass with anger between you and me. I want us to work things out, if we can, and especially when one of us makes a mistake . . . like today. There ain't no need in drawin' lines when one of us hurts the other unintentionally. We just need to understand each other better is all. And the other thing is, we'll be partners. In everything. And I'm sorry I didn't think up that one sooner." Ray shuffled his hat from one hand to the other

and back and turned to leave. "And another thing," he said turning back, "this is as much your house as it is mine. It's ours." He took two steps back. "And you look real pretty standin' there with the light behind you like that."

Lori's hands slipped from her hips as she sighed. "What am I gon' do with you?"

Ray sniffed and rubbed his nose. "I could use some trainin', for sure."

"Well, come on back up here and we'll sit in this swing and shiver while I tell you what I decided." She went back into the house and came out half a minute later wearing her coat.

"I decided," Lori said without skipping a beat, "that you know a lot more about what it takes to keep the business going than I do. If I'm gonna be your partner in this thing, which I figure means I just don't get paid for whatever it is I do, I need to learn. And I want you to teach me."

"I was wrong. I should have talked to you," Ray said.

"Maybe. But, I overreacted. I haven't done anything for you, and yet I go crawlin' all over you for makin' a good decision that needed makin' right then. If I'm gon' be rakin' your cute little butt over the coals, I better learn all about it first."

Ray shook his head and grinned. "I doubt it will make much difference to me whether I get my tail chewed by an expert or some ignorant girl. Seems to me it will be bad either way."

"Yeah, but, if I'm gon' give a tail chewin' I'd rather it be an intelligent one." They laughed and hugged.

"Well, after the beans are in, there'll be plenty of time for teachin'," Ray replied. "Unless I can pick up some cultivating work there won't be nuthin' else for us to do to make money until the hay season. I 'spect we'll do alright from then on."

Lori grew serious. "What about Bob, and Thomas? And Matt, for that matter?"

"Oh, there's plenty for them to do. I want to spend the winter gittin' everything in top shape. Equipment, fences, barns. It'll be tight, but there's enough money in the bank to git us all through. Besides, I been thinkin' about a little sideline for me and Thomas to partner up in."

"Oh? What's that?" Lori quizzed, her interest piqued.

"Well, he's real good at gittin' all this old equipment goin'. And he's just as good at body work and paintin'. I was thinkin' maybe we could get our hands on some old farm equipment, you know, tractors, pickers, implements and such, real cheap. I can buy 'em, and then Thomas can fix 'em up. Then we sell 'em at good prices and do it all over again. And we split the money."

Lorraine smiled. "Sounds like a plan."

After a moment of silence, she turned to Ray, serious again. "It's kind of strange, you bein' such good friends with Thomas and all. I mean, I like him and Linda. They're real nice people. It's just that, you don't see many white folks and black folks with the kind of relationship you two have. Not around here anyway. How did you get to be so close?"

Ray sighed and tightened his lips. He had tried hard not to think of his years at Parchman. True, thoughts and memories would creep in, especially during the long lonely hours on a cotton picker. But, he usually managed to push them away with plans or daydreams. But, the memories were there. Unavoidable. And they were not all bad.

"I had been locked up for eight, maybe nine years. My hard time was mostly behind me. I say hard, because I made it that way. When I first went in, I got picked on a lot. I was young. I was skinny. And I was scared, I don't mind tellin' you. I kept to myself. There were acquaintances, I guess you'd call 'em, but no real friends. I got beat up a lot, too. The same guy mostly kept after me. Him and his cronies'd catch me out somewhere and start pickin' and pushin' and soon there would be a fight, and I would be the one left layin' on the ground or the bathroom floor or where ever they could get me."

"They didn't . . .!" Lorraine gasped in horror.

Reading her mind, Ray assured her, "No! No, not much of that kind of thing goes on up there. Mostly it's guys who used to try hard to prove how tough they were on the outside trying harder to prove it on the inside. The funny thing was, they never did anything by themselves. They always ganged up and his buddies did most of the fightin' for 'im"

"The guards didn't stop them."

"You're pretty much on your own. Oh, the guards kept order and all, but if they didn't see anything happen, they didn't do anything. And the one thing a con doesn't do is snitch. Well, I wasn't in bad shape. I'd always worked and all. But, I started workin' out as best I could. One day, they got me again, early that mornin'. Just bein' mean. I decided it was time to take the offensive."

"By the afternoon, I was feelin' alright. I was sore, but, I could move. And it seemed to be the best way to get the message across to 'em. I sucked it up and walked straight across the yard to where they were sittin'. I bet everybody on the yard had stopped what they were doin' and watched me as I walked. I went right up to ol' Sledge Gibson, the leader of the gang, if you could call him that. Before anybody knew what was happening I had 'im by the shirt and swung 'im around and into a brick wall. Before he could get himself together I was punchin' 'im and shovin' his head right back into that wall. He swung at me and fell and I kicked 'im when he was down. I mean I never let up. Before the guards pulled me off, Sledge had a broke nose and two cracked ribs. The guards held me close enough to where I could kick 'im where it hurt the most, and when they hauled me away ol' Sledge was pukin' and bleedin' all over the place."

"They took you away? Why not him? He was the trouble maker!" Lorraine exclaimed.

"Just doin' their job. I spent some time in solitary for that. But, they told me before they locked me down that they had let me go for as long as they could. They knew Gibson had been givin' me trouble and, all in all, they were glad to see me give some of it back."

Lori sat speechless for a few moments. "What happened when they let you out of solitary?"

Ray chuckled, "Sledge sent one of his boys to warn me that I was in for it big time. Well, naturally, he caught me where we couldn't be seen, so I jumped on him! He didn't expect it, and I was able to work him over pretty good. He was down on the floor groanin', so I took his pants off of 'im and carried them out to Sledge."

Lori's mouth had fallen open. She could not believe what she was hearing.

"Threw 'em right in his face, and beat him up again! When I got out of solitary that time, I went straight to Sledge. I said, 'Sledge, we can go like this for the rest of our time. I can beat you up, and two or three of your girls here can beat me up. But, I'll always come back. Or we can decide here and now that it's over. Either way, I'm through takin' your crap.'"

"And?" Lori pressed.

"He agreed," Ray said simply. "I never had a problem with Sledge or any of his guys again."

Lori thought for a moment before remembering her original question. "So what does all that have to do with Thomas?"

Smiling, Ray continued. "Well, by this time, I had myself a reputation of sorts. The number of fights and the number of people I had whipped at one time multiplied every time the story was told. Worked to my advantage. Most folks left me alone. They had heard that it was the best way to avoid a good whuppin'. I still wasn't interested in makin' friends, so bein' left alone suited me fine. Or at least I thought it did. After six or seven years, my attitude changed. Somebody reminded me of the person I had been, and the kind of person I should be. Well, from then on, I stayed out of trouble, for the most part. Oh, some hotshot would come in and hear some story about me and try to start trouble, but I ignored it when I could."

"And Thomas?" Lori prodded.

"One day, this big black guy showed up. He moped around for a few days and some of the other cons got to callin' him cry baby and mama's boy and stuff like that. Well, he got enough of it and thought the best way to handle the situation was to find somebody to fight. I wasn't the toughest guy there, but, like I said, I had me this reputation and, a lot of the boys thought it was time I actually fought to keep it. So they goaded inmate Thomas Washington into pickin' a fight with me."

Ray chuckled again. "He tried everything. He bumped into me, he stepped on my toes. He accused me of being rude to him, and I guess I was since I rarely acknowledged 'im. One day, he walked right up to me, and got right in my face. He said, 'I want to talk to you.' I looked up at him and said, 'I know you've been tryin' to break the ice an' all, but I don't really think I'm your type."

Lori's eyes widened and she gasped, "You didn't!"

"Yeah," Ray laughed. "I did. Well, that was the end of the rope for Thomas. He reared back and took a swing at me. Luckily, I knew it was coming, so I ducked. I stuck my leg out and pushed him and he fell. When he gets up, I said, 'Buddy, what is it you hope to gain by beatin' me up?' Well, this took him aback! He stopped and thought a minute and said, 'So you're scared I'm gon' beat you?' I said, 'Naw, I ain't sacred. I been beat up before an' I imagine I'll get beat up again.' He looked at me and said, 'So you want to give up 'cause you know I'll beat you?' I just laughed a little and said, 'I haven't said whether I think you can or you can't! I just want to know what you hope to gain if you do beat me.'

'Maybe everbody'll leave me alone,' he says. 'Thomas,' I said, 'If you beat me, you're liable to have to fight half the girls in here now, and most of the hot to trot newbies tryin' to prove something just like yourself!' And then I told 'im. 'On second thought, come on, and I'll let you whup me. That way maybe they'll leave me alone!'

Lori was laughing by now. "So what did he do?"

"Well, by now, everbody on the yard was itchin' to see a fight. As a matter of fact, they were gittin' upset because it didn't look like one was about to happen. A couple of the long timers got three or four new guys worked up and the five of 'em decided to jump on us. They wanted to beat me, and they didn't figure Thomas for a fighter by now."

"Five?" Lorraine asked astonished.

"Five or six. I lose count," Ray replied. "Well, me and Thomas backed up to each other and took 'em on. And we were doin' alright until the guards broke us up. Thomas and me shook hands, ate dinner together, which was a new experience for both of us, and became great friends. We've been tight ever since. . . .'do anything for each other."

"That's a great story," Lorraine sighed.

Ray looked down and shook his head slightly. "There ain't many good stories to tell from that time."

"You never talk about it."

"I try not to think about it, Lori. I'm afraid of what might happen if I dwell on it too much. Besides, I'm out now. I'm fixin' to marry a good woman, and I'm gettin' me a fine family to boot!"

"I know it's hard," Lorraine said in something like a whisper, "but, it may help to talk about it. And when you're ready, I'm here for you."

Rubbing her leg, Ray said, "I know that. Someday, maybe. But, for now, no more prison stories, o.k.?"

22.

The noise that filled the Bennett house all but drowned out the persistent knocking at the door. The usual high decibel levels produced by Jimmy's and Sarah's kids were at least doubled by the happy sounds coming from Lorraine's children as well as Billie Rose and Matt. Pat rose from his comfortable seat in his recliner and ambled to the front door. Wondering who would be coming by so close to dinner time on Thanksgiving Day, he knew it was someone they did not see often. Anyone showing up at the front door, as opposed to the one on the side of the house that was used far more often, was usually selling something he neither wanted nor needed or was bringing information of the same ilk.

Standing at his front door Pat found a rather tight faced middle aged white lady flanked by an older pleasant looking black lady. Neither smiled, though the white lady immediately struck him as the rigid type. The black lady, who looked a bit sheepish and embarrassed, just appeared to have no reason for smiling at this moment.

"Is this the Bennett residence?" the tight faced lady spoke tersely.

Pat rubbed his chin wondering what was going on. "I reckon you already know it is," he replied. "What can I do for you?"

"I'm Mrs. Speakes, this," Tight-face said gesturing behind her, "is Mrs. Collins. We're with the county department of child welfare."

Pat said nothing.

Clearing her throat, Mrs. Speakes continued, "It is our understanding that you have one Matthew Warren and one Billie Rose Warren here."

"There's one of each, for sure," Pat said, "but, what business is it of yours whether they are here or not?"

By now, the house was near silence. Ray, having heard the kids' names mentioned moved to the door.

"I'm afraid, Mr. Bennett, that those children are our business, or more precisely, they are the county's business."

"How so?" Ray asked.

"You would be Raymond Lee Bennett?" Mrs. Speakes asked.

"Yes'm," Ray said. "Now what about Matt and Billie Rose?"

"We've come to take them, Mr. Bennett!" Mrs. Speakes blurted. "We've been alerted that the children have been abandoned by their father and that you have kept them with no legal authority to do so."

"They've been taken care of, and a sight better than they ever knew before, I might add," Ray said trying to control his voice. "Who sent you?"

"We have authority from . . ."

"That's not what I asked," Ray interrupted. "Who sent you? Who paid you to come out here?"

"I believe we've been insulted," Mrs. Speakes sputtered.

"I believe you or someone higher up in your organization has been paid to come out here and harass us," Ray countered. "Why in the world would you ladies drive all the way out here from town to show up on our doorstep at dinner time on Thanksgiving Day of all days, and come up with this nonsense about taking Matt and Billie Rose away?"

"It's our job!"

Ray stepped onto the porch. "I doubt this has anything to do with your job, ma'am!"

Mrs. Speakes' eyes darted about as she searched for something to say. "Never the less, we have the authority to take those children with us and we intend to do just that."

"Ma'am," Ray said evenly, "those two children are about to sit down to what is probably the only real Thanksgiving dinner they have ever had. They are among people who love them like their own and they are finding out what it is like to be a part of a real family. There have not been a lot of happy days in those two young lives, and there's no way I'm gon' let you walk in here and take them away from this one. I promised them a good time today, and I'm gon' give 'em one."

Mrs. Speakes took a step back and clutched at her throat. "If I have to come back with the sheriff, young man . . ."

"You do that, Mrs. Speakes," Pat said. "You go on and drag Sheriff Hogue away from his Thanksgiving meal so he can come out here and help you drag these young'uns away from theirs. See how happy that makes him. And then see how happy your agency head is when copies of pictures we've made this mornin' show up on the front page of the Jackson paper along with the ones we'll make of you and the Sheriff hauling those children away on Thanksgiving Day!"

Angry, but beaten, the lady turned away. "We'll be back."

The black lady, who had stood silent during the whole exchange quietly said, "I hope things work out. Those children are better off here."

Ray nodded his thanks.

Billie Rose was crying in Lorraine's arms. "Don't let them take us. Please don't let them take us!" she sobbed.

Matt stood staring after the car colored in what he called government green as it pulled onto the blacktop.

Ray knelt beside Billie Rose and stroked her hair. "Nobody's gon' take you anywhere today, honey. I promise. I'm gon' do all I can to keep you and Matt right here where you belong."

Looking into each other's eyes Lori and Ray reached a silent agreement. "In fact," he began, "Lori and me would like, that is, if it's o.k. with you, for you and Matt to come live with us from now on."

"You mean like adopted?" Billie asked excitedly.

Ray and Lori again exchanged looks, each wondering if it was right to get the little girl's hopes up on such an uncertain matter.

"That's just what we mean, darlin'." Ray accepted a hug from the girl. "If we can work it out. And we'll do our best. That sound alright with you, Matt?"

The boy looked about the room embarrassed at the tears that filled his eyes. "That's fine with me, Mr. Ray. Real fine."

Maybe we can change that "Mr. Ray" to something else, Ray thought to himself. Turning to his father he said, "I got me a errand to run before dinner."

Knowing what Ray had in mind Pat replied, "We'll wait dinner for you, son."

Ray smiled. "Won't be no need for that. I ain't got that far to go, and it won't take me long once I get there. I ain't about to be late for my first home cooked Thanksgiving dinner in near 'bout sixteen years!"

Just over a mile away, Carl Sullivan was presiding over the Thanksgiving Dinner table at his home. Miss Emily sat at the far end of the great table. Between them on either side sat Emmy, Jason, Laura and Clint, all with somber faces. Carl had long forgotten how to interject joy into such an occasion, if he had indeed ever known how. Despite her best efforts, Miss Emily was unable to overcome the pall her husband's demeanor served like some mood altering drug onto his family's plate.

A look of surprise and slight amusement crept into Carl's eyes when he looked up to see that Ray Bennett, who was now standing in the center of the dining room doorway, was the source of the slamming door and Rona's protestations.

"Had I known you were coming, Bennett, I'd have had Rona set you a place," Carl smirked while sweeping his arm across the table.

Everyone looked up in shocked surprise to see Ray standing once again in the same room with the man he had crippled.

Hesitating and taking his hat into his hands, Ray answered, "Folks, I'm sorry to be disturbing your meal. This ain't a social call. Carl, can we talk in private? Won't take but a minute or two." Ray's eyes swept the room. He hoped he did not allow his gaze to linger on Emmy for too long. She looked so pretty . . . and so angry.

"I don't do business on Thanksgiving Day, boy," Carl barked. "Football's coming on as soon as we finish eating. Call me tomorrow, maybe we can talk then. And I don't like you referring to me by my first name. You need to learn some respect," he added acidly.

The temper Ray had fought to control since entering the room was near the breaking point. "There's ladies and children in the room. I can't call you what I'd like to right now!"

Carl's gaze hardened. "Go on home, boy. I got nothing to discuss with you."

"I'm afraid you do, Carl. You want to do it here, or somewhere private?"

"The last time you got me off alone, I ended up in a wheelchair," Carl scoffed. "I don't plan to give you an opportunity to do worse. You finally come to take your revenge, did you?"

Ray drew a deep breath. "A few of us know why you're in that chair, Carl, and you had a whole lot more to do with it than I did. And a few of us know why I spent half my life in prison, and you had everything to do with that! But, that ain't the reason I'm here. I told you before, I'm not out for trouble, I just want to be left alone."

"So, what brings you here then?" Carl asked chewing nonchalantly on a bite of deep fried turkey. 'As if I didn't know,' he thought to himself.

"How many lives do you have to ruin, Carl, before you're satisfied?" Ray said, his voice trembling, fighting against his control.

Carl's face reddened. "Why, yours is enough for me, boy," he said after a moment.

"Carl!" Miss Emily scolded.

Ray fought to keep his eyes from shifting to Emmy. What must she be thinking now? "You just come on after me, then. But, you leave everyone else out of it! My parents, my wife-to-be and her children . . . and Matt and Billie Rose!"

"What have you done now, Carl?" Miss Emily said slowly. "Ray wouldn't be here like this if it weren't serious."

"Hush, Emily," Carl hissed. "Whose side are you on anyway?"

"I won't take the wrong side again," she replied evenly.

"Mother!" Laura whispered, a hint of desperation in her voice.

"You'd better get on out of here, Bennett," Carl ordered. "You've ruined my Thanksgiving dinner and now you're disrupting my family. I won't tolerate it!"

Ray's eyes narrowed. "Well, let me tell you something, you pompous jack-ass! I'm through tolerating your interference. Black ballin' me at local businesses and burnin' my cotton pickers is one thing. But, messin' with those two children's lives is something else altogether."

"Mighty serious accusations you're throwing around there. You should be careful."

"No, sir! You should be careful!"

"That sounds like a threat. Ain't that a violation of your parole?"

"You leave Matt and Billie Rose alone. Call whoever it is at the county that you have in your pocket, and tell them to leave those kids right where they are. Otherwise, you might see some serious parole violations. If I go back to prison on account of you again, it will be for something more substantial than one of your lies this time!"

By now Laura was standing. Near panicked, she wanted desperately to defuse the situation before any damaging information was revealed.

Already Emmy was questioning everything the two men were saying. "What? What does he mean by that? What lies?" She stood and moved aggressively toward Ray.

As she reached him, Laura shouted, "Emmy! Stop!"

Turning to look at her mother, Emmy's attention was drawn to the mirror hanging on the opposite wall. In the reflection, she appeared beside Ray. In that moment she recognized the eyes, the hair, the chin, even the expression. The features were hers, and yet they weren't. And they were not on her face. She turned and stared intently into the eyes of the man she had so despised for all her life. Connections were forming and fragmenting in her mind.

Rushing to gently shove Ray back through the dining room door Laura said, "Whatever it is, we'll take care of it, Ray. You should go now. This isn't good for the kids."

Ray looked down and shook his head as if to clear it of the violence that was pervading it. His eyes softened. "Miss Emily . . ., Emmy . . ., everybody, I'm sorry about . . . I'm just sorry."

"It's alright, Ray," Miss Emily said softly. "We understand your concern for those children. Don't worry."

Ray nodded slightly, almost imperceptibly. Eying Carl again, his face hardened. A look that had warded off many hardened criminals brought back something Carl had not felt for many years. Fear! Ray's parting remark left little doubt in Carl's mind that the young man would take no more pushing. He must be brought down. "You should end this," Ray said evenly. "Now."

Ray returned home just as the family was gathered for the blessing. In fact, Pat had delayed in hopes that Ray would be back in time to ask it himself. He did. And his anger and resentment left him as he recalled how blessed he had been.

"Forgive me for losing my temper, Lord, and please help Matt and Billie Rose," he silently added to his prayer before his barely audible "Amen" released the fidgeting children to jostle for position in the food line.

With so many mouths and so much food, it was impractical to load the Bennett table with food. Upon such occasions as family gatherings they ate buffet style. As Ray hung back to let the children go first Pat and Lorraine joined him.

"Did you do any good?" Pat said in a low voice.

"I don't know, Pop. I told him to back off. He won't though. He's too stubborn, too hard. Maybe Miss Emily and Laura can keep him off of Matt and Billie Rose."

"Did you see Emmy?" Lori asked.

Sighing, Ray related the confused look on her face. "I almost blew it," he said. "I was so mad at Carl I was ready to say anything." He looked at the children laughing and giggling over their plates. "I think I ruined her Thanksgiving."

Back at the Sullivan home, Carl was seething. "How dare him come in here like that! 'Finish this now', he says. I'll do just that, Bennett. You'll learn just what finished is!" he muttered.

Emily fixed her gaze upon him. "You leave him alone, Carl. And whatever it is you've done to those children, you undo it!"

"Don't be giving orders to me, woman!" he snapped.

"Just take care of it, Carl," Emily continued, her determination surprising her husband. "I mean it."

"You all finish your meal," Carl said rolling back from the table. "I've lost my appetite. I have some calls to make before the games start." Guiding his wheel chair through the French doors he called out behind him, "Clint, Jason, I'll meet ya'll in the den and we'll watch us some football." He almost sounded cheerful.

Later that evening, Buster's place was buzzing. Family time being over, his bar was filled with people who had their own ideas of a "proper" Thanksgiving celebration. Beer flowed continuously and whisky bottles appeared from back pockets, coat pockets, purses . . . and dollar fifty cans of soft drinks provided mixers for those who did not drink it straight. Conversation flowed as the drinks did and, as usual, more than a few secrets passed between people who hardly knew each other.

Two men, casual acquaintances at best, leaned against the railing that divided the bar area from the game area and learned that they had something in common, incentive to bring harm to one Ray Bennett. One was merely for money. The other was to satisfy a hatred. This particular bond made them fast friends in the most literal sense.

Ray kissed Lorraine as he and Matt prepared to leave the house. "Just think," he said, "in two more days I get to stay."

Lori looked at him appraisingly, "Well, we do have a couch, you know."

"Wouldn't be prudent," Ray replied with a weak impression of the vice president.

"Matt shouldn't have to sleep in that little camper of yours on such a cold night."

Ray shrugged. "He wants too and I'll be glad to have the company. Besides, we have to get an early start in the morning and there's no need to disturb you and the kids."

At that moment, Priscilla Marie appeared from the hall leading to her bedroom. Rubbing her eyes, she asked, "Mr. Ray, what am I supposed to call you after you and Mama get married?"

Squatting to meet the girl at eye level, Ray said, "Well, darlin', maybe that's something you and your mama should talk about. I want you to call me whatever makes you feel the best!"

"What are you going to call me?"

Smiling and taking both of the small shoulders into his hands, Ray replied, "Honey, I know I'm not your real daddy, but, I love you like you were my own, and if it's alright with you, I'd like to call you my little girl."

"What about when you leave?" Priscilla asked innocently. "Everybody leaves us."

Ray glanced up at Lorraine, who was blinking back a tear. After a moment he said, "Well, darlin', I ain't never gonna leave you or Susanna or Davey or your mama. Never! And I'm gon' try my best to be a good daddy to you. O.K.?"

Priscilla reached up with her tiny hands and hugged Ray tightly around his neck.

"O.K." she said. "I always wanted a daddy. When ya'll get married, can I call Mr. Ray Daddy, Mama?"

"That's just fine, honey," Lori managed to blubber, "You call him Daddy! Now go on back to bed and I'll come tuck you in."

23.

The day's iced tea and soft drinks pulled Matt from a wonderful dream where Emmy was once again astride her horse, leaning down to kiss him. Just as he told her he loved her and as she was about to say the same, he was sure, he awoke. Trying his hardest to remain in that dream state, Matt shut his eyes tightly. Maybe if he didn't actually see anything, his body would think he was still asleep and allow him to get his kiss. It was not to be, though. Nature was calling him . . . demanding, actually.

Glancing at his watch, Matt saw that it was two-ten a.m. Deciding that he'd better hurry since he had only about four hours left to sleep, he reached for his jeans. Something was different. His sleep numbed mind was telling him that something was different, but it wouldn't tell him just what that was.

He had already stepped from the camper in his sock feet and quietly closed the door before a hint of unnatural warmth brushed his cheek and the strange crackling sound reached his ears through the quiet of the winter night. It was then that an orange glow reflected on the side of the camper brought him around in sudden stunned alarm.

The pounding on the door and the rocking of the small camper drove Ray from the depths of his sleep. It was as if he knew he was sleeping, and at the same time he knew he must awaken. His fatigue had carried him into a sleep so deep that now, within his dream, he fought to wake himself up. He sensed an urgency. His brain . . . his whole head . . . was tingling wildly.

"Mr. Ray! Fire! There's fire out here!" Matt cried as he beat on the aluminum side of the camper.

Ray jerked himself up and stumbled to open the door. That loud crackling and popping noise that he had been unable to identify in his dream was all too suddenly made real and intensified by the wildly dancing shadows around him.

"You gotta get outta here, Mr. Ray! Everything's burning up!" Matt screamed.

Ray looked into the terrified eyes of the young man before him. "Where you been, son?" was all Ray could think to ask.

"I had to go to the bathroom. I came out and there was all this fire!"

Quickly slipping on his boots and coat, Ray walked out onto the tractor lot to see just what was happening. To his horror, he saw the big tractor shed nearly engulfed in flames. The tires on his little tractor were burning. The fire was moving through one of the stalls holding his oldest cotton picker. There would be no way to save it. The other picker would be next.

Suddenly, flames leaped up behind the structure. The pile of old dried hay had ignited. Soon the shed would collapse and everything within it reduced to ashes and worthless junk metal, like the pasture and fields now surrounding it.

Ray ran toward the cotton picker. It was not yet burning. If he could back it out of there, he could save it. He also had to save his big tractor. It was parked at the far end of the shed and was in the least danger. "Least danger", however, was a relative term. Most of the wood that made up the construction of the shed was decades, if not a century, old. And it would not long resist the urge to burn.

"Get your boots on," Ray called to Matt. "I need you to take my truck and run up to Mama's house and call Bob. Get Pop to call the volunteer fire department. And you stay up there away from this fire, you hear?"

Matt reached to catch the keys Ray tossed to him. He would go make the phone calls, but he would be back. Ray's truck, still bearing the scratches and scars of that night at Buster's place responded immediately to the turn of the key. Matt raced out onto the blacktop road that led to the Bennett's house not a mile away.

The cotton picker was not as quick to start as the truck had been. Flames licked at the wire mesh bin that held the cotton, and small pieces of old cotton that had remained trapped in the screen-like walls of the bin sizzled and flared. Ray backed out of the shed as a section of roof toppled down onto the spot the picker had occupied. He quickly maneuvered the lumbering machine out of the lot and onto the side of the road. Jumping down he saw the old combine that Thomas had worked so hard on surrender to the advancing flames. He knew he could only save the big tractor now. Everything else that was under that shed would be destroyed or rendered useless by the flames and the heat.

By the time he had run back to the tractor, the fire was fighting its way through the end wall of the shed. He felt the intense heat as he drove the tractor pulling the big disk Bob had used to plow up the fire breaks through the closed gate that led to his hay field.

Leaving the tractor a safe distance away, Ray ran back to the shed. He hoped beyond hope to save more of his equipment. Without it, he would be finished. There was no insurance. With the exception of the new combine, which was, thankfully, far away at Bing's farm, Ray had not found any one who would offer reasonable coverage. His stuff was all too old and supposedly not worth insuring. But to him, it was everything. Replacing it would be impossible.

The sound of a horn blasting rose above the roar of the flames. Ray saw Matt sitting in his truck blowing the horn and waving furiously. Running to see what the boy was trying so desperately to tell him, Ray turned to follow Matt's pointing finger and heard a primal anguished scream rise from within himself.

The fire had apparently followed the wind and made its way down the row of dry brush lining the fence row. It was taking Carl Sullivan's corn field! The stalks that remained in the field were certainly dry, but they also laid across each other making a horizontal surface of combustible material to feed the fire and lead it all the way to a stand of pine trees that stretched from the edge of the field to the Sullivan's back yard. Ray watched in horror as a tall pine engulfed in flame exploded and fell against the roof of the house. Running as hard as he could now and jumping into the back of the pickup, Ray yelled for Matt to "Go!"

The boy didn't have to ask where.

In the short minute that it took to reach the Sullivan house and speed up the winding driveway, the fire had spread astonishingly fast. It had taken no time for the flames from the fallen pine to melt through the vinyl siding covering the backside of the house. From there, there was nothing but the old original wood siding material, and no stopping the fire.

Ray could not believe what his own eyes were telling him. Flames were shooting through several windows of Miss Emily's house! His exhaustion was suddenly forgotten. He surged forward. "Stay back, Matt!" he yelled.

"Miss Emily!" he screamed. "Miss Emily!" He knew he was still too far away to be heard. He vaulted the five foot chain link fence surrounding the property and ran across the yard. The house was dark except for the flames shooting up the back side and pouring through three windows in the back. The massive front door was locked, of course. It probably had not been used in years. Ray beat on it and yelled but there was no response from within the house. Matt was frantically blowing the horn of the truck, but there was no apparent movement from inside.

Ray ran around the back side, leaping over pockets of fire in the grass and shrubbery. The French doors on the deck would be the easiest way to break into the house. The steps were burning, the old wood crackling, inviting the flames in. Ray climbed atop a small pile of firewood stored below the deck and jumped to reach the railing. Pulling himself over at almost the same place where Carl Sullivan had made his fall so many years before, he bounded across the deck in three quick steps. Using a wrought iron lawn chair, he smashed his way through the glass doors and ran into the house calling for Emily all the while.

The house was filling with smoke. He didn't know the large house well at all. He could only run through it calling and feeling his way along. It was dark, the fire having taken out the electricity, and the smoke prevented any moonlight from filtering through the windows. As fast as he tried to move, it was still slow work.

Doors, walls, beds. He felt his way through the rooms. Miss Emily could be lying unconscious on the floor anywhere in the house. What if he missed her? What if she had been inches away from him and he never knew it? Panic rose within him. Not for himself, but for fear of what would happen if he could not locate Miss Emily.

He knew that there were two bedrooms downstairs, four upstairs. He would have thought Miss Emily would be on the ground floor, and he worried that he may have missed her. But, when he had found and searched the two downstairs bedrooms as best he could, he made his way to the stairs. Ray never knew that his foot had barely brushed that of Carl Sullivan as he lay on the floor semi-conscious. He would make a quick sweep upstairs. If he didn't find her there, he would search again, more slowly and methodically. Even as he formed this plan in his mind, he knew that there would be no time for a second search. The smoke was growing thicker, the air more difficult to breathe.

As he reached the top of the stairs, he heard a loud crash. Then another voice calling, "Emmy! Emmy!" It was Matt!

"Get out, Matt. There's no time!" Ray called back.

Coughing, Matt shouted, "In the back. She's in the back bedroom upstairs. Emmy's there!"

Ray's heart stopped! "What?" he cried. "What did you say?"

"Emmy is in the back bedroom up there!" Matt shouted. "I saw her earlier in the window!"

Ray turned and felt his way down a narrow hall. He could feel more heat, and he saw the glow of flames. 'The back! That's where the fire first took hold!'

Panting and coughing he lunged forward. His foot caught the side of a piece of furniture in the hall and he fell hard, hitting his head on the floor. Dazed, he fought to hold onto consciousness. As he struggled to get to his feet he felt strong hands take hold of his arm and lift him.

"You o.k.?" Matt asked.

"Yeah, I'll make it. I told you to get out of here!"

"There's three people in here, you can't get them all by yourself. I know where Emmy is."

"Follow me."

Matt stayed close to Ray as he made his way to the end of the hall. He turned to the door on his left and thrust it open. "They're in here. Both of them are in here!" Matt said with relief.

Ray entered the room. The heat seemed to scorch his lungs when he breathed. The smoke was blindingly heavy, but in the glow of flames now licking at the walls on the far side of the room he could make out twin beds. What at first appeared to be a pile of clothing on the floor turned out to be Miss Emily. Apparently she had come upstairs to wake Emmy and had been overcome by the smoke.

"I'll get Emmy! You take care of Miss Emily." He knelt beside Emmy's bed and tried to revive her, first by talking to her and nudging her gently. He then shouted and shook her. She seemed to come to. Her eyes opened and then she coughed.

"Come on, Sugar, we've got to get out of here."

"Wha . . . What's happening?" Emmy asked. Then, the realization of the situation hit her. She screamed as a section of ceiling fell on top of her and ignited the covers. Ray beat furiously at the flames with his bare hands. He threw the smoldering material away from the bed and tore at the burning covers. Emmy screamed in pain.

"It's o.k.," Ray said evenly. "You'll be alright. Come on." He lifted her swiftly but gently from the mattress as it burned around her.

"Mamaw? Mamaw!" Emmy cried.

"It's alright, Matt's taking good care of your grandmother."

"She's awake! I'm going to help her out," Matt shouted.

Ray noticed that Matt's voice was shaking. He turned to see what was going on.

"Emmy? How's Emmy?" he said just loud enough to be heard.

"Go ahead. We're right behind you."

Ray pressed Emmy into himself and moved toward the door as quickly as he could. She was coughing violently, gasping for breath. When they reached the top of the stairs, Ray adjusted his hold on her for more stability. "Don't you let go of me!" he ordered. "Matt?" he shouted.

"We're here."

Ray and Emmy moved into the hall. The smoke was very heavy. Almost immediately, her coughing grew worse. "Let's move fast," he yelled. "Go!"

When he reached the bottom of the stairs he drew his first breath since starting down, he shifted Emmy again. She moaned in pain.

"Matt?" he called again.

"Still here," came the reply, only it was not so close behind him as before.

Flames nearly surrounded them now. Ray felt Emmy huddle closer to him. Looking around, he decided that the shortest way out was the best way out.

"We're going to the deck," he called behind him.

"Go ahead."

Matt's voice sounded distant, strained.

Holding Emmy, he trotted toward the french doors. Reaching the opening, Ray saw that the deck was engulfed in flames. Emmy screamed. Tears ran down her face.

"Through the den!" Ray shouted, but he heard no reply. "We're going out the den door," he yelled again. He still got no reply, but he thought he heard coughing. A woman coughing. Miss Emily.

The den had four exposed wood beams running across it. Two of these were now burning. Covering Emmy's head as best he could with his hand, Ray carried her beneath them. He saw that the full length window beside the door had been broken through. This must be where Matt made his way into the house.

"Here we go, Honey. Watch for glass. Through the window!" he shouted, but, again, there was no reply.

Ray stepped through the window. He stumbled, but caught himself before he fell. He carried Emmy to the far side of the wide driveway beside the house. As he put her down gently, he saw that the grass beyond the road was burning.

"God, help us," he prayed.

Just then a loud roaring and cracking sound came from inside the house. One of the beams had fallen!

"Mamaw!" Emmy cried hoarsely.

"Stay here, Emmy! Don't move, you understand me?" he said forcefully.

She nodded her head. Even as she did, she saw Ray running back to the house. His body was silhouetted against the flames. She saw him moving back and forth in front of the window as if he were trying to see inside or to decide what to do. Then, he disappeared through the same opening he had just brought her out of.

"Matt!" Ray called through the roar of the flames. "Miss Emily!"

Coughing! He heard coughing. "Matt!" he shouted.

"Over here," came a weak reply.

The beam had fallen at one end leaving it leaning against the wall. Ray crawled through to find Matt lying on the floor trying to protect Miss Emily from the intense heat now permeating the room. His arm was bleeding and he was gasping for breath.

"Get Miss Emily out of here!" Matt shouted, fighting for the breath needed to speak. "That beam got me. Busted some ribs, maybe my hip!"

"Can you walk if I help you up?" Ray asked.

"Don't worry about me. Just get her out."

"I will, I promise, but I ain't leavin' you in here. We've got to get out now!"

"Get her . . ." Matt looked into Ray's stubborn eyes. "O.K. Help me up. I'll follow you."

"You sure?"

"Sure as I can be."

Ray lifted Matt to his feet. Matt winced and grimaced with pain.

"This must be like Hell, ain't it, Mr. Ray?"

"Closest thing we'll find to Heaven tonight is through that window yonder," Ray replied forcing a grin. Ray turned and lifted the unconscious form of Miss Emily from the floor. "Don't you worry none. Me and Matt'll get you out of here just fine." He squatted and waddled his way back under the fallen beam. The effort caused him to take deep breaths which brought on a violent coughing spell. Still, he moved toward the window. "Come on, Matt!"

Just as he stepped through the window the second beam crashed to the floor sending flames and embers in all directions, including through the window. He fell to the ground still cradling Emily. "That was close, huh?" On his knees he turned back to the house. "Matt?" There was no answer!

Ray scrambled to his feet and ran with Miss Emily across the drive and laid her down beside Emmy. At that moment, Thomas' wrecker pulled up. Thomas and his oldest son jumped out. Ray shouted, "Take care of her!" and ran back to the house.

"Matt! Matt!" he shouted. But there was no answer. The room was now consumed by fire. Ray shielded his eyes with his arm and tried to see through the window.

The boy was nowhere to be seen. He had promised Matt he would not leave him. He grabbed onto each side of the window to help propel himself into the room. The old wood window frame had caught fire when the second beam fell, but Ray didn't notice. He was intent on saving Matt. His hands, though, felt what his eyes had not seen. He bellowed in pain and anger as he recoiled from the window and fell to the ground.

Ray stood shakily and crouched, determined to find Matt and bring him out. Just as he took his first running step he felt the powerful arms of Thomas Washington surround him and hold him back.

"No," Ray cried. "Let me go. Matt's in there. No!"

"He ain't comin' out," Thomas said hugging his friend with tears in his eyes. "He ain't comin' out."

Ray turned and stumbled to the small group huddled beyond the driveway. His hands, throbbing with pain, were cradled against his chest. Emmy was shivering from cold and shock. Her hair was singed and the stench of burned flesh filled the air around her. Miss Emily lay barely conscious on the ground. Trying to take off his coat to give it to Emmy, Ray cried out in pain as his fingers closed around the buttons.

"Carl," Emily managed to say. "Carl's in the front room. There at the corner."

"My, God! I must of missed 'im!" Ray started back toward the house, but Thomas stopped him again.

"You're all done in, Ray. I can git 'im."

As he ran across the yard in front of the burning house, Thomas was a mere silhouette to Ray's eye. His son called out for him, but Thomas ran unhesitatingly to the window at the front corner of the house. He kicked out the window and smoke streamed out, but there were no flames here yet. He disappeared into the house. Ray grew concerned as the seconds turned into minutes and the leaping reflections of flames shone through the window.

Shouts, faint words against the noise of fire consuming the old house, could be heard. Surely there had been enough time to locate Carl. Just as Ray moved to go in himself, Thomas appeared at the window. He was desperately pulling the form of Carl Sullivan through the window. Tears came to Ray's eyes. He was praying that it would be Matt who was carried out of the house. As Carl's lifeless legs fell to the ground flames were licking the top of the window.

"Come on, man! Hurry!" Thomas was shouting. Ray struggled to his feet, trying to get to Thomas with the help he was calling for. "Just jump!"

Coughing and gasping for air young Matt fell through the window. The lower left leg of his jeans was burning. Thomas quickly dropped Carl to the ground and beat the flames from Matt's leg. "Oh, thank you, Lord. Thank you," Ray said through his tears.

"It's Matt! I got Matt!" Thomas shouted as he carried the boy away from the intense heat now pouring through the window he had just fallen out of.

Ray helped Thomas ease Matt to the ground. Thomas turned and ran back toward the house. "I got to get that man!" he shouted. He could only drag Carl across the ground with great effort. When He reached a safe distance, Thomas fell to the ground. It had taken every ounce of strength he had, but Carl and Matt were both out of danger of the fire. He could only pray that he had reached them in time.

Moving by sheer will, Thomas moved to where Matt lay on the ground. "Here," Thomas said softly lifting Matt from the cold of the ground, "Let's get you and the lady here into the truck where you'll be warm." After his son had lead Miss Emily to the open door of the wrecker he gently placed Matt on the seat beside her. They could only lean against each other in their weakened states.

"Where's Carl?" Emily asked weakly.

Thomas looked at Ray and then back at Emily. "He . . . he's out, ma'am. I found him alright. He was on the floor by the bed. He kept saying 'The boy! The boy! He's by the door!' I guess he heard Matt somehow. Anyway, I went and found Matt layin' just outside the bedroom. How he made it that far, I don't know. Anyway, ma'am, what it comes down to is that your husband was willing to give his chance of gittin' out to Matt. But, they both out, ma'am. They both got out." Thomas' voice cracked with emotion.

Thomas started the engine and turned the heat up. "Come on, Ray, there's room for you in here, too. Linda called for an ambulance, but maybe we better get those we can move on up to the hospital."

"No," Ray muttered, "I need to be with Emmy." Looking around, he saw that the fire was still moving through the dry grass of the pasture. "You better go cut a break. The fire's still spreading."

Thomas swallowed hard. "It's dyin', Ray. Nuthin' left to burn, and there ain't nothin' much we can do now."

"Well," Ray said. He nodded his head slightly as if to punctuate Thomas' statement. Turning his attention to

Emmy, he realized for the first time just how badly she was injured. She lay on the ground groaning and wheezing.

Ray knelt beside her. "You just lie still, darlin'. Help's on the way. It's gon' be alright." Tears filled his eyes. He reached for her hand. He clinched his teeth with pain as his hand came into contact with hers, but he would not let go.

Her face stayed straight and still, but her eyes shifted to Ray. "Mamaw?" she pleaded in a harsh whisper.

"She's all right. We got 'er out."

"I always spend the night on Thanksgiving. We're gonna decorate for Christmas tomorrow."

"Why, I bet ya'll can fix this old place up real fine. I'd sure like to see it."

"She always wanted my help. Ever since I was a little girl."

"Miss Emily loves you very much. She's told me so."

"I wanted to ask her about the mirror . . . today." Emmy's voice was growing weaker by the moment. "What I saw."

Ray was taken aback. "Why, honey . . . I . . ."

"I heard them arguing . . . after you left today." Her voice was unnatural, raspy.

"I'm sorry I ruined your day."

"Please. I need to know!"

"You just rest up. You need your strength."

The girl seemed to drift away for a long moment. "I'm real sorry for the way I've acted," she said softly. "I didn't give you a chance."

"Now don't you worry none about that," Ray said gently pushing her singed and matted hair back from her face. It broke his heart to look into his daughter's pained eyes, to see her burned flesh. He forced a smile.

"I think you're really a good man." She could speak only in a coarse whisper now.

"Well," Ray sighed fighting the tears in his eyes and the cry in his throat, "that means the world to me, darlin'. It really does."

"You saved my life." she said weakly. "Matt?"

Turning away, Ray could not hide his grief and pain much longer. "You rest now, Emmy. Everything's gon' be fine. But, you have to rest. I'll just sit here with you."

Her condition terrified him. He wondered if he was successfully hiding it.

His daughter's "O.K." was almost inaudible. Her eyes closed.

Ray looked around toward the road as if that would bring the ambulance to Emmy's aid any faster. When he looked again into her face, he was surprised to see her staring at him. "Please . . . tell me the truth," she pleaded. "Everybody lies to me." She fought for breath. "Are you my father?"

Stunned, he fumbled for words. How could he lie to her now? But, should he tell her now? "Yes, darlin', I am." He decided to be who he was. "And I love you very much. I always have."

Tears streamed from Emmy's eyes. "I knew," she managed a slight smile. "I just knew."

"Everybody loves you, Emmy. People you don't even know love you. And Jesus loves you, darlin'."

"I know," she said looking past Ray. "I can see Him!" Her voice was weak, barely a whisper. "I wish I knew you," she said to Ray.

Before he could open his mouth to speak Emmy had slipped back into merciful unconsciousness. A few long minutes later, Pat and Mary drove up. And almost immediately behind them the Coleman Volunteer Fire Department in its one small pumper truck pulled up.

Mary, in a long terry cloth robe, ran to Ray's side. He recoiled in pain as she reached to examine his hands. Pat, seeing that Ray was able to get around, knelt at Emmy's side. This was as physically close as he had ever been to his granddaughter.

One of the volunteer firemen trotted over carrying a first aid kit. The other firemen went to work on the house. It was heavily involved in flame, and there was not enough water available to save even part of it.

The county sheriff, followed by two deputies, pulled rapidly up the drive, blue lights flashing. Surveying the situation, the sheriff ordered one of the deputies to radio in and find out where that ambulance was. The other deputy, Leon Pitts, strode about the area trying to look as if he were in charge.

"My son is injured!" Mary called.

"Bring him over here and let's have a look," Hogue replied.

Ray refused to leave Emmy's side.

A Cadillac carrying the rest of the McKay family screeched to a halt. Clint and Laura ran frantically toward the house, but stopped when Pat yelled for them to come over to the wrecker.

There, Emily was shivering and crying, and Matt was still unconscious, but breathing oxygen provided by one of the firemen. On the ground in front of the wrecker, bathed in the rays of several flashlights lay the trembling, whimpering form of Emmy. Ray and Mary and Pat hunched silently around her. Laura gasped and fell to the cold ground beside her daughter.

"You did it this time," Clint said as he charged toward Ray. He pushed him hard against the shoulder.

"Now hold on here. Just what are you gettin' at?" Pat growled. He caught Clint by his left arm and pulled him back.

Clint was still intent on getting at Ray.

"We all heard your threats today! You did this. Don't deny it! Are we supposed to think that your little grass burning just got out of hand, Ray?" Clint accused. "You and your ignorant foreman screwed up, didn't you?"

"We didn't . . ." Ray started.

"It's too late for lies and excuses!"

Sheriff Hogue had ambled over to check the disagreement. "Is this true, Ray? You been burnin' off land?"

"Yes, sir, but not . . ."

"And he was out here making threats against Carl earlier today, Sheriff," Clint interrupted. "We all heard him. I'll swear to it!"

"Leon," the sheriff called. "Come on over here." Turning back to Ray, he said, "I'm placing you under arrest for . . ."

"Hold on, Darryl," Pat protested, "You don't know what started this fire!"

~ 337 ~

"For arson," Hogue continued. "I know your son here has been burning off his land. Clint says there are several witnesses to Ray's threats against Carl. This fire clearly came off his land as did that up the road yonder," he said pointing in the direction of the old tractor shed.

"We didn't burn off no piece of land this close by. It wasn't ready yet," Ray said.

"That didn't stop you!" Clint screamed. "Look at this, Ray! My daughter," he stopped for a split second, "is in who knows how bad a condition! My mother-in-law is not much better off. A boy is unconscious. The house is half gone! What were you thinking?" Clint suddenly looked around as he realized that one other person who should be there was not. "Where's Carl?"

"Over there," Ray said impassively. Carl was lying alone on the ground a few yards away.

Clint looked from the rapidly deteriorating structure to his wife and daughter. Laura had not yet realized that her father was not present. "You killed him this time?"

"He's alive," Ray answered. "And the fire is fresh," Ray protested. "We weren't burning anything today! Certainly not in the middle of the night!"

Sheriff Hogue shook his head thoughtfully. "It's a strange thing alright. You could have left something smoldering, wind picked up a spark, and this is the result. In any case, once word of this gets around you'll be safer in our custody 'til we get this all sorted out."

Leon grabbed Ray by the wrist to hand cuff him. Ray groaned. Pain shot through him like lightning.

"Don't worry about the cuffs, Leon," Hogue said. "Take 'im by the hospital and have those burns treated. Then take 'im on in and lock 'im up."

"Ten four," Leon replied pulling Ray to his squad car.

"And read 'im his rights!"

"Where is Bob Riley?" Clint demanded. "He should be arrested, too."

"I'm sure he's on his way," Thomas said quietly.

All eyes turned soberly toward the house. The area around it was lighted by flame. The shouts of the volunteers suddenly became distant, indistinguishable as human voices.

24.

"I need medical treatment."

"You're gonna get your treatment."

"The sheriff told you to take me to the hospital."

"You'll get there soon enough," Leon snickered.

"Look, I have to see about my . . . the people that were hurt in the fire."

Sadistically, Leon replied, "They are much better off than you, cowboy, believe me." Leon jerked Ray out of the patrol car and pushed him up the steps to the Town of Linwood Jail. With one hand holding the door open and the other grabbing Ray by the collar, he shoved him roughly into the small block building, causing Ray to fall against the rickety wooden desk that served all of the administrative needs of the one man "department".

"Marshall, I appreciate you lettin' me make use of your facilities to hold this prisoner for a while."

The skinny disheveled man behind the desk flashed a toothless grin. "My pleasure, dep'ty. Keep 'im here as long as you like. Here's the keys," he said throwing down a small ring holding only two keys. He stuck a .38 revolver into the front of his jeans. "I'll be makin' my rounds 'til 'bout dawn, I guess. That long enough?" he winked.

"Plenty. I'll probably have another man to hold for a little while."

"More the merrier." Linwood Town Marshall Earnest Peters slapped Leon on the back eliciting a scowl from the deputy. "We'll see ya, Leon." And then he was gone out the door. His noisy pickup could be heard long into the darkness.

Leon took three steps over to the single jail cell and unlocked the door. "O.K., get in," he growled.

"How about some water?" Ray asked.

"Drinkin' the water in that cooler would be inflictin' brutality upon you," Leon laughed. "Too much of that stuff might make you turn out like ole Earnest there." He grabbed Ray by the arm. "I don't want it to be said that I ever gave a prisoner something he didn't deserve."

Constant pain had worn Ray down. It was as if he fought to control his own mind. "You take off that badge and that gun and I'll give you what you deserve," he said through clinched teeth.

Leon hit him hard on the jaw. Ray fell backwards into the cell. Moving quickly, Leon jerked Ray up and delivered three sharp jabs into his ribs. A fist to the mouth knocked Ray back onto the floor beside the only cot in the cell.

"Threatening an officer of the law is a crime in itself, Bennett. How many charges do you plan to rack up in one night anyway?" He laughed. Slamming the door shut, he said, "I'll be back later."

Ray got to his feet and dropped himself onto the cot.

The town of Linwood, Mississippi was a very small place. Not really a town, not even a village. Like many small communities of its time, it had once been a fairly busy center of local commerce. When cotton was king, the Linwood gin ran twenty four hours a day during the ginning season. There had been three stores, a bank, a beer joint that thrived with bootleg whiskey, a sawmill, and a small cafe. Now there was one general store, a cafe, the gin (no longer a round the clock operation), a seed and feed store, and a motor parts store. No, it was not much of a town anymore.

The community was nothing more than a crossroads. The only actual residents of Linwood were the owners of the general store who lived in an apartment attached to the back of the store, and Earnest.

There was, of course, no need for a real law man in Linwood. Not that there was no crime. Break-in's had been commonplace in all of the businesses that made up Linwood. The business owners decided it might help curtail the problem if they had a security guard of some sort. So they pooled their money together and came up with a four hundred dollar per month salary and that's just what they got. Earnest was some sort of a security guard. Aaron Young, owner of the general store, provided Earnest with the .38 Special plus gas for his truck. He got free meals from the cafe, oil and power steering fluid, continuously required for his truck, from the motor parts store, and feed for his dogs from the seed and feed. And they let him call himself Marshall. He even had a badge left over from the long ago days when Linwood had an actual law man. He lived rent free in the only intact house within the old town limits. It had been taken for taxes many years earlier before the town legally disbanded and no one knew or cared who actually owned it. Its four small rooms and worn exterior were nothing to covet anyway.

So, Earnest had the title of "Marshall", and the business owners of Linwood had a security guard. And the old jail was rarely used. It had served in years past as a "holding area" during moonshiner raids and such. During the sixties, it housed its share of activists and agitators while charges were "being investigated". But, time, politics, and civil rights lawyers left it empty except for Leon's occasional use. A few dollars or a fifth of cheap whiskey served as a rental fee.

The single cell itself was surrounded on three sides by the cinder block walls of the building. The old bars still made the fourth wall, but Earnest, in one of his few industrious moods, had welded thick steel diamond mesh panels onto the inside of the bars making the cell more cage-like than anything.

Ray didn't know how long he had laid on the dusty, lumpy cot. His watch had been lost sometime during the night. The pain in his hands kept him from sleeping. It seemed like hours. Actually, mere minutes had passed. He was relieved to hear the sound of the front door opening. He sat up. Maybe now he would be able to find out about Emmy. And he might even get something for the pain.

"Brought you some company," Leon said. He opened the cell door and in walked a six foot four, two hundred and forty pound, very drunk gorilla. At least that is what the gin worker looked like to Ray. "Found 'im over at Beany's." Leon closed and locked the cell door. "Red, you be good and do what I told you. I'll be back for you two after a while."

"You gon' help me out, Leon?" the gorilla grunted.

"Said I would, didn't I? You help me, I'll help you."

"Hey!" Ray shouted. "When are we goin' to town? I need something for these burns."

"You'll be out of here soon enough, bad boy," Leon smirked. "Believe me, I want to see that you get what's coming to you even if you are a convict and a killer. Any man that goes around burnin' down crippled folks' homes and tryin' to kill his own farm hands can't reasonably expect special favors from the county, can he?" Leon turned back toward the front door of the jail house. "You think I'm just gonna let you get away with makin' a fool of me in front of the sheriff?"

Ray looked bewildered.

"Insurance fraud sound familiar to you? I'll be back."

"That right? You do them things?" Red slurred.

"No. Well, he did make it easy for that thing with the sheriff."

"You oughtn't to be hurtin' no crippled folk, mister."

"I didn't."

Red stared at Ray. There was a strange look in his eyes. He was thinking, or trying to think. It was a look Ray had seen many times before. Red was trying to find some way to start trouble.

"I'm tired," Red finally said. "You gon' have to git up."

"I was here first and I ain't movin'."

"Oh, yeah? How about if I move you?"

"Look, Red, . . . whatever your name is, I'm tired, I'm in pain, I got plenty of problems otherwise. I've been falsely accused of all kinds of stuff I wouldn't put off on even you. Why don't you just pass out on the floor over yonder and I'll wake you up when Leon gets back?"

"I want the cot."

"Believe me, the floor is more comfortable."

"Believe me," Red shot back, "the floor is yours!"

Ray sighed and shook his head slowly. "Red, if you are intent on doin' this, there's one thing I want you to know."

"Oh, yeah? What's that?"

Turning a cold eye to Red, Ray prepared to utter one word. It had worked before, years before. It took his opponent off focus just enough for Ray to gain a mental foothold. And that could possibly result in a physical advantage. In any case, Ray needed every advantage he could get at this moment. The burns on his hands made just forming a fist too painful to bear, much less using them as weapons. Fancy footwork, maybe.

"Pain." That was supposed to be the word. Ray's own physical pain and his mental anguish at the night's events were driving him into a rage. What if the fire had resulted from smoldering ash somewhere on the pasture he had burned off? What if he was responsible for the fire that destroyed the Sullivan home? And then there were the injuries to Matt and Miss Emily. And poor Emmy! His own daughter!

Had he now brought physical pain, maybe death, to his own daughter? He could not bear to bring her frightened face to mind, her tormented breath. Was history repeating itself, only far worse this time? Had another crime been committed for which he was obviously responsible and yet, again, he had no knowledge or memory of it? His anger welled and grew until he was sure he could somehow stomp to dust this big man looming before him. Hands or no hands, the anger, the bitterness, the confusion, the rage, the . . . revenge of fifteen years was about to be poured out upon this poor disconnected soul locked in this cage with him.

"Pain. I want you to know pain," was what the big man was supposed to hear.

"Jesus." The word stunned even Ray as it fell over his lips. He could hate no more. He could fight no more. His rage vanished and was replaced by unexplainable calm and . . . peace. Yes, peace, here in this violent place. Why even try to hurt the man? Maybe he could help him. But, he would not fight him.

"Jesus," he repeated softly.

"What?" Red blinked.

"Red, you look like a man who needs to know Jesus."

"I ain't talkin' 'bout no church stuff!" Red bellowed.

Ray looked around. His burned hands hurt so badly that the beating Leon had administered just a short while ago barely registered. He fought to control his voice. "Does this look like a church to you? This ain't about no church stuff. It's about you and the one thing you need most in life." Ray slid over to one side of the cot. "Now come on over here and sit down."

Red squeezed his eyes shut and shook his head as if trying to process what he was hearing.

Nodding toward the vacant end of the cot Ray added, "You can always beat me up later if you've a mind to. We have more important things to do right now. I'm in pain and you're drunk, so this may take a while."

Red stared Ray in the eye for a long moment. Wordlessly he walked like a drunk man trying to appear sober the few steps to the cot and sat on the edge of the old iron bed. He looked at Ray expectantly, somewhat like a child awaiting a story.

"Well . . ." Ray began.

Leon Pitts was many things. Most of them reprehensible. He was not necessarily corrupt in the sense that he could not be bribed. If he decided not to enforce a given law it was generally because it would benefit one of his few friends or himself in some indirect way. He did not participate with people he knew to be criminals in what was normally thought of as criminal activity. He liked the power of the badge he wore. He was mean, but he usually inflicted his meanness through people like Red Boetler. And he got away with a lot of "questionable" activity. But this was only because he was lucky. He was not a smart man. He certainly was not smart enough to realize that while a well developed brain will last most of a lifetime, luck was much less dependable.

"What do you mean Bennett is not in our custody!" Sheriff Hogue demanded. "Did he escape from Leon?"

The young deputy stammered, "I don't know, Sheriff. Dispatch says he ain't been booked! Mr. and Mrs. Bennett are there asking questions. They want to see their son. That Lorraine Parker is creatin' a awful disturbance at the hospital!"

"I thought he would have been treated and released by now. You reckon he was hurt worse than we thought?"

"I don't know, sir. I wasn't here to see."

"Well, where were you?"

"Oh, I was . . ."

"Hush, boy! Just 'cause I ask a question don't mean I want an answer."

"Yes, sir."

"What does the hospital say?"

Rookie deputy Travis Burns nervously shifted his weight from one foot to the other.

"Burns!" Hogue bellowed.

"Sir! Uh . . . sir?"

"I asked you a question."

"Yes, sir, but you just said . . ."

"I know what I just said. I just said, 'What did the hospital say?' You see anybody else standin' here for me to ask that question to?"

"No, sir," Travis said thoroughly confused.

Hogue took his hat off and beat his own thigh with it and spun to look into the face of his bewildered deputy.

After a few very long seconds Travis said, "I . . . I . . . I'll call in and see if they've located him yet."

"Please."

Deputy Burns was relieved to have the opportunity to put even a small amount of space between himself and the sheriff. Less than two minutes later, he was back.

"King's Daughter has no record of treating Ray Bennett, Sheriff."

Hogue look at him in disbelief.

"Molly checked, sir. Admissions and her aunt that works in the ER. Nobody there has seen Ray Bennett or Deputy Pitts."

"Raise him on the radio."

"Molly tried and he don't answer."

"It'll be dawn soon. Where could Leon have taken that boy?"

Travis cleared his throat uncertainly. "I can't guarantee nothing, Sheriff, but I have an idea of where they might be."

Leon left Ray in Red's capable hands and drove down the road to Beany's Beer Emporium. Sure enough, Beany was pulling another one of his illegal all-nighters. Not that business was that good. It's just that if a few patrons wanted to stay and drink all night long, Beany was willing to stay and sell them the beer. He considered the company here to be a sight better than that of his wife even if she was asleep. Beany's was an old farm shack that had been turned into a beer joint of sorts. It was lighted by three bare light bulbs, one of which hung over a ragged bumper pool table. The bar was actually two old doors laid across three fifty gallon chemical drums. Two discarded dinette tables and a few chairs, one with three legs, completed the decor.

As Leon had hoped, Patricia McGraw was occupying her usual stool at the "bar". He strutted through Beany's as if on some official mission, but managed to offer a discreet wink at Patricia. Without a word to anyone, he turned and walked back out. Driving another mile and a half, he turned into a gravel driveway and parked his patrol car behind the large mobile home at the end of the drive.

Eleven minutes later another car turned into the drive. He heard the car door slam, then the sound of feet on the deck attached to the front of the trailer, and within seconds, the back door was pushed open.

Once inside, Leon retrieved two beers from the refrigerator and made his way to the end of the trailer to the bedroom.

"What took you so long?" he asked.

"I can't have people gettin' suspicious of me," Patricia replied. "I had to wait a while before I could leave."

Leon laughed. "Baby, you've gone beyond suspicion. Most of the men around here know better than you when your trusting husband heads for that oil rig out in the gulf and when he'll be back."

Her lips pursed. "Take that back, Leon. You know I'm not that loose."

"What I know is that if you had any sense you could be makin' pretty fair money. It's more respectable that way. Why I might even bend my own rule about bribery for you, Patty Lynn."

"Well, Harley makes enough money for the both of us. Besides, I wouldn't want to be the cause of your moral failure." She lay back on her elbows.

"I appreciate your concern for my integrity." Leon sat down and started taking off his boots. "I'm a little pressed for time tonight, honey."

Patricia's leg fell over Leon's nudging him awake. He lay there momentarily and suddenly bolted upright. The commotion brought Patricia out of her deep sleep and she jumped up as well. Her first instinct told her that Harley had come home early and her worst fears were about to be realized. She was greatly relieved to find that this was not to be the case.

Leon spat. "Why'd you let me sleep? I told you I didn't have much time!"

"I'm sorry, baby, I was tired, too."

Without another word Leon was up and dressed and out the door. A faint light was beginning to show in the east. He cranked the patrol car and slammed it into gear driving forward around the trailer. His tires were spinning on the frosted grass. He left tracks in the soft ground that would be there until someone filled them in. But, explaining that to Harley was going to be Patricia's problem

By the time he had driven the few miles into Linwood, Leon had concocted a wonderful story. He would simply say that he had stopped to check on Bennett's injuries before they reached town. Bennett caught him off guard and ran. And he had been looking for him ever since. Of course, they would wonder why he had not called for help. So what! He was embarrassed for having lost a prisoner and he was confident that he could find him. His injuries? Red had probably worked him over pretty good. How could he explain that?

Well, Ray had been hurt more than they thought in the fire, and he had resisted when Leon caught up with him. Apparently, he had taken a few falls while running through the woods in the dark! It was a good story. He would catch some heat for losing Ray in the first place and then failing to call for assistance. But, he could handle that. "Leon, my boy, you're too much for 'em," he said aloud.

Ray lay on the cot and stared at the ceiling. Red, as saved as a man in his condition could be, was passed out on the floor. He had abandoned his mission of roughing up Ray Bennett. After all, they were brothers of a sort now. How much of this Red truly understood in his state of mind, Ray didn't know. But, they would have the talk again when Red was sober. Ray felt that to do otherwise would do both his Lord and Red a disservice.

Ray reviewed the events of the night. He rejoiced in the knowledge that Miss Emily got out of the fire alive. He recalled his grief for his friend, Matt Warren, when he had thought that he had perished inside the house. The image of his daughter lying burned and in pain on the freezing ground in the glow of the fire that had harmed them all haunted Ray. That she was in bad shape, he knew. How bad it may be worried him.

Leon parked sloppily along side of Ernest's truck and ran into the jail. Ernest was sitting behind the old desk sipping coffee from a dirty mug. Leon's mouth fell open at the sight on the other side of the cage. Ray sat on the cot cradling his hands. Red, having been revived by the noise accompanying Leon's arrival, sat beside Ray, appearing to actually be trying to comfort him. Something had gone terribly wrong with the plan. Leon looked from the cell to Ernest.

Ernest shrugged. "I been here for two hours. That big feller there says he's gon' whup me and you both soon as that door is opened."

"And you just left him in there like that?"

"I ain't about to go in there. That feller could kick me into the middle of next week!"

Leon picked the key up off of the desk. "Come on, Ernest."

"I ain't too swuft 'bout goin' in there, Leon, even with you here."

"Red!" Leon barked. "I thought I could count on you. You were supposed to work him over, not become his new best friend."

Red grunted. "You come on in here, Leon. I got something for you. And, yeah, he is a friend. I ain't knowed 'im but half the night, but he turned out to be a real friend. I ain't hurtin' 'im for you or nobody else. And I ain't lettin' you or nobody else hurt 'im either."

"I can't hardly understand what you're sayin', Red. You still drunk? You don't worry me. Come on, Ernest. Help me with Red."

"I seen enough of 'im. You go on and get Red yourself."

"Yeah, Deputy. Go on in there and get Red yourself."

Leon and Ernest jerked around to see Sheriff Hogue standing in the doorway. Behind him, peering over his shoulder, was Deputy Travis Burns.

Hogue swaggered across the room. "Ernest, lay your gun on the desk there." He reached to take Leon's gun out of the holster.

Leon looked at the sheriff with cold eyes.

"Don't you turn them eyes at me, boy."

Hogue's own stern gaze and tone of voice was all that was necessary to compel Leon to turn away.

"You alright, Bennett?" the sheriff asked.

"No, sir."

"Deputy?"

"Sir?" Both Travis and Leon answered at the same time.

Hogue glared at Leon. "I was speaking to my deputy there."

Leon dropped his head.

"Yes, sir," Travis repeated ardently.

"Handcuff Mr. Pitts here to the far side of the cell over there." He placed a heavy emphasis on the "Mr." part.

Leon met Travis' approach with a hard glare. Travis held up the cuffs and glared back.

"Whack 'im with your gun if you have to," Hogue said.

Travis looked steadily into the hard eyes of Leon Pitts. "That won't be necessary, Sheriff. Give me your hands," he ordered. Reluctantly, Leon obeyed.

"Ray, I'm coming in to get you to take you to the hospital before we go on to the station. You take it easy now."

"The way I'm hurtin', I'll be glad to go, Sheriff," Ray said. "You're wrong to be arrestin' me, but I understand you got your job to do. I don't hold nothin' against you. And Red here ain't gonna do nothin' either, are you Red? The sheriff has his duty."

Red sadly shook his head and moved to the far side of enclosure.

"Well, I appreciate that, Ray. I really do." Hogue was speaking more from sincerity than from just trying to placate Ray. He felt sympathy for this young man who seemed to fall victim to the worst kind of accidents. "It looks like you got another mess on your hands."

Ray grunted slightly as he stood to meet the sheriff. "Red, you're a new man now. You can't be fightin' and carryin' on no more, you know."

"I know, Ray. I wasn't so drunk I don't remember what all you said and . . . what all I said. I'll come see you soon's I can. I ought to do this right."

"I was thinkin' the same thing myself," Ray replied.

"Soon as I learn how, I'll pray for you, brother," Red said as if he were ashamed.

Ray smiled through his pain. "Prayin's just talkin' . . ., brother."

When the heavy steel door squealed its way open, Ray stood as straight as he could and walked toward Sheriff Hogue. Exiting the cell, he turned to face Leon. With difficulty, he spoke. "You're a man needs Jesus yourself, Leon."

"You mind you own business, Bennett!" Leon said with a smirk.

"That's all I've been tryin' to do, Leon," Ray replied. "It ain't worked out so well for me up to now. You should learn to mind yourself."

"That sounds to me like a threat! Sheriff, he's threatening' an officer of the law," Leon whined.

"No, he ain't," Hogue snarled. "Me and Travis is the only officers of the law in here. I don't feel threatened, do you, Deputy?"

Travis smiled and shook his head.

"What about me?" Leon cried.

"You ain't on the force. You're a civilian."

"You can't fire me without a hearin' and you know it!"

Hogue motioned for Travis. "Deputy, take Red to where ever it is he needs to go. Since Leon's leavin' us you got a patrol car of your own now."

"Yes, sir!" Travis snapped. He moved to lead Red out to the car.

"Ernest, turn Leon loose after we're gone and take 'im home."

Ernest nodded nervously.

The sheriff continued, "I'll be sendin' a man back out here in a day or so. I 'spect he better report to me that that there cell door has been welded shut."

Ernest nodded nervously.

"Leon, if you don't show up by noon with your badge and all other county property you're holdin' I'll issue a warrant for your arrest."

Leon glared at Hogue. "You can't do this to me, old man."

"You do what I told you without a contrary word, boy, or you'd best get on out of the county," Hogue said smoothly. "'Cause what went on last night will look like a pallet party compared to what's goin' to descend upon you!" His anger burned through. "My department will not be disgraced like this! I will not tolerate it! And I will deal with it in such a way as to discourage any other of my deputies from even thinking along these lines in the future! Do you really want to be my example, boy?"

Leon did not reply.

"Do you?" the sheriff shouted in his face.

Leon was trying to control his trembling. "No. No, sir," he said dejectedly.

"Come on, Ray. Sorry to keep you waitin'," he said gently.

"That's o.k.," Ray mumbled. "I hate to see you run 'im off before I can get my hands on 'im, though."

"You got problems enough, son. Problems enough." Sheriff Darryl Hogue grimaced as he watched Ray Bennett stumble slowly down the three steps clutching at his side and grunting at the pain of each movement. He fell onto the back seat of the sheriff's car and his head rolled back. Ray was as tired as he was in pain, exhausted. Before the sheriff could walk around the car and seat himself behind the steering wheel, Ray had fallen into a fitful sleep.

25.

"I find it hard to believe, Sheriff, that everything I'm treating here happened while running through a burning building," Dr. Belinda Goolsby said matter-of-factly. Hogue said nothing.

"The burned hands, maybe this cut on the forehead. But, facial bruising, a lacerated lip, two cracked ribs on one side with accompanying bruises on the other? This is the kind of case that you try to make us report to you every Saturday night!"

The sheriff remained silent.

"Well, Sheriff, who do we report this to? The D.A.? The Attorney General? The Justice Department?"

Hogue drew a deep breath. "He ain't black. The Justice Department wouldn't be interested." He didn't like this liberal woman doctor. His thoughts were more like 'Why don't you report to the maternity ward and deliver babies or something?' But, she was the best emergency room doctor on staff, and he wanted her working on Ray. He was concerned that Ray's burns had been too long without treatment. "There's nothin' here to interest any of those folks," he finally said.

"I wouldn't say that."

"I would," Ray interrupted.

Belinda gazed skeptically at him over her glasses frames. "Look, Mr. Bennett, you are safe here. They can't get to you. You can tell the truth."

Her motherly tone amused Ray.

"Doc, there ain't nothin' here that I want to take any farther than the people already involved. Sheriff Hogue here has been nothin' but kind to me."

"Sure! And I'm also sure that one of those goons he calls a deputy is involved here somewhere," she snapped back. "I happen to know that you have been . . . missing . . .," she glared at the sheriff yet again, "for hours. And I know that you were in custody, or supposed to have been, during that time. It has not been difficult to connect the dots and see the real picture here, Mr. Bennett."

"I appreciate your concern, Doc, (her mouth tensed every time Ray called her "Doc") I really do. But, justice will prevail in this situation, and that's all any of us really want, so why don't we change the subject?"

"Are we gonna need to transport the prisoner to the burn center in Greenville?" Hogue interjected.

"No! The patient," she replied curtly, "can be treated here. His burns will heal. There will be some scarring, but, I expect he will have full use of both hands. It will take some time, though, before you can use your hands to much of an extent for work . . . or as instruments of justice, Mr. Bennett."

"You ain't from around here, are you, Doc?" Ray asked. Without giving her a chance to respond, Ray continued, "Have you heard anything about Emmy McKay and Mrs. Emily Sullivan?" As soon as the words had left his lips Ray was reminded of Matt. "And Matthew Warren?"

The doctor seemed to nervously divert her eyes to Ray's left side, the same spot she had just examined. At that moment minor pandemonium broke out in the hallway. The door to the examination room burst open.

"You can't go in there," a hapless deputy was saying.

The words were having no effect on Pat or Mary. Lorraine was seething.

"Sheriff, I want to know what's going on here. Your folks told us hours ago that," he stopped in his tracks when he caught sight of his son.

"Ray, oh my God! Ray, what have they done to you?" Mary wailed. Mary and Lori reached for Ray simultaneously.

Pat suddenly grabbed Sheriff Hogue by his jacket and shoved him hard against the wall. Metal trays and instruments crashed to the floor.

"The law in this county pushed us around sixteen years ago," he said through gritted teeth. "Well, it ain't gonna happen again."

The deputy moved to pull Pat away from the sheriff. Hogue held his hand up to stop him. Ray broke from his mother's embrace and grabbed his father firmly by the shoulders. The bandages covering his hands provided a degree of padding, but, near excruciating pain caused him to involuntarily jerk his hands away.

"Pop," he said softly, "It's alright. The sheriff had nothing to do with this. It's been taken care of."

"Well, this arson thing is wrong and it will never stick," Pat said keeping his eyes and hands on Hogue. "Everbody in here knows it!"

"Let 'im go, Pop," Ray urged. "He's got his job to do."

Pat let loose his grip and backed away. "His job ain't harrassin' us."

"I understand your feelings, Pat," Hogue said. "Doctor, when can we transport?"

Doctor Goolsby looked from Hogue, to Ray, to the shattered and distraught parents. "You can't," she said. "We need to keep him for a while."

"What for?" Hogue bellowed.

"For observation."

"You've got 'im bandaged, wrapped, and stitched. There's nothing more that ya'll can do for 'im here."

"And he has done so well in your hands," she quipped.

Hogue turned around and shook his head.

Another deputy entered the room.

"Should I try to locate a larger room for us?" the doctor said in undisguised aggravation.

The deputy gazed at her warily, but still moved to Sheriff Hogue's side. "Sheriff, you better come out here," the deputy said. "They're bringin' in Buck Ammons and he's burnt up real bad, but he's awake, and he's talkin'."

"Burnt up?" Hogue queried. "And where are they bringin' 'im from?"

"Burned bad. They found him just after daylight. He was squattin' by a fence post. His clothes were mostly burnt off and he was too scared and embarrassed to go find help. He was on Bennett's place."

Hogue glanced at Ray.

"And he knows something about the fire?"

"Yes, sir. He seems to know everything about it," the deputy answered. "He's in bad pain and he don't always make good sense, but it sounds like . . . Well, you might just want to come meet the ambulance."

"O.K." Without another word the sheriff and both deputies left the examination room.

Mary moved back to Ray's side and started whispering questions, asking what had happened to him. They could hear hushed voices in the hall outside the door.

Sheriff Hogue stuck his head back in. "Uh . . . Ray . . . uh, I'm gonna let you stay here or go on home, whatever the doctor there says you need to do. I can't say much because I don't know much. But, it looks like we may have another suspect or two." He started to close the door but stopped and stepped back into the room.

"Look," he began, "I know you folks are upset and frustrated and you have every right to be. And the last thing I want is for you to get another raw deal, Ray. I'm sorry about last night. I should've had another deputy bring you in." He stood awkwardly in the doorway.

"You gon' be around later to tell us what you find out?" Ray asked.

"You look tired, Ray. Get you some sleep." Hogue turned to leave. "I'll fill you all in soon as I know anything." He quietly closed the door behind him.

Ray looked at his neatly bandaged hands and his bound ribs. "Well, Doc, looks like everything's all wrapped up in here," he said forcing a grin.

"Ha, ha," she said sarcastically. "Boy, you really have me in stitches. Put this on." She reached into a drawer and brought out a scrub shirt to match the paper pants he had insisted upon wearing when his jeans were cut away. Ray Bennett was not about to sit around anybody's emergency room in jockey shorts and a hospital gown.

"Heard it before, huh?"

"I could swap them with you all day."

"And you might have to unless you let me go on home."

Belinda checked each binding. Then she looked carefully into Ray's eyes for the third time. Ray winced with each touch. His ribs were sore, his hands were in pain, and his swollen face had regained most of its feeling . . . with a vengeance. His head was throbbing.

The doctor sighed heavily and wrote something on the clipboard that was always within reach. She tapped her pen on the clipboard a few times and wrote something else. "You are staying the night, Mr. Bennett. You and your body have been through a lot in the past twelve hours and I want to watch you for a while. If everything looks to be healing well in the morning, we will see about sending you home. You are mine until then. Just be glad you are not going with the sheriff." She quickly scribbled some notes on the clipboard and said, "You all wait here. I'll go make arrangements for a room."

"Now, will somebody please tell me how Emmy is doing?" Ray insisted. "I haven't been able to get a word out of anybody!"

Mary hesitated. "Let's get you settled into that room first, son. You need to lie down. And you need rest," she added.

"I can't go anywhere, just yet," Ray said. "I need to see about Emmy." There was no response. "Mama, you gonna tell me, or am I gonna have to go out in that hall and make a scene?"

Mary tried to speak, but could not. Ray could see that she was barely able to keep her emotions in check. Lori reached to hold Mary and comfort her.

"Pop!" Ray pleaded.

Pat fought to find the words. "She's . . .uh . . . Emmy's not good, son. She took in a lot of smoke."

"She's gonna make it though, right, Pop?"

Pat shook his head. "Nobody knows. She's in ICU. She's bad off, Ray, real bad off."

"I gotta see 'er," Ray said moving quickly for the door.

Lori rushed to stop him, "You can't, Ray! It's immediate family . . . only."

The hurt in Ray's eyes went beyond the physical pain he was feeling. "There ain't much more immediate than me," he said dejectedly, almost pleading.

Lori hugged him tightly. "I'm so sorry, baby. I'm so sorry." Then she stood, holding Ray at arm's length, staring intently into his eyes. "Ray . . ., there's something else."

"Where's Matt?" Ray asked, a sudden chill in the room.

"He's here," Pat answered. "They thought they might have to take 'im to Jackson, but they're gon' keep 'im here. "

Ray thought back to the fire and how Matt had disappeared from behind him. He remembered his panic when he could not get back into the house to bring Matt out.

"He was in the house. I couldn't get to him," Ray said, guilt coloring his words.

Pat reached out and grabbed his son's shoulder. We know, son. That's when you got your hands burned. Thomas got 'im. He went in there and found Matt just a few feet away from Carl. That boy was tryin' to help Carl Sullivan. To his credit, Carl did try to get Thomas to carry Matt out first, but Carl was in the way, so Thomas had no choice but to pull Carl out before Matt. It tore 'im up to do it, but Matt got out in time."

"Then . . . what is it?" Ray asked. "Everbody got out."

Tears fell from Lori's eyes as she struggled to speak.

Pat put his hand on her shoulder and answered for her. "Emily didn't make it," he said in a hoarse whisper. "It looked like she was doing pretty fair, but they reckon her heart couldn't take the stress. She died in the ambulance on the way into town. Nothing could be done."

Ray stood in shocked silence for a few moments, then, "Lori . . . oh, Lori. I don't know what to say. I'm so sorry. So sorry," he repeated as he hugged his fiancée.

A moment later Ray started for the door.

"Where you goin', son?" Mary asked.

"I want to see Matt."

The door swung open silently. Ray walked to the bed where Matt lie sleeping. Across from him, Bob Riley sat in the standard hospital issue uncomfortable chair. He looked exhausted. "How's he doin"? Ray whispered.

"He'll be up and about in a few days," Bob replied. "His ribs took a beatin', his knee is messed up some way or another. And there's a bad bruise on his hip. He'll tough it out, though."

"You know about Emmy," Ray said as more of an observation than a question.

Bob sighed. "I'm sorry as I can be. Aint' nothing I can do or say. No comfort I can give. I'm just real sorry. I wish I was a prayin' man. I sure would be prayin' for her."

Ray nodded slightly. "There ain't no time limit on startin', you know." He looked at Matt. "Tell Matt I came by and I'm prayin' for 'im. I'll be back to see 'im after 'while."

As Ray exited the room, the noise of a cart rolling through the hallway awoke Matt. Breathing deeply, he looked around the room. "Hey, Mr. Bob," he said hoarsely.

"You just missed Ray. He walked out of that door not fifteen seconds ago."

"He's alright then?"

"Ugly enough to make a freight train take a dirt road, but he's gittin' around." Matt smiled slightly, and then he grew very serious. "Emmy," he said, "What about Emmy? How is she?"

Bob stood wearily and looked into the boy's eyes. He'd rather have cut off his right arm than to deliver the news he was about to.

"I'm afraid it's . . . it's bad news, son. You and Ray got her out of the house, but the fire and smoke had done its damage. She's up in Intensive Care fightin' for her life. It's touch and go, son", Bob said running his fingers through Matt's hair. "Touch and go. I'm not gon' lie to you, Matt. They don't think she's gon' make it."

Matt began to tremble and tears welled in his eyes.

Bob sat beside him on the bed and Matt buried his face in the old cowboy's chest. "She kissed me one time,"

Matt said through his sobs. "I was gonna go ridin' with her." He could not talk any more, though he cried unashamedly.

Bob clutched Matt to his chest blinking back his own tears. "You go on and get it out, son," he soothed. "You need a good cry. Maybe we all do. There's so much bad to be found in this old world, it's a shame to lose what little good we have to something like what happened last night. Yessir. You just go on and cry now. Ain't nothin' to be embarrassed about."

Soon Matt was asleep again, his medication having taken over.

Bob stood beside his bed. He took his hat off and held it to his chest, "Lord, you ain't heard from me in a while . . . well, I suppose never. I know I got no right to ask, but will you let them young'uns take that ride, Lord? It's not for me. Yeah, I want to see that. I want Ray to have something with his daughter. I want that girl to live. But, it ain't for me that I'm askin'. Would you do it for them, Lord? Would you just do it for them?"

The sky beyond the small window in Ray's room grew dim as dusk fell on Winstead County and signaled the long awaited end of this tumultuous day. Lori would soon be leaving to go take care of the children including Billie Rose. Jimmy's wife, Diane had driven up from Jackson to sit with the kids. She had been with them for almost two days now and it was time for Lori to go home and explain things to them. Pat and Mary had so far successfully fought Ray's attempts to send them home as well.

A soft knock on the door was followed by the uninvited entrance of Sheriff Hogue. The room quieted and all eyes turned to him.

"Here's what we're told happened and the evidence supports it. Apparently there was some kind of an unpleasant scene at the Sullivan house along about dinner time yesterday. We've heard different versions of just how that went down, but the long and the short of it was that Carl Sullivan didn't like it at all. He made a phone call to Buck Ammons and gave him some instructions. Buck went to the Bodock last night to git his courage up and found 'imself an accomplice with an axe to grind."

"Who was that, Darryl?" Pat asked.

"Felix Warren."

"Oh, no." Mary said almost falling into a chair.

Ray said, "I can imagine the rest, but go on, Sheriff,"

"They were supposed to start a small fire in a back corner of your old tractor shed and get out fast. Buck figured that it would burn down your shed and get your equipment while it was at it. He didn't account for it spreading the way it did. And it might not have, except Felix went crazy and started setting little fires all around the place. The fire took hold faster than they expected and before they knew it, they were both surrounded . . . trapped by their own fire. They were drunk. They panicked. They just ran . . . in different directions . . . through the fire. Problem was, Buck was, um, badly burned by the time he did make it out."

"What about Felix Warren?" Ray asked.

Hogue shook his head. "He's dead. Burnt slap up! Looks like he had a whiskey bottle in his back pocket.

Shoot! The man was a walking distillery!" He scowled and shook his head as if trying to throw off some unseen demon. "That's a sight I wish none of us had ever seen. Won't none of us be forgettin' it anytime soon, that's for sure."

Silence engulfed the room.

"All of our information came from Buck. He's in bad shape. . . .won't never be the same. I tried talkin' to Carl, but he ain't sayin' nothin'. Clint admits to his part in orderin' the sabotage of your equipment. That cut fuel line that we're just now hearin' about," the Sheriff cut his eyes toward Ray, "and the fire over at Perry's place. Says he had nothing to do with last night's fire, but, his previous involvement implicates him very strongly. I expect charges to be filed against him and Carl. Two people dead, four injured counting yourself, property destroyed . . . whatever it was Carl was after with all this, it cost him everything. And I somehow doubt he got what he wanted. Is that about right, Ray?"

"That's right, Sheriff," Ray replied. "He didn't git it. And you can add my grandfather to that list of casualties."

"It's a sorry end," Hogue said as he walked out the door.

26.

As night fell, Ray convinced everyone to go home. Lori needed to be with her children. It took some doing, but he finally convinced Mary that he could survive one night alone in the King's Daughters hospital, having spent fifteen years in Parchman.

Bob would not leave Matt's side. Keeping vigil over the boy kept him from having to deal with his grief over the loss of the love of his life. He had always been convinced that he and Emily would someday be together. He took note that it bothered him so little to fantasize that had Carl died in the fire and Emily lived, his one dream in life might have come true. It bothered him none that the great house was gone. For a third time, tragedy at that house had brought harm to Emily. And for a second time, it had separated the two of them. Old dreams don't die, he reckoned. They just get harder to live with.

Not bothering to knock, Ray pushed the door open and closed it quietly behind him. "I'm not taking anymore pills tonight," Carl Sullivan said brusquely through the darkness. He sounded hoarse, his voice damaged by smoke.

"That's good cause I ain't pushin' no pills tonight," Ray replied.

"Visiting hours are over," Carl said dismissively.

Ray flipped the switch turning on the light above the door. In the room, now dimly lit, Carl lay on the bed. Ray could see that he was attempting to exude the power and authority that had always marked Carl Sullivan. But, he could also sense that the Carl Sullivan he had known was no longer present. A self-defeated shell lay before him.

"Well? What do you want, Bennett?" Carl asked with forced defiance.

Ray sank wearily into the chair nearest Carl's bed. "I don't want anything, Mr. Carl," he said softly.

"You come to gloat? You come so I can be looking at you when they haul me off to prison?"

"Hmpf," Ray grunted, "So you know I didn't start the fire."

Carl sighed. "Yeah. I know." After a moment's pause he added, "If Felix Warren weren't already dead I'd kill him myself." Another moment of pure silence passed before Carl spoke again. "It was just supposed to be your barn . . . your stock. That place of yours was nothing but an old fire trap anyway. They would put it off to an electrical fire of some sort. That, or arson on your part for insurance money. If you didn't get put away for arson, I figured you'd be desperate to settle up on your debt. I would have bought the place and you could have started over at your other barn. If you even belong anywhere around here it's over at Joe Winstead's real place and not right there under my nose on what was rightfully mine to begin with!"

"Mr. Carl," Ray said patiently, "it may grate on you, but you know that that corner of land was rightfully my granddaddy's. His horse was a little faster than yours is all. Pappy won and you lost, and now it's rightfully mine. And as for everything else in Winstead County that you call yours, everybody knows it was rightfully Miss Emily's."

"Now see here, Bennett . . .," Carl started. Ray lifted his hand to silence the man.

"Mr. Carl, I didn't come here to argue about land. It is what it is and I can't help it anymore than you can."

"Then why did you come?" Carl demanded weakly.

Ray let out a long sigh. "I have never lied about what happened that night. I don't know 'cause I don't remember." He sat waiting for a reply that did not come. "Anyway, I've always believed only two people really knew the truth. Miss Emily is gone now," Ray would not offer condolences to the man he considered to be her killer . . . a man who seemed to seek no such sympathy, "so that leaves only you. You know the truth, Mr. Carl. If I did it . . . if I pushed you over that rail . . . or if I didn't . . . I just want to know the truth."

Still, no answer came.

Finally, Carl opened his mouth to speak, but all he said was, "It's late and I'm tired, Bennett. You turned that light on, so turn it off on your way out."

Ray sighed deeply. He stood and walked to the door. He turned the light off, but paused in the doorway. Turning, he walked back toward Carl's bed in near pitch black darkness.

"I thought you were leaving," Carl finally said.

"Do you know what kind of man you are, Mr. Carl?" Ray asked.

"Yeah, I know," he replied. "I never claimed to be good."

"Then you know there is sin in your life," Ray said matter-of-factly.

"More than most," his reply drifted through the darkness.

Ray swallowed hard, not quite believing what he was about to do. "Maybe," Ray agreed, "But, there is at least one thing you do have in common with everybody else in the world."

"And what would that be?" Carl asked as if growing weary of the conversation.

"Forgiveness, Mr. Carl," Ray said, "You need forgiveness just like everbody else."

Carl laughed weakly but bitterly, "Everybody else hasn't done what I've done, Bennett."

"No, sir, . . . maybe not. We've all done maybe the same, maybe different things. But, we've all sinned. And we all need forgiveness."

"I doubt there's any forgiveness for the likes of me."

"Actually, there is, Mr. Carl."

"You offering forgiveness? Are you going to forgive me for what I've done to you?" Carl confronted.

He hadn't really considered that. Ray stood silently for a few moments. Talking to Carl about forgiveness from Jesus was one thing. Did he have it within himself to forgive? And yet, how could he introduce a forgiving savior to Carl if he withheld his own forgiveness?

"Yessir, . . . I forgive you." Instantly, Ray was filled with an indescribable lightness.

"Well, I'm not asking," Carl replied.

"I hadn't thought about it, but I don't guess that matters," Ray said. "I've forgiven you, and I'm not taking it back. You can accept it or not. You can live as if I've forgiven you, or not. As a matter-of-fact," Ray said as if a new revelation had come to him, "it's not my forgiveness you need the most. I can forgive you, but I can't get you into Heaven!"

"Ha!" Carl spit. "Heaven! You think I'm going to Heaven?"

"I'm not the only one who has forgiven you, Mr. Carl," Ray said seriously. "Jesus has forgiven you. And His forgiveness is the one that really counts. I could not forgive you if I didn't know Jesus."

Silence seemed to fill the room in the same way a great noise does.

"And," Ray continued, "you can reject His forgiveness, and you can live and you can die as if you are not forgiven. And then you can go on to Hell."

"That would make a lot of people happy," Carl said.

"Only lost folks like yourself," Ray replied. "No true Christian wants anyone to die without Jesus." Ray paused for a moment, realization flooding over him "It comes to me as I'm saying all this that I haven't treated you like I should. I certainly haven't thought of you in the way Jesus wants me to. I have hated you, Mr. Carl." He swallowed hard. "Will . . . will you forgive me for the wrong I've done you?"

Carl found this to be an incredulous request. "You are asking me to forgive you?"

"Well," Ray almost whispered, "you . . . you've done me plenty wrong, that's for sure. But, that doesn't mean that I get to do the same to you. That doesn't make us even. . . . just makes us the same." He paused again. "And

I don't want to be the same as you in that way, Mr. Carl. I'd rather us be the same . . . saved." He chuckled. "Brothers, if you can imagine that."

"I can't, and it's late, Bennett," Carl spat.

Ray walked, again, to the door. "It ain't too late, Mr. Carl. You just need to accept what Jesus did for you. Stop living for yourself and start living for Him. You'll find it's a much better way of life than the one you've led. I haven't done such a great job of it myself lately. I 'spect that'll change."

"My life is over," Carl said through the darkness, vainly trying to mask his defeat. "It's all in ruins."

"You'll probably find a Bible in that nightstand there by your bed," Ray answered. "In the Book of Isaiah you'll find that it says He will give us beauty for ashes. That means that He will take away the ugliness that is your life now, and He will give you the beauty that is life in Him in its place. You can have that, Mr. Carl. You don't deserve it, none of us do. But, you can have it. It's called grace. You can have a better life here on this earth, and then you will have eternal life in Heaven. Even you, Carl Sullivan."

Ray could see nothing in the darkness. He thought he heard a muffled sniff.

"Good night, Bennett," a hoarse, almost trembling voice said.

"That Bible will do a better job of explaining all this than I can," Ray said before leaving the room.

27.

After his visit with Carl, Ray returned to his room. Despite the pills and the shots, sleep was not coming. The pain in his hands and the soreness all over his body from Leon's beating combined with the myriad of thoughts racing through his mind to hold sleep at bay. Finally, when he could lie still no longer, Ray found the jeans Mary had brought to him earlier and slipped them on,

Ray did not know exactly where the ICU was, but in this small hospital it shouldn't be hard to find. He considered that God was with him. At 2:45 am the halls were dimly lit. Most nurse's stations were abandoned or thinly staffed. In t-shirt, jeans, and sock feet, he made his way past all undetected and then he spied a sign with a small arrow pointing the way to the ICU. Stopping at the door to the cramped waiting room he saw Laura propped up in a chair by pillows and sleeping. The glow from the television was the only light in the room. Ray continued on his quest and slowly, quietly opened one of the doors to the ICU.

The small unit was brightly lit, but he could see that the light did not make its way into the four rooms lining the wall across from the nurses' station. Ray walked slowly and ever so quietly peering into each room. Buck Ammons was in the first one. Only the name "Ammons" taped to the door identified the man. His face, and indeed, most of his body was taped and bandaged. Hoses and wires seemed to fill the room. A ventilator was either helping him breathe, or was breathing for him at this point.

Moving on, Ray was glad to see the lone attendant working with her back to him. He walked slightly faster, but tried even harder to walk silently. The next two rooms were empty. Ray found Emmy in the last room. She was not conscious. A small amount of light filtered into the room. She had been cleaned of the soot and ash which had covered her the night before. Bandages here and there obviously treated burns on her body. It looked as if her hair had been cut. Thinking back, Ray remembered her hair had been singed by the flames as he carried her through the house. Her breathing was ragged, slow.

Quietly moving the one chair in the room closer to the bed Ray sat down and tenderly took Emmy's hand into his own. The second time ever he had touched his daughter. He spoke in little more than a whisper.

"Oh, Emmy. I'm so sorry for this. You were the one true innocent in this whole thing, and look where we've brought you. I never ever wanted any harm to come to you, darlin'." Ray wiped tears from his face. After a moment he said, "I'm your daddy, Emmy. Well . . . I guess I'm your father is more accurate. I wanted to be a daddy to you, though. All those years in the pen, you were all I thought about. In my mind I watched you grow . . . watched you take your first steps. I taught you how to ride a horse. We went to horse shows all over the place and you always won the blue ribbon. Then I taught you how to drive. You learned on a tractor, like I did. After that, the truck was easy for you. We had so much fun! In my dreams . . . you . . . you loved me." Ray corrected himself quickly. "Oh, I understand why you hate me. And it's OK. I was real proud of you that day we first met. You takin' up for your mama and your grandmother the way you did. That was somethin'. But, it don't change the way I feel about you, darlin'. I . . ."

"Sir!" a sharp whisper broke Ray's trance. "Sir, you can't be in here!"

"I ain't hurtin' nothin', ma'am," Ray replied.

"Well you have to leave. If you don't I'll have to call security. Family only! Visitation in ICU is for family only!"

"It's alright, Carol," Laura suddenly appeared in the doorway. "He can stay."

"Now, Mrs. McKay, you know the hospital rules. I can't let him stay, if he's not family!"

Laura put her arm around the nurse to lead her out of the room. "He is family, Carol. He is family."

Moving the nurse out of the room, Laura turned to Ray. "Spend all the time you need to with your daughter, Ray."

Ray could only nod.

He held Emmy's limp fingers in his bandaged hand and laid his head on the edge of her bed. A steady beep from some piece of medical equipment wired to Emmy was the only sound in the place.

"Lord, I ain't been much good to you lately," he prayed. "You've done such wonderful things for me, and look at what I've done. Within hours of leading one man to you I threatened another with harm. When I came home last month one of the first things I did to test my freedom was to go get drunk and ended up in a fight. That did lead to Lori coming into my life, though, and I surely thank you for that. I've carried hate for another man. I've wanted trouble for him as much as he wanted it for me. I took a man's children from him. They needed to go, but you probably had a better way for it to get done than for me to threaten him and treat him like I did.

"And what has that brought us to? If I hadn't of done that, Emmy might be safe at home in her own bed right now. None of this might have happened. I know you love her, Lord. I know she was saved four years ago, and there is no better place that she could be than with You in Heaven. But it ain't time yet, Lord. I'm not trying to tell You how to take care of Your business. But, I am pleading for this girl's life. She should have a long, happy life. This is not her fault, Father, none of it. If you have to take somebody can't you just take me?

"I'm so tired, Lord. It just seems like everything would be so much better for most folks if it was me." He paused. "I trust you, Lord. I'm just tired's all. Help me, God! Help me just to, just to make it through another day of living with myself. I'm so sorry. Please forgive me. Please forgive me," he pleaded. "And let Emmy live, Lord. Let her live. She's precious to you, I know. And you don't like seein' her layin' here sufferin' like this. Touch her, Lord. Heal her little body. Restore her lungs and make her healthy again. It's in your hands. I ask these things in the name of Jesus, with all the power in the name of Jesus. And I thank you. Your will, Father. Your will."

After several minutes of sitting silently, holding Emmy's hand and gently brushing her cheek with the back of his fingers Ray stood to leave. Leaning into her ear he said, "I love you, Emmy. I love you! Can you hear me? Do you understand what I've been tryin' to say? Emmy? If you hear me, can you squeeze my hand? Just a little squeeze, darlin'." There was no movement. No slight squeeze. "It's OK, darlin'. You rest up. And don't be afraid. God is holdin' you in His arms right now." Reluctantly, Ray let go of Emmy's hand and walked quietly out of the room. He waved to Nurse Carol, and mouthed "Thank you" as he walked by the nurse's station.

Six o'clock am was a good fifteen minutes away when Nurse Carol lightly tapped on the door frame to the waiting room. Laura immediately woke and found herself looking into the eyes of Ray Bennett who was sitting directly across from her as if on a vigil of some sort. She quickly wiped her eyes and looked questioningly at Carol, not at all sure if she wanted to hear what the nurse had to say.

"I shouldn't say anything before the doctor talks to you, but I can't keep this from you any longer," Carol said apprehensively.

Laura sat upright in her chair. "What is it, Carol?"

Ray stood, concern shaping his face.

"It's Emmy's vitals," Carol looked down the hall as if expecting to be caught releasing privileged information. "And it is early yet . . ."

"Carol, please," Laura said.

"She has been showing improvement since early this morning."

Laura drew a deep breath.

Ray relaxed his posture. "What does that mean, exactly?" he asked.

Carol looked around again. "Dr. Kirk likes to deliver this kind of news himself. He's on his way in."

"Tell me, please, Carol, is she going to be ok?" Laura pleaded.

"Well," Carol hesitated, "she began to level off around two thirty this morning. I noticed it when I checked on her after, uh, Mr. . . . Mr Bennett left the room."

"Call me Ray."

"Yes sir," she replied as if there were some kind of danger involved in failing to comply with Ray Bennett's command. "And then," she continued, "her vitals began to pick up. It has been slow, but steady all morning!"

"Will she be alright?" Laura snapped.

"That's not for me to say," Carol replied.

"Carol, please," Ray said, "you are a nurse. You know as much or more about this than the doctor. You've been with her all night, he hasn't. He's just going to come in and read off what you are reporting to him. And we'll act surprised when we hear it from him if that helps. Just give us your opinion. We know that's all you can do, but we want to hear what you think."

"I'm sorry, Mr. . . . uh, Ray, I just don't want to raise hope prematurely. But, if her improvement continues for the rest of the morning, she will be considered stable and non-critical. Everything else is treatable." Carol crossed the room and hugged Laura. "I'm hoping you have your daughter back, Laura."

Ray whispered an audible, "Thank you, Lord."

"Thank Him, indeed," Carol added. "Considering where she was this time yesterday, this is nothing short of a miracle." Seeing the emotion building on both of the faces before her, Carol whispered, "I'll have the doctor come talk to you as soon as he gets here," as she left the small room.

Laura reached out to Ray and the two of them stood hugging and crying. "Let's go see our daughter," Laura finally said.

Ray stepped back. "You go, Laura. It might disturb her if she wakes up and sees me there. She's gonna be confused enough as it is."

"But, Ray . . ."

"It's good to hear you say 'our daughter'. I'm O.K." He paused. "I just want to do what's best . . . for our daughter." He smiled and gently steered Laura toward the entrance to ICU.

Laura turned to look at him. "I love you, Ray." Quickly she added, "You know, in the right way!"

"I know, Laura," Ray replied. "I love you, too . . . and in the right way."

28.

Emmy continued to improve. There was no contact with Laura, but Lori kept Ray informed on her niece's progress. Buck Ammons was moved to the burn center at Greenville. And he was talking. Little new information was made public, though the story of that terrible fire and those involved remained a staple of the nightly news on every local station and even some of the network and cable channels.

The local people didn't know what to make of it all. For the most part, they wanted to lay the blame on Ray. But, the emerging fact that Ray had nothing to do with the fire made acting out on that anger hard to do. There were also the sensationalized accounts of how Ray Bennett and "his men" had risked their lives in an effort to save the lives of those inside the Sullivan home. Many of the locals just didn't want to have to refer to Ray as a hero, not that he sought after that description himself.

He had, thus far, successfully avoided all attempts for interviews, and there were many. He couldn't keep the camera from following him at a distance as he worked. By Monday morning, Ray was on site at the pile of ash and rubble that had been his base of operation. He could do little. Padding his gloves helped with the pain, but he could not yet press his hands and fingers into full use and service. There was little to be done anyway.

Thomas and Bob worked silently dismantling the charred remains of the shed and creating a growing pile of useless black wood and twisted tin roofing near the rear of the lot. Matt was still in the hospital. The death of his father had left him and Billie Rose in a real predicament. There was no legal guardian to take responsibility for them. Ray had tried, but the state had no provision that would allow a parolee to take that position. Pat and Mary had applied to become foster parents, but there was no guarantee that Matt and Billie Rose would be their foster children. And there were, in some minds, remaining questions about Ray's involvement in the happenings of the past few days and weeks. Billie Rose was, under the circumstances and for the time being, allowed to stay with Lori.

The shed had burned and collapsed onto most of his equipment. The new equipment, a primary target of the fire, was still on Bing Russell's place and untouched. The only tractor Ray had left was the larger of his two old tractors. The small Ford was unsalvageable. Formulating any kind of plan for the future, far or near, was impossible for Ray at this point. He could not get his thoughts past Thanksgiving Day and those leading to the present moment.

Miss Emily's funeral was planned for late Tuesday morning. Emmy would be there, Ray learned, on furlough from the hospital. Carl, still confined to his hospital bed, was unaccounted for in those plans. Word was that he discouraged visits from anyone, and said little to anyone else, which seemed to be fine with everyone else. It was clear that Carl's plan to burn Ray out of business at best, or out of sight at least, had gotten out of control and resulted in, not only the death of one man, but that of his own wife. Others, including his granddaughter, had been severely injured. Though many had tried and failed, it was Carl Sullivan who had brought himself down. It had been a hard fall indeed.

29.

The small funeral home was packed, mostly with people who had never known Emily Sullivan, but liked to be known as friends of the Sullivan family. There were plenty of family friends in attendance. A crowd stood outside in near freezing temperatures. The newspaper out of Jackson was there, and so was Deborah Leister. She was to be the only reporter allowed in the chapel for the actual service.

Deborah had promoted herself well and now figured prominently in an hour long special being thrown together for "News Point: Weekday Edition" on network television that very night. By Friday she would have appeared on all of the big morning news shows and she would finish out the week in various smaller markets.

A phone call to a sorority sister, who was a literary agent, resulted in a hastily convened conference call which resulted in a large advance on a yet to be written book. All three of the Jackson television stations were present as well as two network news crews. There was a cable news team telling America of this latest "family in crisis" disaster. Any one of the stories within this story may not have been enough to garner this kind of attention. But, the story as a whole was just too big and sensational to ignore. All of the elements that America craved were found within the as yet unfinished story of Raymond Bennett and Carl Sullivan.

The Bennett family was there in force with Lorraine and her children. The Washingtons followed the Bennetts closely. Perhaps they held to the idea of safety in numbers, but, from the glares and shouts of the onlookers, this was not a particularly safe number to be in.

Bob Riley followed in his seldom worn suit. He had dreamed the night before that Emily came into his room, wordlessly took the suit out of its plastic bag, and laid it out for him. She smiled at him and he smiled back. It was as if everything that had gone unsaid for all those years passed between them in those silent smiles. It was their perfect moment, and it happened in a dream, but it left Bob with an unexplained sense of comfort in the midst of his great sadness.

Five city policemen escorted the Bennett-Washington group into the funeral home. The hall was packed and progress to the parlor displaying the remains of Emily Sullivan was slow. It was a mixed crowd, to say the least. Many of the onlookers stood reverently as the small procession passed. Some spoke words of encouragement. Some expressed sorrow " . . . for everything." Many, most probably, were there for the spectacle.

Then there were the haters, those who would never believe the truth just because it might call for some degree of compassion for a wronged family. The Bennetts caught hateful remarks. The Washingtons were subjected to the same hateful remarks seasoned with a bit of racism, some whispered, some shouted, as they squirmed and stumbled through the odd assembly. There were farmers, bankers, a few lawyers (scoping out new business, no doubt), housewives, fast food workers in their mustard stained uniforms, reporters, plant workers . . . lots of lookers, few mourners. Looking into the faces of those in attendance,

Ray surmised that it was a pretty poor turnout for this beloved lady. Those who cared only for the spectacle should leave and make room for those who cared for Miss Emily.

Ray turned his head to find a microphone shoved against his nose. "Mr. Bennett, what do you think about this turnout for the funeral?"

"I think if it was for that fine lady in there it would be alright. As it is . . ." he looked about the jammed hallway, "I just think folks ought to be at a funeral because they care about the person who died or the loved ones left behind. They got no right to make a circus of this. I don't care for it. No, ma'am! I'd just as soon you all go on home."

The reporter pressed on. "You've been cleared of any involvement in this tragedy and all charges against you have been dropped. How do you feel about the hostility that obviously still exists toward you?"

Ray thought for a moment. "I didn't strike the match, ma'am, but I was the fuel that fed the flames. I feel pretty hostile toward myself this mornin'." With that Ray continued down the crowded hallway.

The puzzled reporter was left shouting, "Mr. Bennett, what does that mean?"

The short trip down the hall seemed to take forever. Finally the little group reached the doorway to parlor number three where two deputy sheriffs kept all but the most sincere mourners in the hall. The Bennetts and the Washingtons were admitted with a subtle nod.

Emily's coffin was beautiful, if such a thing can be described in those terms. Glossy white with a very light pink accent. It was finely adorned with flowers of all kinds draped over it and on stands packing the room around it. Photographs of a younger Emily were stationed around the small parlor. Among the Bennetts nothing was said. They all just stood there and wished that they could wake up from this nightmare and find themselves busily preparing for a wedding.

Ray's heart skipped a beat when he saw Emmy sitting quietly in a chair near the casket. He fought back tears as he thought back to Thanksgiving night and his struggle to reach her and get her out of the burning house. There was the helpless feeling that had ruled him as he sat hopelessly in the makeshift jail in Lynnwood. Being denied information about his daughter and the others injured in the fire had taken him beyond worry. And then there was Friday night, finding Emmy in the ICU, and talking to her and praying over her as she lay unconscious, her future in doubt.

Their eyes met, but Emmy quickly turned away and would not look at him again.

The Bennetts and the Washingtons paid their respects to Laura and Lori there by the coffin. Miss Emily lay at peace on a bed of white satin. That she had been a beautiful young girl was evident on a face that still carried traces of a long ago beautiful life mixed with the travail of all that had involved being Carl Sullivan's wife.

They soon made their way into the chapel to await the beginning of the service. Bob lingered over the box that held the body of the only woman he had ever loved. He wept openly as he recalled his brief time of love with Emily so many years before, and how he had always held out hope that they would somehow, some day be together again.

"Mama always spoke highly of you, Mr. Bob," Laura said softly as she rubbed his shoulder.

"She was a fine woman," Bob managed to say. "She loved you girls more than . . . life itself." He stood gazing upon the body that lay before them. "She deserved better than this."

"Yes, sir, she did," Laura agreed. Almost as an act of mercy she added, "She deserved a man who loved her like you did."

Bob looked into Laura's eyes which were, again, filling with tears. She reached for him and they hugged tightly for several moments. Finally Bob said, "I better go find a place to sit. I'm here if you need me."

"You always have been," Laura responded.

Bob gave her that slight nod of his before turning to enter the chapel.

The small chapel of the funeral home was filled beyond capacity. The Bennetts and the Washingtons filled a pew six rows from the front. Lori and her children joined their family in the rows reserved for them at the front. Clint sat quietly, uncomfortably, as if he were a guest among the family. Carl was not there. It was rumored that he was to be released from the hospital on this very day. It was also rumored that he was to be arrested on this very day. As far as anyone knew, neither had yet occurred. Neither Laura nor Lori had been in contact with their father. That would soon change in a very public way.

The pastor had only begun his eulogy when he stopped mid-word and stared toward the rear of the chapel. Every head turned to see what had captivated him so, and every eye in the room fell on Carl Sullivan. He was being slowly wheeled in by a farm hand who was obviously self conscious about his poor attempt to dress up for the occasion. The silence that already filled the place suddenly became very heavy and practically smelled of tension. Carl directed that his chair be wheeled to the front of the chapel and centered before his wife's casket. After a moment of looking at the now closed coffin, he turned to face those gathered to pay their last respects.

Clearing his throat he spoke in a surprisingly subdued voice. "I know this is rather dramatic . . . like something you might see in a movie or read in a book. But, I prefer to say this once. And I prefer that enough people hear it straight from me so that it might not get twisted in the retelling. There will, no doubt, be plenty of that."

His "aide" stood there behind Carl shifting from one foot to the other and looking as if he would rather the funeral be his than to be standing awkwardly before this throng of people who looked as if they would rather the funeral be for Carl.

"And," Carl continued, "I expect that this will be my last opportunity to say anything to anyone as a free man." A murmur swept through the crowd. Searching the crowd, Carl spoke again when he found the face he was looking for. "Ray," (this was the first time Ray could recall Carl having used his first name) "you came to me and asked for the truth. Well, I'm here to tell it. For those of you who scoff, I admit that for most of my life truth has merely been a tool for me. I could use the truth or I could use a lie, whichever served me and my interests best at the time.

And I have lied where Ray Bennett here is concerned."
Gasps and murmuring grew in volume.

"I have several reasons for doing this. Other than Ray and his family, no one wanted the truth to come out more than my wife . . ., Emily. I've done little enough for her over our years together, and, though I can do nothing for her now, I am coming clean to honor her here today. I expect that I will be arrested and that I will spend the rest of my life, possibly, in prison. What I am telling you all here is not an attempt to avoid or lessen the punishment due me. It is merely the truth."

Carl paused to gather his thoughts and his courage. For a man who would have never admitted that he was or even could be wrong the next few minutes would be excruciating. "So, here it is."

30.

Carl drew a deep breath. "The night of July Fourth, 1972 . . ., it is a vivid memory for me, and I took advantage of the fact that Ray could not remember it all." As Carl spoke, Ray's mind raced back to that rainy evening so long ago. A lifetime ago. Carl's words mixed with Ray's memory and it all began to flow back as clearly as if it were happening again, right before his eyes.

"It seems like a long time ago in most ways, and yet it seems like so short a time as well. I suppose that is because it was not very long before my granddaughter was born." Carl searched for a place to start and the words to start with. "Her mother was dating Ray Bennett."

Carl drew a deep, ragged breath. "Emily liked Ray. I never did. She saw a nice, hard working boy. One who was dependable and honest. One who would live a good life. I saw a low class gold digger who was going nowhere because he had nothing to go on. At best, he would take my daughter nowhere right along with him. That, and he was Joe Winstead's grandson. No kin of Winstead would worm his way into my family . . . all that I had worked for.

"On that wet, rainy night Laura and Ray came home earlier than usual. I could tell from the moment they walked through the door that something was wrong." He hesitated. "I'll have to hand it to Ray. He stood up like a man and told us something that neither of us wanted to hear. The problem was that I had been drinking and was not quite sober. I . . . I could be . . . mean when I was drinking, and Ray, well, not just Ray, but anybody that I did not like, could bring out the meanness in me. Only on this night, Ray was the one who was there, and the news he brought infuriated me. It was the last thing any father of a teenage girl wants to hear."

"Mr. Sullivan," the preacher interrupted, "you don't have to do this now."

Carl never liked being told what to do, "I da . . ." He caught himself. "I do, sir, I do. Please let me finish. Now that I am finally saying it, I want to get it all out in the open."

The room remained quiet. It was as though no one wanted to even move for fear of missing a single word.

"It was July Fourth," Carl repeated. "The skies had been cloudy since morning, but it didn't start to rain until after sundown. Laura, you had been out with Ray most of the day. Your mother went to the door when we heard you drive up in that old Chevrolet Ray used to drive. You sat in the car for several minutes . . . talking, I expect. Ray got out first and you slid out beside him. I remember the both of you walking, not running, through the rain to the door. I thought that was strange. You came in with helpless, frightened looks on your faces. Yes, honey," he said looking at Laura, "I remember that."

"Mama? Papa? We have to tell you something," Laura managed to say.

"Well, let's hear it," Carl said, the evening's liquor slurring his voice. "Where have you two been? I thought I told you to get her home early, boy." He glared at Ray. "And don't think you're going to come in here and tell me that you two are getting married or some such nonsense! I don't care if you have grown up together. You've only been going out for a few months. This . . . whatever it is you call it, will go no further!"

"Carl," Emily interrupted sheepishly, "nobody has said anything about getting married. What did you want to tell us, honey?"

"Mama, Pa . . . Papa," Laura was obviously very frightened, "you better sit down," Laura said, her seventeen year old voice trembling.

"I'm about to get tired of this, young lady," Carl snapped as he drank from the glass in his hand. "We ain't sittin' down, because this boy here is leaving in about a minute and a half. You just go ahead and say what it is you have on your mind."

"Well," Laura began.

"Laura is . . ." Ray interrupted, "There is no good way to tell you this, sir, ma'am, but Laura is . . . is gonna . . . have a baby," he finally blurted.

"Oh, children," Emily cried. "What have you done?"

"Shut up, Emily. It's plain what they've done," Carl bellowed. "You got something comin' to you, boy, and it ain't no baby shower either," Carl said shattering his glass in the fireplace.

"Carl!" Emily shouted.

"I ain't tellin' you to shut up again, woman!" he shouted.

Laura, with nausea growing inside her, threw her hand to her mouth and sprinted from the room. Miss Emily instinctively chased after her.

Carl grabbed Ray by the front of his shirt and pushed him against the wall.

"Mr. Carl, I know you're mad and you got every right . . ." Ray sputtered.

"I got every right to skin you alive!" Carl spat. "You think you're going to come in here and get my daughter pregnant so I'll make you marry her, you got another thing coming. Ain't no relation of Joe Winstead marrying into what I've built!" He then spun Ray around and pushed him through the closed patio doors shattering the glass and sending Ray sprawling onto the hard surface. Blood seeped from small cuts in the boy's back and hands as he fell.

Ray crawled to the rail of the patio to help himself back to his feet. Before he could recover his footing, Carl staggered out into the rain and grabbed him from behind. The time worn wooden decking was very slippery in the downpour and this probably saved Ray's life. As Carl was changing his hold on Ray to one that would choke the life from him, Ray's foot slipped and he lost his balance again causing Carl to lose his hold.

"You slippery little . . .," Carl shouted in a rage. "I'll bash your head in." Carl turned and grabbed at one of the short, thick tree limbs that had been cut for firewood and remained on the deck. As he did this, several other of the short round sticks tumbled off of the stack now behind Carl.

Ray, stunned, barely conscious, and unaware of what was happening was struggling to comprehend the violent movement around him. Carl held the limb high above him and took a step back to get a better swing at the back of Ray's head. As he did, he stumbled back upon one of the smaller limbs. It rolled beneath his foot throwing him off balance. Top heavy and falling backwards, Carl fell onto the rail of the deck. The deck was built over a sharp downward slope at the rear of the house. The momentum of his fall carried him over and onto the stack of wood some eight feet below. A large round section of a log there acted as a fulcrum of sorts breaking Carl's back as he landed on it with the full force of his weight increased by the speed of his fall.

"This is where Emily came onto the deck," Carl said. "The first thing she saw was Ray standing at the rail looking over at me. She had no idea what happened. All she knew was what I told her, and I told her that Ray had run at me and pushed me over the rail." Carl sighed. "She never really believed that you did it, Ray," Carl said turning his eyes toward Ray. "And she refused to testify that she did. So . . . I . . . prevented her from testifying at all.

"It helped," Carl continued, "that you could not remember the details of the night. The prosecutor took advantage of that to make it look like you were lying. The rest you well know. Just so you know, Lorraine never doubted your innocence. She had me pegged as the liar in the whole incident from the get go." Carl looked ashamedly at the floor. "I made her miserable over that. I ultimately drove her away. And I've made her pay for it ever since. You have lived anything but a privileged life, Lorraine. I could have helped, but I didn't." Carl looked directly at his daughter, who would not look at him. "I'm sorry."

"So there you have it. Ray, you never touched me. I fell. My own rage threw me over that balcony. I saw an opportunity to get you out of our lives and to get that piece of the Montana Miss back, and I seized it. You, like so many others, were a pawn to get me what I wanted. But you suffered far more than any other." Carl dropped his eyes, shame, a new emotion for him, taking over. Suddenly, he raised his head and searched the faces in the crowd. He lingered on the tear stained faces of Laura and then Lori.

"You all wonder, I'm sure, how it is that I can do this now. The truth is that I owe much of it to the man who has been my nemesis for all these years, Ray Bennett." He paused as the crowd quieted. "Ray came to see me in the hospital the other night. Before he left, he told me something that no one else ever had. And it was not the kind of thing that you would expect to hear from your worst enemy. The long and the short of it is, he . . . he told me about Jesus."

Again the noise from the crowd grew. There were probably as many giggles and snorts as there were "Hallelujah's" and "Praise the Lord's".

"Laugh, if you like," Carl responded. "I know what I was. . . . and, I know who I am. I have done pretty much anything I wanted to do on this earth. I considered myself a powerful man, and in some ways I was. But I am powerless to absolve myself for my sin. And there is much of that in my past. I am here today to confess my sin before you, and to profess to you that I have asked Jesus Christ into my life as Savior . . . and Lord. I cannot change my past, but I declare to you that I am a changed man. The consequence of my past is unavoidable. But, even though I am new to all this, I do understand that I am forgiven. And . . .," Carl was fighting for composure, "I know that I do not deserve any of it."

Those listening to Carl were stunned, some believing, some doubting.

"Laura, Lorraine," Carl addressed his daughters, "I've been no kind of a father to either of you. Laura, I gave you too much in an attempt to buy you off. I couldn't have both of my children estranged from me. Lorraine, I . . . I gave you nothing but trouble. I allowed you and my grandchildren, whom I hardly know, to live in a way that I would have assigned to my enemies. I drove you away and kept you separated as much as possible from your mother and your sister. To both of you, to each of you, I am sorry." After gazing at his wife's coffin, Carl motioned to be wheeled out of the chapel, but he stopped beside Ray. "I want to thank you for what you did for me the other night. Lying up in that hospital bed gave me time to think of nothing other than my past. And, as you advised, I thought of my future. I picked up that Bible and found that I could not put it back down."

"Maybe if I had talked to you about this sooner . . ." Ray began.

"I wouldn't have listened," Carl replied. He cleared his throat. "I didn't want to hear it Friday night. I know it is strange hearing this from me, but, none of this is your fault, Ray. It is all my doing. I doubt I'll ever get to talk to you again, so I want to . . . to . . . to ask you to forgive me."

Ray began to speak but Carl held his hand up dismissively. "I don't expect it. But, I am sincere in the asking." He waived his aide toward the back of the chapel.

Ray stood. "Mr. Carl!" he said.

Carl stopped and turned his wheelchair to look at Ray. Ray looked around the room as all eyes turned to him. Most were thinking that he was finally vindicated, even those who had always looked upon him as guilty. He had the right now to say anything he ever wanted to say to Carl Sullivan. Fifteen years of prison, separation from his family, his own daughter unaware until now of their relationship and hating him for all these years as the man responsible for so much pain in her family. Harassment, sabotage, destruction . . . all bottled up, and now Carl Sullivan is known to be the man Ray Bennett always said he was. This should be good! Lori reached to squeeze Ray's hand. Laura stood and turned to face these men who had affected her life in ways she never would have imagined or wished onto anyone. It was as if the entire room was holding its breath.

"I meant it when I said it the other night. But, I know it took a lot for you to ask. So, yessir, I . . . I do forgive you, Mr. Carl," Ray spoke soundly.

Confusion marked Carl's face. "How can you do that?"

"That Bible you've been reading commands me to, for one thing. And, as strange as it sounds, we are brothers now, just like I told you we could be."

Carl nodded to Ray, looked into Lori's eyes and motioned to be wheeled out of the chapel.

As Ray sat considering all that he had just heard, emotion swept over him in great waves. For half of his life he had lived with the idea that he may actually have pushed Carl over that rail. The responsibility for the devastation of that one moment in time had weighed heavily upon him and he had never realized just how heavy it was until the weight was lifted. But, the damage remained. Indeed, they were all gathered there, many bearing emotional scars, some dealing with physical pain, inflicted by the aftermath of one man's lie about a fall, a simple fall, that changed a community and altered lives. And even with this confession, it was not over yet. There would be more trials, more prison, more families separated . . . there were consequences, as Carl had said.

Ray became aware that the murmuring around him had suddenly stopped. The silence brought him out of his thoughts. He looked up to see Emmy standing and walking slowly toward him. Stopping at his side, she gestured for him to slide over and make room. His heart pounded as his daughter sat down at his side without a word. As the pastor regained his composure and resumed the eulogy, Emmy reached over and squeezed Ray's hand. Ray turned to look into her eyes.

"I hear you," formed silently upon her lips.

Father and daughter, for the first time ever, sat side by side, wiping tears from their eyes with one hand while holding hands with the other.

Clint sat there stunned. It had happened. He felt as if he had lost everything, and now, even his daughter. He realized that keeping the truth from Emmy had never really made her his. Her name, Emmy McKay, did not make her his. The love he had fought to give made her his daughter. And the love that he had so regrettably withheld now seemed to be tearing her away.

By now, Laura was emotionally drained. She was functioning on instinct more than anything. She could not think or reason at this point. Her daughter, along with a stunned community, had just learned that her whole life was a lie imposed by those who loved her most and one who harbored a great resentment of her. The moment she had dreaded for almost sixteen years had occurred in a most dreadful way. The fix she had put on Emmy's life so long ago had very publicly come undone.

There would be an uncomfortable lunch served to the family by the church. Circumstances obligated her to be there. Then the ride home would be unbearable. She just wanted to get it over with.

The remainder of the funeral service was a blur to Ray. He felt people patting his back, hands on his shoulder. Words spoken to him were distant gibberish. He acknowledged it all, but kept no mental record of who he spoke to or what was said.

It was Emmy who asked the Bennetts and the Washingtons to stay and eat the food provided by the church. Everyone was watching them, Emmy and Ray. Their union soon became awkward. Neither knew what to say.

Mary mercifully suggested, with a hug, that Emmy go tend to her mother, who was obviously in great distress.

"I'm not sure I want to," Emmy replied.

Mary took Emmy's hand into her own. "Honey, you are the only medicine that can help your mother right now. I know you are angry and confused. You don't know what to make of all this, and I don't blame you one little bit. But, there will be time for all that soon enough. Go see to your mother, and we will all start working on this whole situation real soon." Mary reached to hug Emmy. "We all love you very much."

"Thank you, Miss . . . " Emmy stopped. "You're my grandmother! What do I call you?"

"There is time for all that, honey," Mary said. "Go and see about your mama."

Emmy looked Ray's way. She felt a strange, uncomfortable obligation to stay near him.

"I'll come by and see you later," Ray said. "Your grandmother here is right. I would imagine that Laura is feeling very lonely and insecure right now. You have every right to your feelings and we all owe it to you to hear you out and help you through this. But, your mama is hurtin' real bad. There is nobody here that can help her through this like you can. You're a strong young lady, Emmy. You're gonna be all right."

"I don't know what to say to you," Emmy said.

"Go on and see 'bout your mama," Ray said nodding in Laura's direction.

Ray would spend days getting used to the knowledge, at last, that he was not responsible for Carl's injury so long ago and all that had happened since. Coping with all that had been lost for no good reason was a battle. "Lord, I know You have a purpose for all this," he would pray. "I'm not sure I have any idea yet just what that purpose was, or is. But, please, Lord, help me to live up to Your vision of me."

31.

A few hours after the funeral, Ray was driving to Laura's house. He felt strange going over unannounced, but he wanted to talk to Emmy. He should not leave it to Laura and Clint to explain everything to Emmy. He knew he had no legal right or responsibility where Emmy was concerned, but he was her father. He should be a part of revealing the truth to her. And, there were questions she might have that only he could answer.

He met a deputy sheriff's car on the narrow gravel road, but thought little of it until he raised his hand to knock on the McKay's front door. There was a great commotion inside and he could hear Emmy's angry voice.

Laura opened the door and immediately said, "This is not a good time, Ray!"

Emmy rushed over. "You didn't waste any time, did you?" she screamed.

"What do you mean, darlin'?" Ray asked, stunned.

"Oh, I'm not your little darlin'" Emmy mocked. "Did you really think you can have my daddy arrested and then just show up here to take your place with my mama and me?"

Ray thought back to the car he had met just minutes before. "That . . . that was Clint?" he asked. "I didn't . . ."

"My Mamaw is gone," Emmy interrupted, "my grandfather is going to prison, and now my dad?" she cried.

"Emmy, I . . ." Ray began.

"I don't want to hear it, Ray!" she said. The way she spat his name cut deep into Ray's heart.

"I . . . I'll just go," he said.

"Please do," Emmy snapped. "I'll let you know when and if I want to talk to you."

The drive home was difficult. Something inside Ray urged him to just keep on driving. Make a few turns, hit the interstate and drive right on through Vicksburg and go until the road just ran out. Everything he thought he had gained earlier in the day had just as quickly disappeared.

"Emmy is young," he reasoned. "She has a lot to deal with. More than any fifteen year old should have to. She'll settle down and she'll come around," he told himself. "And if she doesn't, I'll have to deal with it whether it's here or on the other side of the country."

Ray had expected to find Lori at Laura's house. They had not talked since the funeral, but the sisters had left together. Ray now reasoned that Lori had decided to leave Laura, Clint, and Emmy to themselves. He missed the peace Lori brought to his life. The past week had been non-stop act and react. He realized how the turmoil was affecting him. There was no blaming Emmy for her words and actions. All this had to be too much for her fifteen year old mind to reconcile in such a short period of time.

As Lori opened the door, Ray fell into her embrace.

"I'm so sorry, Ray," Lori said.

Ray looked at her in astonishment. "You're sorry! What on earth for, Lori? You have lost your mother, and your family is dealing with yet another crisis. You have nothing to be sorry for."

"I knew, Ray!" she said crying softly. "I knew!"

"You knew what?"

"I knew you were innocent. I always knew!"

"You saw what happened?" Ray asked, unbelief in his voice.

"No. I didn't see anything. But, I knew you didn't do those things they said you did. I just knew you couldn't have done it. And I told my daddy that. It was like he disowned me right at that moment. He told me that if I could not be a loyal Sullivan that I would never live as a Sullivan."

"Oh, baby, I'm so sorry. That never should have happened."

"I have lived such a messed up life, Ray. Two divorces. My children hardly know their daddies. And I have a reputation that . . . well . . . I probably earned. I'm not the kind of girl your mama wanted for her son. No decent mother would want me in the family. I know people talk about me. I . . . I'm not sure, Ray," she said sadly.

"Not sure about what?" Ray questioned.

"I'm not sure we should be getting married," she cried.

"Lori, I . . ." Ray began.

"Ray, your life has been so messed up by my own father! You have a daughter with my sister! You need someone you can look at and live with who is not a reminder of all the pain in your life. You need . . ."

"I need you!" Ray interrupted. "You sacrificed your relationship to your father to be loyal to me. You have always believed in me, even when I didn't even know it. Sure, you've had a rough life. But all that is in the past. You were a young girl rejected by her father and that set you on a path that God has now saved you from. Do you understand that, Lori? You believed in me and you paid a terrible price for it. I don't think about pain when I look at you. I don't think about the complications that surround us. I am at peace when I am with you, and I am loved. And I love you. And, yes, I want you for my wife! And my very decent mother loves you as one of her own. Shoot, you are one of her own now!"

"Oh, Ray," Lori said reaching for him again. After a moment she looked at him with a confused look on her face.

"What"? Ray asked.

"My niece is going to be my step-daughter!" she said grinning.

"Well," Ray mused, "this is Mississippi."

They laughed and hugged and sat on the porch swing to cuddle in the cold November air.

Before the day ended, Clint was back at home, a free man . . . if free is what you want to call it. Ray had nothing to do with Clint's arrest in the first place, and he told the sheriff and the district attorney that he would have no part in Clint's prosecution.

The family had suffered enough, and he would work things out with Clint to cover his losses. Bill Perry might not be so kind as it was Ray's pickers but his land where they were set afire. No actual damage had been done to his property, so there was little prosecution to be done.

And there was no word from Emmy.

32.

The McKay family had much to deal with. Clint was still living in the house, but the marriage was shaken. From the day Clint had made his deal with Carl back in 1972, when he was still a teenager, he had never been his own man. In everybody's mind, including his own, he was Carl's boy, and that not as "son". Such had driven him to do many things that weighed heavily upon his conscious. Carl's attitude about Emmy had affected his own. Where Emmy was concerned, it had never really mattered that he was not her "real father". He had loved her, but looking back through eyes that could no longer filter and shade reality, he recognized that he had held back in many ways.

Following Carl's lead to more of an extent than he wanted to admit, he had never quite made her his daughter. His name was on the birth certificate. He had accepted her love, pure and sweet, without judgment, while his love was allowed to go only so far. Carl's voice was gone now, that imagined voice warning Clint that he could not fully accept Emmy because Carl did not fully accept her. And that unacknowledged barrier between Clint and Emmy had grown to include his relationship with Laura as well. Clint wanted to blame Carl, and he could. But, he knew the choices were always his to make.

Now, without Carl as the puppet master controlling all who would be controlled, Clint had to face the consequences of his decisions. His family had been living these consequences for years and he was only now able to see that. For the foreseeable future, Clint's focus would be on his family, including Emmy. He would not interfere in whatever relationship developed between her and Ray, but he would not relinquish his place, his position as "Daddy". He and Laura had much to do to help Emmy, and Jason for that matter, move forward from the lie that had always been their lives. For the time being, he would be far less active in the daily affairs of the Walashabou Farm and Cattle Company. This meant eating even more crow.

Much of Clint's conversation over the past few days had pretty much amounted to a sustained state of groveling. For one who had spent each of his privileged thirty two years as more the grovelee that the groveler he performed remarkably well. This trip, though, was the most difficult yet. Three short steps up would put him on the porch, two more steps would put him at the door. And then if he could manage to raise a heavy hand to knock on that door he would soon have the worst of it behind him. The door opened in response to him, but no word of greeting came, only cold judgmental eyes.

"I wouldn't be here if you were not the man I know you to be," Clint said.

"If you really knew me you wouldn't be here at all," Bob Riley replied evenly.

"Look, Bob, you have every right to feel . . ."

"I don't know about the right, but I have every inclination to send you on to where ever it is that Felix Warren is waiting for you," Bob yelled advancing over the doorstep.

Clint instinctively stepped back.

"You could have stopped this! Don't tell me you couldn't do anything with Carl. You could have at least come to me . . . and I would take care of Carl. No matter how it ended, you started it when you sent Buck over there to cut fuel the lines on Ray's picker, and then when that didn't slow him down you sent Buck over to Perry's place to set fire to his equipment!"

"Bob, I . . ."

"The man comes back from fifteen years that he didn't deserve to spend in prison, but that ain't enough for you, is it, Clint," Bob said. "You been holding that little girl at arm's length for all of her life, and then you suddenly can't stand it 'cause you think Ray Bennett is somehow gon' come in here and take away what you was already losin'! And Em. . ." Bob's voice trembled with emotion, "Emily is out there layin' in that cold ground before her time, and don't you even try to think that you are innocent of that! No'sir!"

"I know what I am, Bob," Clint blurted.

Bob silently glared at Clint.

Clint continued, "I am nothing, and I have nothing. Everything I ever wanted belonged to Carl Sullivan and it never will be mine. It will soon belong to Laura and Lori. But none of that matters anymore. I don't care about any of that."

"I don't either," Bob spat, "so what else you got?"

"I am starting from zero," Clint replied. "I've got to try to save my family."

"You destroyed it," Bob said unsympathetically.

"I know. I know," Clint said despondently. "I wish I could go back and change everything, but I can't. I . . . I don't know how I am going to live with myself . . . what I've done . . . what I became. All I can do is take what is left and do my best to rebuild it."

"Why are you here?" Bob asked suddenly aware of a purpose behind Clint's visit.

"Well," Clint began, "Carl is turning the place over to the girls. Laura and Lori . . . and I will form a board, and we'll make the big decisions about Washabow together. The thing is," he broke eye contact, more shame evident in his voice, "they don't trust me to run the day to day operations."

Bob dropped his gaze. He could see how hard all this was for Clint. As little respect as he had for Clint at this moment, he could still understand the difficulties this young man faced. Clint finally seemed to accept the bad turn his life had taken some time ago.

"And that's ok with me," Clint continued. "I understand. And I want to spend my time working on my family for a while. Like I said, I have nothing. I have to rebuild everything. The thing is," he said again, "we want you to come back and manage the place for us. You're better with the day to day than I ever was. And we all agree that you will run it with no one's interest in mind but the family's . . . Laura and Lori, that is."

"I'll have to think about it . . . talk to Ray," Bob said somewhat subdued. He already knew that Emily would want him there watching out for her daughters and grandchildren. Ray would be fine without him. "I probably never should have left," he added. "Maybe I could have seen this coming. . . . done something to stop it." He wiped a tear from the corner of his eye. "You tell the girls I'll be over to talk to them 'bout this, but I 'magine I'll be around. And I'll take my orders from them."

Clint held out his hand. "I hope I can earn your trust, too. I could learn a lot from you."

Bob shook his head. "I don't 'spect we'll be shaking hands for a while yet," he said. "Git all your hands told who's in charge and tell any of 'em that want to stay on to meet me at the tractor shed at seven in the morning." He turned and went into his house, shutting the door behind him.

For the first time in their lives things seemed to be working out for Matt and Billie Rose. Their grief over their father included a grieving of sorts over what should have been. The man who should have provided food, shelter, and, above all, love for his children never showed much of an interest in them or anything he was supposed to do for them. They mourned the father they never had as much as the one they did have. But, beyond the poverty of love and care that had been their lives in years past was the hope of life as it should be. The love and support that they found in Ray and Lori, the Bennett family, and now the McKay family, and even in a community which seemed eager at last embrace them, was more than they had ever known that they could even hope for.

Ray and Lori wanted desperately to adopt them. They had rescheduled their wedding date for shortly after the beginning of the year so the process could officially begin. Preliminary work was already underway. Pat and Mary had quickly been made legal guardians over Matt and Billie Rose. A legally required search was being made for their runaway mother, but no one, including Matt and Billie, were hoping for success in that endeavor.

Matt was healing well. There would be no work for him for a while. His broken ribs were sore and there was little to do on the place for the time being anyway.

Billie Rose surprised everyone with a singing voice that was being compared to that of an angel. Mary had overheard her singing Christmas songs to herself, and now Billie Rose Warren had a solo in the upcoming pageant at church. At long last, life was good for the Warren children.

One of the biggest surprises came a week after the funeral. Ray and Lori were sitting in the Bennetts' living room gazing at the Christmas Tree that had been decorated by all the children on Thanksgiving Day. A soft knock at the door brought Ray out of the trance he was falling into. Opening the door, he was surprised to find Buster standing there, a large jar full of coins and dollar bills held out before him.

"The boys . . . everbody at the bar is real sorry about, well, everything. We didn't know what to do so we took up a collection. It ain't much. Everbody's broke this time of year."

Taking the jar into his bandaged hands Ray replied, "Tell 'em it was real nice of em, . . . very generous, and we appreciate the good thoughts."

"Billy Thompson wanted to make sure you knew he put in six dollars. He's still scared you gon'catch up with 'im and kill 'im for whacking you with that pool cue."

Ray grinned. "Well, you tell Billy that bygones is bygones. 'Sides, it ain't everbody that can say they wacked a known criminal . . . at the time, with a cue stick. I don't hold nothin' against 'im."

Buster turned and walked back to his car. Standing in the open car door he said, "You understand this don't mean we're buddies or anything, but if you want to come by the bar for a beer nobody will mess with you."

"Well, I appreciate that Bust. . .er. I really do, but I've sworn off of it."

"The door's open to you," Buster said as he cranked the car and backed away.

Ray returned to Lori's side. "It's from Buster's place," he said holding up the jar.

Lori sniffed and turned up her nose. "Ewww! They didn't even wash the jar out. That money smells like pickled eggs!"

"Well," Ray replied, "I guess the Bodock has given us a pickled nest egg."

They laughed until their laughter turned to tears and the pain they had endured together overwhelmed them once more.

It was now just over a week before Christmas and a light snow was falling. For the most part, if it snows at all in Mississippi it will be a light snow, so it would not last and there would be no white Christmas. Ray was kneeling to drive a stake in the hardened ground of what used to be his base of operations. His burns were healing well. There was still a bandage on his right hand, but he wore gloves and worked through the pain. There were physical scars from Thanksgiving night, both from the fire and from the beating he took from Leon. He was slowly filing the emotional scars from that night and the days which followed away with all the others accumulated over the years.

He was thinking, just thinking, of rebuilding there. He was also thinking of building on the lot beside the old barn across the road from Gran's house. It would be nice, he thought, to walk to work most mornings. He had more room there than here. But, he had no idea of what he would do with this piece of land if he didn't build on it.

Also, there was the specter of the ruins of Miss Emily's house always in view just up the hill. Someday it, too, would be cleared away, but it would still always be there. What is present in the mind, Ray reasoned, is more powerful than what exists in reality. And there were certainly powerful memories and emotions attached to that old place. Somehow, the ghost of the structure haunted Ray more than the house itself ever had. So, maybe something new needed to be built on this land . . . maybe not. Either way, it was not a decision that had to be made any time soon.

He had decided to talk to Thomas about branching out on his own. The down time at Bennett Farm Services had given Thomas opportunities to work on equipment for other farmers in the area. Glenn Melton was even using him and had, in fact, tried to woo him away from Ray with a very generous offer. People were beginning to take to the Washington family. They had even been invited to church . . . Pat and Mary's church! It seems some people were able to see less color and less past and more heart. And Thomas was already outfitting his wrecker for mobile service since he was traveling to all the work he had at the moment. Thomas could do better on his own than he could working for Ray. And there was the pride a person has in owning their own business. Ray smiled at the thought of all the prospects for a better life Thomas and Linda were now realizing.

Carl was right. He had been arrested the day of Miss Emily's funeral . . . as he exited the funeral home actually. He would plead guilty to all charges and he would go to prison. Two deaths, several serious injuries, property destruction . . . it was likely that he would be incarcerated for the rest of his life. Carl had reached out to Laura and Lori. He wanted a relationship with his daughters and grandchildren. Laura had responded in kind.

Lori was trying to work it all out. Forgiveness that had come so easily to Ray was coming much harder for Lori. So many of her own past attempts to bring her father into her life had been rebuffed. She wasn't going to make it easy for him.

To his credit, Carl had thus far proved to be a changed man. Far from perfect, he was learning what it meant to be a Christian and to live a godly life. Such ideas had been so far away from him for so long that he struggled to believe that God would even give him a chance at a new life. From time to time, the old Carl would win, but then the new Carl would seek forgiveness and take up where he left off. He read his Bible and visited with preachers and lay ministers every chance he got. Carl Sullivan was working hard to live up to the change that had taken place within himself.

Money had already been set aside by the Sullivan legal team to compensate Ray for his losses and his trouble. He could rebuild his facilities and replace his equipment and live in fine shape. Carl's attorneys protested, saying that the matter should be handled in court, and reminding him that his funds were now limited. Carl retorted that his defense should not cost much. He was, after all, pleading guilty. Generosity was new to Carl and he was having trouble controlling it.

Buck Ammons had not yet been called to account for his part in "the Sullivan fire". He would survive his burns, but he had such a long way to go before he would be physically fit to stand trial. In fact, there was already talk of a suspended sentence and probation. His burns were severe. Pretty much half of his body, including half of his face, was forever scarred. One ear and an eye were gone. Buck had already received a life sentence much harsher than anything the State of Mississippi could impose.

Emmy was doing well. Ray had not seen her since that day after the funeral. He had been feeling rather foolish about his visit to her home that afternoon. Her gesture of kindness at the funeral must have been just that. Perhaps she was just caught up in the emotion of the moment. Or maybe she was just being a fifteen year old. Laura had assured Ray that Emmy would come around at some point. He just had to be patient for a while longer. Well, patient was one thing he could do very well on the outside. Inside was something different altogether.

Emmy had so much to deal with and he didn't want to make that worse. Learning the truth in front of an audience had been over whelming to her. At least she didn't have to keep explaining the story. Ray planned to call Laura soon and attempt to set up a meeting between the three of them. He wanted to take Emmy a Christmas present. The whole Bennett clan had presents for their granddaughter and niece. In fact, Mary had a closet packed full of presents that she had been saving for Emmy since before she was born. They all looked forward to the day, if it ever came, that Emmy would be sitting there on their couch opening fifteen years worth of Christmas and birthday presents.

To the outside world, Ray was a picture of calmness. He controlled it well. Somewhere inside, though it churned. And work was his best method of keeping control. Why else would he be out here in freezing weather, pounding stakes of two by four's into frozen snow covered ground to stake out a structure that may well never be built here?

Deep into his thoughts, he never heard the horse's hooves crunching through the inch or so of snow behind him.

"I hope the new one looks better than the old one."

As few times as he had heard it, the voice was still unmistakable. Gazing out over the barren lot Ray hesitated, trying to control his emotion. "Well, I don't know so much about that. None of all this new stuff I've seen quite measures up to what you would call the old stuff." He turned to look up into his daughter's eyes. "Some folks'll count it a sight prettier I reckon."

"You need some help?" Emmy said climbing down off of her horse.

"Don't you think you need to be somewhere nice and warm? How are you gonna get well ridin' around out in the cold like this?"

Tying her horse to the bumper on Ray's truck Emmy said, "I'm plenty well enough to take a ride. The doctor told me fresh air was what I needed to get into these lungs of mine."

"Yeah, well I'm sure he didn't intend for you to git pneumonia in the process of breathin' fresh air!"

"Your concern is noted, sir," Emmy teased. "Can I help?" she asked again.

Ray sighed. He was enjoying this more than he should show. "There's some orange colored string on the seat of my truck there. How 'bout tyin' it off to this stake and then wrap it around that stake over yonder and then those two," he said pointing.

"Where's Matt?" Emmy asked after a few minutes.

"He's at the house helping Mama wrap Christmas presents," Ray replied. "He ain't never had much of a Christmas before, and he's really gittin' into this one. He's itchin' to get to work, but that ain't happenin' for a while yet."

"I suppose so," Emmy said thoughtfully. "He's about as hard a worker as a country boy can get."

"That he is, dar . . . uh, Emmy," Ray caught himself. "That he is."

Emmy looked out the corner of her eye at Ray. After a minute or two of silence she asked, "Can I take his place? Until he gets back, that is."

Ray stood and looked at his daughter.

She continued. "Matt says the best way to get to know you is to work for you. And besides," she said looking Ray straight in the eye, "you owe me some tractor lessons."

Ray looked puzzled.

"I heard what you said . . . in the hospital." She hesitated. "Everything." She paused again. "We can't go back. We have what we have. I've been thinking about that a lot. . . . It's weird, knowing that you're my father. It's not bad weird, though," she hurried to add. After a few minutes she said, "I know it must be strange for you, too."

"We'll work it out," Ray replied.

"I don't know what to call you."

"Daddy Ray is out," Ray said chuckling.

"Agreed!" Emmy laughed. "I'll just play around with some stuff. We'll see what fits."

"How 'bout just Ray?" he said.

"No, sir! I can't call my father by his first name. It doesn't sound right. So about the job . . ." Emmy said.

Ray shook his head and walked to Emmy holding out his hand. "We're gonna have to talk to your mama, but, one way or the other, welcome to Bennett Farm Services." They shook hands in mock formality.

"I'm sorry about the way I acted . . . after the funeral, you know," Emmy said looking Ray in the eye. "I said some terrible things. I just . . ."

"You have a lot to deal with, darlin', Ray," said, and then he added. "I can call you darlin'?"

Emmy smiled and nodded.

"Anyway," Ray continued, "I understand that."

Emmy reached and they hugged awkwardly.

After a much too brief moment, Ray forced himself to take a step back.

"It's about lunch time," he said. "We'll finish this up and Mama'll have dinner ready in a bit. I always like to feed my new hands when I can. Why don't you come on up to the house with me. I know they would love to see you, and you get a good meal to boot! We'll call Laura and let her know where you are. "

"Well . . . o.k." Emmy said brightly, "but Mama's not home."

"Oh?"

"Mr. Bob hooked that old wagon up to the mule, and him and Mama and Aunt Lori and all the kids are on a Christmas Tree hunt!"

"Ya'll don't have a tree yet?" Such a normal conversation was more than Ray could have hoped for.

"Yessir, we do. Jason was at Mr. Bob's house the other day and noticed that he didn't have a single Christmas decoration up. So, they're all out trying to find him a tree and then they are going to go decorate his house with some of the stuff we don't use any more. Mama even went to town and bought him some new ones." Emmy smiled. "He acts grumpy and like he doesn't want all that, but I think it really makes him happy."

Ray smiled to himself. Bob was quickly becoming the grandfather none of those kids had ever had. And Ray knew that Mr. Bob was relishing every moment of it.

They worked on for a short time before Emmy broke the silence.

"Hey, Pa!" she yelled from across the lot.

"Pa?" Ray said turning to look at Emmy skeptically.

"Anyway," Emmy said before breaking out into a grin, "Matt was saying something about a sign-on bonus?"

Ray grinned and shook his head and turned back to his work. "Pa," he repeated shaking his head. Looking skyward, he offered a whispered, "Thank you, Lord."

The End

From your author:

I have thoroughly enjoyed writing this book. I have lived with it for a long time. Through its different versions, changes, and re-writes I have returned many times in my mind to the asphalt, dirt and gravel roads of my childhood and adolescence. I've grown close to each character in the story . . . even the "bad" guys. I find myself wishing I had paid closer attention to all that was around me as I was growing up, 'cause you really can't go back home.

This work began as something I wanted it to be. My only desire now is that it is all God intended it to be. I hope you enjoyed it, and my prayer is that you will somehow be blessed by it.

*Please feel free to visit my blog at **www.wearecrossconnected.blogspot.com**. Also, I would enjoy hearing from you. Feel free to email me at **troubledfields@yahoo.com**. Keep up with the happenings and discussions on our facebook page, "Dennis Manor, Writer".*

Thank you so much for reading my book. I look forward to visiting with you again in a future story.

Dennis

Made in the USA
Lexington, KY
03 September 2017